"FAST AND FURIOUS."
—*Locus*

"An exciting addition to the slim shelf of sword and sorcery written for adults. . . . Bunch manages to keep the tension high. . . . You can almost smell the leather, the sweat, the blood. Bunch's battle sequences are second to none."
—*Oregonian*

"Well-paced and full of fascinating characters . . . subtlety and surprises in an epic setting. Remarkable."
—**Michael A. Stackpole, *New York Times* bestselling author of *Once a Hero***

"A fantasy sex- and violence-fest, courtesy of Bunch's sure grasp of military history and organization."
—*Kirkus Reviews*

"Fast-moving, well-plotted fantasy . . . a solid, three-dimensional world."
—**J. V. Jones, author of The Book of Words trilogy and *The Barbed Coil***

more . . .

THE SEER KING

CHRIS BUNCH

ASPECT®

WARNER BOOKS

A Time Warner Company

WARNER BOOKS EDITION

Cover design by Don Puckey
Cover illustration by Dorian Vallejo
Book design by H. Roberts Design

Aspect is a registered trademark of Warner Books, Inc.

Warner Books, Inc.
1271 Avenue of the Americas
New York, NY 10020

Visit our Web site at
http://warnerbooks.com

A Time Warner Company

Printed in the United States of America

Originally published in trade paperback by Warner Books.
First Mass Market Printing: February, 1998

10 9 8 7 6 5 4 3 2 1

for Kuo-Yu Liang
&
Russ Galen
who helped a lot
and, again, mostly for
Li' l Karen

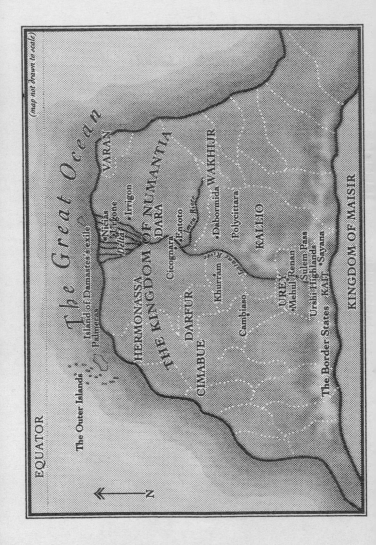

ONE

EXILE

The Seer King, Emperor Laish Tenedos, is dead. A courier boat brought the word this morning, and the prison warden declared a holiday.

I suppose I should not have called him that, but rather the Prisoner Tenedos, just as I am no longer Damastes á Cimabue, no longer Damastes the Fair as some called me in the silken pavilions of Nicias, no longer First Tribune á Cimabue, Baron Damastes of Ghazi, but merely the Prisoner Damastes.

I knew what tidings the ship bore, even before it docked from its gay buntings and the cheers of my guards as they read the signal flags.

They say the emperor died of natural causes, that his heart failed. Perhaps. But it would have taken only one enemy among his guards to cast a sorcerous spell, slip a bit of poison into his mat, or arrange a simple fall when he took his long walks along the coast, as I do, staring off toward the gray horizon, hoping for, but never being granted, the slightest glimpse of the great country of Numantia he brought to greatness and then sent down into ruin.

Sergeant Perak, who heads my guard detail, a man I have grown fond of in the year since my captivity began, said he believes the official tale, but it wasn't disease, but the malaise of exile that sent him to his grave. A broken heart, a romantic might have put it.

But he said this very quietly, after making sure no one might overhear him. It would not do for a jailer to show the slightest warmth toward his prisoner, nor toward the cause the prisoner vowed to serve until death.

At even-meal I noted the garrison's officers looking at me. I knew what they were wondering: How much longer would *I* be permitted to live?

I am, I suppose, the only tribune left of the Emperor Tenedos's great army, save Herne, who betrayed us, and Linerges, who I understand was able to flee abroad. The only other ranking survivor might be Yonge, who vanished long ago into the crags of the Border States.

Perhaps I too will have a convenient accident, or sickness.

It matters not.

I have seen, and done, as much as one man should be permitted. I've cut my way through battlefields where the blood lapped around my horse's fetlocks.

I've loved well twice and been betrayed once. Both those I loved are dead now, as is the part of me that loved them.

I've sat at the head of an army, a thousand thousand men who cheered and charged into certain death and their return to the Wheel on my command.

I've seen the greatest cities of Maisir and Numantia, from Kallio to the jungle borderlands, roar up in flames, flames I ordered to be set.

I've seen battlegrounds torn by demons called by the most evil and powerful wizards, demons who broke a column of charging cavalry when they appeared, ripped a company of spearmen apart with their talons, or sent them screaming away in madness.

I have eaten from golden plates, surrounded by silk and gentle music.

That is the one side.

There is the other:

I've stumbled, bleeding, from the field of war, gut-sick as I saw our banners trampled and torn by the enemy triumphant.

I've snatched a half-burned potato from a low fire and gnawed at it, the best and only meal I'd had for close on a week.

I've screamed on a witch's pallet, while she muttered words and taped dressings around my wounds, and then spent weeks wishing for the softness of death in a recovery tent.

Yet I am not old. I am not yet forty. All that has happened came in less than fifteen years.

Fifteen years, given a few months each way, since I first met the seer named Tenedos, facing death in a deadly mountain pass of the Border States.

Fifteen years, when I rode behind the emperor, his aide, cavalry commander, and then tribune, holding close my family's faith—*We Hold True*—although I now realize that loyalty was felt by only one of us.

He and I were the only two who were there at the beginning—and the end.

Our enemies would have said there were three:

Laish Tenedos.

Myself.

And Death, the dark manifestation of the great goddess Saionji, creator, destroyer, skull-grin tight through the folds of her cloak, swords held high, pale horse nickering, eager to strike again.

Now there are but two of us.

Myself and Death.

My last friend.

TWO

THE SEER TENEDOS

My doom, and that of all Numantia, was sealed on the day I scored five goals at rõl.

This may sound like a joke—how could a horsemen's game make Saionji rip our lands apart, casting millions back on the Wheel to await rebirth?

But there is no joke, nor was there on the day of my disgrace. The Seventeenth Ureyan Lancers took their sport most seriously.

If it hadn't been for those five goals, the adjutant's pride, his lying, and my subsequent disgrace, another officer might have been sent to Sulem Pass, one with less to lose, and Laish Tenedos might have died with a hillman's spear through his throat, and the years of bloody war and dark magic might never have happened.

I was the newest officer of the regiment, having been given my sash of rank not many months earlier. I'd sought frontier duty, wanting to fight instead of drill endlessly on parade grounds, and had been lucky enough to be chosen to be a column commander with the elite Lancers, as my first posting.

My downfall was ironic, because I had been most careful, as I'll tell later, to avoid the usual blunderings and stupidities of a junior legate. In fact, I'd been successful enough in a patrol against a wizard-bandit to be complimented by Domina Herstal, the regimental commander, only days before the rōl match brought me down.

Rōl is a simple game played on horseback across a wide, flat field. At either end is a netted enclosure, a foot wide by a foot high. There are five men to a side, and they attempt, using a mallet with a handle as tall as a man, called a hammer, to drive a wooden ball about the size of a large man's fist into the goal. The game is played to ten points. It was a game I was particularly fond of, since it called for the best in both man and horse, and I was quite good at it—at the lycee I'd ridden forward on the Senior Team.

The regiment was, as I said, very keen on sport, particularly the adjutant, Captain of the Lower Half, Banim Lanett. Perhaps I should explain just what an adjutant is and does, because someone of his comparatively low rank should not be able to ruin anyone, even a junior legate.

An adjutant is the grease a regiment's wheels turn on. The unit commander, Domina Herstal, might walk out on the parade ground one morning and wonder if the stones bordering the field would look better stained yellow instead of white. Captain Lanett would nod, say "What an interesting idea, Domina," and as soon as the regimental commander was out of hearing would bellow for the troop guide and within minutes barracks would be rousted and details of men told off for painting, so when the domina came out for noon assembly, the area would be marked with tawny rocks as if a wizard had wiggled his wand. The domina would never inquire as to the circumstances, and the subject would never be brought up again unless the work had been done unsatisfactorily or the domina changed his mind once more.

Captain Lanett was a competent soldier with but one failing, although at the time I thought him a deceitful, lying bastard I'd call out if the army did not sensibly forbid dueling a higher-ranking officer.

His failing isn't that uncommon, either, and can be found almost anywhere in civilian life as well as the military: a single weakness that hews a deep canyon through a man's honor. For some it is women, for some it is pride, for some it is gaming.

Captain Lanett's failing was his love of sport, more precisely rōl. Off the field, he was a model of rectitude, but once mounted, hammer in hand, he would do anything to win a match, including spearing an opponent if a weapon had been given him and the referees' backs were turned.

The game was a match between the regiment's troops, and I was determined my Cheetah Troop would carry the day. I had been picked to ride forward, the position most likely to score, and things were going very well. I'd driven two goals in during the first quarter and heard cheering from the twenty-five men of my column. The match had swayed back and forth down the field, a grand melee, until, in the final quarter, I'd picked up another two goals and the score was tied, 9-both. We were on the defense, and I was trying to hold back the other side's halfback and back, my pony skittering from side to side of the grassy ground.

Captain Lanett came pelting down on our goal, tapping the wood ahead of him, about to let fly, and I was at full gallop trying to catch him. My mount was slightly faster, and I cut in from his blind side, and slashed, backhanding the ball away from him toward his goal. I heard the captain shout, but paid no mind, wheeling my pony and driving back toward the ball.

Behind me came the thunder of the captain's horse, but I paid no mind, with an eternity to strike, that one-foot-wide goal yawning as wide as an elephant trap, and I snapped my mallet back and smashed the ball directly into the center of the net, and I bellowed victory, and there came another shout from behind.

I pulled my horse up, and turned. The adjutant had reined in, and had one hand clasped to his leg.

"You son of a bitch," he shouted. "You fouled me back there, and now again! I'll have your ass for this!"

He turned in his saddle and shouted to the referees, "Judges! This man struck me twice, and I wish penalty!"

The stands were shouting, some for victory, some wondering what madness the officers had come up with this time, but the two lance-majors chosen to referee the match said nothing. Slowly they rode forward, and the other players rode up with them.

"Sir," one of them began, "I saw nothing."

"Nor did I, Captain," said the other.

"Then you're damned blind! I say this man fouled me! Are you accusing me of lying?"

"Legate?" one of the lance-majors said.

Perhaps I could have phrased my reply more politely, but I *knew* I hadn't touched him—in both cases my stroke would have been put off, and I certainly would have felt the blow up the shaft of my hammer.

"The hells I did," I said, my face no doubt reddening in anger. "The captain is mistaken! He must have struck himself by accident, turning to come after me!"

"I did not, Legate," and Captain Lanett's voice was as cold as a mountain stream. "Are you saying *I* am the liar?"

I started to say what I believed, but caught myself just in time. "I do no such thing, sir," and I put emphasis on the word. "I know what I did, and I expect every man on this field knows as well."

The adjutant stared at me, and when he did I swear the shouts of the regiment went mute. He said nothing, but wheeled his horse and rode off toward the stables.

Cheetah Troop had, indeed, taken the day. But the last few seconds had soured that victory. The men of my column congratulated me, but even their praise was muted. It took only seconds for everyone in the Seventeenth Lancers to know what had happened: The regimental adjutant, a man of probity and respect, had accused the newest officer, an unknown legate from a forgotten district, of illegal play and the gods-damned boy had the gall to deny it.

I hoped the incident would be forgotten or at least ignored, and avoided the mess that night. But it was clear by the next morning that my "fouling" of Captain Lanett was the sensation of the hour, and it would be some time before it was forgotten.

Lanett made it worse by refusing to look at or speak to me save when duty directly called, and so the incident grew.

I felt I was in disgrace such as no officer had ever known and, worse, was being treated as unjustly as any man the gods wished to test for moral righteousness. A thousand plans and plots ran across my mind, from the hope that my family's hearth-god Tanis might reach out and twist Lanett's soul to make him tell the truth, or that the adjutant might be savaged by the next boar he attempted to spear, and even far less honorable thoughts in the deep of night involving cleverly arranged "accidents."

It might seem these events are absurd, taken far beyond proportion, which is true. But such affairs of honor are quite common when soldiers are at peace, their minds not fully occupied with their trade. But on the other hand it's not that foolish—would a merchant hire a young clerk whom another respected colleague has falsely accused of theft?

A soldier, really, has only one possession besides his life, and that is his honor.

I knew not what I could do.

The solution was time, I now realize. Sooner or later another scandal would appear, and mine would move into the background. If I did nothing foolish like desert or strike my superior, there would inevitably come a backswell of support, especially if I carried myself well and gave no cause whatsoever for reproach.

But that is not what happened.

Less than two weeks later, just at the end of the Time of Heat, I was in the riding ring with my column, putting them through yet another round of mounted drill, when I was summoned to the domina's office.

I was worried—thus far the regiment's commander had appeared to take no notice of what had happened at the rõl match, and I was trying to convince myself he hadn't learned of the event. But now . . . junior legates are *never* called before the domina, except in the event of complete disaster.

I hurriedly changed into my best uniform, and went to the

regimental headquarters. The regimental guide, Evatt, ushered me directly into Domina Herstal's office, and I saw real trouble coming.

There was only one man in the office: Captain Lanett. He sat at the domina's table, a great slab of cunningly worked teak, and appeared intent on some papers in front of him.

I smashed my fist against my chest in salute and stood at rigid attention. After a long moment, he deigned to look up.

"Legate Damastes á Cimabue," he began, without preamble, "you are being detached."

I hope I managed to keep an impassive face, but I doubt it. Shit—no doubt I was being sent to some assignment in limbo, caring for the widows and orphans of lances who'd fallen in the line of duty, or elephant handlers' school or something else guaranteed to end my career. The bastard adjutant would not let go.

"Sir!" was all I said, however, in spite of my anger and churning guts.

"Do you wish to know where?"

"If the captain wishes to tell me."

"It's a plum assignment," Lanett said, and a smile, not friendly, came and went on his thin lips. "Something most officers would die for."

I'll interject a rule here that holds true in all walks of life: The more a task is praised by the one giving it, the more likely it is to be dangerous, thankless, pointless, or all three.

I waited in silence. Captain Lanett began reading from the paper in front of him.

"At the pleasure of the Rule of Ten, you are being detached, together with all lances and warrants of Cheetah Troop, to provide security for the new resident-general of the Border States, also known as the Province of Kait, until ordered otherwise. You are also to function as military adviser and aide to the resident-general, and in any other capacity he deems fit, until you are properly relieved or replaced by either the resident-general or the domina commanding Seventeenth Ureyan Lancers. In addition . . ."

He went on, but I heard nothing much. He stopped after a few more sentences, and I'm afraid I blurted, "Sir, if I understand you correctly, I'm being put in command of Cheetah Troop? *All* of Cheetah Troop?" I was completely incredulous. One turning of the glass ago I was waiting to be sent into some sort of exile, now I was being given what I would only be able to dream of for at least five, and more like ten, years: command of an entire troop, over 100 lances, a promotion of two full positions! Something was wrong.

"That is correct."

"May I ask why I was chosen?"

I knew I'd left myself open, and expected a glare and a reprimand from the captain. Instead, he looked down at the desk, as if unwilling to meet my gaze. His tone, though, *was* harsh:

"That was the decision reached by Domina Herstal and me," he said. "You need not question it."

"No, sir. But—"

"If you have questions, you can ask them of Troop Guide Evatt. Your troop is to be ready to ride out, bag and baggage, to Renan, where the resident-general awaits, within two hours. All married men are to be transferred to other troops and replaced by single lances. Dismissed!"

I started to gape like a fish, but caught myself, clapped my hand to my chest, wheeled, and marched out.

Something was *dreadfully* wrong.

Regimental Guide Evatt was—normally—a bluff, paternal man whom a number of new recruits and legates had made the mistake of treating like a kindly and declining grandsire, for which compliment he'd repaid them by verbally removing their hides in small strips and nailing them to the wall of his office. I hadn't made that mistake, but had treated him as what he was: the conscience, judge, and heart of the regiment. If he had not been a warrant, everyone in the regiment except Domina Herstal would have called him "sir." In return, I'd been given the compliment of being addressed as he did all officers under the age of fifty, as "young sir," or "young legate."

But not this day. He acted a bit diffident, as if he was doing something he knew wrong, and, just like Captain Lanett, had a bit of trouble meeting my eye, and his answers were only a bit less evasive than those of the adjutant.

He told me the orders had been received two hours ago by heliograph. I wondered why I hadn't been detailed by Domina Herstal himself—detaching one of his prized regiment's six troops was a big change, and it seemed to me he would want to make sure I was fully instructed.

"He didn't have the time, Legate. Another matter came up."

I wondered what other matter, more important, could have occurred, here in our sleepy garrison, at the exact same moment, but didn't pursue that line.

"Guide Evatt, why me?" I suspect my tone was imploring.

"Because," the older man said slowly, but mechanically, as if giving a rehearsed answer to an expected question, "the domina feels all new officers should be given command training as early as possible."

"But into the Border States?"

"There should be no major problems, Legate á Cimabue," he said. "This is a diplomatic mission, not an expeditionary force."

"I've heard," I said, "the Men of the Hills don't bother to find a difference when they have *any* Numantian soldier within bowshot." I could have also asked if this was expected to be a peaceful task, why the married lances and warrants were to be left behind.

"Legate," the regimental guide said, "we don't have time for jawing. The domina wanted you on your way so you can reach Renan within three days. The resident-general and a company of infantry are waiting there."

That was all I would get from him. I thanked him, trying to sound as insincere as possible, and went for Cheetah Troop's barracks.

They were a swirl of confusion and obscenity as men uprooted themselves from months and even, in some cases, years of comfort. My own column, which would have been given their orders last, after I'd been summoned, and hence had less time to pack, was swearing more loudly and piteously than the others.

There was a line of carts, bullocks already hitched, drawn up in front of the barracks, and bedding and baggage were cascading in.

Fortunately I would keep Troop Guide Bikaner, both of whose wives had left him to return to their native district for ritual purification some months ago, not to return for at least a year.

He was surrounded by chaos, bellowing orders and looking a bit frantic as a steady stream of thankful- or angry-looking married men left for their new troops, and new and unknown lances wandered or rode in, arms and horses cluttered with their gear.

I grabbed one lance, ordered him to my quarters with instructions to pile everything in the room into the bags under the bed and to have my horses, Lucan and Rabbit, saddled and ready to ride and two pack horses loaded with my gear.

Then I set to helping Troop Guide Bikaner, trying to appear as if I were in command, but actually trying to impede him as little as possible. He'd done such moves many times over the years, and I but once, and that a drill at the lycee.

Surprisingly, in one and one half hours we were drawn up on the parade ground, our wagons—loaded with our possessions and the rations for the journey, plus the attached handful of cooks, smiths, harness makers, sutlers, and quartermasters from Sun Bear Troop, the regiment's support element—to the rear.

Domina Herstal appeared and, after I called the men to attention, addressed them briefly, saying they were headed for a new, and possibly difficult, duty, and they were to obey Legate á Cimabue as they would him, *following all proper and sensible orders*, a phrase I found a bit unusual. He also advised the men to be careful on the other side of the mountains and bade them all a safe return when their duty was complete.

It was as uninspiring a speech as I'd ever heard.

At its finish, Captain Lanett gave me an oilskin packet with my orders, Domina Herstal took the salute, and we rode out of Mehul Garrison toward Renan.

It had taken me only a day and a half, riding leisurely, to travel from Renan to Mehul. It took the troop three days, pushing hard. Admittedly, the more the men the longer travel takes, but we were further slowed by our baggage and wagons. I was grateful we were not traveling with families and the motley followers that trail an army on the move, but our pace was tedious for cavalry.

I knew something strange had happened, but could not figure what it could be. It was hard worrying at the matter yet still maintaining a cheerful and firm exterior to the men, who certainly weren't unaware the situation was abnormal. I came up with an acceptable lie, that Domina Herstal no doubt knew of the possibility of this assignment some time ago, but sprang it as a surprise because he wished to find out how prepared the regiment was for a sudden move, such as if war erupted between us and Maisir. That eased the worry, and made the grumbling of "But why is Cheetah Troop so special—couldn't we stay happy, ordinary swine in the rear ranks and ignored like we were?" louder. Ironically, in view of what came later, I'd come up with my explanation as being the most preposterous, since Numantia and the enormous kingdom of Maisir had been long at peace, and our rivalry was only in trade.

Troop Guide Bikaner looked at me wryly, and so I asked him to ride ahead of the column with me, out of the men's earshot. I asked him if he had any better theory. He thrice denied doubting what I'd said, as a polite warrant should, but eventually grinned and agreed that yes, things were most out of whack.

"I'll have t'believe, Domina Herstal was as s'prised by th' orders as anyone. Whatever's goin' on, he's not parcel to. I've known him since he was a captain, an' there's not a sly bone to him."

"I'll ask you," I said, deciding utter frankness was the best, "the same question I wanted to ask Captain Lanett and did ask

Regimental Guide Evatt, without getting a good answer: Why was I chosen to take command of this troop?"

There was a long silence, with only the whisper of the hot breeze through the roadside trees and the clop of our horses' hooves.

"I don't want t'answer that, sir, not knowin' anything, and havin' naught but a supposition t'offer, an' that speaks not well of th' regiment, an' worse of our task."

"I won't order you, Warrant. But your ass—and the behinds of all the other lances—are in the same bucket mine is. I think I'll need all the help I can get, even if it's the most dreadful sort of false augury."

"Very well, sir. You asked, sir. I don't have any idea of what th' crooked die'll be, nor when it'll be rolled, but there's an old army sayin' that when th' floor of th' crapper's about to give way, y' send in the man y' least care if he stinks of shit t'jump up an' down an' test it."

Troop Guide Bikaner's proverb didn't surprise me—I'd already figured something was nearly guaranteed to turn sour, and the regiment wished to have the most sacrificeable lamb to offer the tiger. I thanked him for giving me something to think about, but made no other comment. His morale was easily twice as important as any of the men's, and needed no further lessening. It was my burden. As my father had said, over and over again, "If you want to wear the cloak of command, know it's of the heaviest cloth, with weights hidden in the fabric, and can be worn by only one man."

We reached Renan and went directly to the holding barracks, where my orders said the infantry company would be waiting. It was—125 men, of the Khurram Light Infantry. Troop Guide Bikaner said he'd heard they were considered not the best, but far from the worst soldiery. They'd be a bit of a problem at first, he added, since they had no experience fighting the Men of the Hills. "But they'll learn quick," he added. "Or else there'll be more bones on th' peaks."

They were properly officered, led by a Captain Mellet, who impressed me as a stolid, dependable sort, not fast in the attack, but equally slow to give way. He evinced no surprise that the orders put me, his junior, in charge of the expedition, but expressed hope that I wouldn't give orders to any of the foot soldiers except through him. I reassured him that I may have been young, but I knew my military courtesy, and wished to know where our new superior, the new governor general of the Border States, was staying, so I could report.

"He's already traveling," the captain said.

"What?"

"He received special orders night before last. Heliograph orders, in code, all the way from Nicias, saying he must get to Sayana immediately. The orders came directly from the Rule of Ten, and went on to say they'd had reliable reports from the court seers that trouble was building in the capital, and Numantia had to have an envoy on the spot at once. He set out yesterday before first light, and said for us to join him on the road, after the cavalry joined up."

I was completely astonished.

"Captain, you're saying the governor general set out for the Border States with *no* escort? He's going by way of Sulem Pass, isn't he?"

"Yessir. It didn't seem right to either of us, but he said his orders were most exact. He also told me the Rule of Ten said there'd been a safe passage established through the pass with the tribesmen. He's also a seer, you know, so he thought he might be able to sense any threats before they could be mounted."

"Isa naked with a damned sword," I swore. "The Rule of Ten imagines the hillmen will keep their word?" Even a novice like myself knew better than that. Especially transiting Sulem Pass. Most especially for a dignitary who'd no doubt be laden with presents for whoever was the current achim in the Border States' capital of Sayana. "How many in his party? And is he traveling fast?"

"About twenty. He's got four elephants and their keepers, six outriders, and four wagons heavy-loaded with gear. Eight outriders, two men to each wagon. The beasts'll ensure he's not moving much faster than a man marches."

This was preposterous. Worse, it was insane. I had a momentary flash of what Troop Guide Bikaner had said, but put that thought aside.

"Captain, how fast can your men be ready to move?"

"Two . . . three hours."

"Make it two. I want your command at the gates by then. We've got to get to this damned resident-general before the fool gets himself massacred, which'll happen ten feet inside Sulem Pass unless the Men of the Hills are utter fools."

A look of alarm slowly crossed Captain Mellet's face, and he rose, knocking over his chair, and cried for his legates. I started for the door, then turned back.

"Captain, what's our esteemed and suicidal superior's name?"

"Tenedos. Laish Tenedos."

It was closer to three hours before we set off. My father, and my better instructors at the lycee, had said that patience can be an officer's biggest virtue, and so it was this day. I wanted to shout at the soldiers as they trudged down the winding road that climbed toward the hills to speed up. I wanted to order our bullocks prodded into a stumbling trot. By the armor of Isa, I wanted all of us to be mounted and at the gallop.

But I kept silent, gnawing on my tongue as if it were prime beef, and we plodded on.

If I thought our carts moved slowly, they were racing chariots compared to the infantry's wagons. The KLI seemed to travel with every possession they'd been born with, including several women on the carts who would have fit into Mehul's whorehouse district called Rotten Row without rousing the slightest comment.

We made camp that night without sighting Resident-General Tenedos's party.

At first light, I told a detail of five men to ride up the road, and if they encountered the diplomat, to ask him to please hold until his escort arrived. I also bade them turn back no later than midafternoon—we were close to the mountains, and the Men of the Hills defined that border most loosely and were likely to have ambush parties out.

At dusk we set up for the second night, and as we lit our fires the detail returned. The party must have been moving faster than Captain Mellet had thought, because they'd seen no one. But the resident-general was on the road, or anyway it was someone with elephants, since they found droppings. "Either that," someone in the rear ranks muttered, "or th' damned arm-waver's taken wi' th' worst case a th' shits since Ma told me about corks." I ostentatiously didn't hear the comment, but noted the man, and when time came for a detail to help our cooks clean up after dinner, that lance found himself working.

The mountains were very close now, and we'd reach them on the morrow. Something the patrol had said had worried me even more: They'd encountered no travelers at all coming north. If no one was on the road from the Border States, no merchant, wanderer, or beggar, trouble did indeed threaten.

At daybreak I sent another patrol forward, but this time with ten men, since we were close to hostile territory.

The foothills were bare, and stony, and we kept sharp eyes out to our flanks. Several times scouts reported movement, but we never saw horse nor rider.

"They're out there," Lance-Major Wace said grimly. "But th' only time you see one of them is when they want you to."

The patrol rode back well before dark, and said they'd reached the mouth of Sulem Pass without encountering the resident-general.

We were too late.

We made camp and I set a rotating guard of one-quarter of the men. Now we must be ready for battle at any moment. We only unpacked vital necessities, and fed and watered the unhappy bullocks in their harness.

Two hours before first light we broke camp and when the sky grayed we moved out. I asked Captain Mellet to put out his soldiers on either side of the road, and kept response elements of my cavalry ready in case they were hit. We moved in open order as well, to present a less juicy target.

Just at dawn, we entered Sulem Pass.

The pass, as most know, is the most direct route between the kingdoms of Numantia and Maisir, with the Border State of Kait between. In times of peace it is a prime trading route.

But the Men of the Hills seldom allow that. To them, a trader is nothing more than a personal sutler, who provides all manner of goods and gold as soon as the hillman waves a sword in his face.

Sulem Pass twists for about twenty leagues, until it opens onto the plains that lead to the city of Sayana. Bare ridges climb 600 to 1,000 feet above the floor of the pass. The pass begins in a narrow ravine, then, about halfway through, opens onto a plateau where the Sulem River turns and rushes down a canyon, to the south. From there until the comparative flatlands of Kait, it's more hospitable, the river coursing beside the track.

Twenty leagues—only two days' ride, but no one, not even the hillmen, have ever ridden it in that time. Each twist, each zigzag, each rock may, and most likely does, harbor an ambush.

The pass mouth on the Ureyan side is the narrowest, with the mountains close to a few hundred feet of each other, and the face on either side is unclimbable rock.

We moved slowly through this gut. I had horsemen out in front, and, just back of them, the men Captain Mellet said were his fleetest of foot. If they saw any sign of trouble, they were to double back to the column, giving the alarm.

I sent them out in pairs, with orders that no man was to abandon his mate under any circumstances. The Men of the Hills prize bravery above all, and the bravest can endure any pain without crying out. A captive, wounded or no, will be tortured to death, and if he dies without screaming he will be well spoken of around the hillmen's fires. But that seldom happens, for the tribesmen are most skilled at their recreation.

My cavalrymen, being experienced, had their own rules:

Never leave a comrade unless he is dead, and if you must, kill him yourself. Some of the men carried small daggers in sheaths around their necks, intended for themselves if no one else could grant the last mercy.

A quarter-mile inside the pass, the way broadened, and our progress was even slower. This sounds illogical, but the more open ground was perfect for a trap.

There was an immutable policy regulating how soldiers were to travel through Sulem Pass: First send foot soldiers to take and hold the closest hilltops. Then the road-bound unit moves even with these pickets. A second group takes the next hilltops, while waiting for the first to descend safely. This was the most likely time of ambush—when a soldier thought he wouldn't be attacked, and all that was necessary was to slip back down the hill and march on.

It was then that the sandy rock would become a ululating group of warriors, ten, perhaps twenty, who'd rush the pickets, daggers flashing, and before anyone could move there'd be naked bodies strewn on the rock, the Men of the Hills retreating with their loot and, if Isa was not good, a captive or two for later amusement.

I'd been taught there were seldom big victories when Numantians fought the Men of the Hills—perhaps one or two bodies would be found, more likely only bloodstains and silence, and once again the column would move on.

We went into Sulem Pass at no more than a half-mile an hour, if that. I was angry, angry at these strange orders that had sent a foolish diplomat to certain death, and at the snails I commanded, but mostly at my own inability to think of a plan, any plan.

Again the pass narrowed, and I saw, perched high above, the ruins of a stone fort Numantia had carved out two centuries earlier, when our country had a king, instead of being governed by the Rule of Ten, and before we'd allowed the Kaiti, with the implicit support of the Maisir, to negotiate us all the way back to the flatlands.

These days Kait was as the Men of the Hills preferred it—

anarchic, where every man had an enemy and every tribe a desperate feud. The achim on the throne in Sayana was barely more than a figurehead and, being himself a brigand, someone who used the royal advantage for his clan's private wars.

The pass widened, and there was a small village, and the legend on my map said *They pretend to be allies of any traveler, but turn not your back. Let one of them drink water, taste fruit, before you buy.*

I saw only half a dozen old men, a few babes, and no women at all. The last was unsurprising—the Men of the Hills prize their women as possessions to be kept hidden, for fear a bolder or stronger man will steal them. But that there were no men, leaning insolently on spear or sheathed saber, was alarming.

Troop Guide Bikaner told me this most likely meant the men were araiding. "That'll be th' happiest explanation, though," he said.

As we went deeper into the pass, crawling along, I saw, on the highest crag above me, a bit of movement that might have been someone watching. Then came a mirror-flash, as someone signaled our presence to others, deeper in the pass.

A mile or so farther on, we came on another human presence. Bodies, half-rotten, were scattered in a draw that led up from the trail. They were black, dead more than a few days, and decaying.

One of my men dismounted, and ran to the corpses. As he did, kites fluttered up, skrawking at their meal being disturbed. He reported they were hillmen, and all were naked, stripped bare. He'd seen an arrow shaft protruding from one's ribs, and knew by the markings it came from a hillman's bow.

"I reckoned," Troop Guide Bikaner said, "back there if th' village men were out just raidin', that was the best that could be. This"—and his hands swept across the tiny battleground—"means worse. Feudin' at least. Just as likely buildin' themselves up for war."

"Against whom?" I asked.

"Anybody," Bikaner said. "Mebbe th' folks in Sayana that

they despise for bein' weaklings who give up on th' hills. May-hap south, into Maisir.

"But most likely north. Into Urey. Been a few years since they struck at us, an' th' thought of how rich it's got since they raided's got to be makin' 'em lick their lips, thinkin' of th' sweets t' be had."

He was most likely right—I'd heard in the Lancers' mess it had been almost five years since there'd been a good plague or a better war, which was when promotions fell like leaves in a windstorm. It would make a grand preamble for such a war if the Men of the Hills could parade a high-ranking Numantian head on a lance.

Captain Mellet's sergeants were shouting, and I saw pickets running down from the latest hill they'd outposted, and other warrants were calling for their squad to be ready to mount the next ridge and we were ready for our next round of leap-the-frog.

It was completely intolerable. The day was growing late; the sun was already in the center of the heavens.

Very well, I thought. *I was put in command of this force. Therefore I shall command it.* It was increasingly obvious that I was, if not intended, then surely expected, to fail. I would always rather fail doing *something* than waiting or doing nothing.

I rode to the wagon Captain Mellet was in.

"Captain, I wish you to take charge of this train, including the cavalry's wagons and spare mounts."

The man took a minute to think, then nodded acceptance.

"Very well, Legate á Cimabue. But you?"

"The cavalry will ride on, without stopping, until we find the resident-general."

"But Legate . . ." and he looked about, saw he could be overheard, and jumped from his seat and hurried to my horse. "Legate, that's against standing orders. No unit moves without its support, except in battle or on patrol."

"*My* orders, sir," and I put finality into my tones, "were to escort the resident-general through Sulem Pass to his new post in Sayana. Those are the orders—the *only* orders I propose to follow."

I didn't wait for his response, but shouted for Bikaner. Fill canteens from the water barrels on the wagons, each trooper draw one pound of dry rations—beef jerked with mountain berries—and we would ride. Ten minutes later we clattered off, at the trot, down the trail.

I sent two riders ahead, with orders to stay within eyesight of the troop, to wait short of any possible ambuscade until we drew almost to it, and then to ride through at the gallop. I changed these scouts every half hour.

This was a deadly risk, but I thought it had a chance of succeeding. First, because we were moving faster than the hillmen could, even though they had the fleetness of mountain antelope afoot, and also because *no one* traveled through the Border States in this manner.

I wished we had infantry in support, since sending cavalry through broken terrain without keen eyes afoot to spot a spearman lying in wait is waiting to be destroyed. I had even dreamed of a way to move them faster: either to have them ride behind us, and dismount when we made contact; or even hanging onto our stirrups, which I'd done as a lad when there were five of us and only one horse. Hard on horses, hard on men— but I thought it could work. This later became one of the emperor's most prized tactics to surprise the enemy. But I had not time to explain it to Captain Mellet nor to train his troops in the method.

We moved until it was too dark to see, then made a cold camp, lighting no fires, and keeping half the men on watch.

I slept not at all, and when I could distinguish my hand in front of my face ordered the men up and on.

Two hours after sunrise, we heard the screams of dying horses, the shouts of men fighting for their lives.

I found later that Laish Tenedos had kept his party moving from first to last light, hurrying to get through Sulem Pass to offer the least temptation to the Men of the Hills, not believing in the storied safe-conduct pass. This day, they'd set out at dawn, and had reached the plateau where the Sulem River that came from Sayana curved and left the pass.

They'd seen no enemies, been harassed by no hidden bowmen. They thought that a good sign, none of the party having any experience in these mountains, whereas a Lancer would have taken the greatest alarm, knowing some terrible and vast trap was being laid ahead.

I heard the noise, just as the two men on point galloped back and reported fighting—they thought it was the party we sought, because there were elephants down—at the ford.

I was about to shout for the attack, just as the books say foolish cavalrymen do whenever they hear the clang of swords, but caught myself, remembering there might well be flankers ready, and we could hurtle straight into another trap—this one prepared for rescuers.

I told Lance Major Wace to ready the troop for battle and, with Troop Guide Bikaner, rode forward a ways, then dismounted and went on foot until we could see the valley in front. We flattened and considered the scene.

From this moment until the end of the battle, I shall describe the action as clearly as I can, since this, the Meeting Between Damastes á Cimabue and the Young Seer Tenedos, at the Battle of Sulem Pass, is one of the best-known scenes in Numantia's recent history, familiar in paintings, songs, tales, and murals and presented in a manner either foolishly romantic, absurd, or so filled with Great Portent it should be a religious ceremony. Only our final stand, years later on the blood-soaked field of Cambiaso, is more widely portrayed.

Let us start with the facts of the battle. There were perhaps 600 Men of the Hills on one side, and less than 350 Numantians on the other. This was fairly large for a fight in the Border States, but hardly the horizon-to-horizon clash I've seen it painted as.

I saw no anxious gods overhanging the battlefield, nor demons fighting on either side. Nor had there been any magical emissaries imploring me to hurry and save the emperor-to-be.

Finally I saw no grand sorcerous figure standing in the ruins hurling thunderbolts as if he had become a manifestation of Saionji herself.

What I saw was a desolate, desertlike valley, the ground dotted with scrub brush and, every now and then, a scraggling plot of worked ground that might have been called a farm. The Sulem River curled through this valley, and the road crossed it at a ford.

Here was where the ambush had been sprung. Two elephants lay dead just on the other side of the ford, and there were Numantians crouched behind their corpses, using them for shelter. There were four carts, one on the far shore, one overturned in midstream, and two others on the bank closer to me. Two other elephants were kneeling beside those carts, their handlers trying to keep them calm.

There were bodies of horses, oxen, and men scattered around the wreck of the caravan. But there were still Numantians alive, still fighting.

I looked for the enemy, and finally saw some hillmen, well camouflaged in their sandy robes behind rocks on the far shore. Downstream, I saw another party of tribesmen wading the river, about to encircle Tenedos's men.

"Not bad, sir," Troop Guide Bikaner said. "Th' hillmen waited til th' seer's party was fordin', at th' time of most confusion, when ever'body's worried about the horses breakin' free, and waterin' th' oxen, an' then they hit 'em hard. 'Course, if I were handlin' the ambush I would've hit 'em short of th' river, an' let those that survived th' first clash go mad smellin' but never tastin' water." He looked on, and tsked. "I'm afeared those aren't th' finest hillmen I've seen. I see no sign they've got anything in th' way of a reserve, either."

"Very good, Troop Guide, and I'm sure you have a grand future as a dacoit," I said briskly. "One column detached, put Lance Major Wace in charge of that, to deal with those people crossing the river. The rest of us will take the main body at the charge. Straight down the road at the trot, at the walk across the river, which doesn't look more than hock-high, then charge in arrow formation at the horn. Go through them . . . there," I went on, pointing, "sweep back and mop them up. Pay no mind to the resident-general's party—I don't want them to slow us."

Troop Guide Bikaner made no response. I turned.

"You're sure those're are all th' orders you wish t' give, sir?" he asked, face blank.

I'll wager I reddened, but I didn't snap at him, so the madness of battle had not yet taken me. "What am I missing?"

"Look close, sir. There's magic on th' field."

I gazed more closely, and now saw the haze floating around the ford, something that might have been taken for heat waves or even light dust. I'd seen it only once before, at a demonstration at the lycee. This "haze," and I'm not describing it well, but that is the only word I know that fits, seemed centered around the corpse of the elephant closest to the enemy positions. Not far from it was a white horse, three or four spears stuck in its body.

I heard shouts from below, saw the Numantians rise and volley arrows at their attackers. In their center was an unarmed man, who was waving his hands, making an incantation. I remembered Captain Mellet had said the resident-general was a seer, and rejoiced that Tenedos evidently still lived.

Bikaner pointed to a hillock a bit removed from the fighting, to the east. I saw a man standing atop it, a man wearing long robes that marked him a wizard, and there was the same shimmer about his body I saw around the battleground.

"There's one of their wizards," Bikaner said. He craned. "Another there, back of their lines along th' river. An' there'll be a third. . . ." He twisted and looked upward and to our right. "There's th' bastard. I was wrong about th' battle plan, sir. It's a good un. They've got three magicians, an' th' center of th' triangle that's made, givin' focus to the magic, is where they hit 'em. Th' spells'll be th' same as they gen'rly use—confusion, fear, feelin' helpless—but most of all bein' wi'out skill, not able t'aim a bow right, or strike true wi' y'r sword."

I saw the third man, atop a crag just beyond us, above the

road. I swear I could hear, from three directions, the low rumble of chanting.

"Yon diplomat, sir, may have some magickin' powers," Bikaner went on, "but not when there's three t'his one."

"Then let's even the odds before we take them."

"We c'n do that, sir," Bikaner agreed, ran for his horse, and clattered back to the troop. Twelve of my best archers were dismounted and, with saber-ready escort, split into two parties. The first started up the narrow draw that led to the rock closest to us, where the hillmen's seer continued roaring out his spells, paying no heed to anything around him. The others went for the second Kaiti magician to the east.

Within minutes one party was within bowshot of the nearest wizard, and, aiming carefully, fired. Three arrows buried themselves in the wizard's chest, and it seemed as if the world shook. I heard a screech of pain, as if the man were next to me, and the sorcerer crumpled and fell. Soldiers scurried to the summit, to make sure he was, and stayed, dead.

As arranged, we did not wait to see if the second party of archers was successful in taking out another Kaiti magician, but went into our attack.

"At the walk . . . forward . . ."

Cheetah Troop, Seventeenth Ureyan Lancers, crested the hill into the valley of the Sulem River.

I heard shouts, cries of welcome, and then howls of surprise from across the river as the hillmen saw us, but I paid them no mind.

We reached the ford and splashed into it.

"Sound the charge!" I cried and my trumpeter raised the long bullhorn and sent the challenge echoing across the valley.

As it rang forth, I saw something I shall never forget, one of the most noble sights I've witnessed in battle.

One of the elephants I thought dead, who must have been a war beast before he grew too old and was shamefully made into a cargo animal, heard the blare in the dying recesses of his mind, and rolled up, staggering to his feet, trunk lifting, curling, and his own war cry bugled back at us, and he stumbled a few steps, trying to obey the long-forgotten command, and fell dead.

Our lances were couched and we thundered into the charge, and I was at the formation's arrow-tip. Robed men were before me, one drawing his bow, and my lance struck him fair, the first man I'd ever slain, and sent him spinning away. I wheeled my horse, yanking my lance free, and came back on the line of tribesmen, and took down another hillman, then cast aside my lance and came in with the saber, my troop following like we were a single horseman.

The hillmen may have been bastards, but they were brave bastards. I saw no sign that they were breaking and running, which is usually the case when soldiers afoot are surprised by cavalry.

Instead, the Men of the Hills held their line and then counterattacked, trying to take down our horses with spears, and slashing at us as we rode past.

It was a brutal, bloody melee, men shouting, hacking at each other, gut-ripped horses going down screaming, and rage exploding, sabers too clean for this work, daggers and clawed hands savaging at their enemies.

A line of hillmen came at us, almost like regulars in their order, and I cried warning to my men.

Then the world hummed about me, and I saw something unimaginable. Not far from me a spear was embedded in the sand. I saw it pull free from the ground, with no one close to it, and then arc through the air, hard-thrown, and bury itself in a hillman's chest. Fear coursed through me, and I saw other abandoned weapons—arrows, swords, daggers, javelins—join the battle as if wielded by invisible warriors.

I saw the man who must be Seer Tenedos standing in the open, and I heard his voice, crashing like the thunder as he sent his spell out against the tribesmen.

The hillmen will stand against almost any enemy—but not sorcery.

Now there were screams of terror, and the Men of the Hills broke, throwing their weapons aside in panic and running, but the remorseless spell continued, and men were cut down as they tried to escape.

Then the battlefield was empty of all except corpses, wounded, and victors.

Lance Major Wace's column galloped across the river toward us, shouting victory, and I knew they'd eliminated the attempted attack from the rear.

I prodded Lucan into a trot, toward the ford, to Tenedos and the remains of his party.

Magicians are supposed to tower over all, their fierce beards and clawed hands striking fear into all.

The man who came toward me was anything but that, I saw as I slid from my horse.

He was a little older than I, but still under thirty, and fairly short, more than a foot smaller than I am. He was black-haired, his hair worn short in the current Nician fashion, and his face was round, not unhandsome, almost boyish. He wore dark breeches and a coat, well-tailored, but they failed to conceal his slight paunch.

But it was his eyes that reached out, black, blazing like demon-fire, and took me in their grasp.

His voice came, and it was the commanding thunder of Irisu himself, but the words were completely unexpected:

"I am Seer Laish Tenedos. You must be my executioner."

THREE

A MAGICIAN'S DREAMS

For a moment I thought the seer had gone mad. But before I could respond, a smile grew on his face, and I basked in the warmth of a spring sun.

"Ah, but I see I am wrong," Tenedos said. "I sense you mean me no harm, and I humble myself with apologies. Consider me the least of men who insulted the one who saved his life." He bowed low.

I saluted, and introduced myself, my mission, and my assignment. I explained the problems we'd had, from a seeming error in orders to the slow pace we'd been able to make through the pass. Tenedos nodded.

"We shall discuss this further, and perhaps I can add to your knowledge. I note from your speech that you are from Cimabue, eh?" I braced myself for some probably generous but demeaning comment, but instead Tenedos said, "Then we shall be the closest of associates and in time, I hope, friends, for I, too, am from a land far from the cabals and conspiracies of Nicias and consequently am frequently chaffed about my origins. I am from the islands of Palmeras."

I knew the lands he spoke of, but only from my map-reading classes at the lycee. They are a cluster of islands off Numantia's western shore, the largest giving its name to the archipelago. The inhabitants are nearly as maligned as Cimabuans, infamous for their long memories for a wrong, their willingness to take injury, and their hotheadedness. On the other hand, they're also noted for loyalty to a friend and truthfulness, in so long as it does not interfere with righting a wrong. Also like Cimabuans, they're looked at in Nicias as distinctly lesser beings instead of as fellow Numantians.

"As for that great insult I laid at your feet, allow me to explain why I erred after we have dealt with this mess."

We treated our wounded and put our wounded animals out of their agony. There were no Men of the Hills to succor— their wounded had either been dragged away by their fellows, crawled off, or been killed. War is ruthless on the Frontiers; our wounded would have been treated similarly, although their deaths would not have been the quick ones my soldiers granted.

After that the wagon in the river was righted, and such goods as could be salvaged brought ashore. There were enough bullocks surviving to pull all the wagons, although our pace would be slowed since two of them must be linked in tandem.

The corpses of the two elephants were dragged together by teams of bullocks. I spared a moment to pray that the brave soul of that animal who'd attempted to join my charge would be advanced on the Wheel, and perhaps return as a babe who would grow to be a warrior.

Then the bodies of the bullocks, horses, and men were stacked around the elephants. Already the hot sun was making the blood-stink rise.

Tenedos ordered a chest taken from a wagon, and took out certain items. He sprinkled oil on some of the bodies, then found a small twig, and touched it to the drying blood of men, horses, oxen, and elephants in turn, then finally to a bit of the oil.

He said he was ready, but first he asked if I could assemble my men, as he had a few words to say. It was unusual, but I obeyed, leaving only the sentries to watch for another attack and for our infantry coming up the pass road.

"Men of the Ureyan Lancers," he began, and once more his voice was magically enhanced, so it rang across the valley. "You have served Laish Tenedos well, and your deeds shall never be forgotten. You are warriors, real Numantians, and I am proud to know you, and count you my comrades, even though we met but a few hours ago on this battleground.

"I am a seer, and I will make you a promise, now, here, and seal it in the blood of our fallen comrades. There are great times ahead, great deeds to be done and great prizes to be reaped. You, who have shown your courage and loyalty this day, I hope shall be among those who are richened by what is to come.

"I sorrow with you for your brothers who fell today, although their return to the Wheel is blessed, for they died doing good, and this will be remembered by the gods. Perhaps they shall return, and be among us once more, and live in the glorious times that shall come."

He bowed his head, and we did the same. I marveled at his words—it was as if Tenedos were commander of this troop or a general instead of some diplomat we had been ordered to escort just as we'd done for others from the court of the Rule of Ten. I had heard other soft-handed shifting-eyed government emissaries blather about how they were soldiers at heart, and seen the rudeness or quiet contempt their words were held in. But not now, not by any of the Lancers, nor by me. Laish Tenedos might dress as a government officer, but he spoke as a true leader, and I began to believe I would follow and obey him gladly.

Tenedos had set up a brazier, and he kindled it with a sparkthrower. A small flame rose, and he chanted:

"Listen, unguent.
Feel the warmth
Feel the flame
You serve the gods.
You carry our lost

You serve Saionji.
Fire, burn
Fire, serve."

As he spoke, he touched the twig to the tiny flame on the brazier, and as he did a great fire roared into life on the nearby pyre, soaring high into the sky, far higher than any oil-fed flame could.

Tenedos watched, and a grim smile touched his lips.

"Now, let *that* be seen in Nicias as a portent of what is to come," he said quietly, and I doubt if anyone besides myself heard him.

We moved a short distance upriver, away from the flames, but close enough so we could see the ford, and set up defensive positions. I made sure my sentries were properly posted, then found a rock to sit on while Tenedos's cook, assisted by a few of my men who claimed ability over a camp fire, prepared dinner from the luxurious viands the resident-general had been carrying. Tenedos had told me to take whatever was needed for dinner, saying, "What might have been a boon to the Achim Baber Fergana is better suited as provender for your honest man." Once more, what might have been empty hyperbole I felt to be honest praise.

Tenedos approached. "Now," he said, "since we have a few moments of peace, and there is no one within listening range, I shall explain why I said what I said when we met."

He asked permission to sit, and I waved him to another rock, hoping I'd get a full explanation. I did, but it was as odd as his behavior.

"Have you ever known a man who suddenly decided all the world and all the gods had turned against him and were conspiring to destroy him?"

I had, at the lycee. One of the more promising cadets had gotten the idea the staff was trying to poison him, and he was warned by secret messages from the gods who wrote in private letters of flame across the sky. Seers and herbalists tried to treat him, but with no success, and he was returned to his sorrowing family. A few months later we were told that he'd killed himself, in a frenzy of terror because he now believed even his own blood was involved with the plot. I nodded.

"Good. So then be aware some of what I'm going to say may well sound mad. I will only ask that you keep your judgment of my madness to yourself, and do nothing about it until I'm completely irrational—or else proven to be right."

I was looking at the Seer Tenedos with a bit of alarm by now. That sun-smile flashed again, and I felt warmed, and somehow *knew* Tenedos was sane, perhaps more so than I was.

"I'll start my argument at the beginning.

"Don't you consider it odd a seer like myself has been appointed to the position of resident-general?"

I did, but assumed Tenedos had some friends in the government, and this was a political payment, even if most Numantians would consider it as valuable a gift as a quadruple amputee would think scabies.

"That's hardly the experience one would wish a man to have for such a posting, unless it were to a land ruled by sorcerers, which Kait is not," Tenedos went on. "The reason I was chosen for this post, most dangerous and as far away from Nicias as it is possible to get, is I am an unpopular man with radical ideas."

That, just from his behavior, I might well have assumed. I guess my opinion was obvious, because again Tenedos smiled.

"I was sent out here so honest Nicians would no longer be exposed to my heresies. I also now believe I was intended to die, considering those 'special' orders I received telling me to leave at once without waiting for my military escort, and of the obviously nonexistent safe passage.

"I could now suggest more evidence. I mean no offense, Legate Damastes á Cimabue, but I find it *very* unusual to see a full troop of cavalry commanded by a very junior officer, let alone if his column includes infantry, with a captain at its head, almost as if that legate were being set up to be the skittle the balls will be rolled at."

I kept my face stony.

"Very good, Legate," Tenedos approved. "I would have been surprised and disappointed if you'd made any response. Let me ask a few questions. You only need respond if the answer is yes to any of them: Are you a particular favorite in your regiment? Has your unit suffered a lot of casualties recently among the officer corps? Are you known as having any great skills in dealing with obnoxious and arrogant emissaries such as myself?"

Perhaps a smile came and went at that last, but I remained silent.

"Also as I expected," Tenedos said. "Let us make some assumptions. The first is the Rule of Ten was accurate when they said Kait, the Border States, is preparing to rise once again. Let us further suppose," Tenedos continued, "the Rule of Ten might wish to crush this unrest with an iron boot heel, such as has not been done for a generation or more. If that were the case, would not the death of their envoy be a perfect reason for sending the heavy battalions, not merely a punitive expedition, into Kait?

"With that as Numantia's reason, the Kaiti could appeal to Maisir all they wished, but it would be unlikely King Bairan would respond. Ah, I see you are unaware the Kaiti have always played Numantia and Maisir against each other, so neither country can bring the Border States into its dominion without the risk of offending its great neighbor.

"The murder of a resident-general might also be enough of a reason for the state of Dara to finally extend its borders to include Urey, and end the three-sided argument between us, Kallio, and Maisir about its proper ownership."

"I know nothing about such things," I said. "I am but a soldier, and not political."

This time Tenedos's smile was pitying.

"Damastes, my friend," he said, and his voice was soft, "the time is coming near when *all* Numantians will have to be political."

He was about to go on, but a sentry cried out that Captain

Mellet's column was coming up the road, and in minutes the dust-boil was close enough for us all to make it out.

I had not expected the infantry until the next day, but Mellet said he had been shamed by my dash, and had forced double-speed on the marching soldiers, even allowing them, five at a time, to ride on the carts for a break, and chancing ambush by marching an hour after dark and an hour before sunrise. "I thought," he said, "that'd be unexpected of us, and so the hillmen might not have time to set their traps, and so it's proven."

Camp routine and determining the new order of march occupied the rest of the day. All the while, I kept working at Seer Tenedos's words. I am not a swift thinker; all know that. But I am most thorough, and worry at something until it comes clear in my mind. But what Tenedos had said was still puzzling me when the sun rose and we set off toward Sayana.

Now that we did not have to race on, we could move as common practice and logic dictated, putting flankers out when the country was open, and sending pickets to take each hilltop before we passed under it. The country was less sharp, less broken, so the peaks took less time to clamber up and down, and we made acceptable speed.

The first two villages we passed were as the first: deserted except for babes, women, and ancients. The tribes *were* planning something, and I hoped it was longer-ranged than the obliteration of my command.

The third village was as the other two—almost. Laish Tenedos was riding in front, beside me, on Rabbit. I cannot say I heard anything, but turned for some reason, and saw a boy appear from behind a wall, drawing an old bow nearly as big as he was, aimed full at my chest! I had no time to duck aside, and knew my doom, hearing warning shouts from the column when the rotten wood snapped in two, just below the grip. The boy shouted with rage, and was about to dart away when Lance Karjan swept up at the gallop and caught the lad by an arm, pulling him, kicking and squirming like an eel, up across his saddle.

I dismounted, and walked to Karjan's horse. I grabbed the boy's hair and lifted his head, so I could see his face.

"So you wanted to kill me?"

"*Chishti!*" the boy swore. *Chishti* is a very rude word in one of the hill dialects used to describe a man who has slept with his mother. "*Chishti* Numantian!" What more reason could he need?

Tenedos laughed. "A lion cub always thinks he's full grown, doesn't he?"

"Shall I kill 'im, sir?" Lance Karjan growled, hand on his dagger.

"No," I said. "Set him down. I don't murder babes."

The soldier hesitated, then obeyed, tossing the boy down with one hand. He should have sprawled, but twisted in midair, and landed on his feet. He stood half-crouched, exactly like a trapped beast of prey.

"Go on," I said. "When you try again, remember to use a bow that's been oiled, not your grandfather's that's dried on the wall for a generation."

For this advice the boy spat in my face, and was gone, disappearing into a twisting alley between huts before I could wipe my eyes clear.

"Thus," Tenedos said, mock-mournfully, "is how mercy is returned in these hills. Perhaps you *should* have killed him, Legate. Cubs grow to be lions, and then are hellish to hunt down."

"Maybe I should have," I said, taking a canteen from Lucan's saddle and sluicing the spittle off my face. I saw from the expression on Lance Karjan's face that he agreed completely with *that*. "But I'll chance the boy remembers what I did, and maybe, when he grows up, *if* he grows up, which seems unlikely in these lands, will return my boon to someone." I glanced at Karjan. "Don't bother showing me what you think of *that* idea, soldier. And thank you for being so quick. Next time, I must be a little swifter."

I got a smile from the bearded cavalryman, and we rode on. Indeed, the People of the Hills were all the same. No doubt the women and the old ones were uniformly wishing they could have a dagger and one minute's chance at one of us with our back turned, and then two minutes to rifle the corpse.

Sulem Pass opened out, until it was almost a mile wide, the hills around it low and rolling; so as long as we carefully approached the roadside gullies that cut the land like knife scars, we would have adequate warning of an attack.

Laish Tenedos rode in silence for a while, then said, "Now that boy poses a good riddle for a judge who has yet to take his appointed bench. Should I be merciful, and pray this changes the endless back-and-forth of murder begetting more murder causing still more bloodshed? Or should I choose the other way of ending these problems? Dead men carry no feuds."

I did not wish to comment, but that did give me an opening. "Yesterday, sir," I said, choosing my words carefully, "you said you hold radical ideas. There are many people who believe many things in Nicias, some far beyond radical, but the Rule of Ten does not generally silence them, or . . . send them out to be slain, until they have a following, or at any rate a chamber where audiences may gather."

"A good point, Damastes." This was the second use of my first name, and from then on it was continual, except in formal circumstances, most unusual for the vast difference in rank between us. But for some reason it seemed proper. "I'll tell you a bit of myself.

"I am from Palmeras, as I said. Of my family, I'll say nothing now, save that they gave me enough money so I could devote myself to the study of magic, since I'd shown evidence of the Great Talent as a child and, not understanding me well, left me alone. I returned the favor, although, if circumstances come to pass, I may find use for two of my brothers in the fullness of time.

"When I was sixteen I was fortunate enough to win a competition that enabled me to leave Palmeras for Nicias, and complete my studies.

"Sometimes," he said, "I dream of my island, and the sharp, dry smell of the rosemary under a summer sun, or the tang of our resiny wine, and wish I'd never left. But even then, I sensed my destiny."

I'd begun to let go of the idea that Tenedos was a madman, but this word, *destiny*, made me wonder once more.

"I apprenticed myself to a master wizard," Tenedos went on, "and studied under him for five years. When I was twenty-two, I knew I must set my own curriculum, be my own master.

"I traveled for four more years, visiting every state in Numantia, studying the Art under any savant who would have me. But I knew what I sought would lie beyond sorcery, and so I read greatly about our history and especially about our wars.

"Do not sneer, but I sometimes wish my life had taken a slightly different turn, and I came from a military family, because I feel an affinity for the battlefield, for the army. I wondered then, and wonder now, why magic has played so little a part in the great battles, and know, deep in my guts, this shall not always be the case.

"But that is for the future, and I was talking about my past. One day, sitting at the feet of a hermit in faraway Jafarite, I knew suddenly and completely what actions must be taken, and taken quickly, to save my beloved Numantia. I returned to Nicias last year, and that was when my troubles began.

"I set up practice as a seer, but discouraged the common visitor who wanted no more than a love potion or his future cast, and slowly, slowly, began to amass the clients I needed. At first it was a rich man wanting to know if the gods favored a course of action, or a merchant who wanted spells to keep his caravan safe when it went out. I helped, sometimes with sorcery, more frequently with common sense. Then came others, still more highly placed, men in the government. First they wanted potions or spells, then they stayed for my advice on other matters.

"Two of the Rule of Ten I now count as buyers of my wares who also, and more importantly, seem to be listening to my ideas.

"That was why I was sent out from Nicias, Damastes. The others in the Rule of Ten, and those in their hierarchy, are afraid of my words, afraid that the truth they hold will ring true for all of Numantia."

I looked about nervously, making sure no one else was within hearing. Tenedos saw my concern.

"Don't worry, Damastes. I'm no streetside crazy, collaring anyone who comes close and spouting his babble. What I am saying is for your ears only.

"In its proper time, though, it shall be heard throughout our entire kingdom!" His eyes flamed as they had when first we met.

"My beliefs are simple," he said. "Our country has held too long in the comfortable furrows of the past, like a farmer's ox pulling the plow every season through the same field. Umar the Creator is not paying attention to this world now. We must turn away from Irisu the Preserver, who we've followed too long, and instead follow the Supreme Spirit's third manifestation, Saionji. It is time to destroy, and *then* we shall be able to see clearly how to rebuild!

"Numantia has been too long without a king!"

This was more than just radicalism, but very close to high treason. I should have told him, as an officer of the army, granted my sash by the Rule of Ten, that he must say no more, or I would be forced to take appropriate action, and then spurred my horse away.

Instead, I listened on because, in truth, his words were no stronger than I'd heard my father and others say.

Numantia had been built by royalty, and ruled by several dynasties over the centuries, sometimes changing rulers by violence, sometimes by intermarriage, occasionally when a line died out. Although this is not how history was taught, about 200 years before I was born the king had died in battle, his only son far too young to take the throne. As is common, a regency was appointed. But uncommonly, it was not one man, but a group of ten of the king's most trusted counselors.

Three years later, the heir also died, and the kingdom faced disaster, since there was no one left in direct descent. Whether there were other septs of the family, and whether they had acceptable candidates for the throne, our writings are silent, although years later I had scholars search the archives to satisfy my curiosity, and they said the records had been thoroughly cleansed of any reference to other kinfolk.

In any event, these counselors, who called themselves the Rule of Ten, took charge, and ruled in the beginning with at least as much wisdom and consideration as many kings. The problem arose—and you must remember I knew none of this at the time—when they did not formalize their position, but insisted on the fiction that they were merely caretakers for Numantia until a proper ruler was found. As time passed the counselors grew old, and appointed successors, and so it had gone until the present, never legitimized by law, but limping onward, improvising, through the years. Since the Rule of Ten were always going on about the need for a king, custom did not make their rule familiar, and Numantians were always reminded of their supposedly temporary authority.

Numantia still existed as a country, but barely. Dara, the biggest state, and also the seat of the Rule of Ten in Nicias, was the flagship, although of late our neighboring state of Kallio had stirred awake, led by a firebrand of a prime minister named Chardin Sher.

"Numantia cannot continue as it has," Tenedos said. "Without a firm hand controlling the kingdom, it is inevitable that states will fall away, and eventually come to regard themselves as independent kingdoms. Then we'll see what properly would be called civil war, but that term will be false, since Numantia will be no more than a legal fiction by then.

"Some say," he added grimly, "it's not much more than that now. If the situation is not turned around soon, it shall decline into war, and then anarchy. All Nature agrees: There is either order, or the chaos of the maelstrom!"

I was a bit skeptical. "You paint a dark picture, Seer. But I've heard doom-criers before, and Numantia has managed to stumble on for quite a few years without catastrophe."

"The past, my good fellow, has almost nothing to do with the present or future," Tenedos said. "I can *feel* the unrest of Nicias, in Dara, in all my travels throughout Numantia. The people are without leaders, without direction, *and they know it!*

"It takes no use whatever of my powers to see a small incident in the city suddenly striking sparks, and the mob ravening through the streets. Would the Rule of Ten be able to handle a catastrophe such as that? Would Nicias's own council? I have grave doubts. Even if they called for order, what of the troops I saw stationed around the city? I mean no offense to the army you serve in, the *real* army, but I thought most of the soldiers I saw in Nicias little but perfumed puppets who think their armor serves to hang decorations on."

That had been pretty much my opinion as well, but I said nothing. Families do not take their quarrels or opinions out of the home.

"Poor Numantia," Tenedos went on. "Enemies within, enemies without, and yet we do nothing.

"Consider Kallio. Chardin Sher may be only prime minister, but he rules the country like it was his own. What would happen if he decided to overthrow the weaklings of the Rule of Ten? Would Dara rise in their support? Would the other states? And then would Numantia be swallowed up in civil war?

"What of Maisir? What moots it if we've been at peace for centuries? King Bairan is young, having no more than three or four years on either of us. Youth is the time of hunger, of looking for more. What would happen if he decided to annex the Border States tomorrow?

"That is why I hope my theory that the Rule of Ten plans to exercise more control in Kait is correct, although my neck little loves the manner they possibly planned to institute it.

"But suppose I'm wrong. Suppose the situation continues with nothing being done to settle the Border States? Suppose Maisir does move into Kait? The Border States have always been a buffer between our kingdoms. But what if this ends? Maisir also lays claim to Urey.

"If they sent armies through Sulem Pass, with the intent of occupying Urey, would we be able to stop them? More importantly, since none of us seem to think of ourselves as Numantians these days, but as Kallians, Darans, Palmarans, Cimabuans, would we have the *will* to stand against Bairan?

"What do you think, Damastes á Cimabue?"

I considered what I would say carefully. Tenedos had said much, but one thing he had not told me is who he thought might reign in Numantia. But then, as I thought on, he did not need to.

I finally thought I had the right words.

"I think I've heard too many 'if's,' " I said nervously. "And I'm afraid of running into trouble *if* I start thinking that far ahead, and will be like a man who lets his midday meal be poached by his cat while he's worried about whether his dog might steal the steak he has planned for dinner."

Tenedos looked at me silently for a very long time, then suddenly and unexpectedly burst into laughter.

"Legate," he said, "if anyone ever says to me that Cimabuans are not subtle, but blockheads who can speak only the truth, I shall laugh them out of my presence.

"That was the best nonanswer to a question I have ever heard outside the court of the Rule of Ten.

"You will do very well, Damastes. Very well indeed. So let's start thinking about our midday meal, which is a violent little province called Kait, and how we can keep most of its inhabitants from killing each other and also Numantians, as well as keeping our own heads fairly well connected to our shoulders."

The next day, we rode into Sayana, capital of the Border States.

FOUR

THE TIGER AT NIGHT

I t hardly seems fifteen years ago, as I look back on that young legate, riding beside a master magician whose life I'd saved, my still-bloodied saber in its sheath, looking down from the roadway at those ominous spires of Sayana in the distance, and tasting adventure in the soft breeze.

Who was I? From where had *I* come?

In spite of the turns of fortune, I consider myself the least remarkable of men. I never thought of myself as having been gifted by the gods, as some others have claimed about themselves.

I am taller than most, it is true, nearly a head taller than six feet. Some have said my features are well made, but I have never been able to prate about how handsome I am. In truth, in the pier glass I think myself rather plain.

My hair is blond, and I wear it long, even now when it is sadly thinning on top. I have always preferred to be clean-shaven, finding a beard not only a collector of strange debris, but also something an enemy can use as a deadly handhold in battle. I shall add, since I intend to be as honest as I know in this memoir, that there's a bit of vanity in this, since my face hair grows like a bramblebush, in knots and tangles. When bearded, I look less an imposing leader than a wandering mendicant, a roadside holy man who's chosen the wrong byways to carry his begging bowl down.

I am, as is obvious from my name, from the jungled province of Cimabue. There may be those who do not know the reputation my people have, or the many jokes that are told about our laziness, our unreliability, our dullness and general shiftlessness. Let but one jape suffice: The Cimabuan who sat up until dawn on his wedding night, because the seer who performed the marriage ceremony told him this would be the most wonderful night of his life.

Those tales are not, by the way, told in the presence of Cimabuans more than once, since we also have the not undeserved reputation for being frequently short-tempered and implacable in our wrath. I myself spent many hours stable-cleaning as punishment detail at the lycee for having repaid such "jokes" with my fist.

My family has always been soldiers, serving either our own state or, more often, Numantia, always remembering the days when the country *was* a country, with a king, no matter how evil, instead of a collection of states, each ruling itself badly and seeking any opportunity to do harm to its neighbor.

We were land rich, our estate covering many leagues of hilly forest. The land was worked by freeholders, long beholden to my family, since Cimabue has few slaves. It is not that we are opposed to slavery, since all men who are not fools know that when the Wheel turns a slave may be reborn as a master, so one lifetime spent under the lash matters little, and may serve to teach the soul what errors he committed to be so punished.

Our villa was less a house than a run-down fortress, having been built generations earlier by the first of our family to use his sword and army pension to carve holdings from the jungle, defending it against the savage tribes that have now retreated far into the mountains where no man dares disturb them further, since they are armed not only with savage cunning, but also with dark magic pulled from the earth and blessed by Jacini herself.

Even with little money in the coffers my family lived comfortably, since we grew all that could be desired for the table and had enough herd animals, mostly zebra, cattle, and half-tame gaur used for hauling and plowing that only children and the beasts' drovers could safely approach. A caravan would come through our lands twice a year, and we could trade for the other items—cloth, steel, spices, iron—we could not pull from our own land.

I was the youngest child, following three sisters. I was, they say, a very pretty babe, and so, in a normal household, would have most likely grown up cosseted, frail, and gentle.

My father, Cadalso, would have none of that, however. In the army, he'd seen many battles on the Frontiers, in the Border States, and, in spite of not having any friends in high places, what soldiers call a "priest," was able to reach the rank of captain before losing his leg, and hence being forced to retire, at the famous battle of Tiepolo, ironically a battle fought not against a foreign enemy, but between Darans and our fellow Numantians, the Kallions.

He insisted I be raised as a soldier. That meant mostly outdoors, in all weathers, from the brain-baking Time of Heat to nearly drowning in the typhoons of the Time of Rains. When I was but five, I was taken to one of the estate's outbuildings, a small structure with only two rooms: bedroom and ablution chamber. This was my sanctuary, and no one would be allowed to enter without my permission. I would have no servants, and was expected to turn the vine- and filth-covered building that I suspected had once been a cowshed into living quarters proper for a soldier, and an officer to boot.

I started to protest, looked once into my father's eyes, fierce behind the great prematurely white beard that covered his face, and knew there was no use. Cursing, perhaps crying, I set to work, sweeping and scrubbing. Then I had to take the few coppers he gave me and bargain for my furniture—a cot, a small chest, and an open wardrobe. Father gave me a table of great age that took two men to carry into my rooms.

I was never permitted to slack off. Father inspected my rooms daily, and on the results depended what I would be allowed to do that day.

This, I realize, makes him sound like several species of tyrant, but he was not. I can never remember him raising a hand to me, to my sisters, or to my mother, Serao.

He explained his actions: "You are my son, my only son, and you must learn strength. I sense there are trials ahead for you, and while these will build your thews, you must also have power within. Even the smallest wolf cub must learn to snap before his pack will welcome him and teach him to hunt."

I did not realize until later, when I found real love myself, how close he and my mother were. She had been the daughter of a district seer, a man with a small reputation for honest spells and refusing to work magic that would harm any person, no matter how evil. I know my father could have done better—in our province a soldier is well thought of, and many landowners are proud to give their daughter to a man of arms, particularly if he hails from the area and also owns property. But my father said that when he first saw Serao, assisting her father as he blessed the seeds in the Time of Dews, he knew there could be no other.

She was a quiet, gentle woman, and when they married she struck a pact with Cadalso: All that happened outside the household was his responsibility, all within was hers. This bargain was held to, although I can remember times when a particularly incompetent cook or drunken groom would bring a flush to either's cheeks, and they would be forced to bite hard on the words that wished to come out.

I loved them both very much, and hope the turning of the Wheel has taken them to the heights they deserve.

As for my sisters, not much need be said. We fought each other and loved each other. In time, they made good marriages—one to a village subchief, one to a fairly wealthy landowner, and the third to a soldier in our state militia, who the last I heard had risen to the rank of color-sergeant, and now manages the family estates. All have been blessed with children. I shall say no more about them, for their lives have been fortunate by not being touched by history. The gods let me send gold when I was rich and powerful, and granted them safe and comfortable obscurity when Emperor Tenedos and I met our downfall.

I am told most boys go through a time when they want to be this, be that, be the other thing, from wizard to elephant leader to goldsmith to who knows what. My mind never spun such skeins for me. All that I ever wanted to be was as my father had dreamed: a soldier.

On my name day, I was taken to a sorcerer my father particularly respected, who was asked to cast the bones for my future. The sorcerer cast once, cast thrice, and then told my parents my fate was cloudy. He could see I would be a fighter, a mighty fighter, and I would see lands and do deeds unimagined in our sleeping district.

That was enough for my father, and enough for me when I was told later.

Just before her death a few years ago my mother said the wizard had finished his predictions with a quiet warning. She remembered clearly what he said: "The boy will ride the tiger for a time, and then the tiger will turn on him and savage him. I see great pain, great sorrow, but I also see the thread of his life goes on. But for how much farther, I cannot tell, since mists drop around my mind when it reaches beyond that moment."

That worried my mother, but not my father. "Soldiers serve, soldiers die," he said with a shrug. "If that is my son's lot, so be it. It is unchangeable, and one might as well sacrifice to Umar the Creator and convince him to return to this world, take Irisu and Saionji to hand, and concern himself with our sorrows." That was great wisdom, she knew, and so put the matter aside.

Somehow I knew as a boy what skills I must learn, and what talents would be meaningless. I learned to fight, to challenge boys from the village older and stronger than I, because that was how a reputation was made. I was always the first to climb to the highest branch or leap from the tallest ledge into a pool or run the closest past a gaur as he snorted in his pen.

I listened hard when the hunters taught me archery, when my father gave me lessons of the sword, when stablemen taught me how to ride and care for a horse.

One of the most important things I learned from my father, although he never advised me of this directly, was that the best weapon for a soldier was the simplest and the most universal. He taught me to avoid such spectacular devices as the morningstar or battle-ax for a plain sword, its hilt of the hardest wood without device, faced with soft, dull-colored metal that might serve to hold an enemy's edge for a vital instant, its grip of roughened leather, preferably sharkskin, and its pommel equally simple. Its blade should be straight, edged on both sides. It should be made of the finest steel I could afford, even if it meant borrowing a sum from the regimental lender. The blade should not be forged with sillinesses like blood runnels, since those do not work and only weaken a weapon's strength, nor should it be elaborately engraved or set with gold. My father said he knew of men who'd been slain just for the beauty of their sword—an entirely ridiculous reason to die.

It should be neither too long nor short; since I became taller than most men when fully grown, I prefer a blade length of three inches short of a yard, and the weapon to weigh a bit over two pounds.

He added that if I were to become a cavalryman, I'd likely be given a saber. Most likely I'd have to carry it until I achieved some rank or battle experience, but then to consider well before I kept the weapon. It was his experience that a saber was very well and good for wild swinging in a melee, or for cutting down fleeing soldiery, but afoot or in a man-to-man contest, he'd rather have a bow and fifty feet between him and his opponent than the most romantic saber. This was but one of the quiet lessons I absorbed from him, one of those that kept me alive when all too many lay dead around me.

I pushed my body to the limits, running, swimming, climbing, paying no attention to the tear of muscles and silent scream of exhaustion, but forcing myself to go one more hill, one more lap across the pool, one more hour of sitting, shivering, in the blind with my sling beside me while rain seeped down and the geese did not appear.

One thing came naturally: I loved and understood horses. Perhaps at one time I have been one, since when I was first taken to the stables as a babe, and my father held me up in his arms to see the great beast, I called out, as if recognizing an old friend, and, I was told, the animal nickered a response, trotted across the yard, and nuzzled me.

I don't glorify the animals particularly. I know they aren't terribly intelligent, but what of that? I don't consider myself a sage, either, and some of the finest men I've had serve under me, serve to the death, would be hard pressed to remember today what their lance-major told them last week.

Riding was another part of my schooling, being able to ride a horse bareback, with a saddle, or with the bare blanket and rope bridge someone said the nomads of the distant south preferred. I learned how to make a horse obey without having to use the cruel curb bit, and my spurs had balls on their tips instead of spikes. Some horses became almost my friends; others, while not quite enemies, were not ones I'd readily choose to saddle up for an afternoon's outing.

It was graven into my soul that your horse always comes first: It's watered, fed, groomed before its rider dares provide for his own comfort, or that man is less than a beast himself. I was cursed later by my men for driving them to their currycombs and feedbags, but my regiments would still be mounted long after other units were afoot, their horses foundered, cut into the stewpot, and they themselves stumbling along as common infantrymen.

I spent hours in my father's stables, learning everything I could from old grooms, knowing my fate as a soldier might depend on these beasts. I learned to treat their minor ailments and even, when one of our horses fell desperately ill and a seer would be called, I found a place to lie atop the rafters so I could watch what medicines he compounded, and what spells he cast. Of course, since I have not a single trace of the Talent, when I tried them nothing happened, but at least I was learning how to pick a true magician from the crowd of charlatans that crowd around an army on campaign.

Isa, god of war, who some say is an aspect of Saionji herself, also gave me talents. I grew tall and strong, with a voice other boys listened to and enough brains so they would follow me.

I loved to hunt, not for the kill, although that is the satisfaction the gods give for a task performed well. I would take bow, arrows, a small knife, tinder, and steel, and set out into the jungle. I would be gone a day, or a week. My sisters and mother would worry, my father pretend unconcern. If I were to be eaten by a tiger, then the sorcerer had been wrong and it was the tiger's lifeline that stretched long.

Far away from our estate and the surrounding villages, I learned the real skills of soldiering: to be content while alone; to be unafraid, or at any rate to stay calm when night closes down and the forest noises are very dangerous, even though most of them come from creatures that would fit in the palm of your hand; not to be choosy about your food and to be able to live on raw fish, partially cooked meat, or the fruits and plants around you; to be able to sleep when drenched to the bone and the monsoon pours. Most important of these is always to think of the next step—to be aware that if the rock you jump to is slippery and sends you sprawling, you could be crippled, far from any help. Or that the cave that looks so inviting a shelter from the thundershower may hold a sun bear, and what then, my lad? All of these things I learned well, and they saved my life many times in the years that followed.

There were two other "skills" that are commonly thought of as soldierly that my father spoke little of, but I also familiarized myself with. One came naturally, but I failed at the other.

The latter was drinking. All men know soldiers are sponges, sops around anything fermented or distilled, and I fear it's more than true for most. But not for me. The smell of wine or brandy turned my stomach as a lad, which is hardly uncommon. But the smell or taste never became more attractive as I aged. When young, hoping to learn the skill, I forced myself to drink with my fellows, once as a boy when we found a wineskin that had fallen off a merchant's cart beside the track, and the second time at the lycee, when we cadets finished our first year of studies. I never made a boisterous ass of myself as others did, but became very sick early on and crawled off to be rackingly ill, and then had a sour gut and a huge drum in my head for two days as reward. Of course I never say I do not drink, since the world pretends to respect but actually feels uncomfortable around an ascetic, but I will carry a single beaker of wine for an entire evening without anyone noticing that I but touch it to my lips. I drink small beer by choice, and even water when I'm assured of its purity. There have been a few times as an adult I've gotten drunk, but they were the exception and even more foolish than when I was a boy.

The other soldierly virtue or vice is, of course, whoring. Sex came early to me, and was the hidden blessing of my tiny house in the jungle, since I was alone with no nurse, mother, or busybody of a servant to keep me chaste. Perhaps my father knew this when he gave me those two rooms whose memory I still treasure.

Village maids, more likely infatuated with the idea of bedding the son of the lord than having a real lust for me, would creep into my quarters at night and teach me what they knew. After some time and several girls befriending me, I was able to return the favor of instruction.

There would also be the girls and young women of the caravans. Once trading was finished, there would be a feast, and as often as not the end of the evening would find one of them slipping into the shadows with me.

I remember one such night when a young woman came out with me. Her husband, a great oaf of a silk merchant, had inhaled three wineskins and subsided into a snoring, blubbering pile not long after the sun went down.

She told me, and it might well have been a lie, she'd been sold to him against her will. I said nothing, for such was and unfortunately still is the custom in too many parts of our land. She asked if I knew what could be done with silk, and I laughed and said I might be from the country, but was hardly that much of a fool. She smiled privately and suggested perhaps there were uses I was still unaware of, such as for wall-hangings and, she ran her tongue over her lips, other places in the bedchamber.

I expressed interest, feeling my cock stir against my loincloth. She disappeared into her wagon, and came out in a few moments with a pack.

No one noticed as we left the village square and went to my cabin, being deep in their own vices. She was, of course, telling the truth—there were many, many uses for the silkworm's death I wasn't aware of. I did know how coarsely woven veil, showing more than it conceals of brown flesh, with only a candle to illuminate, can dizzy the mind.

But I knew nothing until that night of the touch of a silk whip, nor how silken restraints can send a woman's passion into flame.

We were resting, curled around each other's bodies, sticky with love, when the tiger coughed.

Her body tensed against me.

"Can he get in?" she whispered.

To be truthful, I didn't know. There were iron bars across the windows, and I knew those to be impregnable. The door was heavy cross-braced lumber, and barred, but I'd seen a tiger kill a bullock with one smash of its paws, then effortlessly pick the beast up in its jaws and leap a nine-foot fence.

But I knew enough to lie.

The woman's breath came faster as we heard the tiger pace around the walls. My cock came hard, and I rolled atop her, her legs lifting as I rammed into her, thrusting as she pumped her hips against me, back arched and hands pulling at my buttocks, the beast outside, and its scream against the night, silencing the monkeys, burying her cry as our sweating bodies became one and I poured into her.

We waited until dawn before I took her back to her wagon, and carried a cudgel with me. We saw the tiger's pugmarks in the mud, but he was long gone. She stopped me when we came in sight of the caravan, and giggled. "We don't need to tell them just how you fought the tiger," and pointed at my body. I saw the nailmarks and bites on my chest, and knew there were others hidden under my loincloth.

She laughed once more, kissed me, and was gone.

I spent the day away from my family in the jungle. I sometimes think of that woman, and wish her well, hoping Jaen made her happy and has given her a long life, and her husband many wineskins for blinders.

So love has been a fine friend, but the soldierly pastime of going into rut anytime there's a female of any age within a league, no. I've not only avoided embarrassments, but disease as well. My father once said, in one of his few references to sex, after making sure neither my mother or sisters were in earshot, "Some people will put their cock where I would not place the ferrule of my staff," and he is certainly correct.

I've also heard it said when a man makes love all the blood rushes to the lower half of his body, thus explaining why men cannot fuck and think at the same time, which sounds quite logical. Jaen knows I'm hardly innocent of that charge. But enough of that.

If it sounds as if I have been bragging, I do not mean to do so, for I have many weaknesses, which should be obvious, considering my present position here on this lonely island as an exile who can expect only death to improve his lot and give him a chance to return to the Wheel and expiate his deeds in another life.

I am but a poor reader, and have little patience with the pleasures that come from listening to the sagas, scholarly debate, or seeing dancers portray the deeds of men. Painting, stone-carving, all these things I can praise, but there is none of the heart's truth in my words. Music alone of all the arts touches me, from a boy tootling on a wooden whistle to a single singer accompanying himself on a stringed instrument to the intricacies of a court symphony.

Philosophies, religions, ethics, all these things are for wiser heads than mine.

At one time I would have said my greatest talent, though, was one Laish Tenedos said was the most important of all. I was gifted with good luck, something all soldiers must carry with them.

Now?

That proud claim has surely been proven a joke, one that would make the monkey god Vachan, god of fools, god of wisdom, shrill laughter and do backflips in wicked glee.

One further thing I learned from my father was always—*always*—to obey the family credo: *We Hold True.* When I swore an oath of fealty to Laish Tenedos within my heart, long before I placed the crown on his head, it was to the death. It is ironic that my vows to him were never equally honored. But that is as may be, and Tenedos is answering for that sin.

I knew, when I approached seventeen, I would enter the army. I assumed I would travel to the nearest recruiter, and take the coin as a common soldier. If I worked hard and mightily, I might be fortunate enough to find a commission and perhaps end my days at the same rank my father reached. This was the highest I dreamed, at least that I'd admit to. Of course there was always the grandness of somehow leading a forlorn hope, coming to the notice of a general and being promoted on the battlefield. But truthfully I knew my most likely fate would be to end my days as a hard-bitten sergeant, such as I met from time to time in the villages. Still more likely was that I'd be taken by Isa on the battlefield in blood, or in barracks from one of the diseases all armies carry along with sutlers and whores.

In theory, I should have been able to apply for one or another of the lycees that produce officers, since our family is more than noble enough to qualify. But the old proverb applies, and my family, and in fact the entire district of Cimabue, was far out of sight and mind of the powerful ones who ruled the army from Nicias.

I didn't care. I suppose this must be counted another of my failings, that I've never been one to think highly of someone merely because the Wheel's turnings makes him the son, or her the daughter, of a grand family. In fact, in spite of my former titles, and my marriage, being around such people makes me a bit nervous, although I've learned to disguise it.

I'm far more comfortable in a barracks, tenting, on the hunting field, or in a common tavern and with the people of those places than in a palace with the grand.

So the thought of being one more spearman or archer didn't disturb or shame me, although I thought I could prove myself a good enough horseman to be allowed into the cavalry.

But once again luck intervened.

My father may not have had a priest, but someone did owe him a favor, a retired domina named Roshanara, who'd been my father's regimental commander at Tiepolo. I do not know what deeds my father did that day—he would never tell tales of his exploits—but evidently they were memorable.

One day, not many months before I was to take the colors, a messenger arrived at the estate. He carried an elaborate scroll that, once its wax seals had been broken and we scanned it, offered me an appointment at the Lycee of the Horse Soldier, just outside Nicias.

This is considered the most elite of the various service schools, attended only by the sons of the noble rich and descendants of particularly well-connected and high-ranking officers.

None of us had any idea how this could've come to pass. My father said at one time there were five cadet postings made available by lot to all applicants, but since I'd sent no letters to the lycee that was an impossibility.

The explanation, of course, was Domina Roshanara, and his letter came in the next post. He said he'd not only named me for consideration to the lycee since he had no children of his own nor friends' children he took seriously enough to propose, but he'd also set aside a sum sufficient to see me until graduation. I could see my father's mustaches begin to bristle, but he read on, through Domina Roshanara's rather weak explanation that he'd heard the harvests had been exceedingly bad in Cimabue, and this was to be looked at not as charity, but as one way to make the army they both so loved stronger.

My father looked very unconvinced, and was, I thought, about to explode and growl something about that would be the last damned time he saved any damned superior's sweetbreads, when my mother took him into another room. I know not what she said, but when they came back my attendance at the Lycee of the Horse Soldier was settled.

The school would commence after the Time of Dews, when soldiers would return from the field, campaigning during the ensuing Time of Births and Time of Heat not being common practice. That was not long distant, and I would need considerable time for travel, since Nicias is far from Cimabue. I spent the short time left with my father, learning all the details of lycees he could remember. Even though he'd not been able to attend such a lycee, but had gone through a training college in our own state, he'd heard many many tales from officers who had, and, he added wryly, still seemed to think their happiest days had been spent there.

Then the time came due and I rode off on the mare I'd chosen, Lucan. She wasn't my favorite, but was quite young, just five, and I hoped to be able to keep her for a great part of my career. I took another mare, Rabbit, named for her overlong ears and thankfully not her behavior when I was astride, and two mules with my gear.

I rode to the curve in the road, and turned to wave my farewell and take one last look at my home. It was hot, but the blur in my eyes was not from the sun. My father . . . mother . . . sisters . . . all the family's servants, and my friends from the village, all were there. I fixed them in my memory, as if I were an artist taking a final look at his models before he hurries to his easel, as if I'd never see any of them again.

And in truth, that is almost how it has been.

I have only returned to Cimabue twice, for the funeral rites for my parents. Sometimes I was half a continent away, other times impossibly busy, and later it became unwise to do so for my sisters' safety. That is not the complete truth—there were more than enough long leaves when I could have gone home instead of elsewhere.

But I did not and do not know why.

Perhaps it would be like returning to a dream only to see what a threadbare fancy it actually was.

THE LYCEE OF THE HORSE SOLDIER

M y two years at the lycee began in a roar, as hardened ex-cavalrymen, all former lance majors, troop guides, or regimental guides, chosen for iron bowels and lungs and eyes that could see a speck of dust on a uniform or a dot of manure on a horse's hoof from across a parade ground chorused loudly, obscenely, and thoroughly about my shortcomings.

Eventually we were shattered enough to be given grudging acceptance, and the army began to rebuild us in the desired image.

I worked hard in the classroom, but never ranked higher than the middle of my class. Some of the required courses made my eyes cross, such as Military Etiquette and Parade Ceremonials. These would be crucial to a successful career dancing attendance as an aide to a general, but that was hardly how I wished to spend my life. I did acceptably well at mathematics, as long as the instructor could show me its use in the field. I can still figure, within an inch, the height of a mountaintop I must assault given its distance and the angle to the top, but as for reveling in the joys of pure numbers that supposedly express our relationship with the universe, well, I think that's no better than what the priests prattle, and I leave such importances for temples.

One course I remember well now was Battlefield Sorcery. It was taught not by a magician, which I found odd, but by a staff officer, which suggested we should not nap through his lecturing, nor harass him with uncomfortable questions unless we wished our first posting to be the Isle of the Forgotten, which all knew to be somewhere between Lost and Nowhere. He explained on the first day that he had a touch of the Talent, and had been selected for that reason. He further explained that the army deemed it important that a "realist" teach the course, rather than some fuzzy-brained scholar who'd fill us up with useless theory and pointless wand-waving.

In his lectures, we learned the army's concept of thaumaturgy's place. It was important, but hardly vital *as long as it is present on both sides*, the officer, a captain of the Upper Half, explained. An army would march into battle, and the sorcerers accompanying it would cast spells of confusion and fear, attempt to influence the weather, cause landslides, make rivers rise or ebb depending on the needs of the commander. But since the enemy would be making their own magic, it would be almost certain the enchantments would cancel each other out. Of course, if one side fought "naked," that is, without magic, it would be quickly destroyed.

One of the more scholarly of my fellows wondered why a battle could not be fought solely with magic, or a real army opposed and vanquished completely by sorcery, given a powerful enough magician.

"In theory," the captain said, and his lip curled to show what he really thought of the idea, "*in theory* this could be done. Just as, with a lever long and strong enough and a fulcrum solid enough, you could lift the city of Nicias to the other side of the Latane River." There was a bit of laughter.

"But we are soldiers here, learning to deal with the facts of the rude day. Perhaps, if your interests lie in such ethereal matters, you might consider applying to a wizards' academy, and leaving your place here for a more pragmatic young man." Some of the less brainy sorts laughed harder at this, since at the time military sorcerers were known as mystical dolts who would die trying to figure why the demon they'd evoked was green instead of the desired blue, and never notice their legs were being devoured.

The young man flushed and sat down.

"I mean no insult," the officer said, for he was not an unkindly man. "We all know of great battles fought magician to magician, especially before war is declared or in the early stages of a struggle. And magic is of inestimable value when unopposed, and again I must emphasize that word, for example when the commander wishes to see if the enemy has concealed reserves. Possibly, if a magician has power enough, and his opponent is weak enough, he might be able to affect the opposing general's willpower to continue a hard-fought battle.

"And finally, magic comes into its own when an army is broken, its willpower gone, just as cavalry should always be used to finish a fleeing enemy.

"But all these purposes, important though they are, are secondary to our real purpose, what we soldiers have dedicated our lives to: battle. When steel becomes the argument, and the battlefield has been chosen, then sorcery must step aside. Magic, just like the quartermaster, the paymaster, or the farrier, exists only to ease the path of the warrior on the battlefield. In no way can it replace him."

I thought of asking a question at this point—I didn't think the questioner had meant that, any more than someone asking if archers should be brought closer to the actual battle zone or kept back to fire volleys at the reserves meant the swordsman should stay home, or someone questioning whether the halberd wasn't vastly inferior to the lance meant it should be scrapped.

But I said nothing.

I also thought something else: The witch in our village could heal colds, ease the shaking bones of the old, make childbirth easier—in short, perform many important tasks. She could not, however, make bones knit overnight or keep a failing heart beating for a while. For that we had to send for a more skilled practitioner. But that didn't mean she denied it was possible to heal a broken leg.

Her attempts to predict and control the weather were complete failures, and so were those of all the district sages I'd seen attempt the labor. But did that mean no one had done such a marvel? Of course not; it merely required a master wizard.

So battle magic was difficult. Perhaps a sorcerer powerful enough had not attempted it as yet, or perhaps no one had devised spells potent enough to rule the battlefield. But that didn't mean it was impossible. All the captain was really saying is that no one to our knowledge had mastered such feats, and not even I, coming from a backwater area like Cimabue, imagined Numantia to be the entire world.

I thought that the army, in this, as in many other ways, was all too ready to say This Is the Way It Is and Must Be, and close its mind. But that was a passing notion, and I, too, accepted Things as They Were.

Until Seer Tenedos.

Where I did well was out of doors, whether on the parade grounds, where I was very familiar with the evolutions, courtesy of my father; in any sport, particularly if it involved riding; or in our war games.

Perhaps I would have ranked higher, but as I've said my temper boiled when any other "young gentleman" insulted me, my accent, my district, or, worst of all, my family, and so there were a number of disciplinary infractions on my record. I cared little, because it's far more important for a man to stand up for what he believes than to bow down meekly. A crawler cannot be a warrior.

This showed another peculiarity of the army: If I was insulted, and touched the hilt of the dress dagger we all wore, the challenge would have been made and my foe and I would have met at dawn with bare blades. A wounding or a death would be shrugged aside as part of the price of becoming an officer. But to seize one of these swaggerers by the waist, as I once did, upend him, and toss him into a slops barrel—why, this was most unseemly, and required three days in the stables for me to expiate my sin.

I made few friends, as I'd expected. Most tales of young

men away from home for the first time tell how they erred and overstepped their bounds, became cocky, or lost all discipline. None of that happened to me, so my time at the lycee is quite a dull tale. Since I was very poor, Domina Roshanara's allowance just covering my expenses with three or four coppers left at the end of each month, the rich cadets did not take me to their bosoms. Since I wasn't a libertine, again more due to lack of funds than desire, the rakehellies thought me dull. Those few who were studious and aspired to be wise needed nothing from someone as thickheaded as I.

Perhaps I sensed the army's cruelty with relationships even then. Soldiers swear the friends they make as recruits last forever, but this is seldom the case, particularly with officers. In the beginning there are the normal differences of class, wealth, and performance that divide young men from their fellows. But it becomes worse once the sash of office is given. Friends fall away like rain. Some die of disease, some in battle, but even more must be turned away—a man who is promoted to captain can no longer roister with his now-lower-ranking legates. Dominas don't relax with captains, nor generals with dominas. My father had warned me of this, too, saying in spite of all the bravado and cheers, a soldier's life is a lonely one. I think he prepared me well for such a truth, for such a fate.

The few men I felt close to were of the lower ranks, although I was careful to remember my father's advice that an officer must never become so friendly with a ranker that he cannot send him off to die. But I did enjoy listening to the tales of the old warrants, of campaigns long forgotten except by soldiers, or being with the stablemen and learning still more about horses and their peculiarities.

I confess my happiest times were alone, when I had no duties, and I'd saddle Lucan, put some bread, cheese, and fruit in a pouch, and ride off into the country with no particular destination in mind. Sometimes I'd take a bow and some blunts, and try for squirrels or birds, or a hook and line for fish. Sometimes, on those back lanes far from the lycee, I'd encounter farmers or fellow hunters-poachers, I suppose they were, which mattered not at all to me, since all men must eat.

More than once, especially during harvest season, I would encounter young women. I guess there was a certain amount of glamour to being a budding cavalry officer, and since I spoke as these young farm women did, I was a friendly presence. Such an encounter might well end on a bed of moss in a secluded glen, lying naked with a maid, and once or twice with a pair of them giggling and taking turnabout. It is only city people who think the countryside is innocent. To this day the smell of new-mown hay or freshly picked berries can bring a smile to my lips and a bit of remembered heat to my loins.

I wonder if my life would have been happier if I'd been born one of these country people, and known no further horizons than they did? Perhaps Irisu intended me as such, and Saionji, in the guise of my father, intervened. I know not.

As the final term came to an end, I began looking for my regiment. Graduates were permitted to apply to any unit they chose, and, if the army grudgingly found a vacancy, it might actually assign you to that formation. As a graduate of an elite school, at least I would be with the cavalry, and not the infantry or, worse yet, the pioneers or some service formation.

I assumed my fellow students, with their "priests" and wealth and families and ties, would get the marrow of the choices, and leave me with the driest of bones.

I'd looked with longing at the cavalry regiments "out there," as the Nicians put it, scattered in cantonments on the Frontiers or within the wary garrisons on the border between Dara and Kallio, in a state of truce that wasn't war, yet never became peace.

Most of all, I wished to serve in one of the three regiments in Urey that kept Dara's vassal state from being ravaged by the Men of the Hills, those fearless killers from the Border States who come down from their hard mountains to loot, rape, and kill.

They also were the front line against Kallio, who also claimed Urey, and, on the other side of the Border States our most dangerous potential foe, the Kingdom of Maisir. These three regiments were the Tenth Hussars, the Twentieth Heavy Cavalry, and the most romantic, the Seventeenth Ureyan Lancers, which guarded the most important passageway into the Border States, Sulem Pass.

As far as I could tell, I stood as much chance of being assigned to any of these three units as I did of being chosen Queen of the Festival of Births to dance around the lingam pole with an orchid between my breasts.

Once more luck intervened, both close and far. I knew one, but not the other. The distant and unknown was that the Frontiers were waking, and on the sheer cliffs and in the sere villages of the Border States, the harsh desert highlands the Men of the Hills called Kait in their own tongue, the tribesmen were stirring, looking lustfully south at the green lands, fat sheep, fatter purses, and smooth-skinned maidens of Urey.

There were others looking at the same lands, but we didn't learn about them for a while, and their lusts went far beyond the immediate joys of rape and raid.

The closer piece of luck became evident, when I heard what posts my fellow graduates were seeking. Either they wished staff postings, preferably serving under the command of one or another of the high-rankers who'd sponsored their career or with one of the "parade-crash" regiments close around Nicias. These units were also considered elite, but hardly by me, since we'd been encouraged to visit these great regiments, to be quietly wooed by them. I'd seen how much time was spent polishing everything from armor to the horses' hooves, and how little they practiced real fighting maneuvers instead of the glamorous but meaningless reviews, charges-in-line, and intricate wheelings. I had not joined the army to worry about whether the horsehair plume on my helmet dangled precisely to the second knot from the bottom of my spine.

I'd sent applications by military post to all three of the regiments in Urey, and then could do nothing but wait.

They say graduation from the lycee is the grandest moment of a young officer's life. Perhaps it is for some, but not for me.

Far greater was the night with the woman and the tiger in my tiny hut, or the day I received welcomes from two of the three regiments I'd applied to. One of them was the Lancers, and I did not think my heart could be fuller.

The days blurred by until graduation, when I galloped Lucan out of ranks, to the platform the school domina stood at, dismounted, marched up the steps, and the sash of rank was wound about my waist.

I went to several of the graduating parties, and swore, with the others, eternal friendship and fealty, but my mind was far south, wishing for those stark, barren hills of the Border States.

THE WOLF OF GHAZI

I t seemed as if every citizen of Nicias was abroad as I rode through the city toward the docks. I kept glancing at the sun, afraid I'd miss my sailing time, but unable to move faster than a walk, for fear Lucan or Rabbit would crush someone.

There were sweating priests staggering along, trying to look dignified, carrying statues of their god or goddess bigger than they were, followed by chanting acolytes; merchants intent on the day's business and paying little heed to the bustle around them; whining beggars; rich wives out to shop in sedan chairs or carriages; a few early drunkards; porters transporting everything from loaves of bread to ceremonial robes to one man—and everyone gave him a wide berth—with an open basket full of snakes.

In the middle of a street a naked religious man sat meditating. The crowd ebbed around him as if he were a rock in a river. Sooner or later either he'd decide to move, a rich man would toss a gold coin into his bowl and he'd mysteriously awake, or he'd be crushed by a freight wagon or elephant. No doubt it didn't matter to him which happened.

There was a slight shimmer about him, and as I rode past, his power was such that I was drawn into his vision.

The two of us were alone in a cool vale, near a laughing brook. A soft breeze caressed us, and the sun was kindly. Birds sang, and a roebuck grazed nearby. The holy man smiled his welcome and peace washed over me.

I was back in Nicias. I wiped sweat, dropped two coppers in the man's bowl, and went on.

Evidently the Seventeenth Lancers were in a hurry for my presence, for they'd authorized me to take passage on a fast packet, the *Tauler,* whose broadside promised to deliver me to Renan in less than two weeks.

The *Tauler* was still moored at its dock and I took a moment to marvel at the craft. It was less than a year old, and a fine example of what the mechanics of Dara could produce, nearly 200 feet long and 40 wide. There were three decks with cabins raised above the main deck, which had storage space for cargo and, amidships, pens for animals. The ship was navigated from a small cupola in the bows. Its upperworks were built of teak that had been crafted into a thousand thousand fantastic images of gods, men, and demons, then painted in as many hues.

But what made it so astonishing was its method of propulsion. At the stern were, side by side, two broad treadmills, such as the ones used in the countryside to power a miller's wheel, but far wider and heavier, as if elephants would provide the energy instead of oxen. But they stood empty. Here was where mighty sorcery would work. A group of Nicias's master magicians had spent years developing a spell that enabled the treadmills, which I had been told were made of elephant hide, not only to hold the great strength of the beast, which would be loosed to power the ship, but also to maintain this power for a week or more before the belts needed replacement. I marveled, and again was reminded how foolish it was that the army thought magic no more than a minor tool.

The rest of the machine was more prosaic, but to me just as wonderful. The treadmills turned wheels, and belts ran from those wheels to a larger one, jutting off the boat's stern, just at the waterline and equipped with paddles. That drove the boat forward, and it was steered with long sweeps that extended from the deck back of the paddle wheel into the water. Commands would be shouted back to the steersmen from the ship's commander in the bows, or, in the event of rain or wind, relayed by signals on pull-cords.

At dockside was the ship's purser, and I arranged for my horses to be loaded, passing a silver coin I could not afford to make sure Lucan, Rabbit, and the two pack horses were properly attended to. I was given a brass token with my cabin number, gave a copper to the lycee attendant who'd accompanied me to the dock, and went aboard.

The cabin was neat but small, and on the lowest deck. Even so, it cost dearly, far more than I would be paid in a Time. Since my possessions fit in one saddle-roll and four leather bags, I had more than enough room.

I went back on deck, and waited for departure. Next to the docks was one of the landings used for bathing. Long steps led into the brown river, and people swarmed down them. Some were most modest—I saw an entire family clad from head to foot in white robes trying to cleanse itself and yet remain modest. Others wore a cloth around their loins, but most were as they came into the world.

In the throng were rich and poor, merchant and thief, and I was reminded that no man can show wealth when he's naked, and, also, unfortunately, that most of us, unclothed, prove the first man or woman who sewed leaves to form a belt had a smattering of good sense.

There were exceptions, I noted a young girl, nude except for a thin silver chain about her waist and a bright smile she turned on me. I winked, she beckoned, I sighed and indicated I was trapped just as horns blasted, the gangways were pulled aboard, and we churned away.

The *Tauler* was worthy of her boasts, and we raced south as if demons were after us. The first few days took the longest, requiring careful navigation as we passed through the huge delta that fed the sea through hundreds of mouths. There were islands no bigger than the single bush that grew on them, and ones I thought as big as Cimabue. The islands were heavily settled, and I wondered, with a shudder, what all these people could do, where they could flee, in the event of a flood. I suspected I knew the answer, and thought on more cheerful subjects.

Once out of the delta, we could move faster. The Latane River was huge, stretching from horizon to brown horizon as it rolled down to the sea. There were many other boats about, from small skiffs to fishing craft to ramshackle barges that were home to huge families. There were trading ships and other transports like our own that the ship's horns hooted at familiarly.

The only time I was in my cabin was to sleep—otherwise I was on deck, marveling at this great and lovely country of Numantia I had sworn to serve.

My fellow passengers were mostly of the monied class, and so I kept to myself. A few times men offered to buy me a drink, and I accepted gladly, since I'd made a private arrangement with the barmen that no matter what I ordered I'd be served a glass of recently boiled water, with that wonderful rarity ice, and a twist of lime, which looked for all the world like some lethal concoction of distilled prune pits or some such.

I made no attempt to make friends, since I was more interested in what I was seeing than in conversation, and I generally dined alone and early. I also had a great deal of reading to do, having purchased books before I left on the history of Urey, the Border States, and even one thin volume on the Seventeenth Lancers themselves. It was a task I did not like, but I knew it was less onerous than appearing a complete fool when I arrived in Mehul.

I remember walking along the promenade deck and seeing a magician entertain a family. The sage was one of the entertainers the ship's owners provided, which included minstrels, players, and mimics. The family was young, and wore their best clothes at all times, clothes that were just a trifle out of the current style. I guessed they'd either saved their money for a holiday, or else this passage had been a present from a richer relative. There were four of them: two boys perhaps three and four, their father, who was about my age, and their visibly pregnant mother.

The magician was quite gifted—a fat, jolly man who prattled on while his hands worked wonders. He took a small toy, a tiger, from one of the children, and turned it sequentially into a cat that meowed, a dog that barked, a zebra that whinnied, and then into a full-size tiger, its mouth wide for a roar. Before either of the children had time to be frightened, the roar became a kitten's meow, the boys laughed, and the magician handed the toy back. The father turned, saw me, and ducked his head in acknowledgment of my superior class.

Embarrassed, I returned the salute and moved on. As I walked back toward the stern I mused about the sense of remove I'd felt watching these people who were living a life I'd never know, one as strange as if they were from one of the other worlds the Wheel surely must touch.

As we went south, the land grew sparser and drier, the cities fewer, and the farms farther apart and scraggly. The people on the banks or in boats were poorer; their clothes were no longer the rainbow hues of the north.

We stopped for supplies at a port that was little more than a long dock and a scatter of buildings. I went ashore for a walk. At the end of the pier squatted a man, the poorest of the poor by his rags. Beside him sat a girl, perhaps nine or ten. Both of their faces held the patient wisdom that poverty gives: There is nothing more the gods can do to me, and the only blessing I shall find is when the Wheel turns. I dug for a coin in my sabertache, although the man had not yet made a beggar's plea.

"Kind sir," he said, as his eyes focused, recognizing that another stood before him. "Would you buy my daughter?"

I don't know why I was surprised, since I'd seen men and women surreptitiously offering their children in Nicias's tawdry backstreets. But I was.

"No," I said. "I'm but a soldier. I'd have no place for her."

"She would be no trouble," he said, as if I had not spoken.

"She is a good girl. She's never sick. She has most of her teeth. She doesn't eat much, either. She knows how to sew, and I'm sure you could find someone to show her how to cook.

"She even can be . . ." and the man let the pause hang, ". . . good to you. Better as she gets older."

He elbowed the girl, and she attempted to put on a smile, such as she'd seen one or another of the whores of this byway paint on. But I saw the fear behind it clearly.

Perhaps I should have struck the man, or something. I did not, but dropped a silver coin in the dust near him and hurried back to the *Tauler,* reminded that Numantia may be a great country, but it was, and is, carrying a horrid burden of despair and poverty.

I wished then, and wish now, that all of us were rich, or at least lacked for nothing. But I suppose such contentment would bore the gods and make them rouse Umar and start over, to make a more fascinating world for their amusement.

As the second week drew to a close, I was weary of traveling, and my bones needed hard exercise. I thought of running up and down the decks, or climbing the teakwork, but thought I probably already behaved enough like Vachan not to need to act more like a caged monkey.

The Latane was now clear, blue, and the land around it green and rich again. We had entered that most blessed of lands, the state of Urey. The river divided again and again, but each branch remained navigable. From atop the third deck I could see, dim in the distance, the mountains that marked the end of the small state, and the beginnings of the Border States. Here is where I would be blooded, and make my name.

We docked, and I saddled my horses and set out through the city on the road that would take me to the Seventeenth Lancers' home in the garrison city of Mehul.

I'd expected to find a beautiful city, but instead I found a magical place. It was very old, and it had been a summering place for the kings of Numantia once.

Elsewhere in Numantia was heat; here it was cool, a pleasant breeze blowing down from the mountains and stirring the trees of the many parks in the city. The trees themselves were of a type I'd never seen, sixty feet in circumference, with multicolored leaves big enough to use for umbrellas in the gentle rains that fell occasionally.

In the center of the city, rather than a palace or a grim fortress, was a garden, where fountains rose and sang among pillars of black marble, worked with gold, and the water ran laughing down cascades into small pools.

Canals stretched through the city, connecting the district's many lakes. Huge multistoried buildings, old beyond age, stretched up, their balconies and lattices arabesques of beauty, and flowers growing on their roofs.

There were sidewalk cafés, and I smelled roast duck, spiced fish, chile-drenched corn, and other delights.

The people seemed uniformly cheerful and friendly. While of course there were beggars, they looked as if they'd bathed and been fed within the week, and even pled their cases as if they were respectable men and women working a trade, asking no more than their due.

On the lakes I saw drifting islands of flowers, black-faced swans, and moored houseboats, each with wonderfully carved decorations in many kinds of wood stained in rainbow hues. Behind each of these houseboats, which were almost 100 feet long, was a smaller, canopied craft fitted with cushions, perfect for a lazy idyll on a warm day like this. This, I thought a bit wistfully, would be a perfect place for a lover and a long holiday.

I rode on into the countryside. The land was very green, rolling farmland, broken by forests and lakes, each inviting the fisherman, boatman, or swimmer.

It was said that all men have two homes—their own and Urey—and I knew it was true. What that province is now is yet another example of the doom the Emperor Tenedos—and, I must admit, myself—brought to our country. Mourn, Numantians, the glory that was Urey and is no more.

But that day I swear even the dust Lucan's heels kicked up smelled sweeter than any other.

I understood why Urey, although under the protectorate of Numantia, was also claimed by the neighboring province of Kallio and even, along with the Border States farther south, by Maisir, although at the time no one thought they meant their assertion to be taken seriously.

I rode on, toward Mehul. If Renan is one point of an equal-sided triangle and Sulem Pass is another, then the third point, to the west, is Mehul. It guards not only Sulem Pass, but another fearsome area, the Urshi Highlands, as well. They're also part of the Border States, but the legend says the men who live there are those who are too fierce for their brothers in the rest of Kait, who keep the same customs and speak much the same language, to tolerate. Certainly they've caused the army and the people of Urey as much grief over the years as any raiders who boil out of Sulem Pass. This I would learn well within a few weeks.

I camped that night beside a stream, and stretched out my bedroll under the stars, listening to, far in the distance, the belling of a maned deer as I drifted away.

The next day, I rode into Mehul. The town is a fairly typical border settlement, with perhaps three or four thousand people, most of them working directly or indirectly to support the Lancers.

Their camp is five minutes' walk beyond the town. It's been there for generations, time enough for the saplings planted in the dim hope the regiment might be there long enough to cut them for kindling to grow into great plane trees that give welcome shade during the Time of Heat. The barracks are of stone, with wooden interiors and tile roofs that shed heat and let the water run off freely during the Time of Rains.

The grounds are perfectly kept, from green lawns to seasonal flowers, which might be expected when you realize there are several hundred men who are only a lance-major's frown away from being ordered to trim the grass with nail-clippers.

There are, or were anyway, around 700 lances in the regiment, assigned to six troops and headquarters. The troops were Sambar, which is for scouting; Lion; Leopard; Cheetah; Tiger;

and Sun Bear, which rides in support of the four combat troops. Each troop contains four columns of twenty-five, which are numbered and *always* referred to by the ordinal or it's time to buy the mess a round.

I rode in, reported to the regimental adjutant, and was assigned to Three Column, Cheetah Troop.

The next few days blurred past in a haze of happiness, as I was given necessary weapons, uniforms, the Spell of Understanding for the local languages, equipment, and met my fellow officers, and most important of all, the men of my column. I can still name them all, even the ones who did not choose to follow me later as members of my household guard when I rode with the emperor.

They also brought the only fear I had: fear that I'd somehow fail them and myself, and bring needless deaths. Fortunately, my father had told me every one of the stages I'd go through in my first command, and had warned me to leave well enough alone, admonishing, "Do not start fiddling with your column like a spinster who constantly arranges her sitting room and is never satisfied," and instructing me, "At the beginning, be no more than a presence to your men, and a pupil to your warrants." I tried to obey him.

I also knew full well that I was the youngest, newest member of the mess, and so kept well into the shadows, staying silent unless spoken to, and then making my answers as brief as possible.

Some of the other junior legates chaffed me, trying to find a weakness. I responded in kind, but stayed a bit remote, practicing another of my father's preachings, the one that said the cheery man who first befriends you in a new post will borrow money, steal your gear, and finally abandon you in battle. Friendship isn't a spring flower, he went on, but grows like an oak. He warned me there were of course exceptions, just as there are, he added, in love.

Two months passed, and I swear I grew happier with each day. Then came the pinnacle: I was ordered to take my column out to a village not far distant that had been hit by raiders from the Highlands and, in Domina Herstal's words, "put whatever's right back in its slot, and deal with whatever's wrong as you see fit."

Some might gasp at a man in his fifties being stupid enough to assign the task of warden, judge, and possible executioner to a boy just short of his twentieth birthday, but Herstal was a long spear-cast from being a fool. He'd told off Cheetah Troop's troop guide, a bearded man named Bikaner who'd been with the regiment for twenty years, and, I found later, a warrant who'd broken in more than a dozen fresh legates, to accompany me. My lance-majors had nearly as much experience, and the column was liberally salted with long-service lances. There were, in fact, only two recruits holding the rank of horseman. With twenty-five men such as these, I would have had to be a complete moron to fail.

I was also given, since the raiders came from across the border, a renegade tribesman named Ysaye we used for a scout. I thought him a complete scoundrel, and Troop Guide Bikaner cheerfully assured me I was correct, but he was inexorably loyal to the regiment, if for no other reason than that he'd been named outlaw in his native Highlands and had also committed murder here in Urey. We were his last and only safety, the troop guide said, " 'less he c'n figger somethin' else, an' then he'll turn on us like he did ever'one else."

We rode to the village, and set up a tribunal in the square. The situation was simple—or so it appeared at first.

The raider was an Urshi chieftain and reputed sorcerer who called himself the Wolf of Ghazi. He'd hit the village near dawn, killed two herdsmen, gravely wounded another, and stolen seven bullocks. But this was not the main plaint of the villagers. He had also broken down the doors of a local merchant, beaten and robbed him, and stolen his only daughter.

Through the weepings and wailings of his family, I asked for what purpose. The babble became worse—the Wolf would either take her to wife, make her a common whore for his men, or, and this was the consensus by volume, sacrifice her in some terrible ceremony, for, as the merchant said, "she was a virgin, blessed by the gods, the favorite of us all." I asked how this bandit had known which house to break into, and was informed no doubt he'd seen this beautiful flower of Urey, this peerless wonder of young womanhood, this pearl of beauty, when he'd traded in the village.

I was about to ask why the villagers were so foolish as to let a bandit window-shop for what he needs, especially when trade with the Border States was illegal save on certain days clearly specified by the government. But Troop Guide Bikaner shook his head slightly, and I said nothing. Later he told me all of the border towns trade regularly with their enemies, and not infrequently intermarry, which, he said, "makes enforcin' th' law interestin' at times, not knowin' whether you're steppin' into th' middle of a feud or not."

We must ride out immediately to save this merchant's daughter, whose name was Tigrinya, before she was sacrificed to some dark demon, and bring the Wolf to bay, not forgetting, the village chief reminded us, payment not only for the bullocks, which we should also return if possible, but for the deaths and sore injury of his man.

So I rode across a border on my first military campaign—twenty-seven men after a ragamuffin bandit and the peasant girl he'd kidnapped.

Ysaye knew where the Wolf's lair would be: no more than three leagues from the border, just north of the village he came from and claimed lordship over.

We followed a track into the hills, and twice saw cattle droppings not two days old—we were on the right path. I felt very confident, very sure that we would destroy this man and I'd win great honor.

The lance riding point shouted a warning, and I saw three men ahead, just where the truck entered a narrow defile. They screamed defiance, and lobbed arrows at us that fell well short.

Now we had them! I was about to call for the charge, and Troop Guide Bikaner said, "Sir!" There was something imperative in his tone, and so I held back, although anger touched me—battle is no time for a conference.

"Beggin' th' legate's pardon, but it's not strange for th' tribesmen t' suck so'jers in, sendin' a few out t'challenge, with th' main body lyin' in ambush."

As he spoke, my confidence, my bravado, vanished, and I cursed, knowing Bikaner was right, and that in addition the Wolf had sent a spell out, seeking a fool who'd allow it a home in his mind and make him bloodthirsty and foolhardy.

"Column . . . halt!" I snapped. "Dismount! Troop Guide Bikaner, I want four men on foot to go forward as flankers atop those rocks. Five archers halfway to that pass to support them. Make sure they aren't waiting for us on the other side."

As my scouts went out, moving like cautious lizards from shelter to shelter, I heard the clatter of horses' hooves from beyond.

"We've sprung it," Bikaner announced. "There'll be no one waitin' now."

But I'd learned my lesson. There could be a double bluff being played, and so had the men proceed. There was a small pocket beyond the narrow canyon, perfect to tether horses in while their riders waited for twenty-five or so idiots to stumble into the trap, a pocket with fresh, steaming horseapples on the ground. But the Wolf's riders had broken off.

"That's th' way a th' Men a th' Hills," Lance-Major Wace said. "They'll on'y fight y' t'yer back, ne'er t'yer face."

I guessed he thought there was something dishonorable about a handful of poorly trained men not willing to stand up to twenty-seven regulars. *I* thought anyone who'd fight as he wanted was not only foolish, but destined for a short life as well.

We went on, farther into the mountains, but encountered no other trap.

We rounded a bend, where the track ran halfway up a low hill, with tall, barren mountains on either side, and saw the stronghold of the Wolf of Ghazi.

It was a round tower, perhaps fifty feet high and a bit more in diameter, that'd been laboriously built with flat stones piled atop each other, and crudely mortared with clay from the nearby stream. There were firing slits in the walls, and I counted three floors, and a deck with raised stonework for archers to fight from. The upper floor's slits were wider, almost windows.

It wasn't much of a castle—but then, it didn't need to be to stop us.

There were men atop the tower, and suddenly arrows rained out. They fell well short, but I prudently ordered my men to withdraw, leave their horses with handlers, and come forward prepared for battle.

Before they could, a tall, bearded man stood up on top of the tower. He wore boots, bright red robes, had a belt around his waist with several weapons stuck in it and a blue cloth wrapped neatly around his head. This could only be the Wolf of Ghazi.

"You are dead men!" he screeched, and his voice was sorcerously magnified. "Flee, or face my wrath!"

I called for my two best archers, and rode forward. Perhaps I should've dismounted, since a horse under fire can be skittish, but I needed all of the presence I could manage. I stopped at what I estimated was extreme arrow range.

"I am Legate Damastes á Cimabue, of the Seventeenth Lancers, and I speak for the villagers of Urey!" I called in return. "You have broken the laws of our land, and you must pay!"

The Wolf roared laughter.

"*I* am the only law I obey! You are a fool!"

"Return the woman! And pay for your misdeeds," I called back. "You must also bring gold for the families of the men you slew, and the one you maimed."

"Leave my land, or you die!"

Clearly, we were not communicating any too well.

"You have four hours to consider," I came back, I'm afraid rather weakly. All that came back was another laugh. We started away, and very suddenly one of my archers, a very alert man named Curti, cursed and his bowstring twanged. There came a shriek from the tower, and a tribesman flopped forward, from one of the windows, his bow dropping from dead fingers before he'd had time to loose a shaft at me.

I was grateful I hadn't been stupid enough to use a white flag of truce when I rode up—it might have given the man a better aiming point. But now I had my second lesson in the way war was waged in the Border States.

I went back to the men, and we held a council of war. Our options appeared fairly limited, and none were enchanting. We had the Wolf besieged, but how long could twenty-seven men seal off his stronghold? I assumed no more than a day or so before either his bandits would slip off through secret ways we knew nothing about or, just as likely, we ourselves would be attacked by other Men of the Hills. I doubted if the Wolf had many allies, but figured most of the Highlanders would forget a feud for a chance at the head of a Numantian soldier.

We could attack the tower frontally, and be shot down as we charged.

Or we could give up and retreat.

I would accept none of the three, and set my troops to building a breastwork—carrying rocks to build a low stone wall around a tiny hillock near the redoubt, enough to slow down a charge if we were attacked. There were mutters at my order—since no cavalryman prizes physical labor—which were quickly subdued by the warrants. While they set to work, I went out a few yards and sat studying the tower.

There were two doors, both of wood and certainly heavily barred and blocked from the inside. Would it be possible, come nightfall, to set fire to them? This was doubtful: What could I use for firewood? If I had a seer with me, I could've had a spell cast that would have made them roar up in fire, but even so, what would that have given me? There would still be a dozen yards of open land to charge across. I stared on. A slight idea came, and I called for Ysaye.

I pointed to the windows on the third floor, and asked if he thought a man could fit through them. He looked closely, and said yes—if he was thin. Very thin. Troop Guide Bikaner would never make it. I looked at the stonework of the tower.

"Can that be climbed?"

Ysaye didn't need to look.

"*I* could climb it. To me, to any Man of the Hills, it would be like a highway. But you . . . the soldiers? I do not think."

I *did* think, having a bit more respect for my men than he did. But what was the possibility of getting enough men to take the tower up the wall in silence? I started to discard that as another stupid idea, then another possibility came.

"Ysaye, would the Wolf fear magic?"

"Of course. Doesn't the swordsman always worry that one day he will face someone better with the blade than he? But we have none. Unless the legate has talents so far unblossomed."

"I surely do," I said firmly. I asked him for the small jar of blue kohl I knew he would have about him, that all the hillmen used to make up their eyes, thinking it made them more handsome. He puzzled, but handed it over.

I sent for Curti, and borrowed one of his arrows. Then, with two other men, I went back to my vantage point and shouted for the Wolf. He came after a bit, pulling his clothes on.

"What do you want, fool? I was just about to enjoy the woman."

I paid no attention to what he said, and held up my arrow that I'd stained blue with Ysaye's kohl. I pointed it at the Wolf, then to the four corners of the compass.

"Wolf, O Wolf," I cried, trying my best to sound like a magician, "this is thy doom, this is thy end. Cease thy sins, make thy peace with Saionji, with Isa, god of war, or hear the Wheel creak. Obey me, O Wolf, and ye shall live. Send forth the woman, send forth the gold, and I shall not loose this arrow."

The Wolf ducked reflexively behind one of the outcroppings, but when nothing happened, he peered out.

"There is no use to hide, O Wolf. Your doom is sealed," I cried. "Do not make me send forth my arrow, which needs no bow, needs no string, but can seek you out and kill you. O Wolf, there is no shelter from my arrow, there are no walls thick enough to keep you safe. O Wolf, hear me, and obey! Do not make me send forth my arrow!"

He waited for a spell, then started laughing, bellowing, and I half-hoped he'd strangle himself.

Without making an answer, he vanished.

I walked back to the men. Troop Guide Bikaner made sure none of the men could hear him, and said, quietly, "Nice thinkin', Legate. But bluff'll not crack *that* one. He's too hard f'r words. We'll have t'try another plan."

I shook my head. "We may, Troop Guide. But not until tomorrow, because my scheme's just begun."

I waited until dark, called Ysaye to me, and told him now was the time for him to prove his boasting. I wanted him to climb that tower and perform a certain task.

He paled, and his eyes shifted, and he licked suddenly dry lips before agreeing.

"I will obey, Legate. It shall only take a few moments."

"I have full confidence in you, Ysaye," I said. "I'll go forward with you, and Lancer Curti as well, who shoots most accurately in the dark. He will be able to give you supporting fire if you're found out. Or . . ." I let my voice trail away, not needing to add what he would shoot at if Ysaye tried to flee. "If you do not return in one fingerspan of the moon, we shall assume you became lost, and make a great outcry to guide you back."

His face fell. I'd closed off his possible escape. I took the arrow I'd cast my "spell" on, and told him what to do.

We crept forward. The tower was all alight, and I heard the sounds of laughter and singing. The Wolf's men weren't taking my presence heavily.

Ysaye looked at me, at Curti's ready bow, cast away his robes, and said, "I think, Legate, in another life you were one of us," and vanished into the darkness. I strained my eyes, and thought, after a bit, I saw something move up the tower wall like a great cautious spider.

Half an hour later, Ysaye reappeared. He was breathing hard and his skin was bruised and scratched.

"I was wrong," he said, slipping into his clothes. "The climb was almost impossible. I think I am the only man in these hills who could have done it."

"I'm sure you're right," I said, grateful that the darkness hid my grin. "I'll ensure Domina Herstal hears of your bravery and rewards you—*if our plan works.*"

We went back to the others and waited. In two hours, the lights began going out in the tower. Then I heard a man scream in sudden terror.

Very good, I thought. Now we wait for the dawn.

At sunrise, the door to the tower came open, and the Wolf himself came out. Behind him was a not unpretty young woman I assumed to be Tigrinya, and three men, carrying chests.

I heard the lowing of cattle and saw half a dozen being driven toward us from the village beyond.

As the Wolf came closer I saw he had not slept well—there were great circles under his eyes, and he was deathly pale. In one hand, he held the arrow I'd had Ysaye toss through the upper window of the tower, which must have shocked him when he came on it. I wondered if Ysaye had been lucky enough to throw it into the Wolf's bedchamber.

I walked to meet him, but stopped well out of sword range, even though neither the Wolf nor his men appeared armed. My archers had arrows nocked.

Without speaking, the Wolf knelt, and held out the arrow.

"O Seer," he whined, "forgive me my sins. I knew not what mighty wizard I'd offended, and swear on all the gods I shall never offend thee again.

"Take the woman—I swear I treated her gently.

"And here is my gold." As he spoke, the men opened the chests. "Take all, take what you deem fitting, but leave me my life."

"I grant you your life, O Wolf," I said, solemnly. "And I am pleased that you took the warning I was gracious enough to grant you.

"But I still hold this arrow. If I ever hear of your crossing our border and harming the innocent, know I shall launch it, and it shall seek you out and slay you wherever you are."

"I swear, I swear I shall behave as a man of the law." There was a pause as he considered, and then cocked an eye up at me.

"At least in Urey."

"What you do in your own lands matters little to me," I answered, afraid to really press my luck. The Wolf would *never* become a sheep.

I ordered the men forward, and they led Tigrinya back to the horses. She seemed angry about something, and pulled away from our assistance. Certainly it appeared as if the Wolf was right: She didn't appear the victim of rape and savagery.

I looked into the chests, and learned the lot of a petty raider against poor villagers is slim. There were only a dozen gold coins, three times as much silver, and about the same in copper coins. The rest of the chest was full of rubbishy brass jewelry, beads, and gems I thought to be cut glass.

I took the gold and the silver and bade the Wolf sin no more. Bowing and scraping, the Wolf retreated to his redoubt, and I never saw him again, nor heard tales of his reiving against Urey.

We rode back for Tigrinya's village, slowed by the cattle. I felt pleased with myself: Not only had I accomplished my task easily, but we had done it without any bloodshed in my column. Blood is the natural end of war, certainly, but the less spilled the greater the commander. It is ironic that I always tried to follow that precept, yet served under the bloodiest of history's leaders.

That night, camping just on the other side of the border, intending to arrive at the village early the next morning, I heard a scuffle from where we'd made a crude tent for the young woman. After a time, Troop Guide Bikaner came to me, barely holding back laughter. I asked him what had happened, and he explained.

It seemed that Tigrinya was most angry. Here she'd had the one adventure of her life, getting out of what Bikaner said she'd called "that gods-damned village I was rotting in," into the arms of such a romantic rebel, and then we had to show up and ruin her dreams.

"But she's a wily one, Legate, an' went an' offered one of th' men a chance wi' her charms if he'd let her ride wi' him back t' Renan. Cursed him, an' then me, most eloquent when we said it could not happen.

"What'll y' wager, sir, that within th' month we'll see her on Rotten Row wi' th' other whores?"

Such were the realities of life along the border.

We returned a sullen Tigrinya to her father, gave the coins from the Wolf to the village chieftain, who seemed very pleased, and I guessed the widows of the slain men would be lucky to see any of the money, and rode back to our cantonment. Domina Herstal nodded approval and allowed I showed signs of learning my job. The regiment adjutant, Captain Lanett, bought me a glass of wine in the mess that night, a glass I was most pleased to drain to the dregs.

My life with the Seventeenth Lancers was beginning.

A month later I scored five goals at röl and it appeared ended.

SAYANA

Sayana is an old and evil city.

Legend has it the city was built in a single night by a horde of demons, under the control of a master warlock, who was thus able to extend his claws over the entire region and untie it in a commonality of greed and blood lust. This might be true, but as I'd already learned, demons could have taken lessons from these Men of the Hills.

As we rode toward it, the Seer Tenedos told me briefly of its past and at greater length what must concern me to represent the interests of the kingdom of Numantia properly.

Sayana stands on a low rocky plateau that juts from the plains of Kait, the Border States. It's a walled city, and eminently defensible against foreign attack or the far more common internecine warfare the Men of the Hills call polite society. It controls all approaches to Sulem Pass from the south, so the Kaiti have always been able to dictate who passes between Maisir to the south, and Urey and Numantia to the north.

Kait is a snake's nest of intertwining clans and families, most of whom seem to have blood feuds with most of the others. Whoever holds the throne in Sayana is called achim, and deemed overlord of the Border States, at least until the next poisoned cup, arrow-dart, or dagger-strike from behind.

The current achim was Baber Fergana, whose history was positively dynastic by Kaiti standards: His family had held the throne for three generations. Baber Fergana, as was customary, had signaled his intent to rule by having all his brothers murdered and his sisters married to peasants. However, unlike his father and grandfather, he'd erred slightly, and a younger brother, Chamisso Fergana, had escaped the slaughter and now held the loyalty of those tribesmen who were not on Baber Fergana's list of friends. "Sooner or later," Tenedos said, "either he'll come down from the hills, take the city, kill his brother, and become the new achim, or else Baber Fergana will succeed in inserting an assassin into Chamisso's tents, and there shall be peace everlasting until one or another of their children become strong enough to pull sword from sheath . . . or else woo enough warriors and sorcerers to once again topple what these people think constitutes government."

This was the normal state of affairs for the Border States, and of little concern for Numantia. However, there'd been a new force come into the hills of late, one that worried the Rule of Ten.

This was the Tovieti, which Tenedos told me the Rule of Ten had variously called "a dangerous revolutionary order," a "cult of fanatics," and "crazed bandits." "By which," he said, a smile touching his lips for a moment, "I took it to mean our rulers are terrified of them."

Little was known of the organization, save that it was very loose, with cells scattered everywhere, and that most of its members came from the peasantry, the landless, and the lower classes. Its prime tenet was that those who followed its banner would inherit all from the rich—not in some future paradise, but right now, and might speed that inheritance by killing anyone whose goods they desired, "except, of course," Tenedos went on, "those who also espouse their creed." They also required absolute loyalty and obedience to their leaders and complete secrecy about the organization.

I listened, but without a great deal of concern; it'd seemed my betters were always going on about some nefarious organization that was about to attack the state or at any rate absolutely corrupt the morals of the citizenry. As a soldier, I paid polite attention, but until I was actually faced with these folks as real enemies, and not chimerical apparitions of a fevered politician, I didn't waste time peering under my bed for these mischief-makers.

I suppose my unconcern showed itself to Tenedos, who I'd already seen was an astute reader of men's countenances. "There's been more than just scare-talk," he said. "The Tovieti have killed across the borders of the Border States into Urey, Dara, and even Kallio, or so the Rule of Ten's agents have reported. Most of the victims have been merchants whose caravans or houses were stripped bare, with nothing left but the bodies.

"The Tovieti kill by strangling with a yellow silk cord, when they can, and the cord is left knotted around the neck of their victims.

"The agents' reports also say the murderers have powerful magic on their side, since not one of them has been caught making his kill. Also, when their tracks are followed, they vanish inexplicably.

"I myself wonder just how ambitious a pursuit some village warden would mount after finding, say, half a dozen merchants dead and their gold and trade goods vanished, but I was assured that the reports of the Rule's agents was most accurate in this regard."

"How has this group been traced to the Border States?"

"That was a question I had as well, and received no answer other than that this was to be regarded as 'dependable information.' " Tenedos shrugged. "I was also told Chamisso Fergana appears to be either the leader or among the leaders of this organization, which is adding members by the day. Soon he will lead them down from the hills, seize Sayana, and mount a great war into Numantia. The Rule of Ten believe the Tovieti are responsible for all the unrest along the borders of late.

"Now you see what a wonderful ferment of evil and dark magic we are about to enter."

Sayana, not more than a mile ahead, was dazzling white under the sun, as white as a bride's robes. But between us and the walls was a truer symbol of Sayana. Iron stanchions, about thirty feet high, stood on either side of the road. Hanging from them were wrought-iron cages. Inside each was the rotting remains of a man. Some were no more than bones, picked almost clean by the kites and crows. Others were more recently dead, corpses blackening under the sun, eyes pecked out, grasping hands reaching for a mercy that was never granted until Saionji allowed them to return to the Wheel.

I heard a croak, not from any charnel bird, but from one caged man, or perhaps a woman, who yet lived. I could not distinguish through the filth and rags. A single eye stared, and a hand fluttered, asking for the last gift.

I knew I must not grant it, as much as I wanted to take a bow from one of my men and send a merciful shaft into the heart of that caged wretch. Such a boon would have been instantly punished, most likely by my replacing the one I'd granted mercy to.

I turned my eyes away, and we rode on.

Just ahead were the city's gates, and waiting in front was a formation of some fifty horses, with a single figure at their head.

"I see we're expected," Tenedos said. He eyed me to see if I was about to issue a string of panicky orders for my men to buff up their uniforms and blow the dust of the road off their trappings. I said nothing—I had full faith that my troop guide and lance-majors had done any necessary smartening-up before we set out that morning. Besides, I doubted the Men of the Hills held gleaming brass in as high esteem as razor-edged steel.

This honor guard was hardly the rigid line of soldiery a state visitor to Nicias would have been met with: The horses blew and chafed, eager to be on the gallop, and the formation was motley at best. Their riders were fantastically caprisoned, wearing many-hued headgear that billowed down like a boat's collapsed sails, ballooning sleeves on their gaily colored tunics under leather hauberks and breeches. From each cap draped a brightly colored feather that floated back almost to their horse's haunches.

But the sheaths of their swords were plain leather, and well worn, as were the unadorned hilts of their blades. They carried long spears, and these were also simple in design, and as I neared I saw their heads gleamed not from polishing but from frequent sharpening.

These gentlemen might be a palace guard, but they bore no relation to the parade-ground bashers like the Golden Helms of Nicias that clattered attendance around our Rule of Ten. These were warriors, not popinjays.

For a moment I thought the man at the head of the formation was their commander, but then I realized differently.

He wore robes of shimmering green that changed hues as the sun's rays struck them. In one hand, he held a staff, and colors ran up and down its shaft as if it were hollow glass, and fires played within. The man was tall, only a bit shorter than I, far leaner, and his coal-black hair had been waxed and was pulled back in a queue that ran halfway down his back. His beard was also waxed, and divided into two spears that reached to midchest. He could only be a sorcerer.

"I greet you," rumbled his voice, and I knew it to be magically augmented, "Seer Laish Tenedos and soldiers of Numantia. I am Irshad, chief *jask* to the Most Noble Leader, Achim Baber Fergana, and his Most Humble Chief Adviser in Worldly Matters, as well." He spread his arms in greeting, and from nowhere came a gentle mist that smelled of rosewater and musk.

I'd expected murmurs of surprise from my men—but was surprised and most pleased that there came nothing but silence.

"I thank you for your welcome, *Jask* Irshad," Tenedos replied. "Since you have seen our coming, and divined the craft we both share, perhaps I may return your compliment and gift. But I fear mine cannot be cast through the air, for fear of hurt.

"May I ask your brave soldiers to lower their spears until they point at my heart?"

"I can and shall," the magician said, and motioned. Instantly fifty lances came level with the ground, and I saw some of the men grin tightly. "You have great faith in their willpower, since some of them have declared death-feud with all Numantia."

"I need no faith," Tenedos said carelessly, "for I come as a guest, and is it not a mark of honor that a man who comes to you as an invited visitor has naught to fear? Or have I heard wrongly about the Men of these Hills?"

Without waiting for a reply, he nudged his horse forward, touched each of the outthrust spears, one at a time. I saw he had something small in his hand, but he kept it palm down, half-curled, so I could not make out what he held. His lips moved slightly as he touched the spears in a spell.

He'd laid his hands on only three or four of the lances when shouts of surprise came. The spearheads had gleamed of steely death—now they shone of golden wealth.

Discipline—what there was of it—of the honor guard broke, and they pressed their mounts forward, to make sure each of them received the touch of gold.

Irshad's face clouded, then he forced calm. "You give great gifts, and you are obviously a seer who has few equals in this land," he said. "My men thank you. I can only hope you have equal munificence for a man as great as the Star of the Mountains, my master."

Tenedos waited until the last lancer was gifted and he'd ridden back to my side before he responded. Gold glittered as his hand slid inside his robes, then came out empty.

"I have indeed brought great things to Achim Fergana," he said. "But they are not of gold or silver, for I know a man of his wisdom and taste puts a bauble at its exact worth, no more, no less.

"A man of such nobility might well consider himself slight-ed by gold, even if I were to change the very gates of this city to that metal, knowing his price to be far beyond any material thing."

Now Irshad smiled. "Numantia may have chosen well, Seer Tenedos, in sending a man whose own tongue is more precious than bullion. No doubt Achim Fergana will be equally impressed, although he's been known to have men of lesser speech's tongues removed when disappointed."

"I am sure our time together will be mutually valuable," Tenedos said, an equally insincere smile on his face.

And so we entered the city of Sayana.

The cobbled streets were narrow, filled with carts and men on foot or horseback. I saw few women, for these men consider their women capable of the most astounding immoralities if not watched closely, and so keep their wives and daughters mewed up. The few I did see smiled boldly, and one or two allowed their robes to slip open for a moment, to show a daring bit of ankle or even calf, and I knew their trade for what it was.

The street opened periodically into a square, and each one was filled with merchants hawking clothes, melons, fruit, vegetables, brass jewelry, questionable-looking meat with flies buzzing about it, and such. But a significant number—I thought every other one—seemed to be selling some sort of charm, spell, or magical potion.

Tenedos leaned over and said, "I see from the vendors I may have erred when I said it was a strange thing for the Rule of Ten to have posted a sorcerer as resident-general. Perhaps I am the man best suited for the task. Either myself . . . or a village witch."

A smile quirked his lips, and I returned it. I was beginning to like this small man, and his occasional self-deprecating humor, rare in someone with such a rarefied position.

The stone houses on either side of the street showed nothing to the world but a single, heavily barred door and, on the larger ones, a larger gate as well, equally well secured. Tenedos commented that he could tell the achim's tax-gatherers were most efficient: Men made no display of their wealth only when the land was rife with taxmen or thieves. "Most would say," he went on, "the occupations are one and the same."

Jask Irshad led us to the center of the city, where the streets were broader and the houses larger, mansions filling nearly a block. Outside one walled compound he halted, and announced this was the Residency of Numantia.

"Your servants await you, and the house has been provisioned as its previous occupant, also a Numantian, wished. If anything is lacking, your staff will be eager to assist.

"You have the rest of this day and the morrow to rest, and then my master, the Hand of Peace that Stretches Everywhere, would be pleasured by your company."

Bowing servants swung open gates—spear-tipped at the top, the spears looking like they'd been recently filed sharp—and chorused welcome.

Thus began our stay in Sayana.

We had little time for relaxation, however.

The mansion was huge, and there were many tasks that had to be accomplished instantly.

First, we sacrificed to Irisu and Panoan, god of Nicias, for our safe arrival. My men made further worship to Isa, and I added gifts of fresh fruit to Cimabue's monkey god, Vachan, and my family's hearth god, Tanis. Tenedos also held a private sacrifice—I was certain it was to Saionji the Destroyer, a god few wished to acknowledge, let alone bring themselves to her attention, except, perhaps, in the male aspect of the war god Isa.

After the ceremonies, Tenedos set his retainers to setting up a dispensary where the wounded from the ford battle could recuperate, then to preparing his own quarters.

The Kaiti servants, even though they certainly would report anything and everything to either Achim Fergana or *Jask* Irshad, were well skilled, surprising in a land where men so prized their independence. The household was run by a shifty sort named Eluard, whom I felt most comfortable around, for the rogue would have so many petty fiddles going he would hardly want to upset the cart by reporting us to anyone, unless the rewards were greater than he was already reaping. Laish Tenedos also knew him for what he was, and put him on our payroll.

Tenedos took various magical tools from his gear and screened the mansion, searching for various items of sorcerous interest, as he described them. I wondered what he meant.

"Oh, let us say there could be several things a wise seer might leave in a house that will be occupied by those his master might be interested in. In one place I might lay a spell that would carry any words spoken within its range to another place, perhaps my master's palace. In another, I might leave a different rune. For instance, in the bedchamber to be occupied by my honorable opponent, I might leave a conjuration of susceptibility, so a properly seductive young woman or man might achieve influence. A more concrete spell could be cast on a door, so all who look at it see naught but a bare wall. But if I or my soldiery needed emergency entry, I would not be left outside the gates foolishly imploring, or forced to mount siege to settle the matter."

"Your world is a shadowed one," I said, probably foolishly.

Tenedos looked at me in considerable astonishment.

"What one is not?"

I had no answer, and he went on about his business. I asked him later if he had, in fact, found any spells such as he described.

"To talk is to give away," he said. "I shall not be specific, but I will tell you the mansion is now safe, but *Jask* Irshad has a considerable talent."

I was busy with my own tasks.

The mansion could have served as barracks for the entire Ureyan Lancers, with every sort of room imaginable, from great dance floor to audience chamber to stables to troop quarters. The house filled four sides of a square, with a garden and courtyard in its center.

I assigned quarters for my men, and Captain Mellet's Khurram Light Infantry. In addition to the Numantian troops, I also had call on another 100 native levies to keep the Residency secure, commanded by a mercenary Maisirian named Gyula Wollo. How he'd found his way to the Border States, and into the service of Achim Fergana, he did not say. I liked him little, and trusted him less.

Troop Guide Bikaner took one look at the scruffy, loutish Kaiti soldiers and suggested I dismiss them out of hand, since the least they could be was spies, and would certainly betray us at the earliest possible chance, and quite likely murder us as we slept.

I thought this not unlikely, but determined to try something first, although I did order Bikaner to detail a handful of men and make sure the doors to the Kaiti barracks could be bolted from our side. The rest of my plan would have to wait until later. I had to prepare for the meeting with Achim Baber Fergana.

My rooms were palatial, larger than those the domina commanding the Lycee of the Horse Soldier occupied, being a sitting room, a bathroom, a study and library, a dining room, and a bedroom so plushly laid out I might have entertained several harems without running out of space. It was dizzying for a legate as young as myself.

To make sure I did not lose track of who I was, nor forget how momentary these splendors would be, I chose a servant from the ranks of the Lancers. I picked Lance Karjan, who was as little like a kowtowing lackey as could be imagined. I asked him if he liked the idea, and he grumbled, thought of spitting, decided there was no place convenient, and said it was "a duty." That would be the best I could expect.

Both of us set to, cleaning uniforms and weapons, just as all my lances and the infantry were doing. We would decide how we'd train to maintain our fighting edge later. Now it was time for square-bashing and gleaming regalia.

Achim Baber Fergana's castle loomed down over the city around it, rectangular, six stories, with the first story closed off and used as a storeroom. Achim Fergana's dungeons ran down into the living rock below. There were crenellated square towers at each corner. Entry was made via a ramp to a gatehouse, and then on a raised causeway into the castle proper. Eminently defensible, of course, but what a pain to the poor butcher who must drag carcasses up the ramp before Achim Fergana could feast.

Four Numantians rode to the audience with the achim: Resident-General Tenedos, myself, Troop Guide Bikaner, and one other soldier, Horseman Svalbard. He was chosen not only for the neatness of his turnout, but also for his stolidity and skills at hand-to-hand fighting. Captain Mellet and Lance-Major Wace had been left in command of the troops.

Tenedos wore ceremonial robes, white with the colors of Numantia worked into a frieze down the left side, and a sash in matching colors. He carried a short stick, not quite a staff, longer than a wand, made of ivory with elaborate carvings.

Bikaner and Svalbard wore full-dress uniform, with roached helmet, breastplate, greaves, and sheathed sword. Svalbard also carried a rolled leather case that contained the presents Tenedos had brought from Nicias for the achim.

I wore boots, chain armor under a linen tunic with a chest-blazon of the Numantian emblem, my sword, and a dagger sheathed opposite. Rather than a helmet, which I would have preferred, I wore a ceremonial pillbox hat, also in the blue of Numantia.

We were met inside the castle by two escorts and taken to Achim Fergana's audience chambers.

It was a very strange room. It began at the third level of the fortress, and stretched all the way to the roof of the castle. The ceiling wasn't solid, but elaborate spiderwebs of wrought iron supported multicolored glass, so the crowd below were constantly bathed in changing colors as the sun moved.

Cunningly wrought iron filled the huge room, providing benches, sculptures, dividers, and decoration. But where we Numantians would leave the metal bare, craftsmen had painted their work to closely resemble real life. I thought a bush beside me was a torrent of brilliant color, quite alive, until I brushed against it and bruised myself.

The floor was one single level, and mosaics were worked into its stone. At the far end of the room was a low dais, just high enough to make the step uncomfortable, which was evidently deliberate on Achim Fergana's part. In the center of the dais was his throne, a seat large enough to seat three. Its back rose ten feet in the air, and swept out like a peacock's display. But a peacock would have been shamed by the colors of this throne, which was set with every precious stone imaginable.

The walls of the chamber at ground level were irregular, with many nooks and crannies perfect to take a fellow into for a quiet conversation. I found out later that behind each of these convenient cubbies was a tiny room where one of Irshad's agents would be stationed, making careful note of any treasonous words.

The room was about half full of people. They were dressed in everything from the rags of the hillmen to colorful and ornate robes. Some men, regular members of the court, I was told, wore conical caps of leather intended to suggest war helmets. There was a scattering of women, all finely dressed. A few were wives or daughters of nobility, but more were unattached women of the higher stations who, without a father or husband, were seeking a protector on whatever terms were offered.

It seemed as if every level of Kaiti society was present, and I found out that despotic though Achim Fergana was, one of the ways he held his throne was to open his court to any supplicant or even the curious, as all achims must. An armed culture like this certainly encouraged the murderous and made the meek meeker, but it also kept people from putting on too many airs.

I noted one man standing near the throne, flanked by two retainers, who looked very much out of place. He wore an outfit I'd expect to see in the finest palaces of Nicias: a red silken tunic, black breeches bloused in high horseman's boots, with a black riding cloak held by a chain across his chest and a scarlet skullcap to match his tunic. His beard was blond, and closely trimmed. Only his weapon fit in with the rude society he was party of: He carried no sword, but he did wear a ten-inch-long fighting knife, its sheath mounted horizontally just beside his belt buckle.

Above the main floor ran a gallery, but it was impossible to see if anyone occupied it, since movable wrought-iron screens blocked my vision. This level was for Achim Fergana's women, to listen to the words of their master and "learn greatness from his wisdom."

Above that was yet another gallery, this one with a very different purpose. Three sides were filled with archers, who held arrows ready-nocked, who changed places and relaxed their wariness every few minutes. Until I discovered this secret, I'd wondered why, in a land of treachery, the achim didn't seem to care if his retainers were armed. I wondered no longer. Just to make sure of the achim's safety, the fourth side, the one directly behind the throne, held a full complement of *jask*s, ready to magically strike anyone who dreamed of endangering their master.

When I learned of these precautions, I wondered why any man would lust after a throne if he must surround himself with so many safeguards. I puzzled for a while, then gave the matter up. Would that I had pursued the thought to its inevitable conclusion. There might be many millions still alive, and I might not be waiting to die on a desolate island.

But all that lay in the future.

I save the two greatest marvels for last.

The first: Wandering among these men and women were wild beasts, the creatures of the Border States. I saw a tiger, a small honey bear, a pair of antelope whose horns intertwined above them, two small jackals, and other creatures. Overhead flew or sat birds of Kait—owls, chickadees, hawks, sparrows. Near the roof sat, in dark majesty, a horned eagle. All behaved as if they were as rightfully members of this court as any animal who walked on two legs.

Now I was truly impressed by the magic of the Border States. Not only were these creatures peaceful, not savaging each other or their mortal enemies they walked among, but they were carefully controlled, since none of us stepped in ordure, nor did we smell the reek of the wild.

Of all the displays I've seen in the courts of kings, that still is one of the most impressive.

The second and final marvel was the man sitting on that great throne, Achim Baber Fergana.

He was a big man. In his youth, he would have been a frightening warrior, not only from his size and muscles, but also from his dark hair that, like his beard, was waxed, brought to a series of points with gems mounted on each tip.

He was perhaps in his middle fifties and had gone somewhat to seed—his belly threatened to overcome his lap, and his beringed fingers were chubby, as were his cheeks.

But he was still a dangerous man. If I'd faced him in the wrestling ring, my best tactic would have been to keep out of his crushing embrace, and try for a back-heel knockdown. In armed battle, I imagined, he would prefer an ax or perhaps a double-handed sword. His tactics would be that of the woodsman, the hewer, rather than the delicacy of a fencer.

His voice rumbled out, a bearish tone quite fitting his appearance:

"I seek speech with the nobleman of Numantia."

Tenedos bowed, and started toward the throne. As he did so, *Jask* Irshad came from behind the throne and stood beside his master.

"Bring your fellows, Seer," Fergana went on. "I desire to meet all new faces within my realm."

The three of us followed Tenedos. When he stopped, we stopped. When he bowed, thrice, we followed his lead.

"You may approach my throne and name yourself."

"I am Laish Tenedos, appointed resident-general to the great Kingdom of Kait, and ambassador plenipotentiary to his Most Royal Highness, Achim Baber Fergana."

"Honorable sir, do you have papers so identifying yourself?"

"I do indeed. . . ." and Tenedos produced a properly beribboned and sealed parchment scroll and handed it to Achim Fergana, who untied its ribbon, opened it, pretended to study it, summoned his Most Honorable Aide and Most Puissant Sorcerer, *Jask* Irshad, and the ceremony went on. In the course of it, Tenedos gave the achim his presents.

He'd shown them to me before we left the compound, and I'd been most impressed. The case contained handmade knives, each one unique to one or another of the states of Numantia. So there was a thin-bladed fishing knife from Palmeras, a long, broad-bladed cattleman's knife from the state of Darfur, a brush-cutting blade of Cimabue that I can attest was also useful in brawls, and so forth. Each of them was made of polished ondanique steel, their hilts, grips, and guards of exotic woods and metals, with gems set into them.

It was evident that Achim Fergana liked them well, for I heard growls of pleasure, not of rage, from the bear. Then the ceremonies went on.

I shut off my ears, and pretended to be most attentive. I was somewhat surprised that a rough warrior like Achim Fergana truckled in such time-wasting, but guessed he felt it added legitimacy to his bandit's reign.

Eventually Irshad and Fergana decided Tenedos was no impostor, and was welcome at this court, so long as he held to the laws and customs of the fair country of Kait, and Achim Fergana was most interested in hearing the latest news from Numantia and its never-to-be-sufficiently-venerated leaders, and friends, the Rule of Ten.

I heard a very quiet snort at this last, and looked out of the corner of my eye to see who objected. It was the man with the red skullcap and dagger.

Evidently Fergana also had good hearing, because when the ceremony was over he motioned to the man.

"Landgrave Malebranche. Come forward, please."

The man obeyed.

"We are most honored," Fergana said, "to have two representatives of ancient and honorable courts with us. It is truly warming that Kait, which has been dubbed the Border States by the outside world, and we Kaiti, sometimes called no more than the Men of the Hills, as if we were wandering peasantry, have attracted such notice.

"Resident Tenedos, allow me to present the Resident from the country of Kallio, Landgrave Elias Malebranche."

I managed to hide my astonishment—surely Achim Fergana knew Kallio was but a state of Numantia, just as Nicias was. Before anyone could make anything of it, Malebranche bowed. "Perhaps, O Achim," he said, "because our two states differ in so many ways it's easy to think of us as being of different nationalities. But we are the same, which some are proud of, and others regret."

Tenedos turned slowly to the landgrave, a rank about equivalent to our count.

"I greet you in the name *of your proper rulers,*" he said, putting just the slightest emphasis on the last three words, "the Rule of Ten, and am sure we shall be the best of friends. But Landgrave, you said something that perplexes me. You say some regret being citizens of Numantia. Why would anyone be so foolish?"

"I spoke carelessly," Malebranche went on. "I did not mean that anyone regrets being Numantian, but there are those—of course I am not one—who feel Numantia is being, shall we say, led in a rather haphazard fashion these days."

Achim Fergana bellowed laughter.

"Ah, there shall be good times, I can tell, if two representatives of the same kingdom begin a catfight before they're even fully introduced. I predict great entertainment for myself and my court."

Tenedos allowed a smile to show, then vanish.

"I am pleased Your Majesty is amused, and I hope to gladden him in other, more important ways as part of my mission. However, do not think a small disagreement about semantics is a catfight. In the end, Numantians are brothers."

Fergana laughed even more loudly.

"Is that correct, Langrave Malebranche? Do all your folks hew together when times grow hard?"

Malebranche's grimace might have been intended to show private mirth, but he made no answer. Nor did Fergana press him for one. Instead, he turned back to Tenedos.

"Interesting times, yes." He looked past the seer, at me. "You, young man. You are the one I have been curious to meet."

I'm afraid I goggled.

"You are the clever soldier who convinced the Wolf of Ghazi you were a magician, and made him yield his prey, are you not?"

This did not make me any the less mazed, but I managed to recover control of my face. Did this man . . . or rather the sorcery of his *jask* . . . have all knowledge of the borders?

"I am that man, sir," I said.

"You have a quick wit," Fergana said. "I am curious to see how it shines in the future, and hope that you will have more opportunities to display it."

"Display it carefully," Irshad put in. "Some of us are not as easily amused as the achim."

I bowed. "Thank you for the compliment . . . and for the warning."

Both men looked hard at me, as if graving my features— and soul—into their minds. I started to step back, but held firm. After a moment, they both looked to Laish Tenedos.

"I am moved," Achim Fergana said, "to admit you to this court as an honored representative. All you need do is fulfill one final duty."

"You have but to ask."

Irshad gestured, and the entire dais, with the throne on it, slid back, until it was flush against the wall. I could have sworn the stone had been firmly cemented against the floor. I reminded myself that merely because the Men of the Hills had barbaric customs, they were not to be taken lightly, neither in their crafts nor in their thinking.

Where the dais had sat was a round iron plate, wonderfully painted as a wheel, with, it seemed, all the creatures and men of this world on it.

Irshad motioned once more, and the plate slid away, revealing a low pit.

"Step closer," Achim Fergana ordered. "All four of you."

Below us was a miniature of the first level of the chamber room we stood in. Not only were the details of the room exactly worked, but it was filled with dolls, each about a single hand high. I studied them, then looked about me, recognizing the courtiers who'd modeled for the mannequins. Each member of the court was represented in this shallow depression, his face most exactly carved of ivory, and costumes equally realistic.

There were far more dolls than people present that day. The other difference was that there were no dolls on the tiny dais to represent either Achim Baber Fergana or the *Jask* Irshad.

Irshad stepped down into the pit and picked up one doll. It was an amazing replica of the Kallian, Landgrave Malebranche.

"This is not a child's conceit, Resident Tenedos," Fergana said.

"I have already sensed that, O Achim," Tenedos said. "Remember, my main craft is not that of diplomacy."

"Ah yes. I forgot. Each of these figurines contains at least a bit of hair from the man—or woman—it represents. I require anyone who chooses to attend my court to provide such matter."

"I must protest," Tenedos said. "That could give magical control of the person into your . . . or your sorcerers' . . . hands."

"It could," Fergana said. "But I am a man of honor, and would never take advantage of that, nor would I allow any of my *jask*s to commit such an offense."

"Then why do you require it?"

"Honor begets honor . . . and the reverse is true as well," Fergana said. "I am afraid there have been men come to my court who intended evil. But once they were confronted with this choice, with providing *Jask* Irshad with the necessary items, they either fled, or else remained most honorable while they were in Sayana.

"When your service here is completed, the doll will be given to you as a memento. I also require such items from any of your representatives, such as the clever Legate Damastes á Cimabue, who will attend my court."

"I cannot provide such items," replied Tenedos, "and again must protest the lack of trust you show in a properly accredited representative of the court of Numantia."

"Your protest is heard and rejected."

"Then I have no other choice than to withdraw my credentials."

"If that is what you must do, then do what you must," Fergana said, amused.

"The Rule of Ten will be most displeased."

"No doubt," Fergana said. "But it is a *very* long way back through Sulem Pass, through Urey, and down the Latane River to your capital. By the time word reaches the Rule of Ten, *if* it ever does, and they decide to take whatever course of action necessary to protect the rather imagined interests of one man . . . well, a great deal of time will have passed, and in that time many things will most likely have occurred."

Landgrave Malebranche smiled, and I could well imagine what he was thinking: With the Numantian envoy, who of course in his view spoke only for Dara and Nicias, discredited, there could well be opportunity to make a pact with Kallio's new prime minister, Chardin Sher. Which no doubt was exactly why the landgrave was present in Sayana.

I glanced at my men: Bikaner's face was set in stubborn refusal, as was Horseman Svalbard's.

Tenedos looked at me, and his lips were pressed together angrily.

I saw one of the court's animals—a strangely striped antelope—wander past, and an idea came me.

Supposedly magicians can transfer their thoughts one to another, without the necessity of speech. I've heard of, but never seen, such a marvel, even though I doubt it not. Nor do I believe very highly in omens or people somehow sensing a dear one in dire straits many miles away.

But in that instant I stared hard at Laish Tenedos, willing my idea to go out, to enter his brain, to sweep across the few feet between us like an invisible wave. I allowed myself to nod . . . just a bit. Tenedos blinked, and his expression became bland once more. His eyebrow lifted, questioningly.

Again, I chanced a tiny nod.

Tenedos turned back to Achim Fergana.

"I . . . see," he said, slowly. "This is a very new, very shocking idea."

"But one that must be obeyed."

"May I have a day to consider it?"

Irshad started to say something, but Fergana's glance silenced him. "I do not mean to insult, but there is no way this edict can be gotten around, by trickery or any other way. You must provide a bit of hair, at the very least. Most are willing to give a drop of blood and saliva as well, to assure me of their loyalty.

"But I shall not require all such items from outlanders.

"Very well. This time tomorrow, you are to present yourselves here, to me. No. Make it two days distant. That will give my artisans a chance to make the dolls, and you may have the pleasure of seeing them.

"At that time, you must either clip a bit of hair from each of your heads to be inserted into the figures, or else forever depart my court, the city of Sayana, and the Kingdom of Kait, as a declared enemy of this country.

"Is that completely understood?"

Tenedos looked at me, and he appeared slightly worried. I was not. Either my idea could be accomplished in seconds, or not at all.

His lips firmed.

"I agree."

"Very well," Achim Fergana said. "In forty-eight hours, we shall meet once more. You have leave to go."

EIGHT

THE DECEIVERS

A s soon as we'd returned to the compound, Tenedos took me to his quarters, said a few quick words at each corner of the room to ensure there were no magical listeners present, and said, "I assume you were not wriggling your eyebrows from an itch, Damastes."

"I was not. Perhaps I've a solution to our, er, embarrassment."

"Tell me. I would far rather find a way around this quandary than be forced to confront it directly." He smiled wryly. "What a strange predicament I am in. If my theory is correct, and the Rule of Ten wishes something to happen to me, I'm afraid the minor disaster of being rejected at Achim Fergana's court would hardly be enough to send in the heavy regiments. It would, however, be enough to ruin my reputation in Nicias. I can hear the jests now—a highly trained seer, a great magician of Numantia, foxed in his first state assignment by a barbarian with dolls. Well, *I do not propose to fail,*" and steel was in his voice. "So what is your plan, my friend?"

"A question first, sir? When we first entered the city, and you turned the guards' spearheads into gold, you held something hidden in your hand—held like this, am I correct?"

Tenedos nodded. "Good eyes, my friend. I held a small

golden amulet that's been given certain powers to transmute base metal, although of course the amount of magical energy required for the task makes it prohibitively expensive, or else the lowliest peasant's geegaws would be golden, and the metal would lose all value.

"I assume, when you were a boy, the sleight-of-hand artists who attempted to deceive at the local bazaars hated you on sight."

"Nosir. I never let on when I spotted how they did something. I told a friend once how a conjurer did a trick, and he got angry, and said he would rather not know where the scarves or doves are hidden. So I never did again. But I thought you were quite good—the only reason I could see what was in your hand was I was behind and to the side. If I'd been in front, like the Kaiti were . . . I would have seen nothing."

"Still, I had best spent more time exercising my fingers," Tenedos said. "No one likes to be found out. So you think my legerdemain might provide a solution?"

I explained what I had in mind. A smile slowly grew across Tenedos's face.

"Indeed. That sounds a definite plan. I like it. I think it could well work, because I shall be performing in front of another magician, and no one is easier to fool than the man who himself wears a mask.

"Yes. However, I had best begin practicing. We will also need to involve your troop guide in our little conspiracy."

Two days later, we returned to Achim Fergana's court. This time, there were but the three of us. We arrived a little earlier than the hour set, and spent the time moving among the people of the court. There was quite a crowd that day—no doubt the thought of seeing the humiliation, one way or another, of the loathed Numantians guaranteed a crowd.

Tenedos was the perfect diplomat, speaking to a man here, a woman there, introducing himself as he went, pausing for a sweetmeat from one of the passing servitors, patting one of the court animals as it passed, Troop Guide Bikaner behind him like a proper retainer, and then there came a shouting of soldiers' voices, and Achim Baber Fergana stalked into the room. Behind him was *Jask* Irshad.

Without preamble, he walked to the throne, and waited until all finished bowing, in our case, or prostrating themselves, as the Kaiti were required.

"Resident-General Tenedos," his voice boomed, "you heard my orders two days gone. Are you now prepared to obey them, or are you defying my edict and our customs?"

"I still resent the implication I, or any of my retinue, would consider harming Your Majesty," Tenedos said. "However, in the interests of national amity, I am prepared to agree." He walked forward, and took from a pouch at his belt three tiny golden boxes. He opened them.

"Troop Guide Bikaner of Numantia, are you prepared to sacrifice for the good of the country you serve?"

"I am," Bikaner said, and the slight quaver of his voice seemed real. He walked forward, and removed his helmet. Tenedos took a tiny pair of silver scissors from his pouch and, with a bit of difficulty considering Bikaner's close crop, snipped off a bit of hair and let it fall into the box. He snapped the box shut, and touched it to his forehead.

"Nothing is in here that came from outside this court," he announced, and set it on the edge of the dais.

"Legate Damastes á Cimabue, are you ready for this sacrifice?" Tenedos said.

"I am."

Hair from my head was cut and put in another box, and again Irshad checked to make sure we had not somehow managed to substitute someone else's hair that we'd brought into the castle with us. Then it was Tenedos's turn.

When all three boxes were on the dais, Irshad stepped behind the throne and brought out three dolls. They were marvelously made, each of them not only exactly clothed as we had been at the previous ceremony, but the expressions on the ivory faces were very recognizable, although, truth to tell, I did not think I looked quite *that* young.

The clothing of each was opened, revealing that the dolls

had been carved from wood. In the center of the wooden skeleton was a small hole stuffed with clay. *Jask* Irshad, his lips moving in an inaudible incantation, opened each of the boxes he'd been given, took out the bits of hair, and pressed them into the clay of the appropriate dolls.

He finished, and stepped onto the dais. Again he motioned, again the dais slid back and then, with another gesture, the miniature court was revealed.

Irshad put the three of us into the scene—just beside the doll that represented Landgrave Malebranche. Then the pit's cover slid back, and the dais returned.

Irshad bowed.

"I thank you, in the name of the Most Bountiful of Monarchs, Achim Baber Fergana, and wish to congratulate you in being able to bask here and learn from his wisdom and decisions."

"Very well," Fergana said. "Enough of magic. Now, let us to business." He sounded relieved, and I suspected that he, like many of us, was most uncomfortable around any sort of sorcery, even though it was intended to benefit him.

And so the slow dance of diplomacy was finally allowed to begin.

Our deception had succeeded.

Our tasks in Sayana were three-fold. First was to represent Numantia, and attempt to keep Achim Fergana from making any decision that would be harmful to our national interests. Second was to provide information on this new organization called the Tovieti. Third was the long-range and probably impossible job of trying to encourage the Kaiti to change their warlike ways, or at any rate direct them away from Numantia, especially Urey.

It had been five years since there had been a Numantian resident-general in Sayana. The previous holder of the office had died quite suddenly and mysteriously; we were variously told of drink, of an overly heavy intake of the spice leaves the Kaiti were partial to, or of some disease brought on by insanity. Tenedos said he believed none of them but had no conjectures of his own.

The Rule of Ten had given Tenedos the list of agents the previous resident-general had developed, and we were to contact them and put them back to work.

This was almost impossible, since any Numantian who went out of the estate was instantly spotted and followed, either by one of Irshad's agents or by a mob that would grow in size and anger, shouting threats and hurling an occasional stone at the hated enemy.

But it took little investigation, no more than a cursory visit to the neighborhoods these agents supposedly lived in, to realize there was little need to worry about exposing anyone to the wrath of the achim and his torturers. Either the former resident-general had made up his spies entirely and pocketed their pay, or else they'd fled when he died—and I believed the former most likely. A stable in which the blacksmith was one of ours had burned to the ground. A tavern was now a fortune-teller's shop. A residence where our man was described as a strapping youth held nothing but doddering crones.

If we were to have spies of our own, we would have to grow them from our own seedlings. Since I had little knowledge and less inclination for this dark world, we were severely handicapped, and I wondered why Tenedos's retainers had not included an experienced warden who knew about informants and agents and duplicity. Tenedos himself, a bit shame-facedly, said he'd always been interested in spies, and had some theories, but this land was a terrible place to test them, so he'd be no real help.

We found out a great deal about *Jask* Irshad, and very little of it was favorable. He was the kingdom's most talented sorcerer, and was also blindly ambitious. He'd come late to Achim Baber Fergana's court, and some whispered that he'd waited to make his declaration until he was sure the achim had a firm hold on the throne. Since then, he'd ensured he was Fergana's most needed servant, providing him not only with magical resources, but with a network of agents that ran from the top to the bottom of Sayana. I thought him a loathsome being, and he seemed to return the opinion. One of his few honestly held beliefs was a complete hatred of any non-Kaiti.

I mentioned my dislike once to Tenedos, and he shrugged, and told me he felt no particular hatred for the man. "He is, in his way, a patriot," Tenedos said. "He is ambitious, but what of that? Aren't we all? Frankly, I am learning some things from him, and I suggest, Damastes, you follow my example—I've found no man so monstrous that something in his character is not worth the study." I had better ways to spend my time than studying a sewer, but kept that thought to myself.

My main concern was with our native soldiery, since they were the most dangerous, being close to us at all times.

I called them into the courtyard, and bade them watch while I put my own troop through a series of drills. They were unmoved, since they fought singly, and believed soldiers fighting in formation were no better than puppets. I then had the best of my swordsmen and fighters show their abilities. This the Men of the Hills understood, and were impressed by.

Next I invited their best bladesmen to try their skills, with sheathed blades, against my men. The hillmen did their best, but only beat my Numantians one out of four times.

Finally, I divided them up into small groups, did the same with my men, and set them against each other—one on one, one on two, two on one, three on one, and all the desperately unfair combinations that real war brings. Once more, they were bested by Lancers and the KLI.

I then put them in formation, and said I proposed to turn them into soldiers, and if any of them objected, they were welcome to leave Numantian employ. There were mutters and dark looks.

Before mutiny could develop, I announced the first four changes: Their old, reeking uniforms would be burned, and replaced with much smarter regalia Tenedos had sketched and ordered local seamstresses to make; their filthy quarters would be cleaned and painted by outside workmen and thereafter kept spotless; their cooks had been discharged as the incompetent slop-handlers they were and the men would now eat at the same tables and from the same menu as we did; and finally their wages would be increased 20 percent, paid weekly in gold.

This got the darkest of looks from their leader, Gyula Wollo, but the rest of the men were shouting enthusiasm.

While the romance still bloomed, I put my lance-majors and the KLI's sergeants to work, drilling the tribesmen hard, but not that hard, and with orders never, ever to swear or treat these hillmen as if they were anything other than the noblest of Numantians. When my warrants were satisfied, I would order the levies to be integrated into the Numantian forces. Hopefully the tribesmen would learn how to soldier by example—and, of course, I would have the added security of having a trusted man at each hillman's side at all times. A double advantage of this was that my men were also being trained, yet in a way that was fresh to them, so the various drills kept their interest.

I sent for Wollo, and informed him I would be making an accounting of the monies paid to the hill soldiers, to make sure there'd been no errors.

He glared at me. "S'posin' that things don't look straight," he said. "Rememberin' I'm not one f'r numbers."

"You'll have a chance to explain any discrepancies."

"Y'know," he tried, "there's nobody honest in Sayana, so it wuz necessary sometimes t'slip a coin or two under th' table."

"No doubt," I said. "If I have any questions, or if Resident-General Tenedos has, of course any explanations will be listened to."

"E'en if it's naught but my word?"

"You are an officer, and any officer under my command is assumed to always tell the truth, or else he's cashiered. Besides, Resident-General Tenedos is a seer, a *jask*, and his sorcery can instantly scent the truth.

"An honest man has nothing to fear."

Wollo tried for a smile, failed, and made his departure. Of course, he was gone by the time we shut the gates for the night, leaving his few possessions behind. But my investigation of the levies' funds showed that, unless he were a complete wastrel, he would have been able to buy himself a new wardrobe handily—and a mansion to closet it in.

I'd expected nothing different.

Similarly, Tenedos's retainers put their efficient hands to work on the household staff, and little by little we made the Residency into a livable part of the world. They were given invaluable assistance from our castelan, Eluard, once he was assured we had no plans to audit *his* accounts. That thief was firmly on our side.

Time would bring even greater changes—but none of us was under any illusions that we would have that commodity.

It did not take spies, or magic, to realize that Sayana was seething. We dared not ride into the countryside, but assumed that whatever was happening in the capital would be occurring throughout the Border States. Worse, we heard feuds were being reborn throughout the country, with the promise that "all would be settled soon . . . when the Change came." All Kait was abubble with the steam of war, as we'd seen coming through Sulem Pass.

We Numantians were hated, as were all outlanders. A favorite slogan chalked or painted on any open wall was: *M'rt tê Ph'rëng!*

Death to Outlanders.

It took little conversation in a tavern to find most Kaiti felt that meant *all* foreigners, without fear or favor. Whether you were Ureyan, Nician, Kallian, or any other Numantian, or Maisirian or any other breed, including natives of the other Border Regions, you were enemy, and legitimate prey, either by shortchanging or a spear through the chest.

There were other Numantians in Sayana besides our own soldiery and Tenedos's retainers. There were about 300 civilians, in various occupations from merchant to mendicant to swordmaker to a handful who'd married Kaiti and come back to live with them or their children. Both Tenedos and I wished they would flee Sayana before the storm broke, but we could say nothing. In the event of catastrophe, it would be our duty to try to protect them.

One thing I could learn nothing about was the Tovieti. Mere mention of the word was enough to end a conversation and silence any tavern. There weren't even any rumors to be heard—or at least none that would be repeated to a Numantian. However, Tenedos pointed out that this hushed silence *did* indicate the Tovieti were not a fever-dream creation of some Nician bureaucrat. "All information, my good Damastes, is valuable," he said. "Even in its absence." I definitely was not cut out for a career in espionage.

I was able to find out a little about Fergana's brother, Chamisso. He was mentioned in only two ways—mostly as if he were the biggest monster in the land. This came from anyone who held any position of authority, or anyone who wasn't sure of the allegiance of the person he was speaking to. Other people, servants and workers, the poor, spoke of him as if he bore all the virtues of the Fergana family, while his brother, the achim, had all the evil. This was not a good sign: It was clear the Pretender in the Hills was far more popular than the court believed, and that popularity was growing.

I allowed my Lancers to go out only in fours or more, with at least one warrant in each group. They didn't like that much, and Captain Mellet thought I was being overly severe. But after a half dozen of his infantrymen were nearly beaten to death in "spontaneous" tavern fights, he gave similar orders.

Not that many of my men wanted to go outside the compound anyway. I set up our own tavern, bought wine and spirits in bulk, and sold them just above cost. Food, well cooked in the Numantian manner, was always available from our kitchens.

As for sex, there were the whores the KLI had brought with them, and the native staff was mostly women. Since they were in the employ of Irshad or Fergana's spymasters, they'd been chosen as much for their social abilities as cleaning talents. They were almost all young, quite striking, and most friendly. Whatever arrangements they made with my men was not my business, and so I made no inquiries as to who slept where when he was off duty. I'd been taught, in the academy, that spies value pillow talk, and worried for a few days until I hit the obvious solution: Pillow talk is completely harmless if the talker doesn't know anything important.

We had few secrets, really, and most of those we did were held by Laish Tenedos, myself, and Captain Mellet. There were other things an enemy might wish to know that a foolish lance might confide, such as when guards were changed, or where the posts were, but those I changed frequently.

I, myself, slept alone, remembering my father's teachings, although I still recollect one young woman, one responsible for the floral arrangements in each room. She was dark, with a quick and easy smile. She also had roseate nipples and curvaceous legs that I saw once when she'd "thought I was out," and changed her dress in my room—while I "just happened" to be drowsing in the bath. I am sure we would have ended in the same bed in time, but time was not there.

I was a bit surprised by Laish Tenedos; more than once I saw women slip into or out of his quarter at an unseemly hour, and once I heard a bit of a giggling conversation when I passed by a larder: "Ay, yes, th' wizard's ripe for love, an' with an eye for th' unusual, but there's one strange—" but my footfall was heard so I never learned what was unusual. But the more I thought on it, the less it mattered. Tenedos was not married, or if he was he never spoke of his wife. What did it matter whether he slept alone or with someone? Kaiti customs were hardly straitlaced, and the higher in society the more open they were. I paid no more mind to the matter. He was my superior, and besides I assumed he had sense enough not to babble in his lustiness.

Suddenly I had other things to contend with.

It was well after midnight, and I was sitting with Tenedos in his study when the screams came.

We were relaxing after a long day with one of Achim Fergana's greedier assistants working on a proposed pact, wherein Numantia would agree to provide a sizable amount of gold to the achim, in exchange for which he promised to do "all that lay within his powers and authority" to dissuade the Men of the Hills from raiding into Urey. Tenedos wanted a more concrete assurance, such as the achim's willingness to permit cross-border pursuits or even cooperation with our border-patrol units such as the Lancers, and the achim just wanted more gold.

I was listening to Tenedos hold forth on just what was wrong with the way Numantia was ruled, and how each of the states must be required to provide more support for their kingdom, for which they'd receive far greater benefits than at present, when the peaceful night air was ripped apart by screams.

Before the echoes died, I was up and out, bare sword in hand. The screams came from belowstairs, in the building we were in. I heard shouts of the duty warrants turning out the guard, and outcries from civilians.

The screamer was on the first floor, standing just outside the entrance to Eluard's quarters. It was one of the scullery wenches, and I wondered why she was abroad at this hour.

She was hysterical, and could only point inside.

I pushed her aside and went in.

The apartments were very luxurious—as plush as those of Tenedos. Eluard's little thieveries mounted into quite a sum, I saw.

Slumped in a fat padded chair was Eluard.

Two glasses of liqueur were on the table in front of him. One, the closest to him, had been drained. The other was full to the brim.

The ends of a long, yellow silk cord dangled on his chest, and the cord was buried in the folds of his purpled neck. Eluard's tongue protruded grotesquely, as did his eyes, and I smelled shit from the voiding of his bowels.

He was still warm to the touch, but very, very dead.

There were people behind me in the doorway, and I heard that word that didn't exist in Sayana:

"Tovieti!"

* * *

An hour later the body was gone, reluctantly lugged away by what the Kaiti called their wardens. They were terrified of touching the corpse, and refused to offer any explanation of what could have happened, nor any theories as to why Eluard would have been a target.

All of the estate's gates were still locked or barred from the inside.

The wardens made no attempt to search the house or interrogate any of the staff. The wench had been one of Eluard's bed companions, and this was her night to sleep with him, no more.

I made brief inquiries of the warrants of the watch, and ordered a close check of the building for previously unnoticed entryways, but doubted I'd find anything with such a physical search.

What clues might be discovered were in that silk cord.

It lay across Laish Tenedos's desk. He had both of the trunks that held his magical implements open, and an assortment of tools ready. He'd cleared the rugs back from the floor, and scribed certain symbols within a small triple circle that held a triangle inside its innermost round. For some reason, looking at those unknown characters sent a slow chill along my spine, and I tried to keep my eyes away from them.

He had a small brazier on his desk, and was adding herbs to it from vials. I saw the labels on a few: *Wormwood, Broom, Mandrake, Elder, Maidenhair.*

He finished and set the brazier at one point of the triangle. He took the Tovieti's silk strangling cord and then stood in the circle with his feet touching the other two tips.

"Now, my friend, if you'll be good enough to take that taper and hold it to the brazier when I tell you, I would be appreciative. After that, please have your dagger ready. If any-thing . . . unforeseen happens, or if it appears I am in any danger, you must cut through all three rounds of the circle. Please do it quickly, because events might occur rather rapid-ly and I feel I am going in harm's way."

I nodded understanding. I was far more nervous than Tenedos—I'd never even been present at a magical rite, let alone assisted in one.

"Light the brazier." Tenedos's voice was calm.

I did, and jumped back as a blue flame roared up and touched the ceiling, but it was a heatless flame.

Tenedos began chanting:

"Now we go
To the heart
Whence you came
Where you were gifted.

"With your brothers
With your sisters
Whence you came
Now we go."

The flame lowered, but still was the height of a man. More flames appeared, around each circle that had been chalked onto the floor, and darted around them as if they were being chased or were chasing.

Dark-green fire flashed at each of the triangle's tips, and then it was as if Tenedos vanished.

He still stood there, but his spirit was elsewhere. His head moved, back and forth, and I was reminded of a hawk, looking down from the sky for his prey. His gaze swept back and forth, then looked up, as if the "hawk" were approaching a cliff. His lips drew back, in a snarl, half fright, half rage, and he shuddered.

I started to make the cuts, but held back.

Again his eyes went back and forth, and then flared open, as if in astonishment. He gaped, and terror gripped him. His mouth came open to scream, and I slashed once, then again to make sure.

The fires vanished and Laish Tenedos returned. He dropped the silken cord and tried to take a step, but staggered. I helped him to his seat, and started to pour brandy.

"No," he said, his voice a croak. "First, water."

I poured a glassful, and he drained it, then another.

"Now I know our enemy," he said, and his tones were grim. "But now . . . brandy. Pour yourself one."

I obeyed, though I wanted it not. He sipped at his, gathering his thoughts.

"The Tovieti certainly do exist," he said. "I followed the trail their strangling cord gave me to their stronghold. Or, perhaps, only one of their redoubts. It is in a great cavern, some distance from here. Perhaps two, perhaps three days' travel, deep in the mountains. I suppose, with someone to help me with the maps, I could find it once more.

"I found the cave, and I entered it, but without using an entrance. There was a huge center room, and I noted passageways leading off to the side. I do not know where they lead.

"There were people inside. Men and women. A thousand at least, more likely more. They were all dressed in white, although some of them were quite dirty. I think all, or most of them anyway, were Kaiti. To one side was a great pile of gold, gems, other treasure.

"It seemed as if these people were waiting for something.

"There was a throne, man-made, and in front of it was what might be called an altar, but one such as I've never seen nor heard of. It was cylindrical, like a field drum, and quite high, perhaps twenty feet above the chamber's floor.

"Standing around it were men and women, also wearing white, but each of them also wore a yellow sash. I think, although I may have imagined it, that one of them looked a great deal like a younger, and less rotund, Baber Fergana."

"His brother," I guessed.

"Perhaps. I tried to move my presence closer, and then someone . . . something . . . sensed me, for all at once the crowd began howling in rage. The people with the sashes—the leaders, I guess—seemed to see me, because they, too, shouted in rage, and began pointing at me.

"I wasn't sure what to do, then a horrible feeling of dread washed over me. Dread, and then fear, as if I were suddenly confronted by a raging tiger.

"I was about to be seized and torn . . . and then you cut the circle and saved me.

"For the second time, Damastes. Once more and you shall have to adopt me, for only kinfolk should have such a debt." Tenedos smiled weakly, trying to make a small joke.

I paid no mind to that.

"What was that something, sir? Another magician? Or magicians? Did you sense Irshad?"

"I don't know. If another magician, a powerful one. Perhaps a group of sorcerers, or *jasks*.

"All I know for sure is the Tovieti most certainly do exist, and, if their reaction to my presence is any indicator, are hostile toward Numantians or, at any rate, *this* Numantian. Perhaps if I wore a sign reminding everyone I am from Palmeras and am not much more fond of other Numantians than they are, I might be safe." He shuddered and knocked back the brandy. "The Rule of Ten are not the panicky fools I feared they might be. There is something here, something dangerous. When we find a way to send a confidential pouch back through the pass, I shall inform the Rule of what occurred."

"And as for ourselves?"

"I do not know," Tenedos said. "The cord revealed no secrets as to how entry was made to this mansion by the assassin, nor if one of our retainers pulled the strangling cord tight. Their sorcery is thorough. I imagine the only reason I was able to track the cord to its home was there are few magicians here in Sayana with powers to match mine.

"As for what we do next, I can increase the magical wards I've placed around these buildings, but that's nothing more than a temporary, defensive maneuver. All we can do is be most wary, and hope we will be able to discover their plans . . . if they pertain to us . . . before the Tovieti can put them into execution. My apologies. That last was a terrible choice of words."

He drank another glass of brandy, not noticing that I'd barely tasted mine, then I returned to my quarters.

But I did not sleep.

Nor, from the number of lighted windows in the mansion, did almost anyone else.

Two days later, we received an invitation for a banquet at the court of Achim Baber Fergana. The invitation was a command, since the occasion was the joyous celebration of the anniversary of Achim Fergana's ascent to the throne. Any member of the nobility not actually on his deathbed was required to attend, with appropriate presents, or his absence would be deemed a declaration of blood feud against the achim.

I'd already weathered a few of the achim's feasts, and wished there was some way I could avoid this one. His idea of merriment was to listen to endless speeches, songs, and poems extolling his brilliances in every field from bed to politics to war, while nibbling at a continuous flow of delicacies. These were washed down with spice leaves, which convinced the chewer, in his dreamlike state, that he was gifted with all the virtues Irisu had given Mankind. To keep from falling asleep, one drank *â'rag,* an oily, lethally effective distillation of the juice of oranges. By the next morning death would be counted one of Umar's greatest blessings.

Since there could be but one unutterably excellent person per banquet, the goings-on tended to produce arguments and, the Men of the Hills being as they were, duels. This Achim Fergana thought capital, and encouraged his nobility to hack away at each other with swords or daggers until at least one fighter was too bloody to continue.

But there was no alternative.

Things went badly from the beginning.

The throne room was filled with tables, and the animals had been banished to a mews outside, where they would be given their own feast. The room was packed with Kaiti nobility. Men were the only ones allowed present. Tapers along the walls and small oil-filled lights on each table provided illumination.

Achim Baber Fergana sat on his throne, a table in front of him. At such a banquet particularly honored noblemen and foreign dignitaries were seated at the first long table, directly in front of him. This night, it was Seer Tenedos, myself, and, three seats away, the Kallian, Landgrave Elias Malebranche. He caught my eye, and raised his glass with a rueful smile. I returned the mock toast—it was clear he was enjoying the evening no more than we were.

Achim Fergana was in a foul mood, and its reason took little investigation. The center chair at our table was empty—the chair reserved for *Jask* Irshad. There were three of his high-ranking sorcerers present, but no sign of the master magician. I wondered how anyone, even of his high station, could dare defy the achim. Something terribly unforeseen must have happened.

Naturally, the achim assuaged his anger by drinking and chewing more than usual, and barely touched the delicacies offered to him. The great pile of gifts to one side of the throne was ignored.

Matters peaked as a particularly untalented bard was holding forth, in wretched doggerel:

"Fergana struck in that hour
Feeling the strength within him flower.
Sword in hand he made them cower
Blood would fill that peaceful bower.

"With his sword, that fearsome blade,
The Mighty One—"

The Mighty One had enough and, with a roar of incoherent rage, hurled a golden plate at the poet. He realized his masterpiece was unappreciated, and fled hastily.

"Where in the hells is my *jask*?" Fergana roared. "How dare he shame me in this hour, as I celebrate my triumph? Guard captains! I want this castle searched until he is found! Turn out the watch . . . turn out a regiment and search every street in Sayana if necessary!"

He roared on. I was staring in fascination, never having been close to a monarch's wrath before, and then I shivered. It had suddenly become very, very cold. My breath was steam, and my fingers were growing numb.

Then I saw the fog.

It crept in from nowhere and everywhere, as if doors had been flung open, and the mists of a winter night had come rolling in on us. But it had been clear and temperate when we arrived. The mist came more thickly, a dark, seething ocean with flecks of light within it. I thought it would fill the throne room solidly, but it formed into near-solid, shimmering shapes.

A voice crashed into our ears:

"Baber Fergana . . . this is the hour of reckoning. Now is the moment of my revenge, my brother."

Chamisso Fergana! Yet I saw no human form.

The fog swept toward the throne. One of Achim Fergana's nobles leaped to his feet, sword in hand, and slashed vainly at the mist. It took him, lifted him, and tore him in twain, blood gouting and entrails spattering, steaming in the cold. He had not even time to scream before he was dead, his torn corpse cast aside.

Fergana was up, his own blade out. The fog seized and pinioned him, pulling his arms apart until he might have been stretched helpless on an invisible rack.

Gratings above us clattered open, and the achim's archers in the gallery took aim, and arrows volleyed. Some of them struck home—in Kaiti bodies—but most clattered against the flagstoned floor.

The fog swept up, and there were screams as it fell on the guards, held them helpless like pinioned kittens, and throttled them.

Tenedos fumbled in the small pouch at his belt, and down the table the Fergana's *jask*s were yammering magical phrases, trying to devise up a counterspell.

Laughter rang through the room, laughter I thought I'd heard before. Then came *Jask* Irshad's voice:

"You fools can save your efforts. My magic is far greater than yours could ever hope to be, just as I am the greatest jask in this or any other land.

"Baber Fergana, O False Achim, this is the time you shall rue all of the shame, all of the humiliation, you have dealt me over the years, even though I was once your most faithful servant. I fled your tyranny before dawn this morning, knowing I would return after nightfall, and finally strike back at a time and a manner Chamisso Fergana desires.

"A long time ago, when first I realized the depths of your evil, I came up with a device I told you would provide perfect safety. Dolls, each of which would contain the life-element of everyone around you.

"You, fat roaring fool that you are, thought it an extraordinary idea. And so you let whoever owns the dolls own the heart of Kait.

"Look not beneath the dais, O false Achim whose doom comes. For I have the dolls, and I am fled into a safe place, where I have sworn eternal fealty to your brother, the achim-to-be, Chamisso Fergana.

"Know this, too, dog of an achim. Over the years, little by little, I was able to make another doll. A doll of you, although it could easily be mistaken for some peasant's pig, so foul and misbegotten does it appear.

"It holds your hair, your spittle, a bit of your blood, even some of your life fluid one of the whores you call wives permitted me to scrape from the inside of her thigh.

"You are mine, Baber Fergana, and you shall die most slowly, in a manner that will be told of in whispers until the city of Sayana has fallen stone from stone.

"I shall now give you the pleasure of seeing what that death is, and making your agony even more dire.

"I thought of wreaking it on someone you hold dear, but realized there is no such being.

"The only one you love, Baber Fergana, is yourself.

"So I asked permission, and the achim-to-be was kind

enough to grant it, to rid Kait of two of its enemies, from a land that we'll deal with most harshly when Chamisso Fergana sits the throne.

"Your fate is here, Seer Laish Tenedos and Legate Damastes á Cimabue. I hold the mannequins you were foolish enough to give your substance to, and I give them to my wraith!"

The fog lowered from the balcony, and I pulled my sword, as stupidly as Fergana or that nobleman, but knowing nothing else to do. It formed tentacles, and the tendrils hesitated, then began flailing about, like vines in a windstorm, as if the fog were unsure of its victims, suddenly blinded. Then, from outside the castle, I heard the sudden screams of animals in agony, the poor beasts the fog now was tearing at.

When Bikaner, Damastes, and myself had donated our hair for the dolls, Damastes had switched the tiny golden boxes before handing them to *Jask* Irshad. Since he suspected Irshad might test them, to make sure we hadn't smuggled in matter from outside, he and Troop Guide Bikaner had secretly clipped bits of hair from three of the court animals. That animal hair had gone into the boxes and thence into our dolls, and now, those beasts died our deaths.

Time stopped, no one moved, and the fog itself was immobile. But next to me Laish Tenedos's fingers blurred.

The Seer Tenedos cast far greater spells later, spells that held or broke entire armies. But this might have been his most impressive, since he had no time to prepare, nor materials to choose from. He later told me he had rue and red eyebright in his pouch, and used mustard and horseradish from the table condiments. He muddled them together on his plate, then dropped the mixture into the tiny flame of the oil lamp in front of him. He said the real strength of the spell was in the words, and not the materials used. I do not know the language he spoke in, and Tenedos never offered to tell me what the words meant or what they summoned. But I can recollect them precisely, and set them down as they sounded in my ears:

"Plenator c'vish Milem
Han'eh delak morn
Morn sevel morn
Venet seul morn
T'ghast l'ener orig
Orig morn
Orig morn
Plenator c'vish Milem."

I felt warmth, warmth growing into heat, and in seconds it was hot in the hall, very hot, like the heat of a summer day in the desert outside.

The fog coiled, then shriveled, like a slug in a saltcellar, and a long, dying wail came, like a man falling into a bottomless abyss, and the throne room was clear.

Baber Fergana stood next to his throne, sword forgotten on the stones beside him, his face a gape of amazement.

Men stared at each other, realizing they yet lived. But in that instant before the babble started, *Jask* Irshad's voice came:

"Very well. Fergana, the magic of the Ph'rëng *has given you life once more.*

"But I still hold the dolls, False Achim. And my sorcery has barely been tested.

"Chamisso Fergana and I have another idea. You have three days, Baber Fergana. If you give up your throne, I will give you an easy death, far easier than that you've granted your enemies. This is only because of the Most Benevolent Chamisso Fergana's concern for the people of Sayana.

"But if you do not abdicate, in three days I shall return. And I shall bring another death to you, death in its most terrible, most lingering form.

"It shall not come just to you, but to everyone in your court, every man . . . and woman . . . whose spirit I possess in my mannequins.

"If you still cling to your throne, I promise I shall kill everyone who now hears me very slowly, in an awful manner.

"Then Chamisso Fergana will loose his secret allies, the Tovieti, to ravage the streets of Sayana.

"Consider my offer, False Achim.

"Consider my offer, princes who serve evil.

"In three days, I shall return for my answer."

There was silence, silence broken by a babble.

I saw Landgrave Malebranche hurry from the room, and wondered why Irshad had ignored the other *Ph'rëng* in the throne room. But other things were more important.

Tenedos was on the dais, talking to Achim Fergana. He went to the back of his throne and touched a level I'd never noticed, and the dais swung away, revealing that the trick was mechanical, not magical.

The cover of the pit was gone, and the depression was empty, of course.

Now the babble redoubled, and despair, rage, and fear roared through the chamber. But that went almost unheard.

I was staring across the chamber, into Laish Tenedos's eyes, and their message was clear:

If Kait was not to be turned over to anarchy, and the always-turbulent kingdom explode north into Urey and Numantia in its chaos, somehow I was going to have three days to find and steal back that collection of dolls.

NINE

THE RAIDERS

Sayana was atumble with noise, confusion, and fear. Achim Fergana's troops were alerted, and were trying to bring some sort of order, but with little success. There were men running in all directions, shouting the most nonsensical things about doom being upon us all; women shrieked in panic; and the taverns and temples—man's two favorite shelters—were packed, despite the late hour. Obviously word of the horror in the palace had spread through the city like oil across water, growing in awfulness as the story traveled.

Some merchants were taking advantage of the disorder, and their stalls or shops were open, and they stood outside, loudly shouting the efficacy of their magical wares. Buy an amulet and turn away the wrath to come. Let a seer cast a spell, and you will be unharmed when the dread Tovieti come to ravage Sayana. They were doing a brisk business.

Since everyone was busy with his own destiny, we went unnoticed as we made our way back to the compound. I noted the Time of Heat was almost over and the Time of Rains was to begin as I heard thunder growling on the horizon. I smiled. Bad weather would be a definite advantage when we went out next.

I ordered my soldiery to full alert, summoned all officers and warrants, and advised them of what had happened. I did *not* tell them exactly what my plans were, only that I wanted twenty volunteers for a dangerous task, ready to march out in three hours. I could have made up a band right then, but of course could hardly have stripped my tiny command of its leaders. I added that I wanted five of my men to be Kaiti, chosen from the best of our native troops.

My plan was very simple: to ride hard for that cavern Tenedos had "seen" in his vision. *Jask* Irshad and the mannequins must be somewhere nearby. I would strike at dawn as soon as we reached the cavern, find the mannequins, and steal them back. If we could not make our escape with them, if there was any free-running water, I could render the sorcelled objects harmless by casting them into it—something I remembered our village witch had told me.

My idea might sound absurdly simple, but I felt confident. Irshad and Chamisso Fergana would assume that everyone in Sayana, whether Kaiti or Numantian, would be paralyzed with fear and indecision. If we struck secretly and ruthlessly, the gods might favor the bold. Also, if we did nothing, there seemed no way to keep the government of Kait from tumbling and a bloody holy war against Numantia from beginning. I knew that we in Sayana would be the first to die. Viewed coldly, it was a case of a certain death in three days, or a possible one before that. The choice was easy.

There was no time to spare—if my idea had the slightest chance, it must be undertaken before anyone, either from Achim Fergana's forces or from the rebels in the hills, could begin to think about what might happen next. I must be away before sunrise.

I was a bit surprised when Captain Mellet was the first to volunteer—he was hardly the sort I'd thought for a dashing raid. I refused him, and he, a bit sourly, said, "I suppose yet again I'll be keeping the home fires toasty. Well, don't let me stop you from having a good time," and stamped away peevishly. From his command we chose Legate Baner, an exceptionally eager and boyish officer whom everyone, including myself, felt like an older brother to; Sergeant Vien, a deceptively fat man who moved like a snake; and six infantrymen, all of whom swore they knew which end of a horse ate, and which shat. I was taking foot soldiers as well as Lancers because I planned to approach our target on foot in the final stages.

From my own troop I took nine, making Troop Guide Bikaner senior warrant, and my choices included the always-glowering Karjan; Curti, my best archer; and the stolid Svalbard.

The five Kaiti were headed by Yonge, the sharpest of the hillmen, and the most likely to be worthy of command. With Tenedos's permission, I promoted him on the spot to sergeant, and planned to commission him if we returned with our lives. To the demons with the whines I'd get from our masters in Numantia about so honoring one of the not-quite-equal Men of the Border States.

I took my men into one of the mansion's libraries, where Tenedos had laid a spell guaranteeing there'd be no magical eavesdropping, and told them how I wished them armed and dressed. I watched closely as I spoke: Too often a man will volunteer in the heat of the moment, but once he realizes how hazardous the task, has qualms. If I'd seen the slightest tremor, I would have found some pretext to drop that soldier from the roll—there were many volunteers eager to replace the hesitant. But all of the volunteers remained steadfast.

I went to my own quarters, followed by Karjan, to ready my own gear. Pinned to the door was a note to please go to the resident's quarters at once.

I should have known what I would see when I entered his rooms. Instead of a well-dressed prosperous diplomat and magician, I was greeted with a scruffy-looking sort in sandy robes, hood, and sandals, who might well have been one of the Kaiti wizards who opposed us at the battle of the ford. "I promised you wards against any enemy being able to eavesdrop on your orders session in the library," Tenedos said, a bit smugly. "I said nothing about myself. A very interesting plan you have, Damastes. It will be worthwhile to see how it develops. I, by the way, borrowed these rags from one of our gatemen—but he will have no memory of the loan."

"Sir," I said. "You cannot go with us. I will not permit it!"

"You," Tenedos said, his voice suddenly frosty, "Legate á Cimabue, may offer all the suggestions you wish, but you cannot give me orders."

"Oh but I can, sir. I was ordered by my superiors, whose orders I must follow exactly, to keep you from harm. And—"

"And pahfiddle to that," Tenedos said. "I am going with you for two very good reasons. First is that I am the only one who's been to this cavern where the mannequins are most likely held. How were you proposing to find it?"

"I planned to ask you to pinpoint the location on a map. I assume your sorcery can relate actual locations to a topographic picture. Sir." I was veering slightly toward insubordination.

"Perhaps, although you'll not know this time. Second is that you are no magician, Legate, nor is any other Numantian besides myself. We will be opposed by sorcery, in case you've forgotten. The Tovieti use magic, as we discovered, and *Jask* Irshad is hardly a novice seer."

"Sir. What happens if you're killed?"

"Then you flee to Urey, give the Rule of Ten the gladdening news that will give them the excuse to mobilize the army, and probably get promoted."

"Hardly," I said. "I'd best die beside you."

"How noble," Tenedos said, a bit of a smile touching his lips. "Just as I'd expect from a dashing young subaltern of the cavalry."

"Not noble, sir. They'll flay me alive if I came back without you, and that's a very slow death." I was only half jesting. Certainly my career, such as it was, would be completely finished. Not that I was concerned about that—I had sworn to protect this gods-damned little magician, and he seemed determined to make me disobey my oath at every turn.

"Be that as it may," Tenedos said, "I see you have no grounds to argue, since you've already changed the subject."

It was true—logic and sense were in his camp. When I first thought out my plan as we rode back from Achim Fergana's palace, I'd wondered just how I'd deal with Irshad's magic, and vaguely thought I'd ask Tenedos for a protective spell or something.

Since I'd learned well from my father not to argue with a superior when his mind is set, and also never to belabor a cause that's lost, I came to attention, clapped my fist against my chest, and said, "Very well, sir. Please be ready to move out within the hour. I'll have a horse and provisions ready. One other thing—you are now under my command, in *all* matters save the application of magic. Is that understood?"

Now Tenedos's smile was very broad. "Yes, Legate á Cimabue, *sir.* I'll obey precisely, Legate á Cimabue. *Sir.*" I swear the man was as excited as any recruit horseman who's about to see his first action.

Less than an hour later, as villainous a crew as the mansion had ever seen was gathered in the courtyard: twenty-two hill bandits, raffish in their dirty robes, and dripping weapons. The robes, hoods, and sandals were most authentic, perhaps a little too much so, I thought, scratching at a Kaiti flea who'd decided Numantian blood was palatable, and wrinkling my nose a bit at the smell. Under the light-brown robes we wore loinclothes and our own chain mail shirts. On our heads were the hoods most Kaiti travelers wore, and we had strapped boots on our feet. For warmth, we wore heavy sheepskin jackets.

We'd rough-curried our horses to look a bit like the ragged mounts of the Kaiti, although they were still too clean and well groomed to stand a close examination. Each man had two horses, not only for a reserve, but to carry the mannequins back, if we gained our objective. Our provisions were in saddlebags and we had sleeping robes rolled behind our saddles.

All of my Numantians had been given the Spell of Understanding earlier, although they hardly had the accents of native Kaiti when they spoke. Tenedos himself spoke like a native; he must have either studied the language hard or, more likely, finely honed the Understanding Spell to perfection. We also could use Sergeant Yonge or one of the other Kaiti soldiers.

Our arms were Numantian, but we had no intention of passing that close a scrutiny.

It was as well that Tenedos was accompanying us, since I'd looked at the only map I could find of the region. Beyond the thin track that led back into the hills, and some roughly sketched-in villages, it told me nothing.

Tenedos had asked how I planned to slip out of the mansion, since of course we were always watched. I said one at a time, through one of the back gates, and he'd curled a lip and said, coldly, that he could do "vastly" better than that. So he did.

I had ordered everyone indoors; my Numantians were keeping close watch on the Kaiti soldiers and our household staff. Captain Mellet had been ordered to keep the compound sealed until our return—or until circumstances proved that it was no longer necessary, for good or evil. The pretext was the resident-general's shock and horror over the events at the palace.

Rain spattered down and it was but three hours before dawn. There was only one person in the street outside, and he was huddled in a doorway a distance down from the gates. He kept himself back in the shadows, as much to keep out of the chill wind as to avoid discovery. The man was blowing in his hands, trying to warm them, when Curti's arrow took him in the throat. The spy's corpse sagged, and two soldiers dragged him back into the compound. We'd dispose of the body later.

The more impressive part of the deception I could barely see and hear. In the probable event that Achim Fergana's or Irshad's *jask*s were keeping watch by sorcery, Tenedos had arranged a more spectacular display for them. A wizard would have "seen" a dozen men standing around flickering oil-fed fires, Kaiti who so hated the Numantian presence that they watched us day and night. I didn't see anything, although I thought I caught a dim flicker of flames from the corner of my eye, and heard a ghostly shout of *"M'rt tê Ph'rëng!"* That sorcerous watcher would have known no one could come out of the compound without attracting attention and known we were all still within.

The spell cast, the twenty-two of us rode for the city gates.

There were still people abroad at this hour, but they were either crazed with rumors, spice weed, drink, or intent on their own goals, and had little interest in us. We held weapons ready under our robes as we rode.

There was no problem leaving Sayana—Achim Fergana's guards were more afraid of what lay outside trying to enter than the other way around. The officer of the gate didn't bother coming out of his gatehouse when he saw the party of hard-looking hillmen ride up, but motioned to the two soldiers at the levers to open them.

We rode out, into the night, into the wilds of Kait, at a trot.

There was just enough light, despite the overcast and occasional rain, to see the rough track we were following. I wasn't worried about being ambushed; even thieves must sleep sometime, plus very few bandits would risk hitting twenty-two armed opponents. The dirt track was narrow, less a road than a path—at no point could more than three horses have ridden abreast.

Every hour we rested for a few minutes. I checked the horses the infantry and Kaiti were riding carefully, but none of the mounts were mishandled. At sunrise we stopped long enough to brew a pot of the fragrant tea the Kaiti loved, and gnawed dried strips of beef.

Four times that day we rode through tiny villages, each a handful of mud huts around a small square. The Kaiti were ragged, dirty—and their eyes gleamed hatred for us rich men who actually owned horses. But they saw our ready arms and grim faces and behaved as if we did not exist.

Five times we encountered parties on the track. One was a merchant's whose guards nearly panicked, sure we were about to attack. They dove from their horses, frantically yanking out weapons and buckling up armor. We paid them no mind whatsoever. Three others were hard-faced men intent on their own purpose, spears carried ready for the casting. They glared at us, eyed our weapons calculatingly, and decided the prize was not worth the game.

The last group we came on just before dusk.

We heard them before we came on them—the wail of a baby crying, and the murmur of hopelessness. There were perhaps forty of them, no more than two or three young men, the rest women, children, and four or five ancients. They were raggedly dressed, and carried makeshift packs and bundles.

There was a wail of fear when they saw us, and then babbling pleas for mercy and they scrabbled off the trail out of our way, some prostrating themselves.

This was the other side of the golden banner of war: the poor civilians caught in its midst, easy prey for all. I felt pity, and wished we could help, but knew better.

"We mean no harm," I shouted, and the babble changed to thanks and promises the gods would reward us. I noted, though, that their faces showed disbelief as we rode slowly past—they were waiting for us to show our true colors and the rapine to begin.

The flock had two shepherds—an old, dignified man, who must have been a village elder, and a young girl, no more than fourteen who, in spite of her dirty garments and face, was astonishingly beautiful.

"We thank you, kind sirs," he said.

I found a few coins and tossed them to him. He bowed gratitude, and we rode on.

About a mile farther, I found a safe shelter for the night. A tiny village sat abandoned, about a hundred yards from the road, on a small, rocky hill that made a perfect redoubt. The rain was about to turn from showers into a full storm, and the huts, ramshackle though they were, would at least let my men sleep dry. This would be the last rest they would have before we made our raid, and looked ideal.

We stabled our horses in one of the larger huts, and fed

them oats in nosebags. I made sure Lucan and Rabbit were taken care of, then broke the party down into four teams, one for each of the remaining huts, and we made ourselves as comfortable as possible. The huts were very big, more byres, actually, and in surprisingly good shape, and each of them had a fire pit dug in the center. The former occupants had used these buildings as barns and living quarters—there were ricks and stalls at the end of each of them. We used our horses' blankets to cover the windows and doors. I ordered small fires built and, in the gathering darkness, walked around the hilltop to make sure no gleam of light could betray us.

I heard footsteps up the path from the road, and put my hand on my sword. Out of the gloom came two figures—the old man and the girl who headed the knot of fugitives we'd passed a short time earlier.

Suddenly, beside me were Bikaner and Tenedos, their weapons ready.

"Good evening," the ancient said. "Although I doubt it to be that. We saw you turn aside, and thought we might, in the name of the merciful Irisu and Jacini, ask a boon?"

The girl stepped forward.

"We are the only survivors of the village of Obeh," she said. "All our men were either killed or forced into the service of that dog Chamisso Fergana, and our village was burnt, our few treasures stolen, many of us outraged, and our livestock slaughtered for sport.

"We were told only by Chamisso Fergana's mercy were we allowed life, but this was a temporary gift, and we had best not chance further indulgence but flee at once.

"Now we have nothing but the road, and fear.

"We would ask one gift of you. Could we travel with your party? I sense you are good men, men of mercy, and we could be safe until we reached some settlement."

"I am sorry," I said. "But we are sworn to a task, and must travel fast and far."

The girl's face fell. "Could we at least take shelter here, with you, for the night?" she said after a pause. "One night's safety, one night's sound sleep, just for the babies, would be like the breath of new life."

I started to say no once more, but stopped, thinking. I turned to Seer Tenedos. He motioned me aside.

"I see you may be thinking what I am," he said. "These poor people might well provide an excellent cover for us, for the night. If Irshad has magical guardians out, might they not think we are no more than a group of villagers on the move, our men appearing to be part of their band?"

That *was* exactly the thought in my mind. I nodded, and as I did, a wave of warmth came. I'd felt badly enough having to ride past these folk on the road with nothing more than a few coppers to give them; one of a soldier's duties is to protect those who are helpless.

Bikaner, too, was nodding. "Aye, sir," he said. "That's a rare idea. I've not liked th' idea of those poor bastards wanderin' the roads with no man t'stand between them an' a reiver's pleasure."

And so it was decided. The young woman, who introduced herself as Palikao, wept her thanks.

"You are most generous," the old man, whose name was Jajce, said, "and you have given us two great gifts. Not only this night, when all may sleep soundly, but also reminding us that not everyone in this world is evil, and wishes nothing more but harm to the helpless."

He shouted, and the refugees shambled out of the darkness. We were not completely artless in our trust—I turned my men out, and we patted each of the civilians for arms. Beyond a few small knives for cutting up a meal, they were unarmed.

Just as no one can be more brutal than a soldier, the same man can be the most generous of all mankind. So it was with my men. They took charge of the poor wanderers, made sure each had a bed of straw, patted the infants, and tried to get the children to smile. But they'd seen too much horror, and the best jest or most outrageously pulled face received no better audience than a solemn look. Since we had more than enough food, we were glad to share what we had.

In my hut were Tenedos, Yonge, Karjan, and two others. We had an equal number of the refugees, including Jajce and Palikao.

The storm broke, and the rain roared, but in our huts it was almost comfortable, if you ignored the fleas, the reek of ancient manure, and the smell of bodies too long unwashed— none of which concern themselves to an experienced campaigner.

We were not like turtles, tucked blindly into our shell; the men on watch outside moved in pairs, never keeping the same route as they patrolled around the tiny hill. I checked hourly, and was pleased they remained very alert, although I was unsurprised. We were too deep in enemy territory and there were too few of us to relax.

Tenedos was on the other side of the low fire, listening to Jajce talk about what had happened, trying to winnow through the old man's memories for information that might aid us when we came on Chamisso Fergana. I leaned back on my bedroll, listening idly. Palikao sat not two feet away from me. I noted, to my considerable surprise, that she smelled quite good, unlike the rest of us unwashed heathens, and wondered what scent she wore. She suddenly turned her attention away from Jajce.

"I cannot listen anymore," she said softly. "It hurts too much to think of Obeh. All that is gone."

Her shoulders sagged, and I wished I could comfort her.

"I suppose for someone like you, it might not have appeared much," she said. "But I was happy. I was betrothed, and my husband-to-be and I had just begun our trial conjugality. Then, one day, a week before Chamisso Fergana's savages came and destroyed Obeh, he announced he had determined to become a soldier, and, in spite of my tears, left me, promising he would return in two months, with great wealth.

"I cared nothing for that. I just wanted him."

She looked directly at me, her gaze not shy.

"He should not have left," and her voice lowered, "just when it was so . . . wonderful."

My loins stirred.

"It is hard," she went on, "trying to sleep in the cold, in the wet." Her hand stretched out, brushed mine, and her finger ran down the wool facing of my bedroll. "Your sleeping robes look very warm."

She smiled, and stretched, and somehow her robe became slightly disarranged, and I saw smooth, bare leg, and a momentary flash of darkness above her inner thigh.

Her flesh was clean, and on her ankle she wore a gold circlet.

Lust took me and shook me, and I almost could have taken her then, but forced myself to be calm, to wait until the fires were banked and we would settle down to sleep. Yonge and Karjan were already snoring. Then would come pleasures such as I'd never seen.

I looked at Tenedos, and saw his eyes start wide. I came back to myself a little, and looked at what he was staring at.

Jajce's small pack sat between him and Tenedos. It had fallen on its side, its flap open.

Coiled inside was a long silk cord, gleaming yellow in the dying firelight.

Tovieti!

Shit! The spell broke, my cock shriveling as if it had never wanted Palikao's false wet warmth, and the foolishness, brought on by their magic, that had allowed us to permit strangers, no matter how innocent looking, to come into our midst, was gone. I looked at Palikao, to see if she'd sensed the change, but she was staring dreamily at the fire. Her bare foot crept out and caressed my booted ankle.

Hells! I wondered if they'd already struck in the other huts, and if my men were now sprawled in death, my mission ruined before it could even be launched. The spell we'd been ensnared in was complete—my sword belt lay all the way across the hut, and Tenedos's lay beside it.

The seer saw I'd noted the cord. I saw his brow furrow in thought, then his hand slip to his side, and pick up one of the long leather thongs used to bundle his sleeping robes. He then looked pointedly at me: Do something!

I suddenly sat bolt upright, coughing uncontrollably. Both Jajce and Palikao pretended concern, and Damastes used my diversion to reach across and, in a flash, touch the leather to the silk strangling cord. His lips moved, and he ran the leather through his fingers, coiling it to and fro.

My coughing spasm eased, and I reached for a canteen, to continue the charade, when Palikao spoke, very calmly:

"They know who we are."

Her hand dove into her robe, and emerged with that deadly cord. I threw myself on her, trying to pinion her hands, and it was as if I was in the ring, wrestling the strongest opponent I'd known. Palikao had greater strength than any man I'd ever fought, including professional strong men at local fairs, and she easily broke her wrists from my hold, down to my chest, and pushed, and I went spinning away, through the firepit, embers flying, to sprawl on the other side.

She was on her feet, cord in her hands, a look of savage glee on her face, coming toward me, and now I heard shouts of surprise and horror from the other huts. Jajce was standing, his own cord ready, when Tenedos began to chant:

"Hear me
Hear me
You are one
We are the same thread
We serve one master
We have one master
There is one master.
Hear me
Turn, Turn
Obey me
Bind, bind
Bind and hold
You must obey
You must obey
Bind, bind,
Bind and hold."

The yellow cord in Palikao's hands writhed, came alive, as if it were a snake, and twisted its way around her wrists, twisting, turning, knotting, holding, and she struggled vainly, and then fell. Jajce's own cord was tying him, and again I heard shouts from outside, but these were from women and children as Tenedos's magic turned their craft against them.

Palikao tried to get up, her strength now no more than it should have been, but I was up and across the hut, reaching for my blade, then it was out, and I had its point at her throat. "I've not yet killed a woman," I said. "But there is a first for everything."

She stared up the long steel at me, saw truth in my eyes, and ceased struggling. I wondered if she would have killed me before or after we made the beast with two backs, but had no time for rumination.

"Karjan!" and my Lancer was beside me, his own weapon out. I looked about the hut. All of the Tovieti were safely bound by their own cords. I darted out, into the night, and checked my men.

By the grace of Panoan and Isa, none of my men were injured. They'd all fallen deeply asleep, and woke to chaos. Evidently the deaths of Tenedos and myself were to mark the beginning of a general slaughter. I told them what had happened, and who these "innocents" actually were, and ordered them into full fighting readiness. The team outside, on guard, had seen and heard nothing until the shouting started. I put a second pair out to back them up, and returned to Tenedos.

Karjan had pulled the Tovieti into a line along one wall. Their feet were now tied with conventional rope. Their eyes blazed helpless anger.

"Now what do we do?" I asked Tenedos.

"Kill the shit-heels, rip their gods-damned guts out slowly," Yonge snapped, still shaking from the terror.

I waited. Tenedos thought carefully on the matter.

"No," he finally decided.

Palikao laughed mockingly.

"Do not mistake me," the seer said. "I have no objection to your death. Know that, woman." He stared at her, and she nodded reluctantly. Tenedos took me aside.

"I think," he said, "no, I know for sure that my magic is sufficient to bind them for at least two days. Also, I don't think any of them are magicians themselves. What sorcery they used to fool us is vested in those cords, or perhaps they have been given an amulet to use. I didn't sense their spells because all my awareness is reaching out toward that cavern, waiting for Irshad's magics to search for us.

"I said we wouldn't kill them because we want our men ready for battle—not shaking from having murdered babes and women, no matter how bloody-handed they might be."

I agreed, and, quite frankly, was and am not sure I could have given the orders for such a slaughter.

Tenedos turned his attention back to Jajce.

"I propose to let you live, because the god I serve is stronger, as is my magic.

"But I am new to this land. What *is* your god?"

"We serve no gods," Jajce said. "Gods, from the vanished Umar to the lowliest piss-souled hearth godlet, are all part of the Wheel, the Wheel we are going to shatter for a New Way."

"Break by killing all?"

"Break by killing all who do not join us," Jajce said flatly. "Kill them, then when they return from the Wheel, kill them as babes in arms, kill them in their wombs until the Wheel collapses from the weight of all the souls it carries. My own group has killed over a thousand, sometimes pretending to be woeful refugees, sometimes occupying an abandoned village and telling travelers we are its residents."

"All men, even gods, serve someone," Tenedos said. "Whom do you obey?"

"Our leaders," Jajce said, looking uncomfortable.

"Thak," Palikao whispered.

"Silence, woman!" the old man snapped.

"Who is Thak?"

Palikao pressed her lips together, said nothing.

"Thak, eh?" Tenedos said. "Is he human or otherwise?"

Once more, no reply, and I knew we would get none.

"One question you might answer," Tenedos said. "I understand you are permitted to keep whatever you loot from your victims, correct? And that if you kill enough, you Tovieti will live in the palaces of the rich, and so on and so forth. Correct?"

Jajce nodded. "That is the truth."

"What laws will you live under in that golden time?"

"We shall need no laws," Jajce said firmly. "Just men behave justly."

Tenedos lifted an eyebrow, bent, and picked up one of the strangling cords.

"I see."

An hour later we rode off into the night.

"You s'pose," Bikaner said quietly, "they'll work their way out of th' ropes 'fore they starve?"

"I would imagine," Tenedos said.

"More's th' sorrow," Karjan said. "They ne'er would've given us mercy."

We rode on in silence.

Before dawn, we chanced leaving the road for a nest of rocks, and chanced an hour's sleep, watch-on, watch-off.

At first light, we moved on once more.

It rained steadily all that day. The track was deserted.

The villages we passed were either ruined or shut tight against the elements. We saw no man or woman all that drear day as the road climbed into the hills.

Through the rain and the mist hanging like curtains, we dimly saw a great mountain, black, wet, and evil.

"There," Seer Tenedos said, "there is the mountain I 'saw.' In it is the Tovieti's cavern."

TEN

THE CAVERN
OF THAK

The mountain, about three miles away, looked like a god-child had built it of sand, and then haphazardly carved away with a spoon. The nearer side would be the easiest to climb, although its slope was steep enough, which meant it would be the most heavily guarded. I could see, even through the rain, where a trail had been cut out. The trail led about two-thirds of the way up, where the entire mountainside had a nearly symmetrical scoop out of it.

"There," Tenedos pointed. "There is where we'll find the entrance to the cavern."

The face farther from us was far more precipitous, almost a cliff.

I saw no sign of life, either on the mountain or the approaches.

Not far away from where we sat was a draw. We left the trail, and rode up the narrow canyon about half a mile, until it widened into a cleft. There was enough of an overhang to give some shelter.

I ordered the men to dismount, and assemble. From here, we'd move on foot. For the first time, I explained exactly what our mission was. I watched the men's faces closely. Even as tired, dirty, cold, and wet as they were, I saw no signs of discouragement or fear. My warrants and I had chosen our men well. When I finished, I asked for questions.

"How'll we gie up t' th' mouth of th' cave?" one man asked. "Creepin up th' trail?"

"No," I said. "We'll go up the cliff."

A couple of the men groaned.

"Remember," I said, realizing I sounded a bit like one of my more pompous tactical instructors, "the easy way's always ambushed."

Troop Guide Bikaner gave me a look of mild approval.

We assembled our gear into backpacks and, leaving four men to watch the horses, started for the mountain. The land was desolate, with never a tree to be seen, but only the stark brush. In the dry season, it would have been desert, but now it was a sandy, sticky mire.

It was dusk when we reached its base—our timing was perfect. I looked for a dry place to rest, where we'd eat and wait until full dark, but the entire world dripped dankly. We found some thick bushes I imagined to be a bit less sodden than the rest and crawled under.

I remember the meal I ate, wondering if it might be my last: dried beef that had been shredded and mixed with berries and rendered fat, which was extraordinarily nutritious, but as easy on the stomach as digesting a rock; cold herbal tea we'd brewed back in the village the night before; and soggy flatbread dipped into a fruit jam. I admit, though, I felt better afterward.

I decided it was dark enough, and we set out. I put the hillmen in the fore of the column, since they'd have the best feel for the terrain; then the fat infantry sergeant Vien, myself, Tenedos, the rest of the party, and the rear was brought up by Legate Baner and Troop Guide Bikaner—with this small a party, I must have someone I had absolute confidence in for my rearguard.

We climbed for almost an hour, the grade growing steeper, but still no worse than a hill-scramble. Then the way grew more difficult, and I signaled a halt and ordered the men to rope up—we'd brought twenty-five-foot-long ropes with us. They were fine—no more than a quarter-inch in diameter—but had been given a strengthening spell by Tenedos before we left Sayana. We pulled off our sheepskin jackets and tied them to our packs.

The way was wet and slippery, but fortunately the boulders were small enough to move around, and those we had to climb over were cracked and split, giving us sufficient handholds.

I tried to keep an idea of where we were in my head—there was nothing to be seen but darkness against darkness and the black rock all around. The going grew worse, and we had to traverse left again and again to find a passable route. We were being forced closer and closer to the face with the trail, but there was little I could do to change things. At least the rain had lessened, which was a mixed favor. We could move more easily, but the likelihood of us being seen or heard was greater.

Fingersnaps came down the line, and we froze. A whisper came: "Officer up."

I untied and laboriously crept over five men, to the front of the column. Sergeant Yonge was on point. When I reached him, I didn't need any whisper to see what the problem was. I cursed silently. Just above us was mortared stone. We *had* been moving too far left—the road to the cave's entrance was just above us. We'd have to go back and shift right to a new route. I decided to slip up onto the trail, and see if I saw any sign of the Tovieti.

I was about to lever myself over the parapet when a noise came. I don't know just how to describe it, but it was a low swishing, or perhaps hissing. I ducked back, and became one of the stones around me.

Something came up the path, something enormous. The sound took about ten seconds to go past, then there was nothing but the night and the rain. I forced myself to peer over the parapet, saw nothing, and pulled myself up onto the parapet and over onto the cobbled pathway. I slipped and almost fell, going to my knees. The slickness was not from the rain, but from a horrible slime that whatever had just passed left in its trail. My stomach curled, and I decided there was no valor in continuing this reconnaissance. Now I knew what that hissing had suggested—it was the sound my mind thought an enormous slug might make as it moved past. I do not know in fact what it was, though, nor do I wish to.

Laboriously we reversed our course, and went back to our right. Eventually we found another way that seemed to go. The closer we climbed to the cave's entrance, the harder it rained. At last we'd climbed to the same level I thought the cavern to be on, and once more we traversed left. Again we came on the mortared stone, and I peered over it. The path came to an end here, on a level, parapeted terrace, a balcony with the cave mouth behind it. I saw no sign of guardians, human or otherwise. I ducked back, out of sight.

We'd made good progress—it was still two hours before dawn, I guessed. We would wait for at least an hour. Climbing had raised a sweat, and we'd paid no attention to the wet and the chill. We put our jackets back on, but clinging to the near-vertical rocks, the cold seeped through into our bones within minutes, and I was hard-pressed to keep my teeth from chattering.

Over the howling of the wind, I thought I could hear chanting, or perhaps only shouts, from the cavern. I tried to forget about my misery, and go through, again and again, just what Tenedos had told me he'd "seen" in his brief seconds inside the cavern.

The sounds from the cavern stopped, and there was nothing but the storm. I heard another sound: boot heels that I hoped were human, clattering on the cobbles above us.

Sentries. There were two of them. Once again, we became lumps of sandy stone. But there was little real danger. I doubted the guards would bother peering over the edge—there was nothing at all to see, and they must be near the end of their watch. I'd never really entertained the hope that the entrance to the cave would be wholly unguarded.

Very slowly, as slowly as anything I've known, the sky changed from black to the darkest of grays. Now I heard more footsteps above, and the clatter of armor and weapons. Voices came—a challenge, a response, inaudible words, then some laughter and the sound of the relieved watch marching away.

It might have been better to take care of the other sentries, knowing how cold and tired they would be, and hence easy targets. But when their relief showed, they would have cried the alarm. I listened for another space, and was somewhat impressed. These sentries did march their complete rounds, rather than huddle against the weather. Nor were they talking and telling stories. I listened to them pass, then return, counting the interval. I would rather have done that half a dozen times, to ensure I had the exact time, but the sky was growing lighter all the time.

I crept up to Sergeant Yonge, and motioned. Two fingers, two fingers—fingers stiffened whisked across my throat, fingers pointing at the ground, then looping back in an arch. Yonge nodded, and I saw the stumps of his teeth flash in the dimness. He pointed to three other hillmen. They slid out of their packs and gave them to other men. Knives came out of sheaths, and the four moved up to just below the parapet.

The footsteps came back, passed, came back once more, and four figures went over the wall. I heard the scuffle of booted feet, the very beginnings of an outcry, then, over the hiss of the rain, a falling gurgle.

I went over the parapet in a leap, Sergeant Vien behind me. The two sentries were sprawled, their seeping blood being washed away by the downpour. I saw in the growing light one of the hillmen looking shamefaced, and knew he must have been the one who almost spoiled the killings. Sergeant Yonge would deal with him harshly if we lived through the next hour.

The rest of our party came over the low rampart.

"Yonge," I ordered. "That body . . . throw him far out."

Yonge frowned, not understanding why I didn't wish to dump both corpses, but motioned to his men, and one of the sentries was hurled into blackness. I listened, but heard no sound of the body striking.

"The other, put facedown . . . there." I pointed to a rock

about fifty feet back down the rise, a rock it would take some scrambling to reach.

Four men maneuvered the second corpse downhill, then carefully positioned the corpse as I'd wanted.

It would be in plain sight to anyone who peered over the railing, which was exactly what I wanted. Not even Troop Guide Bikaner seemed to understand, so I briefly whispered why I'd arranged matters as I had. If someone came out on the terrace, and saw it unguarded, the first thing they would think was there'd been an accident. They'd rush to the parapet, peer out, and see poor dead Mathia, or whatever his name might have been, where he'd fallen. They would shout for help, for men to climb down and see if their comrade yet lived. That hue and cry would warn us that our escape route had been blocked, and that it was time to find another exit or plan. Or so I hoped.

Now I took the lead, Laish Tenedos just behind me. I put my best men behind him—they'd already been told their deaths were a small matter compared to Laish Tenedos's and I knew they'd obey.

Then we entered the cavern of the Tovieti.

The cave's mouth was V-shaped, and reached almost 100 feet above the floor. About fifty feet inside, it rounded, and became an arch. Now we were out of the wind and rain, and a warm, soft wind blew toward us. It was far warmer than the caves I'd explored as a boy, and I wondered if this mountain had once been a volcano, and if its heart still held fiery lava, or if the Tovieti heated it sorcerously.

The light from the outside grew dimmer, our way now lit by torches set in niches cut into the rock. The torches were burning low, and I hoped mightily that all those inside were sleeping.

The tunnel's roof lowered sharply, until it was about ten feet above us, and the passage narrowed, no more than thirty feet wide in places. I saw some of the men look a bit worried, and hoped the way grew no narrower; there is no way to keep from giving in to certain terrors, and the fear of being closed in is one of the strongest. But the passageway grew no smaller, but twisted and turned between natural stone columns, like mushroom stems, that stretched from floor to ceiling.

This cavern was not only excellent shelter, but eminently defensible—a tiny force could use those columns as cover to fight behind, or mount sudden counterattacks from behind them.

The passageway increased in size and there were side passages that led in different directions. But Tenedos's sense of direction was sure, and he unhesitatingly waved us on, keeping us in the main tunnel. There were also rooms opening off the sides, and from some of them we heard the snores and shifts of sleeping people.

The cave opened into a great room, its ceiling at least 200 feet above us. There were several levels in the walls of this chamber, with openings like balconies of some enormous tenement, such as I'd seen in Nicias.

Torches weren't needed here. Instead, mineral formations hung from the roof and grew up from the floor. These growths were translucent, and lights of many colors ran up and down inside them, sending a constant color kaleidoscope shimmering across the cave.

I thought for a moment this could be the great chamber Tenedos had seen, but he shook his head and led us on, across the floor, toward one of a myriad tunnels. He chose one, the widest and tallest, and we followed.

This passage ran as straight as if it had been laid with a plumb for about 200 yards, and then the cavern opened once more.

This was a truly enormous room, its walls made of the most wonderfully colored minerals. Again, there were landings and balconies studded everywhere in the walls, and those startling colors from nowhere provided the illumination.

This was the chamber Tenedos had "visited." I saw the throne in the room's center, patterned closely after the one Achim Fergana sat in Sayana, although it didn't look as gem-encrusted.

Behind it was the drum-shaped altar, and, to one side, high-piled treasure the Tovieti had looted from their victims.

The room was full of sleeping people, the white-robed Tovieti, sprawled everywhere. It looked as if their priests had stopped in midceremony and cast a sleeping spell over their flock. I hoped that was true, and that it would take another incantation to rouse them.

Tenedos pointed toward the throne, and I saw, on either side of it, rows of elaborately carved chests. I lifted an eyebrow, and he nodded—he sensed that in those was what we sought.

So we crept onward, weapons in hand, stepping over and around these sleeping people. There must have been several hundred in the room. Tenedos's lips were moving, and he touched his eyelids several times. I guessed him to be casting a spell of sleep, or perhaps increasing the power of the one the Tovieti masters had already laid.

The chests were made of wood, and locked, and we used spear-shafts and daggers to pry them open. The wood screeched, and I shuddered, but none of the sleepers stirred.

The one I opened held all manner of marvelous things: I saw a queen's diadem, a skull, a wand, a stone too large to be precious else it would be worth a kingdom, and many more things. But no mannequins. I tried another, and this one was equally full of wonders, but again, none of the dolls we sought.

Fingers snapped, and Svalbard was beckoning. I hurried to the chest he stood over, Tenedos behind me, and there were some of the dolls, stuffed unceremoniously inside. I waved my men over, and we hastily began stuffing our packs full. Other chests were opened, and we found more dolls.

I was beginning to hope we'd accomplish our task and escape unseen when a shout echoed through the stone chamber. A half-dressed man stood on a balcony halfway to the roof of the room, crying a warning.

Curti's bowstring twanged, but the shot missed, clattering against stone. Another arrow went after it, truer than the first, taking the man in the stomach. He fell slowly forward, off the rocky ledge, screaming as he pinwheeled down.

The screams woke the sleepers, and the befuddled ones stumbled to their feet.

The last of the dolls went into packs, the packs were shouldered, and we ran for the exit. There was as yet no opposition, other than one or two of the white-clad Tovieti who stumbled into our path and were knocked flying for their pains.

Then *Jask* Irshad appeared.

He stood on a balcony about thirty feet above the cave floor. He saw us, and screamed in rage. As his shout rang through the chamber, he grew, until he was nearly fifty feet tall, and stepped easily from the balcony to the floor.

"Numantians! The False Seer Tenedos! Now you shall perish, interlopers, *Ph'rëng!* How dare you! How dare you!"

He picked up a pebble, and cast it at Tenedos. It grew into a mighty boulder, coming directly at the seer. Tenedos spread his hands, chanting, and the boulder was struck aside. It smashed down into Tovieti, and red spurted across white robes.

Tenedos grabbed a spear from one of my soldiers, tapped it against a nearby stalagmite. I could hear bits of his spell over the din:

"... change ... change now ...
Free yourselves
Free ...
Like a dart, like ...
Strike now
Strike hard
You are ..."

He tossed the spear at Irshad gently, and as he did the stalagmites around the *jask* snapped off and smashed through the air at him, like hard-thrown javelins. Irshad was crying a counterspell, shrinking to his normal size as he did, and a curtain of colors rose around him, and the mineral spears shattered as they struck it.

Irshad began a spell of his own, and other *jask*s ran into the chamber, some with wands, some with relics, and their chanting and cries added to the din.

While magic fought magic, I saw something I might do.

"Lancers," I cried. "Follow me!" I charged forward, and my men came out of their trance. Tovieti rose against us, and we cut our way on, heading for Irshad and the other magicians.

Irshad's spell was building. I heard the roaring swell, the sound a wind makes as it becomes a cyclone, growing louder and louder.

Tovieti guards, still buckling themselves into their armor, rushed forward, blocking our attack on the wizards. At their head was a banner with a device I could not make out, and beside the standard-bearer charged a huge man I instantly recognized, having spent enough time around his elder brother.

Chamisso Fergana was armed with exactly the weapon I'd imagined Achim Fergana would prefer: a single-headed beaked ax. He saw me—I suppose *Jask* Irshad's magic had told him who I was—and cried a challenge, one I was glad to meet.

Legate Baner dashed in front of me, shouting some sort of a war cry. He cut wildly at Fergana, leaving himself open, and Fergana ducked Baner's stroke, hooked Baner in the shoulder with the ax's beak, and yanked the screaming boy toward him. As Baner stumbled forward, Fergana jerked his ax free and sent it crashing into the back of the legate's head.

Sergeant Vien was there, lunging, missing, and Fergana blocked him hard with a hip and sent the foot soldier stumbling away, and then there was nothing but the two of us.

Fergana held his ax ready in front of him, left hand just below the axhead at shoulder height, right on the haft. He danced back and forth, looking for an opening. I struck for his face, and his ax flashed, almost taking me. I cursed myself for trying for an easy strike, ducked as he cut at me, and struck for his leg, missing again.

We went back on guard, moving, moving. I moved to his weak side, and he turned as I did. I vaguely was aware of Karjan and another Lancer guarding my flanks.

The ax came at me once more, and I jumped back, landing

on some gravel. I almost slipped and went down; Fergana shouted victory and came in for the kill. I knelt, grabbed a handful of gravel, and cast it full into his face, jumping aside as his ax came down. Before he could recover, I struck, this time as I'd been taught, not for the vital parts, but to cripple to make the killing easy.

My slash hit his ax handle about halfway up, slicing wood, and then Fergana's fingers. His shout was a roar, and he dropped his ax, but his unwounded hand reached for a long dagger at his side.

But there was no time left for the rebel leader, and my full lunge took him in the throat, the point of my sword coming out the back of his neck. As he went down I pulled my sword free, recovered, saw Sergeant Vien belabored, and killed his opponent. Then I faced the enemy standard-bearer, trying to defend himself with a short sword. I parried once, again, cut his legs from under him, and gave him the deathstroke as he fell. Chamisso Fergana's banner fell, landing a few feet from its dead lord. Troop Guide Bikaner had the standard then, waving it triumphantly in victory.

Over the battle din, I heard the keen as *Jask* Irshad saw his lord's death, and his concentration broke and the wind-song died. Then, over all, the Seer Tenedos's voice boomed:

"I have you
I have you
Your force is mine.
Your strength is mine."

Tenedos stood with his arms stretched out, his fingers closing into fists, as if he were squeezing something invisible. Tenedos's voice came again:

"Your blood
Courses through my hands.
I hold your heart
You are mine

You are mine.
Take your death.
Take the gift.
Take your death."

Jask Irshad screeched in agony, clutched at his chest, then fell. He writhed briefly, then lay still.

The Tovieti screamed with him, both their leaders down in death, screamed in panic and desperate need, and louder than the fear came their chant: "Thak! Thak! Thak!"

From somewhere their overlord heard them.

Thak appeared, atop the drumlike altar.

I do not know what strange world Thak came from, nor, really, what he was. Perhaps he came from deep inside our own world, in awful caverns where metal flowed like water and all life was like him. I suppose he was some sort of demon, but one whose form was not flesh nor blood. He was about sixty feet tall, roughly manlike in shape, but crudely formed, his limbs of equal proportion, his cylindrical head sitting squarely atop his torso. Faceted like a jewel, his body sent out blinding shards of light.

The screams from the Tovieti became louder, and I knew they feared their god or demon as much as they worshiped him.

Thak saw us, although there were no eyes or other features to his head, and stepped down from the altar toward us. His joints screeched like ungreased metal as he came, and his thick, stubby fingers reached for us.

As he came, a high-shrill ringing began, a ringing that drove against my eardrums like invisible nails.

Tenedos was digging in his pouch, and he brought out a large, clear gem, cut like a cylinder with the facets coming to sharp points at either end.

I couldn't hear his spell over the whine, but he cast the gem out, and it landed on one end about twenty feet away. Thak was no more than thirty feet beyond. The gem began spinning, as if Tenedos had whipped a top into motion.

As it spun, it, too, sent flashes of light striking into all corners of the cave, and a low hum started, a hum that quickly rivaled the whine in volume.

"Come on," Tenedos shouted. "I don't know how long that will hold him."

Two men started to run, and both Bikaner's and Vien's bellows caught and held them, and their discipline came back.

At the trot, we went out of the cavern, withdrawing in good order, not retreating. Later I'd have time to marvel at how a handful of men had been able to strike and paralyze many times their number, with no more than boldness, surprise, and some sorcery to aid them—a device I was able to use time and again in the service of Emperor Tenedos.

One or two of the Tovieti, dazed by all that had happened in the last few minutes, tried to stop us, but were easy to knock aside or slay—they offered no real resistance.

I chanced one final look at the chamber's exit, and saw Thak gather himself and stumble forward, like a man driving into a hard wind, step by step toward Tenedos's gem.

I realized I was the last Numantian in the chamber and hurried on to catch up to my men.

It was a gray, dismal morning, and I delighted in it. We lost three in that cave, counting Legate Baner. Four others were wounded, but were being supported along by their fellows.

In battle order, we went down that trail, now having no reason for concealment, and there were none to oppose us.

Within an hour, we'd regained our horses, lashed the packs with the precious mannequins to our saddles, ridden out of the draw to the track.

Tenedos stared back, up at the mountain and the cavern entrance. The rain had died, and there was no wind. I could hear nothing from the cavern's mouth, neither screech nor hum.

"Did you kill him?" I asked.

"I don't know. I was certainly lucky, providing a spell and talisman where like could strike like, although I had no idea what we would face when we entered the cavern," Tenedos said. "Perhaps I hurt him sore. Perhaps I sent him back to where he came from." Tenedos's voice was most unsure. "Or perhaps not." He gathered himself.

"Come. We have what we came for."

We rode hard for Sayana.

ELEVEN

THE ACHIM'S
BETRAYAL

We were heroes at Achim Fergana's court. Not only had we saved the lives of the courtiers and the achim himself from some terrible rending, but we'd killed the traitorous *Jask* Irshad *and* the rebel's most evil brother, Chamisso Fergana.

As for the demon Thak, Achim Fergana was unconcerned. With no one to guide him, even if that powerful spell the ever-brave and never-sufficiently-praised resident-general and Most Powerful Seer Laish Tenedos cast hadn't, Thak must now be impotent and would soon return to his own dark realms. Similarly, the dreaded Tovieti, without any leaders, would fragment and disappear as if they'd never been.

Achim Fergana, sure that his rule was secure and his family would hold the throne forever, promised us anything, *anything* we wished, especially since we had returned his dolls. I'd quietly drawn Tenedos aside and wondered if this was wise. He'd shrugged and said that firstly, he doubted if any of the Kaiti would be able to use them without *Jask* Irshad's magic, and second and more importantly, it did not matter to Numantia how the ruler of Kait held his throne, so long as the Men of the Hills killed within their own borders.

As for Achim Fergana's rewards, unfortunately there was little the kingdom of Kait had that we wanted. Gold would have been more than acceptable, for neither Tenedos nor myself nor any of us was wealthy. But this was against the rules of the kingdom, Achim Fergana explained, most regretfully. Besides, the treasury was in a deplorable state, and all hard currencies were desperately needed for the benefit of the people. But anything else . . .

Tenedos attempted, once, to tell Achim Fergana that mere ratification of the pact he'd been sent into the Border States to present would be the greatest reward of all, for Kait, Numantia, and Urey. Achim Fergana smiled blandly and said he had the matter well under advisement. Even someone as artless as I knew what that portended.

No one, not Tenedos, not me, not any officer or ranker, could come up with an idea for an individual reward. Each of us could have had an estate in the country, and been murdered the instant we rode out of Sayana's gates to visit it.

Titles were meaningless.

Food—the Kaiti diet wasn't exactly prized by my men.

The Achim Fergana offered women or young boys, as many as each man wanted. Some of my men were licking their chops most lasciviously, planning orgies of a prehistoric nature. Here I had to step in firmly: If a woman wished to enter the compound by day, *of her own free will, and she would be asked by me,* and the man involved was off duty, what they chose to do was their business. However, the security of the compound was too important to allow strangers to pass the night. Army laws fortunately forbade enlisted men keeping slaves, so that kept another door closed.

I knew that few Kaiti women would wish to involve themselves with the hated *Ph'rëng* beyond whores or our staff spies, who of course were under orders to be accommodating, especially if they would be forced out into the streets of Sayana at nightfall.

We were left, then, with the undying gratitude of Achim Baber Fergana, a gift that would live, as Resident-General

Tenedos cynically but correctly said, for at least a full week beyond its presentation.

There were some rewards—all the men who rode with me were mentioned in my dispatch back to Domina Herstal and the Lancers, and Captain Mellet did the same for his men. Some we could promote: Legate Baner would be posthumously raised to captain of the Lower Half, which might provide some consolation to his family. As I'd vowed, with Laish Tenedos's full approval, Sergeant Yonge was commissioned legate, as were other hillmen.

As for my own men, I could hardly promote Bikaner to regimental guide, since there was but one such rank in the entire regiment of Lancers and that held by Evatt, back in Mehul. Lance Karjan refused my offer of promotion, saying, "Havin' rank-slashes means givin' up y'r friends an' soul both, an' hardly's worth the few coins extra." Curti was too ashamed of his having missed his first shot in the cavern to countenance reward. At least Svalbard allowed himself to be raised to lance, and grunted, I think in thanks.

Resident Tenedos insisted on writing a dispatch to Domina Herstal that was so commendatory I nearly blushed. I wondered if it would change what Captain Lanett thought, but doubted it. People of his nature never change their minds once someone's played into that fatal flaw of theirs.

There was other praising to be done, and this Tenedos handled most skillfully, although it left a sour taste in my mouth.

He waited less than a day after our return to begin rolling out a ream of letters and dispatches. The first was the necessary report to the Rule of Ten.

He let me read it before sealing the packet. I was polite, and voiced none of my criticisms. It was accurate, but it sounded as if we'd taken a gigantic step to bringing peace to the Border States and bringing Kait firmly under Numantian influence. I noted, however, that the dispatch left several options open, constantly saying *if* certain obvious measures were continued by Achim Fergana and the present government, *assuming* Achim Fergana provided proper justice now that inroads had been made against the Tovieti and the constant feuding within the country, these thoughts being mere *conjectures* dependent on the current situation continuing undisturbed for at least half a year, and so forth.

But Tenedos's use of such slippery words was not the worst. Before he sent the official dispatches off in the hands of a twenty-man patrol to make sure they reached Urey safely, Tenedos produced a second round of correspondence. Some of these missives were private, intended for Tenedos's friends and mentors, including those two men in the Rule of Ten he counted as his allies. Those, of course, he did not allow me to read.

Other writings were intended for various of Nicias's broadsheets. I read part of one, which was filled with references to the "heroism" of the "stalwart young officer of the famed Ureyan Lancers Legate á Cimabue," the "dauntless bravery" of the Numantian soldiery against "overwhelming charges" by the evil tribesmen, and so on. Legate Baner was cut down after killing at least a dozen of the rebels, and died in Tenedos's arms, with his last words being "Promise me, Seer, that the deaths we die this day shall not be in vain, and one day Numantia will recover its past glory and more."

I felt a trifle ill.

Tenedos saw my expression and guessed my thoughts. He smiled, a bit grimly. "You are thinking, What shit—am I not correct, Damastes?"

I grunted noncommittally.

"But what is a lie? Wouldn't Baner, for instance, have killed that many Tovieti if he'd lived?"

"Perhaps. But you make no mention of the Tovieti, either."

"That, young fellow my lad, is because I know the Rule of Ten would have my hide nailed to the city wall if I mentioned such closely held information. Let me continue. As for Baner's last words, well, I admit to putting some words in his mouth. But can you guarantee he didn't believe that?"

"I never heard him say anything about politics."

"Then who can tell? Besides, there is a greater truth here,"

Tenedos went on. "You remember when I spoke to your man, back at the ford? I promised them great times, great deeds, and great prizes.

"Very well. The men who fell, and were returned to the Wheel, can yet serve. Baner is one and gives an example to other young Numantians.

"Should I have told the truth about Legate Baner's death? That he was killed foolishly attacking a man who had twice his skills at fighting? That he dove in front of his superior, no doubt hoping to win the great glory of killing Chamisso Fergana himself? Shall I say that his death did nothing to bring peace to this benighted country, since it will continue to be as it is, as it always has been, unless every gods-damned Kaiti is slain and the land repopulated with sane folk? Shall I say that these Border States matter little to Numantia, that most Numantians cannot find them on a map and care nothing of what happens on their frontiers?

"Do you think that would please the legate's family, if family he had? Do you think that would serve Numantia?"

Tenedos, warming to his subject, was becoming slightly angry. I did not answer his question, but professed ignorance about such abstruse matters.

Instantly Tenedos became charming again.

"Damastes, my friend. You concentrate on what you are very good at, soldiering and doing what you can with very little to work with. I promise, one day, you too shall be rewarded and given a chance to do truly great things that shall make your name ring down the annals of time.

"Let me worry about the politics and the chicanery. But think of one thing: After these accounts I'm writing reach the broadsheets, what chance do you think the Rule of Ten will have of casting me back into oblivion?

"All I'll have to do . . . all *we'll* have to do, is survive this assignment and our names shall be forever known in Numantia. And what can be the matter with that?"

I was still uncomfortable, made my excuses, and left. Over the next few days the matter gnawed—I'd seen officers who made sure their every favorable action was noted by their superiors, and my father had told me, scathingly, of others. I had nothing but contempt for them.

But on the other hand Laish Tenedos was *not* a soldier, and fought in an entirely different arena, one I knew little of and wanted to know less. Was I right in disparaging him? Especially since what he'd accomplished in the cavern *had* kept the peace in Kait, *had* kept Achim Fergana, Numantia's ally, no matter how untrustworthy, on the throne, *had* kept the Kaiti from exploding north into Urey and Numantia with thirsty swords, at least for the moment.

Finally, he was my superior, and I had little right to question his decisions or policies.

Fortunately, there were other, far more important concerns, and I set the matter aside.

One matter appeared minor, but curious: The Kallian, Landgrave Elias Malebranche, had vanished, disappearing from the palace he'd been assigned on the morning of the day we returned, just about the time we'd escaped Thak in the cavern. The coincidence seemed quite remarkable to me, and seemed not at all a coincidence to Resident-General Tenedos, but all questions about him at court were shrugged away.

Our biggest worry was the Tovieti. They did not disappear, as Achim Fergana had blithely promised. Instead, the movement grew and grew. No longer was their name forbidden; instead, it could be heard almost everywhere. They may have been leaderless, but their ideas had not changed: destroy the rulers, destroy the landed. Take what you want. Until the old order is destroyed, there will never be peace, never be riches for any but the overlords. And, of course, *M'rt tê Ph'rëng!*

I saw this painted on many walls, and no Kaiti ever seemed to paint over the slogan. There was also a new wall-painting—a rough circle, sometimes painted in red, intended to represent the blood of the slain Chamisso Fergana, the martyred *Jask* Irshad, and the others we'd killed in the cavern, and, rising from it, a nest of hissing serpents, fangs bared. It could be painted most elaborately, or merely scrawled as a circle with arcing lines coming up from it, depending on how much time and ability the artist had.

There was a Tovieti motto: "From one body, many fighters. From many fighters, one will. Death to the outlanders! War against their kingdoms!"

Now mobs always surrounded the Residency, in spite of it being the height of the Time of Rains. At any hour, there'd be outbursts of chanting, singing, always promising death to the evil foreigners, the *Chishti* who were determined to destroy the fair kingdom of Kait.

When we rode out, we had to wear canvas cloaks, to keep the offal from staining our uniforms. Our Kaiti staff were shouted at and pushed around, and we were forced to escort those who did not live at the compound to and from their homes. Finally, we had to dismiss them entirely.

I called our Kaiti troops together, and offered them the chance to leave our employ. I was pleased, and a bit surprised, that only half, about fifty, took my offer. The ones that remained, including Legate Yonge, were among the best.

Then the first Numantian was killed. His name was Jeuan Ingres, and he was five years old.

His father was a traveling Numantian silversmith, his mother Kaiti. He'd been playing kickball with his four brothers and a wild shot had sent the ball over a wall, into a neighbor's tomato garden. He'd gone after it. Suddenly three men had darted out of nowhere, a yellow silk cord yanked around his neck, and with a sharp pull the boy's windpipe was crushed. Before his brothers could cry out, the three men vanished.

The Kaiti wardens said they were unable to find any clues, and none of their agents heard anything about the deed.

Resident-General Tenedos protested the atrocity to Achim Fergana.

The ruler put on a most distressed face, and went on about how horrible it was for such a deed to have occurred, and how shamed he was, although he certainly understood how some people, remembering the traditional evils Numantia had wreaked on hapless Kait, could be so blinded by their rage that they took a mere babe for an enemy.

"What evils are you referring to, Your Majesty?" Tenedos inquired icily.

"Those that are known to us all, and hardly worth going into at this time, although they are of great shame."

"Since I speak for the Rule of Ten, for Numantia, I must insist on specifics. I understand our countries to be at peace."

"We are," Achim Fergana said. "Of course we are. But that does not alter the truth of what I said."

Tenedos stared at him coldly, then bowed, and we withdrew. Our time as heroes was clearly past. Now we were back to normal—*Ph'rëng* scum.

When we reached the compound, he hurriedly wrote up a summary of recent events, and ordered me to send it at all possible speed north to Urey.

"I'd suggest you send more than one rider, Damastes. Send someone clever. I doubt they'd risk killing an official representative of Numantia, but still . . ." Tenedos looked worried.

I said I would—and requested he prepare a second letter, this one to the army leaders in Urey, asking for reinforcements for the Residency.

"You feel things have gotten that much worse?"

"I would feel a lot more comfortable, Resident, if we had at least two more companies of infantry and a column of heavy cavalry. The lines between us and Urey are very long and thin."

"I'll do that, and I'll use my most cunning phrases. I'll have it ready by the time you detail the men."

I chose Lance-Major Wace, and four of my better lances. I ordered them to move quickly but carefully, and to trust no one between here and Urey, especially not in Sulem Pass. I would have sent a larger party, but with the situation aboil I couldn't spare the men.

"Thankin' th' legate for his advice," Wace said, "but I know better'n even dreamin' such a thing. No, sir. We'll move at th' gallop an' with all our senses at th' raw."

I further ordered him not to return through the pass without reinforcements; I was sure that they could pass through once safely, having surprise with them, but most likely all the hill bandits would be preparing for their return. He growled, said he little liked leaving Three Column in such a fix, but it'd be as the legate ordered. They rode off within the hour.

That evening, Tenedos called me to his study. Once more sorcerous material was spread around the room.

"Since you performed so well before, I'm asking for your assistance again as my acolyte, Damastes. This time, though, there's considerable less risk. I propose to go looking for our demoniac friend Thak, and see if he still exists on this plane."

There was a large, circular brass tray with a raised lip worked with elaborate symbols on the table in the center of his study. Tenedos lit three candles, and put them equidistant around the tray. He motioned twice over a small brazier on a stand, and incense fumed up. He said a few words in another language, then uncorked a metal flask.

"This particular bit of thaumaturgy depends less on material than on training," he explained. He poured a thin layer of mercury into the tray, until I stared down at a dully reflecting mirror.

"You are welcome to observe, if you wish," Tenedos said. "This particular device is most handy in that regard—a novice or nonsorcerer will see as much as the magician. Of course, if the sorcerer happens to be having a bad day, or is a hoaxster, this could be a definite disadvantage.

"There is no risk save being revealed, and we needn't worry about that."

He moved his hands, palms down, fingertips curled, back and forth over the tray. The dullness faded, the mirror was crystal sharp, and then I was looking down at rugged land, as if I were a high-flying bird, except at a height I doubt any bird, even an eagle, could reach. It took me a moment to realize that I was staring down at the city of Sayana, and its outskirts. It was mostly quite clear, although there were places where it was blurred, as if small clouds were between us and the city.

"The indistinct places," Tenedos explained, "are sorcerously blocked—for instance"—and he pointed to one spot—"here is Achim Fergana's palace, and his *jask*s have cast counterspells to prevent interlopers such as myself from spying on him.

"This is one of the greatest advantages this spell gives—it can unerringly show the watcher where a magician is working his craft. But since magic is always double-edged, it also can show the watcher's location as well.

"Now, we shall take a look at the area of interest. I could move our perspective area by area like so. . . ." and his hands shifted, and the view swooped dizzyingly, and Sayana shifted to one side of the picture, and we were looking at a road that led to Sulem Pass. "But there's an easier way to get there. Here's a bit of a mineral I pocketed when we were in the cavern." He tossed it into the brazier, and the mercury pool swirled. "When it clears, we should be looking down at our mountain, and can move inside."

"If a wizard can see us looking for him," I said, a bit concerned, "couldn't a demon like Thak?"

"Possibly—but it matters not, because there's nothing he could do, save block our vision."

The bowl swirled once more, then its edges cleared, and I saw rugged, mountainous terrain. But the center was a gray blur just as I'd seen over Fergana's palace, except covering a far greater area.

"Mmm," Tenedos said wryly. "The Tovieti *jask*s have their wards up. Let us see if we cannot move closer, and go through it." He pushed his hands down, and the grayness filled the plate as our perspective came closer to the mountain.

The gray darkened to black, except here and there were light streaks. "Very good," Tenedos said. "We're now cutting straight down through the mountain. The brightness you see is crevasses that carry light from the outside. Very good indeed."

Then the mercury roiled sharply, and began whirling, like a maelstrom. Tenedos looked alarmed, but before he could explain what was happening the vision cleared, and we were looking at Thak!

I do not know where he was—there was nothing but the crystal demon in the tray. Thak's head creaked back, and he "looked" up at us. The mercury spun faster, and now there was a funnel, and we were about to be sucked down into it.

Thak's arms came up, and his hands reached for us, coming up, closer and closer, and I felt the cold horror of death.

Somehow my muscles obeyed, and I kicked hard, against the table's bottom, and the shock sent the tray spinning, globules of mercury flying across the room. The brazier flamed, and then went out, and that Presence was gone.

I turned to Tenedos. He took a long moment to recover, then made a wry face.

"Well," he said finally, "that spell *used* to be considered quite safe." He went to a sideboard and poured brandies.

"So Thak not only is alive and well, but knows us," he said. "These are not circumstances that send a thrill of joy through me, I must say."

"Do you have spells against him?"

"Unfortunately, no, at least not a spell powerful enough so I could take the offensive. Perhaps if I knew his intent, why he's chosen to enter this plane, assuming he's not a native, I could devise something. But as yet our best defense is to stay out of his way. If we're attacked, I have weapons, but don't know if they're effective enough to destroy him."

"Why," I wondered, "would a demon have come up with the ideas he seems to have taught the Tovieti?"

"I doubt he did. Creatures of another plane generally aren't that familiar with what makes men do what they do. I'd guess some time ago he was invoked by a man who preached the gospel the Tovieti are trying to put into practice, and Thak absorbed enough so he can broadcast it, without really knowing what it means, other than it brings him worshipers."

"What might have happened to the sorcerer who called him up?" I asked.

"It's not unknown," Tenedos said dryly, "for a seer's magic to overwhelm him. Regardless, Thak now appears to be his own master, fulfilling his own desires."

"Is Thak aspiring to become a god?" I wondered. "I mean, someone who has temples and priests, and control over some part of this world?"

"Now we're getting into matters I don't understand," Tenedos said. "Were gods once demons? I don't know. It would make a certain amount of sense, since we know a minor god can sometimes be revealed as an aspect of Irisu or Saionji herself and is given even greater veneration. Are there really gods at all? I don't even know that, although if there are demons and lesser spirits surely there must be greater ones, and there must have been a single spirit at one time—call him Umar if you will—with power enough to create this universe. Or perhaps it just came about. Perhaps there is another Wheel beyond the one we return to that controls all. I become dizzy and want to take a cold bath when I think of such matters.

"As for Thak, I think those we call demons thrive on disorder. Their own planes must be always changing, chaotic. Perhaps they resent any attempts we tiny creatures called men do to bring the world we see into some sort of system. Again, I don't know. Those small spirits I've summoned from time to time to help me certainly resent being required to perform a constructive task, and take positive glee in doing harm.

"I wish I had the leisure to study the matter. Thak is quite a fascinating manifestation. But I fear this is not the place for calm contemplation. Nor do we have the time to develop theories that would gladden the hearts of academicians, unless we plan on them being our final monument.

"For us, it's enough that Thak is our enemy, and the enemy of all that we believe in. As he is, so are the Tovieti."

The next morning the Residency was attacked.

It was a cold, gray morning. The sky threatened rain, but as yet none had materialized.

The mob filled the streets around the Residency. There were at least a thousand Kaiti, shouting, jeering, screaming rage. They were throwing things—stones, filth, masonry, and such. As yet, no real weapons had been used, but it was only a matter of time before things grew worse.

They were all men, of course, from boys to doddering gray-beards. The men of Kait would never allow women the sweet-ness of being able to vent some rage in public. In view of what was to come, I was, for once, grateful for this piece of Kaiti chauvinism.

I had my men at full alert. I'd had eight platforms built ear-lier, in secrecy, and now had them moved to the positions I'd planned, two along each wall of the estate. They were three feet lower than the wall, so the outer wall now became a pro-tective rampart.

Our weakest point was the main gate, which was no more than heavy iron bars. Not only could it be seen through, but we had no way of solidly reinforcing it.

I briefed my soldiers on what they were to do. It took only a few moments, since the very first drill we'd learned was to repel an attack on the compound.

While the mob roared, building its rage, my soldiers and Tenedos's staff stacked heavy furniture as barricades, and overturned freight wagons in front of the main gate to serve as a bastion. They filled bags of dirt from the garden and used them for reinforcing bulwarks.

Resident Tenedos was a pillar, here, there, and everywhere, helping men shift unwieldy objects, giving men encourage-ment, even holding bags open for a shoveler to fill.

I took him aside, and asked if he "saw" any magic behind this.

"No. I sense nothing but a sort of black foreboding aimed at us. If it is a spell, it is such a general one, and so large, it is hardly worth concerning ourselves about compared to some idiot out there in the street who's planning to hurl a cobble-stone at our skulls."

That worried me, because I'd gone to the roof of the main building and tried to pick out leaders of the mob. If the situa-tion worsened, I wanted to have archers pick them off. The way to destroy a mob is always to cut off its head. But I spotted no chieftains, so I wasn't sure at what point to attack the snake; rather, the mob seemed to be more like one of those enormous poison-worms of the swamps that must be cut into fragments before each part ceases thrashing.

Of course there were no signs of the wardens, nor of Achim Fergana's soldiers.

"He won't help the mob," Tenedos theorized. "He's not quite convinced it's time to back the Tovieti completely. But he'll do nothing if they take the Residency, either. Probably he'd use that as an excuse to send his army against them, although I think he'd be most astonished to find out that his soldiers are now about half-converted to Thak's persuasions.

"I suppose we just wait for further developments." They weren't long in coming.

It began with a shower of spears over the wall. They clattered against the cobbles harmlessly, but a few moments after that, arrows arced over, one of them wounding one of the KLI foot soldiers.

Then came shouts, and they charged the gate. They slammed into it with their shoulders, trying to smash it in. They could have tried that tactic for the remainder of their lives without accomplishing anything. Planks appeared, and they tried to lever the crossbar up.

I shouted for them to disperse but no one paid any attention—I doubt if I was even heard over their chanting. I ordered my archers on line, and to fire directly through the bars. The first volley was blunts, flat-headed arrows used for killing birds. That produced yelps of pain, and a few men staggered away, bruised. But there were ten to take the place of one.

The next shots were war arrows, and the crowd fell back, screaming pain and rage.

I ran to one of the platforms, climbed it, and peered out. Far down the street I saw a cluster of men. They were carrying a long wooden pole, about a man's shoulders in diameter, intending to use it as a battering ram.

That was quite enough.

I'd asked Tenedos to hold a spell in readiness, and motioned to him to begin casting it. It was a fairly standard confusion conjuration, intended to produce no more than nameless fear and distraction. Soldiers were routinely trained to expect this when battle began, and to ignore the feeling and obey the orders of their warrants and officers. I'd thought it might be effective against untrained men like those shouting around the gates, and so, by the confusion of shouting and terror, it was.

I put the next stage into motion. Since there seemed to be no leaders to cut down, I thought I'd give the throng a handy exit. So I ordered my archers to send a high volley far down the main street, just as, in time of battle, they'd launch arrows over the front ranks, hoping to strike deep into the enemy's leadership in the rear.

Five volleys went out, carefully aimed, and now came howls of pain. Again, I peered over the wall, and was nearly brained by a rock from a sling. But I'd spotted bodies in the street. Now the rear of the mob was suddenly the most dangerous place, and those heroes who contributed only pushing and shouts found it better to go elsewhere. Now the mob had a way out, which they'd need shortly.

"Assemble!" I cried.

Men slid down from the towers and ran to where they'd been instructed to form up. Our flanks and rear were left defenseless—I intended to strike for the enemy's heart.

With a clatter of hooves, my lances rode in from the parade area, where I'd had the horses saddled and ready. Each lance held the reins of two other horses belonging to the cavalrymen who'd been posted on the platforms.

"Mount up," I shouted, then, "Open the gates!"

Four men lifted away the crossbar. One was struck by a missile and fell, his body thudding limply like a grain sack. Those of my cavalrymen not armed with the bow stepped into their saddles.

"Archers!" The bowmen doubled through the gates as they swung open, nocking arrows. Their warrants shouted, "Any target . . . fire!" and razor-edged war shafts hummed out, some fired no more than fifteen feet into their targets.

"Archers . . . mount!" and the cavalrymen ran back.

"Captain Mellet!"

The captain's voice boomed, "The Khurram Light Infantry will advance!"

The KLI went forward in five even ranks, javelins ready. Behind the battle array were their three drummers, striking an even cadence. They marched through the gates, into the street.

"KLI . . . halt!" Boots crashed obedience. "Into battle lines . . . move!" The men shifted into three open lines, filling the street from side to side, as smoothly as if they were performing the drill at parade.

"Javelins . . . throw!" The spears flew out, and thudded deep into their targets.

The Kaiti mob broke, and men ran for safety.

"KLI . . . wheel right . . . march!" The foot soldiers swung back against the outer walls of the compound as I pulled myself into Lucan's saddle.

"Lancers . . . forward!" and we rode into the streets of Sayana.

Shrieks of terror came as they saw us.

"Lances . . . down! At the trot . . . charge!"

We slammed into the mob like a juggernaut, and broke them and sent them running. I took down one man, who was running hard and waving a forgotten saber, with my lance and sent him whirling away.

The blood-mist was rising, and I heard battle shouts from my men. Now was the time to ride the rabble down into their own filth. But we were fifty yards from the compound, and must not be sucked to our deaths in the dark, twisting streets of Sayana.

"Lancers . . . halt!" We reined in and pulled our horses around, riding back through the gates, the KLI moving smoothly in behind us, and the gates clanged shut and we were safe.

I shouted for the civilians to help tend the wounded, and ran to one of the towers.

I counted forty bodies sprawled in the street. We had two men dead and half a dozen wounded.

We'd given them a lesson, but the next time it would be our turn to learn. The next time they would be armored and armed, and the moment might well be theirs.

We must maintain the edge we'd honed, or else we were doomed.

Before dawn of the next day we were in motion.

I left only a handful of troops to guard the Residency—I doubted if the mob would have recovered its courage in such a short time—and divided the rest into three-man teams.

Neither Tenedos, myself, nor his clerks had any sleep the previous night. All Numantians in Sayana had been required to list their current addresses with us, and we divided the list into groups.

The orders were to bring all Numantians to the compound. Captain Mellet's infantrymen would screen the inner part of the city and my Lancers would try to save those living in the outskirts. One soldier would guard against attack, the other two would help our people pack what they could carry. They were also instructed to make sure the civilians took warm clothes and practical foodstuffs—I remembered as a boy, when a neighboring farm had burned, its master had run out of the flames proudly waving what he'd saved from the flames: a single pewter candlestick he'd seized from a cabinet full of silver and gold.

We had to move swiftly. Each team was told to give no more than a few minutes to each house, then move the people out, by force if necessary. The Kaiti would quickly learn what we were doing.

We set out, hoping for the best and expecting the worst. Again, there were no wardens or soldiers abroad; Achim Fergana had them either restricted to barracks or surrounding his palace to keep his own neck from feeling the touch of yellow silk.

My companions were Lances Curti and Karjan. I dismounted at one house, a neat little cottage set apart from the other Kaiti dwellings. This had some hardy plants in window boxes that still showed green despite the nearing winter. The door had been painted a welcoming red. But it stood open. My sword was out as I entered.

I was too late. There had been four Numantians living there, a man, his wife, and his two sons. I don't remember what had brought them to Sayana. All four of them were dead, the Tovieti strangling cords still wound around their throats. The house was stripped nearly bare.

I cursed and ran to my horse. As I remounted, a mocking laugh came from somewhere, but I saw no one.

My next address was luckier, although I nearly had to knock a grandsire out to convince him he *must* leave. He kept trying to tell me he'd lived in this city since he was a boy, the Kaiti were his friends, and nothing bad would happen. I dragged him to his doorway and pointed to where a knot of glowering men stood, held back only by Lance Karjan's menace. He looked at his neighbors and erstwhile "friends," and I thought his heart would break. But he, his equally aged wife, and their grown son then obeyed my orders.

As we rode off, I heard cries of triumph as the Kaiti began looting their house.

A half-dozen other addresses went smoothly.

The next I sensed something strange about, even though there appeared nothing untoward. It was a large building in a wealthy part of town.

I slipped out of the saddle and went to the door. I was about to lift the knocker when I *felt* something. My sword was suddenly in my hand. I began to knock, and the unlocked door was pulled open, and a blade flashed.

But I was not there. I'd slipped to one side without willing the motion, and as my mind "saw" the attack I lunged, and put my sword deep in a Tovieti's guts. He gasped helplessly for air that was rushing from his lungs, dropped his blade, reached for mine, and died. I yanked my sword free, and went into the house. Curti and Karjan were behind me.

There was the body of a young woman on the floor, her head half-severed. An infant lay beside her, the silk strangling cord around its neck. I heard the sound of crashing from another room, and crept toward it.

A man was pulling drawers out of a cabinet, eyeing them for valuables, then dumping them on the floor. An open sack sat on the table nearby, half full of loot.

"Will y' stop admirin' your skills with th' blade an' gimme help," he snarled, half-turning.

His eyes had time to widen just a trifle before my sword took his head off, and sent it tumbling, blood spraying in a half-circle against the walls.

I was about to search the house for other Tovieti when a voice came from the larder:

"Thank you, soldier."

A little girl, no more than six, her hair as golden as mine, walked into the kitchen. She looked at the headless corpse and nodded soberly.

"That's good. I think he's the one who killed my father." Then she looked at me. "Are you going to kill me now?"

I almost burst into tears.

"No," I managed. "I'm a Numantian. Like you are. I've come to take you to a safe place."

"That's good. I wish you had come a little while ago. While my sisters were still alive."

I could stand no more. I picked her up and rushed her out of the house, telling Curti to prepare a bundle for the girl. I'd stay with her at the horses.

I set her down, and she looked up at Lucan.

"Is he a nice horse?"

"He's a very nice horse. His name is Lucan."

"Can I pet him?"

I nodded, and she walked forward as Lucan lowered his head. He nickered when she rubbed his nose.

"Hello, Lucan. I'm Allori."

In a few moments Curti and Karjan came out. He shook his head in response to my unasked question. There was no one still alive inside. He had a full armload of clothes, stuffed into a heavy storage bag.

"I took mostly heavy clothes," he said. "There was some coins in the bag that bastard in the kitchen had. I stuck 'em in here. She'll need 'em when we get her to safety."

I told Allori we must leave, and helped her mount in front of me.

As we turned away, she looked back at the house, then up at me.

"I don't want to live here anymore," she announced quietly. Her eyes were dry, and I never once saw her cry.

We rode back to the compound. The Kaiti watched, but stayed well out of our way. There were grumbles and occasional shouts, but the tale of what had happened the day before had spread, and no one was willing to chance our wrath.

Of the 300 or so Numantians in the city, we'd managed to save more than 250. The others either had changed addresses without telling us, been killed, or fled from their rescuers, sure they still had nothing to fear.

But real safety still lay more than 100 miles distant.

The officer of the watch shook me awake just after midnight. I came to groggily, since I'd been asleep for just over an hour, and the first thought that wandered across my mind was that the greatest blessing peace can bring is an uninterrupted night's rest.

"Sir," the man said. "You'd best come to the main gate."

I'd fallen asleep almost completely dressed. All I had to do was pull on my boots, my heavy coat and helm, sling my sword belt, and we hurried out.

It was seething rain, and the torches the watch held smoked, sending shadows against the water-walls that washed across us. But I could see well enough.

Lance-Major Wace's head was impaled on his broken-off lance just outside the gate. Piled against the lance were the heads of my other men.

We were cut off from Urey.

* * *

"But what is it you desire of me?" Achim Fergana asked, trying to sound concerned.

"Since Your Majesty evidently can no longer govern his own city, cannot guarantee the safety of the public streets to men and women of my country, I must ask for permission to depart, along with all other Numantians and those who've chosen me as their protector."

"What will your masters think of that?" he said.

"The Rule of Ten will be most displeased," Tenedos said. "That I can guarantee. What action they may choose to make, I cannot say, but I know it will be harsh, and not in the best interests of Kait."

"I do not see why my kingdom should be made to suffer because of the actions of a handful of fanatics." Achim Fergana actually looked worried; perhaps he'd never considered the course of his actions, or, more correctly, inactions.

"Where were your soldiers when my Residency was attacked, O Achim? Where were your wardens when innocents were slaughtered yesterday?"

"Sayana is experiencing great unrest," Fergana said. "They were occupied with other duties."

"I noted what those were when we entered your palace," Tenedos said. "Tell me, O Achim, are you so afraid of the Tovieti you must have *all* your army protecting you?"

Tenedos's guess the day before had been correct: Soldiers packed the palace, and the gratings were lowered on all levels of the balconies above, and archers lined them.

Fergana's face engorged in anger, but I wasn't watching him that closely; I'd seen, with fascination, the effect the word *Tovieti* had on the handful of courtiers around him. It was as if a bloody corpse had been cast in front of them.

"You cannot speak to me in that manner!"

"Forgive me if I spoke in error. But this is a waste of both of our time," Tenedos said, steel in his tones. "I ask you for one thing. Nay, I do not ask it, I demand it, in the name of the Rule of Ten, and the vast armies they command, armies who seek but an excuse to pull free the long-time thorn that is the Border States. I demand you provide myself and those men and women under my charge safe passage to your borders."

Fergana breathed deeply, forcing control. He gained it.

"Of course you have that," he said. "You need not threaten me with your soldiers. Seer Tenedos, your presence in my kingdom has not been a happy one, in spite of a certain service you managed to perform for me.

"Now I bid you go, and take your fellow *Ph'rëng* with you. You will not be troubled, you will not be bothered. But never return to my kingdom again, not you, not your soldiers, nor your people.

"I hereby proclaim the Kingdom of Kait to be closed to all Numantians from the time you cross the border into Urey until the end of time itself!"

Achim Fergana rose and stalked from the room.

That was when the nightmare began.

TWELVE

DEATH IN THE ICE

We'd expected mobs to jeer us out of Sayana. But—and this was most ominous—there were only a few scuttling figures on the streets when we marched out.

We left the Residency at dawn. It had taken us three days to prepare for departure, setting up the order of march, making sure the civilians had proper clothing and footgear, assigning as many elderly or infirm to wagons as we could, preparing rations, and so forth.

We chanced going outside the Residency to buy extra food and horses, although we were hardly welcome in Sayana's marketplace. We bought with one hand holding gold and the other on the grip of our swords. We had just enough food, I hoped, counting the iron rations and dry reserves in the compound, for the journey back to Urey.

My final task was to call together the fifty remaining hillmen. I told them their duty was finished, and to line up for their final pay. I said that once they'd gotten their gold, Seer Tenedos would cast a spell so they could slip out the gate and disappear into the city without attracting notice. I thanked them for their faithfulness, said I was proud to have known them, and wished things had gone differently.

About ten of them drew aside, Legate Yonge at their head.

I went to him, and he said quietly, "We wish to serve on with you, Legate á Cimabue."

I told him how honored I was but that, quite frankly, he was being foolish. "There is a long journey between here and safety, and I know we face enemies at every turn."

"Life itself is nothing more than that." Yonge shrugged. "I took an oath to serve you *Ph'rëng,* and do not wish to be released from it."

"Yonge, think, man. Even if we make it to Urey, you'll be an exile. You'll never be able to return to Kait as long as Fergana lives."

"Do you honestly believe," the hillman said, "that lizard shit who calls himself achim will let any of us escape his punishment for serving you? I know he'll have his *jask*s cast seeking spells for anyone who swore fealty to the resident-general, and a slow death will follow their discovery.

"No. I would prefer to take my chances with the seer, as would my fellows." He started to say more, but broke off.

"Go ahead," I encouraged.

"Two other reasons. You treated us as equals when you came, as did all your Lancers, in spite of what I know they feel about Kaiti. This is the way of honor. I wish to learn more about it.

"Besides"—he grinned—"I have never seen Urey, and would like to learn what skills their women have when they come willingly to your bed."

I could do nothing other than accept. For their safety on the march, I told them to dress themselves as Numantians, although I wished them to keep their native garb ready. There might be a need for a Kaiti spy on our journey.

We planned to cover the nearly 100 miles in about ten days, weather permitting. The rains were coming to a halt, and while it was bitter cold, so far the winter storms had not begun.

The order of march was One and Two Columns, Seventeenth Lancers, at the front; then two platoons of the Khurram Light Infantry; then the civilians; a third platoon of the KLI; Four Column; our wagons, which I asked Captain Mellet to take charge of; the last of the infantry and Three Column, which I personally regarded as the best of my troop, at the rear, under the command of Troop Guide Bikaner. I half apologized for always giving him the hardest task. He half smiled and said, " 'S alright, sir. I'm gettin' so used to eatin' dust now I've grown t'like its taste."

The city gate stood open, and the guards were withdrawn. Sitting on horseback, just on the other side, was Achin Baber Fergana, surrounded by some of his courtiers and cavalrymen.

Now we heard jeering, but it was muted. Even these lackeys were afraid of Tenedos's magic, which had killed *Jask* Irshad and saved us from the demon.

Tenedos held up his hand, and we reined in. He stared long and hard at Fergana, his eyes harsh, as if he were cutting a steel engraving of the man. Fergana grew visibly nervous under the stare, then wheeled his horse and galloped around us, his men streaming after him, back into Sayana.

One of them turned as he rode through the gates, and shouted, *"M'rt tê Ph'rëng!"*

Tenedos turned to me. "Ride on, Legate."

I shouted commands, and the long train creaked forward.

Behind me, I heard Lance Karjan grunt, "Good, that. Don't give th' bastard no satisfaction. 'Though it'd do me good t'see th' seer send a bolt a lightnin' up that shit-heel's arse, 'twould."

It was a charming thought, and I did wish Tenedos had cast some sort of spell, even though my rational mind knew the achim was well surrounded with protection from his court *jasks*.

It gave me something to think about as we crawled north toward Sulem Pass. If I'd had to watch my words before, when we'd first made the slow passage, now I must be doubly careful. I must not try to hurry these civilians, for fear they'd panic, or else lose all belief in themselves and lie down to die.

Another thought occurred: I told Lance Karjan that he might have chosen to be my servant, but the best way he could serve was to stick close to Seer Tenedos. I could manage for myself, but the resident-general *must* survive. Karjan muttered darkly, but obeyed, and from that time on stayed as close to Tenedos as he'd permit.

This was fairly open country, so I was able to keep Two Column out as flankers. The few Kaiti we saw stayed distant from the road.

I'd expected harassing attacks the moment we went beyond the gate, but nothing happened. I knew better than to expect Fergana's safe-conduct to be better than before, and wondered when we'd be hit.

We camped the first night, having made almost twelve miles, which sounds like very little, but on a first day's march, with inexperienced people, it was quite respectable.

Seer Tenedos said he would put out magical wards, so no more than a third of my men were needed as guards. He sensed no spells being cast against us as yet.

The second day went even better, and I grew quite worried—the longer the wait, the nastier the surprise.

Captain Mellet chided me for my gloom.

"We *could,*" he said, "be the first Numantians to have good luck in Sulem Pass, now couldn't we?"

We broke into rueful laughter at the same time.

That day we made fourteen miles, and the weather held as it'd been, cold, with a chill wind coming down from the mountaintops.

It was almost noon on the third day when the hillmen made their first move. The ground was no longer so open, and the icy river ran to one side of the road, so I had pulled my flankers back into the main column.

From nowhere about a hundred mounted men appeared in front of us, blocking the road. I heard cries of alarm from the civilians, but paid no heed.

The hillmen trotted toward us, only stopping when I shouted for them to halt or be fired upon.

One man walked his horse forward. He was tall, quite thin, and his beard was braided. He wore a long multicolored coat, made of different animal furs, and his long saber hung below his stirrups.

He pulled up about twenty feet from me.

"So you are the Numantians, eh?"

"Your perception is almost as acute as your eyesight," Tenedos said.

The man grinned, showing blackened teeth.

"I am Memlinc, and my word is law in Sulem Pass."

"I know some other Men of the Hills," Tenedos said, "who might argue that."

"Pah. Bandits, no more. They all kneel when I come before them."

"No doubt," Tenedos agreed. "So why have you honored us with your presence, Memlinc the Great?"

"I wished to see the *Ph'rëng* that pig Fergana ordered out of Sayana. You have some women I might fancy, or one of my warriors might like. One of my elders has the Gift, and he's shown me, in a vision, a girl or two worthy of attending me in bed.

"Yes, women. And perhaps half your gold and jewels. I am a reasonable man, but since you must pass through my domain, I think it only reasonable for you to pay some sort of tribute, eh?"

Tenedos waited a long moment, then leaned forward and said softly, "Fuck you."

Memlinc blinked.

"To be precise," the seer went on, "fuck you, fuck the whore who called herself your mother and fuck the father you never knew because he never paid for the first time."

Memlinc's face paled.

"You cannot speak to me like that! No one can and still live!"

"Ah?" Tenedos's voice was still mild.

Memlinc's hand flashed to his dagger, just as my blade slid half out of its sheath.

"Very well," he said, and pulled his lips back into something resembling a smile. "Let your words carry their own penalty. I offered you peace . . . now see what my other hand carries."

He picked up his reins, and made as if to turn his horse.

Instead, he spurred it forward, straight at the column, in a full gallop.

I guess this was his way of showing his courage to his fellows. They shouted encouragement, and made as if to charge. My archers' bows were up, a volley went out, and the hillmen's ranks became a cluster of plunging, wounded horses.

Memlinc hurtled down our column at full speed. No one had time to draw a sword and strike at him, and he was too close for bow or lance.

But he didn't reckon with Lucan. I spun my horse in his tracks and shouted him into a run.

A spear almost took the hillman, but he ducked under it, then drove his horse through the last few infantrymen into the column toward the second wagon. On it were a handful of women, a few old civilians, and some children. Riding beside the driver was one of Tenedos's retainers, an assistant pastry chef named Jacoba. I'd noted her before—a small, exceptionally striking young woman, a year or two older than I was, with long, dark hair she normally wore tied into a bun—but had never so much as spoken to her.

She must have been one of the beauties Memlinc's elder had magically pointed out, because with a shout of triumph the Kaiti leaned from his saddle, scooped Jacoba across it, spurred his horse away from the road.

I turned my own mount through the column after him. One of Mellet's men was fumbling with his javelin, and I yanked it from his grip.

Memlinc rode for a twisting ravine. Once he was away from the road, no one would dare follow him. He was crouched in the saddle, his face far forward on his horse's neck.

I stood in my stirrups, balanced . . . and cast. Perhaps he thought Numantians were gentlemanly at war, or fools, because I did not aim at him, but at the far better target. The spear took his horse in the haunches. It screamed, and fell, sending the woman and her kidnapper tumbling. I pulled Lucan up hard, skidding, and came out of the saddle as Memlinc rolled to his feet. His saber had been lost in the fall, and he ran at me, yanking a long dagger from inside his coat. His hand swooped down to pick up a rock as he came. As he started to pitch it underhand into my face my sword snaked out, and his hand, still holding the rock, fell to the ground. He had an instant to stare in disbelief at his blood pulsing out, then my blade ripped into him on the counterstroke, cutting deep into his chest, smashing through his ribs and into his heart.

Behind me I heard battle shouts, but paid them no mind. I ran forward, I lifted the stunned Jacoba, and turned to find Lucan. He was beside me, sensing that we had but an instant. I mounted, yanking Jacoba across the pommel of my saddle, and then we galloped hard for the safety of the train.

A handful of Memlinc's riders had attempted to ride to the aid of their leader, but my men cut them off. There were a handful of bodies, men and horses, down in front of the column, and the rest of the bandits were fleeing up a wide draw.

I waved to Tenedos to resume the march. I returned Jacoba to her wagon just as she got her wind back. Her nose was bloody, her coat dirty from the fall, and I suspected she'd have a black eye on the morrow. She tried to find strength for words, but it had not returned as yet. I touched my helmet and rode back to the head of the formation.

As I rode past Two Column I heard a low whistle, the mocking signal the men used to show exaggerated awe at a particular piece of grandstanding. I buried a grin, and put a scowl on. Two Column would be my choice for rotten details for the next few days.

I pulled my horse in beside Tenedos.

"Now I wonder," he said, without preamble, "if that was Memlinc's plan from the beginning, or if he was merely improvising?"

"Probably the last, sir. I'll guess he needed to do some showing off to make sure his men still thought he was worthy to lead them."

"Speaking of showing off," he said after a few seconds,

"what, Legate Damastes á Cimabue, do they teach you at the lycee about a soldier who abandons his command to do something perfectly stupid, if noble?"

"Generally, sir," I said, realizing I had been a gods-damned fool but not regretting it for a moment, "he gets praised, then taken behind the barracks, given a thumping by one of the bigger warrants, and told never, ever do something like that again."

"My congratulations, then. When we reach Urey," Tenedos said, "I may wish to borrow Troop Guide Bikaner for an afternoon. Until then, however, do me the favor of *not* performing any more daring rescues that can get you killed. I really do not wish to command a troop of Lancers in addition to my other responsibilities."

"Yessir. And while we're talking about responsibilities, sir, may I say how shocked I am at the language a professional diplomat sometimes uses?"

"Tut, young Legate," Tenedos said, mock-magisterially. "Consider this: Our opponent is defeated, is he not? His forces have retreated, have they not? Our way lies unobstructed, and we wasted little time in the colloquy, correct?

"Perhaps," he said, mock-mournfully, "I should have attempted similar tactics with our friend the Achim."

That was the last time I laughed for a long time.

The next day the raiders came back—or perhaps it was a different clan of bandits. They lay concealed on the other side of the riverbank until the cavalry passed, then about thirty archers rose from concealment and showered arrows into the front two platoons of foot soldiers. The infantrymen instantly charged; the best way to survive an ambush is to attack the least-expected direction. The archers turned and splashed away through the shallow river without fighting.

On the other side of the road men darted out of their hiding places and ran toward the wagons, screaming war cries. They cut down the thin screen of guards, and in seconds grabbed what they fancied from the wagons and were gone. At the same time a third group struck the civilians. They stole ten

Numantians—five women, including two of the KLI's camp followers, a ten-year-old girl, a baby, and three men.

Then there was nothing but the keening of the wind through the rocks and the cries of the wounded and dying. Seven soldiers, six men of the KLI and one of my hillmen, died in that skirmish, and another half dozen were wounded.

We reformed and marched on.

An hour later, we heard screams from the rocks ahead. The Men of the Hills had begun their sport.

Around the next bend, we found the baby. Its brains had been dashed out against a roadside boulder and its tiny corpse left for us to find.

We went on, and eventually the screams were lost in the distance.

An hour later we came on the village where the boy had tried to murder me with his grandfather's bow. This time there was no one at all in the settlement. It was growing colder, so Tenedos suggested that we send a search party through the huts, to see if there were blankets or other bedding material we might acquire.

I kept the main column outside the village, and sent our searchers in on foot. The first two huts were empty, already stripped bare. The lance leading the search party set foot in the third hut, and a crossbow clacked and he came stumbling out, looking bewildered, and tugging at a small bolt, scarcely big enough to bring down a sparrow, stuck in his chest.

The crossbow had been cleverly rigged so anyone coming through the doorway would trigger it.

The lance cursed, pulled out the bolt, and tossed it aside, saying it was nothing. He started for the next hut, then screamed in pain, clawing at the tiny hole the shaft had made. He fell to his knees, then on his back, convulsing, biting his tongue almost through. Before anyone reached him, he was dead.

The tiny wound already smelled of putrefaction from the poisoned arrow.

We found only a few things worth taking, but when we went on the village was a sea of flames. I remembered the gift of life I'd given the boy, and grimaced. I'd learned how war was fought in these lands—to the knife, and the knife to the hilt. The Kaiti would learn that Numantia could fight as brutally as anyone.

The next two villages we also put to the torch, the second, after we'd spent the night in it.

Late in the afternoon of the sixth day, we reached the ford where I'd met Tenedos. We'd barely made camp when the long-threatening storm broke, and icy gales lashed over us, driving snow hard into our faces.

Tenedos cautioned us to be doubly alert, for he sensed sorcery swirling around us. I needed no caution, though. This was ideal weather for the hillmen. I put my men on half-alert, and doubled all guard posts.

Captain Mellet set up stoves next to the wagons, and stretched canvas roofs over them. After I'd seen to my men, and those off watch had been fed, Tenedos and I went through the line for our own supper. It was nothing more than rice with some meat in it, and herb tea, but praise the goddess Shahriya for her gift of fire, it was hot.

One of the servers was the young woman Jacoba. As I thought, she was sporting a wicked black eye. She looked at me, started to say something, then looked away. I was just as pointlessly embarrassed, and went on without speaking.

The little girl, Allori Pares, came up to me while I ate.

"Hello, soldier. Do you remember me?"

I did, and told her to call me Damastes.

"I've been helping that other soldier with the food." She pointed to Captain Mellet. "He said he's got a daughter just my age."

I knew Captain Mellet was unmarried, and smiled inside myself at the craggy bachelor trying to be nice to the child.

"I like cooking. Maybe . . . if I grow up, I'll want to have an inn."

If she grew up. Part of me wanted to cry, part of me wanted to lay waste to this whole gods-damned country.

"You'll grow up," I said finally. "You and I, we're partners. I'll make sure nothing happens."

"Is that a promise?"

"That's a promise."

At midnight, I went the rounds relieving my guards, then thought I could chance a bit of sleep, giving instructions to the commander of the guard to wake me when it was time for the watch to change.

The wind roared even louder, and the snow was drifting on the ground. I found a place to lie, thought wistfully of those civilians who had found sleeping room in or under one of the wagons, wrapped myself in Lucan's saddle blanket and my cloak, and do not remember my head touching the saddlebag I'd set for a pillow.

The air was rich with the scent of orange blossoms and tamarind. I lay back on the silk pillows, wearing only a loin-cloth, feeling the houseboat move slightly as gentle waves washed under it. There seemed to be no other craft on the lake, its water echoing the blueness of the sky. A soft summer breeze touched me and was gone.

I felt a touch of thirst, picked up the goblet from the tray beside me, and sipped a cooling punch, its scent a marvelous combination of peaches and strawberries.

Jacoba lay on pillows beside me. She wore nothing but a sleeveless vest and flaring pants of a material thinner than silk.

She leaned toward me, and slowly undid the fastening of my loincloth and it fell away. My cock rose to meet her fingers. She bent, and her tongue flicked around its head, then caressed it down to its base, then she took me in her mouth.

I felt my pulse hammer.

She came lithely to her feet, and untied the yellow silk cord that held her pants, and stepped out of them as they fell away.

Jacoba knelt across my thighs, and as I arched my back her fingers guided me into her. She moaned, and her hands slid across my chest, still holding the cord. She raised herself, came back down, raised once more, and as she did she slipped the cord around my neck, and pulled it taut, twisting it hard, her head going back as she cried in passion.

The universe was nothing but my cock in her softness and the wonderful feel of that cord as joy rose within me, and I opened my mouth to shout . . .

. . . and a child screamed and the face above me was bearded and twisted in evil, silent laughter. The blood crashed against my temples and I was looking at him through a tunnel as I brought my feet up and booted the Tovieti back into the snow.

He came to his feet, reaching for a knife at his waist as I dove at him, the back of my fist smashing into his face, then drove the heel of my hand against the base of his nose. He cried out and fell, spattering blood and cartilage on me as I dropped on him, my rigidly braced forearm crushing his windpipe. I rolled off as he died, and I had my sword in hand.

The camp was alive with shouts and screams, and I saw the dim form of men running away, into the snowstorm, as torches flared up into life.

The Tovieti's cord still hung around my neck, and now I could feel its red burn.

I ran into the center of the rounded wagons, shouting for full alertness. Tenedos, Lance Karjan behind him, came out of the darkness, blearing awake.

But the Tovieti were gone.

Six of my soldiers were slain at their posts. How the Tovieti were able to creep up on paired sentries and slay them without any alarm being given, I do not know. Then they'd crept into the camp and begun their killing.

Ten civilians had been killed, eight of them, including a month-old baby, strangled, the other two knifed in their sleep.

I paid no mind to the wails of fear and mourning, but pulled Tenedos aside.

"What happened to your wards? Didn't you sense anything?"

"I felt nothing," the seer said, and a bit of fear showed on his face. "My magic should have worked . . . but it did not. I don't know why."

I felt a flash of anger, then common sense prevailed. Why should Tenedos's craft have done any better than a soldier's?

Both were but men, and their skills imperfect. I wondered what child had greater prescience than any of us, but never found who had screamed.

We collected the bodies, and prepared them for burial. The ground was frozen hard, so I ordered well-guarded parties out to gather the rocks we'd use to build tombs.

We built the fires up, and made more tea. Once again, I saw Jacoba, buttering bits of hard bread. She set her knife down and walked over.

"I never had the chance to thank you," she said.

"It's not necessary."

She was silent for a moment.

"Just now . . . when *they* came, I was dreaming of you," she said, her voice no more than a whisper.

I'm afraid I colored, although she could not have seen it in the dark.

"I, uh, well . . . I had a dream of you, as well," I finally managed.

"We were in a boat," she said dreamily. "Just the two of us. It was on a lake. Perhaps it was one of the houseboats I've read about, in Urey." She fell silent. I said nothing, amazed. There was a long silence. Then she looked up at me.

"Perhaps . . . perhaps, if we live . . ." She turned away, suddenly, and went back to her task.

The next morning the storm was worse. The icy walls of Sulem Pass closed about us, and the wind blew hard from the north.

We were struck four times that day by hillmen. Two or three men would rush out of hiding, seize the person or goods they wanted, and disappear. We could not post a soldier every five feet, so we made no kills.

The column was straggling, no matter how hard Troop Guide Bikaner and Three Column at the rear chided or threatened. I rode up and down the long line, trying to encourage, and when someone was obviously exhausted let them ride Lucan for a spell while I walked alongside. Rabbit and our other spare mounts were already carrying the sick, lame, or old—and there were still too many of the helpless afoot. Each time bandits attacked, we'd take casualties, and the wounded would go into the wagons, further displacing someone who should not be walking.

I learned another lesson that day. I'd disparaged the camp followers the KLI had brought with them as no more than whores. But it was they who nursed the wounded and sick, bringing a bit of mercy and softness to someone's last hour.

We halted an hour before noon, and it took another hour for the last laggard to stumble into camp.

I could have broken up the infantry and sent them into the civilian column to help, but then I'd have lost half my fighting men, and would have no coherent unit to support the middle of the line.

The best I could do was order Two and Four Columns to dismount and use their horses to carry more of the helpless. If we were attacked, they were to help the people out of the saddle, then mount and form up. It was stupid—the time wasted would be more than enough for the Men of the Hills to escape—but I could not watch people in my charge just die.

Laish Tenedos had said little that morning, and now I found him at the front of the column, seemingly unaware of the gale, the snow, or his always-present companion, Karjan. He became aware of me, and turned. His nose and cheeks were beginning to pale with frostbite.

"Snow," he said musingly, and I thought he was in shock from the cold, "Damastes, we need more snow."

I knew he'd gone mad.

"Come. I think I've derived a spell that can help us, if only briefly and slightly."

He hurried to the wagon that held his magical gear, and took out various bits of paraphernalia. I helped him lug the materials back to where I'd found him. He paced ten steps out into the undisturbed snow.

"Best I cast this where man has not walked," he said. He used four small candlesticks, each ending in a spike, to make a square on the ground about two feet on each side. Into them he put four small candles, one green, one white, one black, one red.

In the center, he put a small brazier set on a tripod that brought it almost to waist level.

Awkwardly he sprinkled herbs onto the brazier, shielding it with one hand to keep the wind from scattering his material.

Then he prayed, first to our goddess of the earth, then to the god whose realm was water:

> "Jacini, hear
> We are your children
> We are the earth
> Varum take heed
> I seek now a boon
> I seek now a loan.

> "Grant me this favor
> Grant me this wish."

He touched a finger to each candle, and they spurted fire, a high, narrow flame three times the candles' height.

He held a finger, without burning it, in each of those flames, his lips moving in an incantation, then touched it to the herbs in the brazier. He raised his voice:

> "There is peace
> There is calm
> All is still
> All is frozen.

> "Time will stop
> Time must stop
> You will hear
> You will heed."

The herbs began smoldering, and then I saw something truly marvelous. The snowflakes swirling in the space defined by the four candles froze, as if they'd been cast in an invisible amber, a cube two feet on all sides.

"Good," Tenedos said. "Someone . . . god or not . . . approves my wish. Now for the hard part."

His hands moved in a strange series of gestures, and something was born in that brazier. It was dark, speckled with light, and had form, yet no form, and my eyes hurt trying to make it out and I looked away.

Again, Tenedos chanted:

"I have a need
  You owe a debt
  I did a boon
  Now you must serve."

The dark shadow, or cloud or form, shivered, as if taken by the wind. There was a humming.

"Thak?" Tenedos said. "He is not of your realm, nor do I wish to strike against him. You will obey me."

The shadow hummed once more.

"I said you *will* obey." Tenedos's fingers moved in quick gestures, and the humming came once more, and I oddly thought it a groan of pain. The shadow bent, as if bowing in obedience.

"Very well." Once more Tenedos touched the brazier.

"There are those beyond
  They are filled with hate
  They would do us harm
  They must be turned away."

The shadow grew tall, taller than a man. Tenedos continued his chant:

"Varum gave me water
This shall be our tool
It shall be your weapon
It shall not be seen.

"Snow that blinds
Snow that hides
Cloud the mind
Cloud the eyes.

"They shall not see
They shall not know
We shall pass
We shall pass."

The magical square was empty.

"Now take your weapons and go," Tenedos said, then resumed the chant:

"I bid you once
I bid you twice
I bid you thrice
You must obey
You will obey."

Now it was the shadow's turn to vanish. Tenedos motioned, and the four candles smoked and went out.

"Now we shall see what we shall see," he said. "If that spell works, it should act as a fog to those robbers. They'll somehow *know* we're not on them yet, even though we're in front of them, or else *know* that we passed hours ago. They'll *know* we left the road and seek us up side tracks, or else comb the villages, *knowing* we took shelter from the storm.

"If the spell works."

"What was that shadow?" I asked. I'd been fascinated, completely oblivious of the cold and storm.

"Something from . . . somewhere else," Tenedos said,

deliberately vague. "Something I performed a service for once." I knew he'd tell me no more, but I had one final question.

"Is Thak more powerful than that being?"

"Who knows?" Tenedos said. "My wraith is a lazy one, and hardly gifted with what we mortals call courage. But I'd suppose he is less powerful than the Tovieti's demon."

"Will Thak attack us, as he did in the cavern?"

"I don't know," Tenedos said. "I've been preparing some spells if he does . . . but have no notion if they will work. I don't think they will. I need something more."

"Such as?"

"No, Damastes. That I cannot, must not, tell you. Not now, not ever."

That was the first moment I touched on what was the Seer Tenedos's great secret, the secret that would bring him an empire. When I reveal it, it shall be obvious, but it never was to Tenedos's friends, tribunes, army, or his enemies until far too late.

"Now, let us travel on," he said.

After we'd reformed for the march I saw there were still four people huddled in the snow. I went to the first. It was one of my cavalrymen. His mustache and eyebrows were thick with frost, and his eyes were glazed.

"On your feet, Lance."

He stared up, without seeing, rocking back and forth. I pulled him up, but it was as if he were boneless. He sagged back to the ground.

Troop Guide Bikaner ran up, and yanked the soldier to his feet, as I'd done. Once more the man fell. "Son of a mother-stabbing bitch," he swore. "Th' shortcock's given up!"

And so it was.

"Shall we leave 'im?"

I thought about it. The Lancers never abandon their dead or wounded except in the last resort, and this man, someone with a weak spirit, was as much a casualty as if he'd been slashed by a hillman's sword.

"No," I said. "Find a place for him on one of the wagons. Ask Captain Mellet to put one more civilian into his saddle."

I went on to the next huddled figure. It was an old man, and he was quite dead, frozen as he sat. So were the other two. One was an equally aged woman, the other a boy in his teens. I was startled.

"Don't be s'prised, sir," Bikaner told me. "There's somethin' at I've learned, an' that's th' young don't cling t'life that hard. Damned if I know why, but they'll lay down in their tracks long afore a mean old bastard like me's even feelin' puny. Mebbe they're so fresh from th' Wheel they don't mind returnin'."

We moved on without burying the dead—we had no time to gather rocks for their tombs. I muttered a short prayer as we rode away.

The road climbed, not steeply enough so a traveler in normal times might even notice, but it was like a mountain to some of us. Now men and women started dropping, falling off to the sides of the column. Soldiers would kick, curse, help them, but too often to no use. Sometimes these people, desperate to be left alone, desperate for some final peace, would just wander off the track and be lost in the storm.

A KLI warrant, already staggering, trying to shepherd two young boys, told me he thought he'd seen someone stumble away a few minutes ago, a woman he'd tried to help before.

I rode back, and found a path leading to the side. I dismounted, and saw footprints, rapidly being filled as the snow drove down. Leading Lucan, I went after them.

I allowed myself a count of 100 before I must turn back, or chance losing my own way.

I'd reached seventy-five when I heard the snarls, and Lucan whinnied in terror and tried to pull away. Four wolves growled around the sprawled figure of the woman. There was blood on the snow. They saw me, and bared their fangs.

I dropped from the saddle, drew my sword, and started forward, perhaps unwisely, but I could no longer, must no longer, be helpless.

The wolves waited until I was about five feet away, then yapped, turned, and bounded off.

I knelt beside the woman. Her throat was ripped out, but her eyes were closed and there was a peaceful smile on her lips. I lifted her across Lucan's saddle, vowing I'd not leave her for the beasts, and made my way back to the column. We found a place for the corpse, lashed to a wagon's tongue.

The wagons were full, now, and we began mounting people double. At least the horses were strong and well fed, although I knew the strain would drive them under in just a few days.

So it went that day, and halfway through the next. The road wound on and on, never offering any respite. Sometimes the storm clouds blew away, but all they showed us was gray, wet rock, snow, and ice. Tenedos's spell seemed to be working— we had no more encounters with the hill tribes.

None of us looked like soldiers. We were unshaven, with dark circles under our eyes. We'd tied rags around our heads and pulled our helmets down over them, and those of us who had the shabby sheepskin coats we'd used to disguise ourselves as Kaiti wore them over our armor and thanked Irisu for their warmth. I'd given mine to one of the civilians on the second day of the march, and secretly hoped he might fall dead and I'd stumble on his corpse and recover my coat.

I noted a cruel irony. Someone who was weak, unable to walk, would be moved to one of the wagons. But riding produced no warmth, and the storm cut through the rugs and blankets. At each halt there'd be frozen corpses to lift off the wagons, but there'd always be new riders trying for a place to sit.

One wagon was set aside for the dead, and they would be cremated at our noon halt. We had forty soldiers and about seventy civilians as casualties of one sort or another, more than half of them dead.

There was no time, no energy, to bury them, but we could not just abandon the bodies or we might as well be beasts. Tenedos produced a spell. The corpses were piled, words said, and they burned without smoke, without smell, without any more of a flame save a low blue one that looked like the one produced when brandy is ignited.

We had been traveling now for—and it took some thought—eight, no, nine days, and I knew my hoped-for pace of ten miles a day was a joke. But all we could do was push on, push on.

About an hour after the midday meal of the tenth, Tenedos sent down the column for me. I'd been walking with Captain Mellet, and we'd been trying to think if there were some unnecessary baggage aboard the wagons to dump, so even more could ride.

Allori had been riding Lucan, and listening to our conversation intently. Without being bid, she slipped out of the saddle and I mounted, and sent Lucan at a slow trot to the head of the train, just as it was stumbling to a halt.

"It seems the spell is working better, if a little differently than I thought," Tenedos said without preamble. "My little friend appeared a few moments ago, and said that there were enemies ahead, waiting. He'd not been able to blind them with the sorcerous snow, but owed me the duty of a warning.

"Your department now, Legate."

I felt my lips form in a tight, humorless smile.

I turned to Lance Karjan.

"Ride back, Lance, and ask Troop Guide Bikaner if he'd care for an outing. Also tell Captain Mellet I'd like a dozen volunteers."

Karjan nodded, turned to his horse, then stopped.

"Sir," he said, and his eyes were pleading. "Can I—"

I was about to say no, but Tenedos spoke first.

"Take him if he wishes. I'll fend for myself."

I wanted a total of twenty-five volunteers, split between the infantry and cavalry. I could have had 250 if I'd wanted. Among them were Yonge and his hillmen. I chose him and two of his fellows.

I knew approximately where we were on the map, which I'd looked at as little as possible to avoid the heartbreak of seeing how slowly we were progressing toward safety.

I could imagine just where the hillmen would be waiting. It was a very good place indeed, where a small valley belled between two narrow draws. They would wait until we were in the valley, then attack from their hiding places, at the same time sealing both the front and rear exits, and cut us to ribbons at their leisure.

But I saw, even though the map was vague in its details, where I thought the Men of the Hills might well lay themselves open, especially remembering how they'd not bothered to guard their rear in the ambush at the ford.

I assembled my twenty-five volunteers and issued orders. We'd carry swords, knives, bows and arrows, no more, plus ropes. We tied off in five groups of five men and scrambled up the side of the pass. It was a hard climb, moving from boulder to boulder, never sure of our footing, slipping often. I nearly fell half a dozen times, and was pulled to safety by Karjan. I returned the favor four times myself before we reached the ridgeline, perhaps 400 feet above the roadway.

The map was now useless, but I had a feel for the terrain. I closed my eyes so there was no storm, and I was looking down on that tiny valley as if it were a clear summer day. The ridgeline ran almost due north, following the invisible road far below.

We moved along it, just on the far side, so even if there'd been a momentary break we wouldn't be spotted. It was hellish hard, the rocky mountain steeply slanted, sometimes almost vertical.

It took us four hours before we reached the point I wished—or, rather, where I imagined the point to be. We should have been just at the far northern end of that little valley. I gave the last orders and signals.

Now to find a way down—and the only one was little better than a cliff. As commander, I should have gone first, but pride was secondary to logic. I chose Yonge to go first. He unroped, and then tied off on a fresh line, looked over the edge, winced, and checked his knots once more. "Tell me again about those Ureyan women, sir."

Before I could say anything he was gone. At the end of his rope another hillman tied a line onto it and went down, then one of my lances, an experienced man from the eastern mountains, named Varvaro. He'd barely gone three feet when the rope went slack, then was pulled twice, the agreed signal that Yonge had reached safe ground.

We went over the edge after him, and found ourselves on a tiny plateau. It was hardly what I'd call safe ground, since it slanted off at about forty-five degrees. But a small spring bubbled out, still unfrozen, that had carved a ravine that, to my eyes, looked like a highway leading to the road below.

We rolled socks over our boots, so there'd be no clatter as we descended. It didn't make our footing any easier, but we managed to reach level ground without falling or raising an alarm. We were just where I'd hoped to descend—at the far northern end of the valley. Weapons ready, we started forward.

We smelled burning wood and heard the crackle of the fire before we saw anything. Then we saw, dimly through the snow, the hillmen who were one of the ambush's "corks," sealing the valley's northern end. There were sixteen of them.

We went out on line. I waited, then yelped as much like a jackal as I knew how, which was not very, and we rushed them.

We were on them before they had time to cry out, and then it was too late. They scrabbled for their weapons, but our steel was searing into their bodies. In a few moments, the last was down. Without bidding, some of my men went from body to body, making sure all were dead. We needed no betrayal from *our* rear, and mercy had died somewhere along the cruel track from Sayana.

Following the road, we went across the valley to the south. We crept from cover to cover, thoroughly scouting each ravine, each draw, before we passed it.

We came on the rest of the ambushers in one of them, as we'd expected. The hillman, and their horses, had found shelter from the raging winds in a canyon cleft. It was only about fifteen feet deep, but gave excellent cover. Vastly experienced at lying in wait, they knew better than to man exposed positions until they must, and their scouts posted to the south would not have given the warning of the column's arrival. Obviously Tenedos's spell was working, since their *jask*, if any were with them, hadn't sensed us.

We crept out on the rock above them. When we were ready, our bows strung and arrows nocked, we stood as one and fired down into them. There were a few screams, and even pleas for mercy, that went unheard. When the last man was down, the snow splashed with blood, we went into the cleft with our swords. We'd carefully avoided shooting their horses, for they'd be needed.

When we moved on, they were the only living things left in that draw.

They'd posted three scouts at the southern end of the valley. We surprised and slew two of them—the last fled into the growing darkness before we could stop him.

Yonge swore. "It would've been a mighty tale," he said, "if we'd killed every last man. *That* would be a legend that would live long in the hills."

"It'll live longer now there's someone t'do th' tellin'," Karjan pointed out, and Yonge grinned agreement.

We were blood-covered and exhausted, but felt no fatigue, trotting through the pass back to our fellows. The word went down the column and I heard some low cheers. We weren't always helpless victims.

We hastened back through the draw, stopped at the cleft long enough to secure the horses and loot the bodies of their coats, then went on, forcing ourselves to move beyond that second narrow place, out of the valley.

Finally, just before full dark, the pass opened once more, and we found a place to circle our wagons.

I sat huddled against a wagon wheel, Lucan tethered beside me, using a stone to touch up where my dagger's edge had been nicked on the bones of one of the men I'd killed that day. I smelled bad, worse than before, but I was almost warm, wrapped in a stinking sheepskin cloak I'd taken from one of the corpses.

It had even stopped snowing as hard as it had been. I looked up and saw the little girl Allori. She held a cup out to me. I took it and drank the hot tea it held, and felt the warmth spread. She sat beside me.

"I have been thinking, Damastes."

"Oh?"

"You said we are partners."

"And so we are."

"Well, if we are partners, and if I want to open an inn, doesn't that mean you'd help me?"

"Well, that's an idea," I said. "But I'm a soldier, so I'd have to spend a lot of time away."

"That's all right. My mother . . ." and the girl's voice caught for a moment, then she recovered, "always said a man shouldn't be allowed in the kitchen too much or he'd start thinking he was better than he was."

"Your mother was probably right."

"Maybe Jacoba would help, too. I know she likes you. Do you like her?"

"I . . . well, yes. I do."

"Do you like her more than you like me?"

I chose my words carefully.

"I like you both . . . but in different kinds of ways."

"Oh. When I'm older, would you like us both the same way?"

I didn't answer *that* one at all. Instead, I changed the subject.

"Allori, do you know if you have any relatives you can live with until you get old enough to open our inn?"

"I don't think so." Her voice became wistful. "I don't know where I'll go."

"I do," I said. "I know of a place where there's no cold at all."

"Not ever?"

"Not ever. It's warm, and everything's green, and there's all kinds of animals to play with." I talked on, telling her about my parents' estates. If she had no one, they could take her in—

there were more than enough women who'd delight in the little girl. Allori listened intently, her eyes wide. When I ran out of nice things to say about Cimabue, we sat in silence for a minute.

"Maybe I could have my own kitten," she said. "I had one, back . . . back there. But it ran away."

"You can have ten kittens if you want," I promised.

"That would be nice." She got up, then quickly bent over and kissed me on the cheek. "Phew," she said. "You smell awful!" She laughed and was gone in the darkness.

We crept on for two more days without attack. But men, and women, still died from the cold as the storm came back, seemingly doubling its fury. We went on, dully, forcing ourselves, because there was nothing else to do.

Then, less than a day's journey from the end of Sulem Pass, Tenedos came to me.

"The spell's been broken," he said. "I can't *feel* it out there anymore."

"Thak?"

"I don't know. I was afraid to cast any runes, for fear, if it is him, he'd sense us and know just where we are."

I decided when we halted next, about two hours from now, we would reform into proper formation before moving on. If our magical shield had been ripped away, even if we lost half a day, the lost time would be worthwhile, since we were no more than a shambling herd of walking wounded.

But we were not given the chance.

They hit us an hour later. We were about halfway across another of Sulem Pass's occasional valleys when the attack came. It was only by the grace of Isa that we had a bare moment's warning when one group who couldn't stand the suspense broke cover and, screaming, ran toward us.

The hillmen never attacked in an army, we'd been told, because they were too independent, with no minor chieftain willing to give up his small authority for any reason, even the finest of loot. But as with everything else in the Border States, this law was only sometimes a truth, because now the Men of the Hills came at us in close-ranked battalions.

All we had was a few moments to get the civilians to the far side of the road and down.

From somewhere I felt energy surge, and tore away that stinking robe and the headcover that made me look like a beldam, and shouted for my Lancers to turn to.

Other officers and warrants found hidden strength, and the sorry remnants of a company of the Khurram Light Infantry and Cheetah Troop, Seventeenth Ureyan Lancers, formed what would be our last battle line.

"Wait for them," Bikaner was bellowing from the rear. "Let them get close or I'll have th' hide of anyone wastin' a shaft."

The first wave of screaming tribesmen rose before us, and bows thwacked and arrows buried themselves in their targets. The hillman hesitated, took a second volley, and fell back.

Another wave charged through their ranks, and they were hit by our arrows, but had too much momentum.

We cast our bows aside, and they were on us, and the world was a whirling mass of blood and steel. I cut a hillman's legs from under him, parried a slash at my head and impaled the man who'd made it, spun, brushing a spear-thrust away with an arm, feeling another spear clang against my armor, slashed at that man without knowing if I hit him, then felt a searing burn as a blade cut into my upper thigh.

Then there was no one to kill, and the tribesmen were ululating their war cry as they fell back.

I looked down at my wound. It was not severe, but it was gory. I looked around for something to tear up as a bandage, and Karjan was there, with a strip of dirty cloth, winding it around my pants leg.

Another charge came, but this one we drove back with arrows.

The tribesmen pulled back, shocked by their heavy losses, and gave us time to confer.

We were in little better shape—the road was littered with dead.

Tenedos was beside me.

"What can I do?"

"Give me a spell that . . . no. Magic later. Go down the column and get all the civilians forward."

Tenedos was about to ask why, then remembered the way of a soldier, clamped his lips closed, and hurried off.

Captain Mellet came up beside me. We looked off, across the valley. Even through the drifting snow it was easy to see there were many, many hillmen out there.

"Well," Mellet said, "I've killed my ten, but it looks like we've got some slackers. I guess we'll have to go for twenty or thirty each, eh?"

That brought a smile from me. Mellet looked around to make sure no one was in earshot.

"I don't suppose you have anything resembling a plan, Legate?"

"The best I have, sir, is to put the civilians ahead of us, try to keep them moving, and we'll hold them from the rear."

"All the way to Renan?"

"Do you have a better idea?"

"I do." Mellet sighed. "But it's not that much better. The problem is, there's a small matter called death that keeps intruding."

He explained his plan. It wasn't much superior to mine, but it did offer a chance.

"As I said," he finished, "it's either some deaths, or everybody's. Most likely it'll be everybody's regardless. For some reason they didn't use magic this time, but I know they'll set their gods-damned *jask*s on us when they attack next."

The civilians were moving now, coming past us, stumbling, some crying. I saw Jacoba, Allori with her, and managed a smile.

I explained to Tenedos what the infantry captain proposed.

"I do not like it," he said.

"You do not have to like it, Resident-General," Captain Mellet said formally. "We are now dealing with matters in *our* area of supposed expertise. I mean no disrespect, but if you have a demon or two up your sleeve that could turn the tide, now would be an ideal time to produce him, and I'll shut up with a smile."

Tenedos looked at him, and his expression was sad.

"I can offer but three spells," he said. "None of them can prevent the sacrifice. One may reduce the potency of whatever magic they plan to use. I imagine they used none this last time because of the arrogance of their chiefs, who sought to conquer with only steel and cunning.

"I can probably stop that.

"The other two . . . I'd best prepare them now."

He hurried away. In a few minutes, he was ready with his apparatus. The first spell was a weather spell, meant to do no more than increase the strength of the storm. This sounds bizarre, but it could well be vital in our escape.

The second spell was the one against the *jask*s. I do not know what it was, nor if it worked.

As for the third . . .

Captain Mellet paraded his men on the road. We had archers out on the flanks, to make sure the hillmen wouldn't seize the moment and rush us. I thought they were waiting for dusk, to use the gathering darkness as a shield for their final assault. But we still had three hours of light before then.

It tore my heart to see the sorry remnants of his company trying to stand at attention. There'd been 125 of them in Renan. Now, there were no more than fifty, and many of them were wounded.

"Men of the Khurram Light Infantry," Captain Mellet began. "When we took our oath, we swore to serve until death. This is our day.

"This is the time for our final gift to our fellows, the men and women of Numantia we vowed to die for.

" 'That others may live' is a saying I've heard now and again. I cannot think of a better one to light our way back to the Wheel.

"I choose to make my stand here in this valley. Those who wish to fulfill their vows . . . join me now."

The warrants and two surviving legates were the first to cross to him. Then the privates followed, first by ones and twos, then in a stream. At the end, there were only three foot soldiers standing by themselves, shamefaced.

"Very well," Captain Mellet said, and his voice held no anger or scorn. "You have found your vows too heavy. I release you from them. Put down your weapons and go with the civilians, and obey all orders they give you."

One man did just that, but the other two looked at each other and hurried over to where their fellows stood.

"The Khurram Light Infantry will form up," Captain Mellet shouted.

I saw something wonderful then. There were seriously wounded KLI men who'd been in the wagons that'd gone past us. Now I saw some of them coming back, hobbling toward us, the blind led by the halt, a man with but one arm and a wounded leg using his sword as a crutch. We tried to argue, but none of them would listen, and so we let these bravest of the brave join their fellows.

Tenedos was ready with the final spell, and he anointed each KLI man in turn.

We moved off, just as the magically enhanced storm roared in. We moved as fast as we could, in the strangest order imaginable. At our front were ten lancers, then the civilians and the wagons. The Lancers were behind them, in mass, and to the rear, the KLI.

We'd marched only a few hundred yards when our movement was seen, and the hillmen rushed once more. But they'd made no plans and the attack was ragged and easily driven back.

They tried again, and then we were at the end of the valley.

"The Khurram Light Infantry will take battle positions," Captain Mellet shouted, and the foot soldiers spread out, across the narrows.

"Legate á Comabue," he shouted. "Tell them in Numantia of us!

"Tell them there are still men on the Frontiers who know how to die!"

He saluted, and I ordered my Lancers to attention and returned the salute, unashamed tears cutting through the dirt on my cheeks.

Then we marched away, through the pass.

The third spell Tenedos had cast was to make the foot soldiers feel little pain, so they could be struck and struck again and still fight on.

I heard battle begin behind us, and I began praying, to Isa, to Panoan, even to Saionji herself, to grant them an easy return to the Wheel and elevation to the highest in their next life.

The Khurram Light Infantry's last battle was still raging when we went out of earshot.

The tempest crashed around us as we went on and on. We stopped for a few hours to rest and eat. Now there was more than enough room on the wagons. Seer Tenedos examined my wound closely. "A nice clean slash." He muttered a spell over it. "This takes its strength from your own body's reserves. If you were old and feeble, it would be like a vampire on your energy, but you've got more than enough to spare."

There were no more enemies with swords. Now our foes were the cold, the wind, the wet, and they slew as gleefully as the bloodiest-handed hillman.

I found Jacoba and Allori, and mounted them on Lucan. I walked beside them, at the head of the column.

Behind me were the Seer Tenedos and Lance Karjan. I never saw either of them stumble or weaken as we went on and on, the road winding through the cliffs close on either side.

We stopped somewhere, ate, and, I suppose, slept for a while, then went on.

I was moving numbly, limping, holding my last reserves close, knowing there could well be a final battle before we reached the end of Sulem Pass. In my heart, I felt we were lost, doomed. None of us would ever reach the flatlands and the safety of Urey.

I looked up once at Jacoba, and could barely recognize her,

a scarf pulled close around her face, ice caked on the shoulders of her coat.

Allori was a small bundle of woolens sitting in front of her. I saw a wisp of blond hair from under her cap and with fumbling frozen fingers tucked it back. The little girl said something, I guess it was thanks, but the wind blew her words away.

We went on.

I don't know how long the snow had stopped before I noticed it, but all at once there was no knife-wind cutting me. It was a miracle.

A second miracle came. The rock walls closed in, until they were cliffs only a few hundred feet apart. Then they were gone, and the land was flat around us.

We were on the far side of Sulem Pass. We were beyond Kait, beyond the Border States. We had reached Urey. I felt life, and hope, surge.

I looked back. There was a line of staggering men and women behind me, and behind them, wagons and then, to the rear, ragged men who were Cheetah Troop, Seventeenth Ureyan Lancers.

I tried to smile, and felt the skin of my cheeks crack. I caught up with Lucan.

"We're safe!" I shouted.

Jacoba pulled her scarf aside, and looked at me, numbly at first, then my words penetrated. She gave Allori a hug. "We're alive!" she said, her voice as shattered as mine.

But there was no response from the little girl. Her head was sunk on her chest, her eyes shut. I pulled her cap off, held the back of my hand in front of her nostrils.

A single snowflake fell on my hand and stayed there, not melting.

Allori Pares had died, without our realizing it, within the hour.

My triumph was ashes.

JACOBA

The crew had barely set the long houseboat's two anchors when dark clouds raced across the sun, and a freezing rain shattered the lake's mirror.

I sprawled on pillows covered with silk and furs in an open pavilion on the boat's top deck, wearing nothing but a long kilt loosely tied at the waist. But I felt no cold: The four sides of the pavilion were covered with a marvelous witch-spelled fabric, a thin cloth as clear as glass that blocked the winter's chill, and an open fire of sweet-smelling woods burned to one side.

It was midmorning, and there were no other boats on the lake, since the Time of Heat was the most popular season for these craft, not midwinter. The crew, twenty-five strong, had gone into their own below-deck quarters when they were satisfied the boat was secure and we lacked for nothing. If we wished anything more, I had but to ring the small bell set on a table nearby.

There was a pewter mug of a warm, dark drink infused with spices beside me. I sipped, then continued staring at the lake. The cold and pain of the long flight from Sayana drained, and warmth crept into my bones.

"Is this what I was wearing in your dream?" Jacoba asked.

She wore a long robe with a high collar that cradled her smiling face like a loving hand, and then reached to the rugs on the boat's deck. But it was hardly modest, since it was made of a diaphanous black material that hid nothing from the dark areolae around her nipples to the tuft of hair at her sex.

"Not quite," I said. "Nothing so virginal."

"Then away with it," and she slipped her shoulders back, and the robe fell away to pool around her ankles.

She stretched one foot out, as graceful as a dancer, and ran it up my inner thigh, lifting my kilt.

"In your dream, what did I do?"

"Uhh, you strangled me."

"Nothing before that?"

"There *were* some . . . goings-on I seem to recollect," I said.

"In my dream," she said, her voice becoming throaty, "here is what *I* recollect doing."

She knelt, untied my kilt, and pulled it away. Her tongue traced the ridge of my cock, then she took me into the warmth of her mouth.

"What you're doing . . . meets with my own memories," I managed. Her tongue caressed me for a few moments more.

"Next, this is what happened," she said, and, as in my own dream, she bestrode me and I thrust into her. Her hands caressed my chest as we rose and fell, her long black hair brushing my face. Her sighs came closer together, and merged with my own harsh breathing, and then she cried out once, twice, three times, as I drove hard and then we collapsed on our sides as we died the small death.

It had not always been like this. . . .

We'd marched only a few miles from the mouth of the pass when a roving patrol of the Tenth Hussars came across our column. Their commander wanted us to stop where we were and they'd ride for help. But all of us were obsessed with one thing: to get as far away from the nightmare of Sulem Pass and the Border States as we could, and so we kept moving. I learned later the legate in charge of the patrol drove his men at full gallop to the nearest heliograph tower, and that day word of the tragedy went out to all Numantia.

When we stopped that night near a small settlement, villagers came out to help, to do what they could, bringing warm food, firewood, tents, and blankets. All that night wagons arrived with more comforts from Renan and the other cities of Urey. When we moved on late the next morning, none of us were afoot. I was particularly grateful to be able to ride Lucan again, since my leg was throbbing and stiff.

But men and women kept dying from wounds, cold, exhaustion—another thirty of us returned to the Wheel before we reached Renan.

A small part of me wished to curl in a ball and sleep forever, but I could not. There were Lancers to take care of, and Numantians to be responsible for. My discipline held me in a mailed fist.

We were met by a host of dignitaries outside the city, and told we were granted the honors of Renan, and all Urey was honored to provide all we needed—shelter, food, anything— until we recovered.

We listened numbly, not knowing what to make of anything.

I myself had expected to be met with by the provost and arrested. I considered my performance the most dismal of failures. I'd left Renan with about 300 soldiers, including the company of KLI. There were only six of the foot soldiers still alive, only because they were too sore wounded to climb out of the sick-carts and join their fellows. Of the 150 Lancers I'd ridden so proudly away from Mehul with, sixty-five were left, and most of them were sick or wounded. Of the others, about half of Tenedos's staff lived, and only one-third of the Numantians we'd tried to rescue. If there was a bright note, it was that only one of Yonge's hillmen had been killed in the flight. To me, this was dark catastrophe.

Yet when we rode through the gates of Renan, it was as heroes. The city had declared a holiday, and the lamp standards and flagpoles of the city fluttered with bright banners, and the streets were lined with cheering men and women.

I felt I'd never been party to such a fraud. I suppose Tenedos guessed what I was thinking, because he issued orders that no soldier was to talk to anyone, not officials, not cityfolk, not inquirers from the broadsheets.

We were quartered in a huge palace on a lake, each of us with his own room.

Luxurious sprung wagons arrived for my Lancers, to return them to Mehul, but they refused. They'd ridden out on horseback, and they'd return the same way.

I'd wanted to return with them, and bury myself in the safe routine of garrison duties, but Tenedos's orders had been very firm: I was, by the gods, assigned to him until otherwise ordered, and there had been no orders, so my duty was clear.

I was presented with an oilskin pouch by the young legate who was to take the men back to Mehul. I thought him young, even though he was slightly older than I was. I thought the last of my youth burned away by the horror of Kait.

There were other surprises to come, but none as great as what the pouch contained. It was a single sheet of parchment, containing but one sentence:

> *Legate Damastes á Cimabue:*
> *I find that your performance commanding Cheetah Troop to be in the highest tradition of the Seventeenth Lancers.*

It was signed by Domina Herstal.

To a civilian, that sounds like nothing, but to a soldier in a unit with as high a standard as the Lancers, there could be no greater praise. But I still did not believe it.

I showed the dispatch to Tenedos, and he nodded. "It is but a beginning, Damastes." I had no idea what he was talking about.

I bade Bikaner and the others farewell, and do not know how I was able to keep from crying like a child. I said some words, which were completely inadequate, and wondered if any of them knew how much they meant to me, and how they would always hold a place in my heart. I thought I saw Troop Guide Bikaner swallow convulsively when I saluted them, and Lance Karjan seemed to have acquired a cold, because he kept blowing his nose as the last of Cheetah Troop went slowly out of the gate.

I returned to the quarters I'd been assigned, rooms even more palatial than those I'd had in Sayana. Not that it mattered—I would have been as happy, or unhappy, in a single-room hovel.

Sitting on the floor just inside the door were two small cases and on the bed was Jacoba.

I made myself smile politely, and asked her how I could serve her.

She looked deep into my eyes, then shook her head, as if not finding something she'd been expecting. Finally, she said, "In the pass, we talked about how I might repay you for saving me, about what might happen . . . if we lived."

I remembered, but said nothing. For some reason, I felt a bit of not-rational anger. All I wished was to be left alone, and it seemed that wish would never be granted.

"Is this Tenedos's idea?"

Anger flashed in her eyes, she began to snap an answer, then caught herself.

"Laish Tenedos pays my wages to make his desserts. No more." She stood. "Do you wish me to leave?"

I almost said yes. But there was one tiny bit of sense left, and I shook my head. She put her hand on my shoulder. After a moment, I put my hand over hers.

I felt little hunger, but forced myself to go to one of the dining halls and have a bit of soup. Then I walked in one of the gardens, not feeling the chill for the greater cold within, until it was quite late.

Jacoba was already in the great bed, carefully curled to one side. I undressed as quietly as I knew how, and slipped in beside her, lying on my side. I felt no passion, no lust, not much of anything in particular.

Her hand touched my bandaged leg, then moved up to my back and caressed it, not so much sensual as reassuring. But the ice within me was too thick, and after a moment she sighed and rolled over. After a time her breathing became regular, and after a longer time, I slept.

The next day, Tenedos summoned me.

"You remember I said yesterday that your congratulations from your domina was just the beginning?" He held up a sheaf of dispatches. "Here are special orders, sent by heliograph. You and I, and my staff and some of those who were with us on the terrible journey from Sayana, are requested by the Rule of Ten to attend them immediately, and give them a full accounting of the evils worked on Numantians by the barbarians of the Border States.

"We are to await the arrival of the paddleship *Tauler,* which will be dispatched within a few days," he went on, half-reading, "during which time we are to gather our strength and enjoy the comforts the city leaders of Renan have been directed to provide.

"Then we are to proceed directly to Nicias and await their pleasure." He looked up. "This is where it shall start, my friend. They thought they were sending me into exile or perhaps my death, but Saionji wanted something else.

"Now they shall be forced to listen to me and realize the time has come for change.

"I tell you, Damastes, none of those who died with us died in vain if it brings about the great renaissance I've dreamt of." He stood and paced back and forth excitedly. "Yes, I can sense it, I can feel it. This is the beginning."

I found polite words, but felt no inner thrill. But if Laish Tenedos, the Seer Tenedos, wished me to accompany him to Nicias, that was as good a place as any. Why not? Far from these mountains, perhaps the ice would melt.

But it did not take that long.

That night, both Jacoba and I walked through the gardens. It was cold, and we wore heavy cloaks. We found ourselves standing side by side under one of the huge trees of Urey. Even though it was the Time of Storms, the monstrous multicolored leaves still clung to the branches. A few feet from us was one of the many sculptures the palace's gardens were filled with. I paid it little mind.

Jacoba lithely pulled herself up onto a thick branch that curled a few feet above the ground, so her eyes were at the same height as mine.

The night was sharp and clear. I looked out at the mountains, the awful peaks that marked the border to the Border States.

As I watched, a shimmer grew on them, the borealis. Someone spoke to me, a voice of thunder, a voice of silence, and perhaps it was the voice of a goddess, perhaps the voice of a little girl. Perhaps it came from the gods, perhaps from my good, hard common sense.

What the voice said was not in words, but it was very clear.

The world is death, the world is nothing but pain and a desperate fight to avoid returning to the Wheel, and then an equally headlong rush to be taken by it.

If that is how you choose to see it that is the way life is and always shall be, the voice went on. *But do you think Captain Mellet and his men wanted death? Didn't they want life, want warmth, love, and the giggling embrace of a woman?*

So Saionji took them, took them and the girl Allori. Does she also now own you?

"No," I said, and wasn't aware I'd spoken aloud, vehemently, until Jacoba said "What?" in a startled manner.

"I'm sorry," I said, and turned away from the mountains and death and realized she was very close. Her lips were parted, and her breath was very sweet.

It seemed appropriate to kiss her, and so I did. Her arms fumbled for a moment, then found the entrance to my cloak and pulled me closer to her. I kissed her again, a very long kiss.

"I'm back," I said.

Somehow she understood, or appeared to.

"That's good."

I opened my cloak so it covered us both and we held each

other, me standing, her on the branch, for a very long time, without moving. I kissed her once more, and her legs came around me, and took me into another embrace.

It was warm, comforting, welcoming me, and I felt my spirits lift.

Jacoba giggled.

"What's funny?" I asked.

"That statue."

I peered at it through the gloom, and was grateful for the darkness. I still had some innocence. The stone showed some god loving a nymph. He held her lifted above the ground, hands cupped around her buttocks, her legs wrapped around him, and on both their faces were expressions of goatish glee.

"What's funny about it?"

"You *know* a man carved it."

"How can you tell?" I wondered. "Other than it's, uh, fairly exact."

"Ah, my handsome young cavalryman, but that's where you're wrong. It's not exact at all."

"Why not?"

"Men aren't that strong," she said. "At least not for very long. If anybody . . . even a god . . . tried to make love like that, he'd be sure to fall. Probably on her, too."

"Ah-hah," I said. "Further proof, my pastry chef, you should stick to matters of the kitchen, and not theorize wildly."

"Prove I am wrong," she said. "That is, if your leg is up to it."

"It's not my leg that's up," I murmured, as my hands slid beneath her cloak, and lifted her tunic, and her small breasts sprang against my palms, nipples hard and firm. I massaged them, while my lips sought hers, then kissed down the silk of her neck. Her breath came faster against my ear.

She wore some sort of belted kirtle, and her hands unfastened it and pulled it away, then busied themselves with the ties of my trousers.

I moved both my hands down her sides and across her stomach, fingers entering and gently caressing her. She gasped pleasure. I slid my hands under her thighs and picked her up from the branch. Her hand held my cock steady, and I let her slip down onto me, and she shuddered as I drove deep, breath shrilling, gasping and then she buried her shriek into the wool of my cloak as I shuddered and spasmed inside her.

We stood like that forever.

Then she murmured, "You cheated. You used the branch for a brace."

So I had, holding her against the tree as we drove together.

"You still haven't proved you were right," she said.

Still inside her, I lifted her away from the tree and carefully knelt, until she lay on her cloak, mine serving as blanket. I felt myself growing strong, and moved within her. Her legs slid up around my waist and she lifted against me.

When we came back into the palace it was very late, and I was very glad no one was about, for we looked exactly like what we were, with damp leaves everywhere and clothes muddied in the most obvious places.

I was back from that dark realm of death and ice.

I sought Tenedos out the next morning to apologize as subtly as I could for not showing the proper enthusiasm for our summons to Nicias.

"The very man I was about to look up," he said heartily before I could speak. "Tell me, Damastes, poor lad, do you feel sick?"

"Not at all, sir."

"Oh dear," he said. "The disease you have is truly dreadful, since one of the signs is the carrier is unaware of his state."

I noted the smile on his face, and waited. I was becoming accustomed to Tenedos's way of dealing with matters.

"So I am sick, sir. Why?"

"Sit down, and I'll explain. What do you think will happen when we reach Nicias?"

I thought about it for a few moments. "Forgive me if I sound like a fool, sir. But I'd guess that the Rule of Ten want us to testify as to what happened."

"Of course. So they said in their orders. What comes next?"

"Now I'm using some of what you told me, about them wanting to settle the Border States, and using you as a pretext for action. I'd guess they'll mobilize the army and, as soon as the Time of Dews permits campaigning, march south against Kait.

"As for us . . . well, I suppose I'll return to the Lancers, and you'll do whatever you want."

"Let's ignore us for the moment and go back to the former matter. Before this morning, I would have agreed with you as to the Rule of Ten's intents. But I breakfasted with the domina of the Twentieth Heavy Cavalry this morning."

The Twentieth, the Lancers, and the Tenth Hussars were the three elite formations responsible for keeping peace along the border.

"I imagined," Tenedos continued, "that he would have been alerted to such a plan, or do I still not understand the military mind?"

"No, sir. You're correct. Of course the Rule of Ten would send some sort of confidential missive to him, since his unit should be one of the first to take the field. If I were planning the campaign I'd use the Lancers to drive through Sulem Pass and the Twentieth to hold it, so soldiery from the flatlands could enter Kait with the fewest possible casualties."

"Well, he's heard nothing. I gently sounded him about the matter, and he was most surprised he'd not been alerted, given what happened to us."

Anger flooded me. "Are you saying the Rule of Ten won't do anything?"

"I'm afraid that may be exactly what will happen. They'll be terribly outraged at the horror of it all, and then send some sort of threatening note, which Achim Fergana will ignore, and life will continue."

"Son of a bitch!" I said.

"Yes. I've often thought of our rulers in similar words."

"What about the Tovieti? What about Thak?"

"Ignore it and it shall go away. They've ruled Numantia for

generations with that policy. Why should things be different now?"

Tenedos still smiled, but his expression was utterly humorless. I controlled myself. Very well. If that was to happen, I was a soldier, and I would continue to serve. Politics were not my affair.

"What does this have to do with my being sick?"

"After I returned from my meal with the good domina, I considered the options. What I need is time, time to send some dispatches north."

"As you did when we recovered the dolls?"

"Exactly. Perhaps if I sound our horn quite loudly it shall be impossible to mute when we arrive in person. So I sent a message north to the Rule of Ten just an hour ago that you had fallen ill. I said that we would be delayed for a week, and apologized for the delay. Certainly I could not entertain the notion of coming without you, since you have knowledge of important military matters far beyond my ken, so the *Tauler*'s passage can be put off for a few days."

The anger ebbed, and I grinned.

"Just how sick am I to be while you're being a one-man symphony?"

"Quite invisibly ill."

He handed me an envelope.

"You mentioned once, back in Sayana, that you wished to spend time on one of the Ureyan houseboats. Well, it is not spring nor summer, but arrangements have been made."

"May I ask a favor, sir?"

"You need not," he said. "That also has been taken care of. I guess I can live without my desserts for a week." He looked down at his body, which was regaining its former sleekness. "Someone commented last night I was putting on weight. I suspect she prefers the emaciated look, but be that as it may.

"I want you to perform your disappearing act within the hour. There shall be an ambulance at the rear entrance to the palace to take you and Jacoba to your 'hospital.' "

I saluted him, and hurried off.

* * *

Jacoba had already gotten the message, and her case was packed. I'd seen her open but one, and asked her, as I rolled my kit, what was in the other.

"My cooking tools."

"Those two cases are all you own?"

"All I wish to, right now. When the time comes to own other things, I shall know it, I believe. But at the moment I prefer to travel fast and quickly."

The week on the lavish houseboat floated past easily and quickly. I'm afraid we didn't avail ourselves of many of the services that were available. The lavish meals were all too often eaten cold, the moment having seized us. Since Jacoba was not much more fond of drink than I, the expensive wines went untasted. Nor did we see much of the winter splendor of the lake, even though the crew moved us every day from place to place.

What we did was make love. Sometimes it was carefully planned, a building crescendo in one of the luxurious bedchambers. But it was as likely to be a sudden burst of passion.

Once, when we'd sent throw rugs and a small table flying, Jacoba murmured afterward, her head against my chest, that whoever owned the boat would have to have it most thoroughly cleaned, since every room now smelled of nothing but musk and semen. "Or, perhaps he'll leave it as it is, and try to find for his next client some rich old fool with a young wife who wishes some aphrodisiacal assistance."

I said I was delighted to be doing such an altruistic service, but that her knee was digging into my side, and could she move a little?

"I could," she said. "Tell me how. Should we consider whether my heels would fit comfortably behind your neck?"

I said I thought that could be a marvelous experiment, and the world swam away yet again.

"I think I need a vacation from our vacation," I murmured as we left our carriage and reentered the palace.

"Weakling," Jacoba said. "I've been looking forward to getting back, and having a few hours to show these foolish Ureyans a sabayon is *not* a custard." Her superior had not survived the journey from Sayana, and so Jacoba had been promoted to his place.

Resident-General Tenedos found me in my rooms, where I was contemplating a nap. I'd found that the *Tauler* had not arrived, although it was expected momentarily.

"My sorcery says you are most miraculously healed," he congratulated me.

"You appear most jovial, sir," I said.

"I am, I am. I have had some response to the small missives I sent to Nicias that suggest the Rule of Ten may not commit its usual vacillations after our testimony, although I frankly believe cowardice will always out."

"What happens if it does?" I asked. "I'd hate to think my men and the others died in vain."

"Damastes, don't ever think that. The battlefield is always changing. If it is not fought here, well then, it shall be mounted on another day, in another place.

"History cannot be turned back on itself, which the Rule of Ten do not know as yet.

"My day is drawing very near. Which is why I wished to speak to you. I've considered how we should appear once we reach Nicias, and think it would be best if we appear most wonderful and exotic.

"To that end, I sought our hillman Yonge, who is making a most disgusting satyr of himself in the whorehouses of this city. I think the harlots were glad to see his back.

"He was delighted at the thought of accompanying us on our journey, especially when I told him he was to be assigned directly to you. He's quite determined to copy your style of leading, for which I wish him nothing but luck."

Tenedos's light tone vanished. "I'll also be taking four of the poor foot soldiers with us. Perhaps when the Rule of Ten see these men who've given an arm, a leg, or an eye they might be less likely to pass the matter off with an empty threat."

Tenedos took a deep breath, visibly forcing a change of mood.

"I've also written a letter to your domina, and he agreed that certain of the soldiers in Cheetah Troop could be detached to join us.

"I'll welcome your suggestions. Remember, we wish men who'll be very colorful, sending the starkness of the Frontiers deep into the hearts of these city men. And wasn't that a well-turned phrase?"

I thought.

"Lance Karjan . . . the one who was your bodyguard in the pass. I'd also be very pleased to have Troop Guide Bikaner," I said, "but I doubt if the domina will give him up. Besides, he'll be busy rebuilding Cheetah Troop up from fresh recruits.

"The archer, Curti, although I'd take him more for his talents than appearance. If I'm allowed one other, that gaur who walks on two legs, Svalbard.

"Maybe if we can't get the Rule to listen, we can turn him loose with a bludgeon and let him provide his own brand of logical convincement."

"Careful, Legate," Tenedos warned. "You're spending too much time around me. You're starting to sound positively treasonous."

I grinned. "One question, sir. Who are you taking to provide this, umm, color you seem to think is vital?"

"Why I'm surprised," Tenedos said. "First, a sorcerer worth his potions needs no outside bullshit to baffle.

"Secondly, Damastes, what do you think *you* are?"

A day later the *Tauler* churned its way to the docks in Urey. It was decked with bunting from stem to stern, and a band played gaily on its foredeck.

Its officers and crew were uniformed, and the ship shone as if it had just been launched.

There were barely seventy of us to make the journey, less than a quarter of the usual complement of passengers. The

Tauler was to be ours exclusively, and we were told again and again that anything we wished would be provided for, nothing could be too great for the heroes of the Border States. I tried to lead Lucan and Rabbit aboard myself, and I thought the hostler would die of shame. I tried to give him a coin, and he was even more shocked.

Two stewards led me to my cabin, which was on the top deck of the paddle wheeler, its large portholes looking directly over the ship's bows. There were three rooms, a bedchamber, a sitting room, and an enormous bathchamber. There were four attendants whose sole duty was keeping me happy. I wondered what the suite cost in normal circumstances and shook my head. I would most likely have to loot an entire province to afford it.

The Seer Tenedos had his cabin across the passageway. Its door stood open, and I noted three young women making themselves easy within. The first was one of the women who'd shared his bed in Sayana, the others were maidens he'd met in Renan. One I'd been introduced to as the daughter of one of that city's elders. The city *had* given its all to make us happy.

As for me, I had Jacoba, and wanted nothing more.

She bounced twice, experimentally, on the springs of the large bed.

"I wonder what my mother would say if she could see me now," she said.

"Perhaps . . . shameless doxy?"

"Not likely, since she was kept by one of our district's counselors, and she told me she was never quite sure who my father was, other than he was certainly not that old lecher.

"She'd most likely be proud of me," Jacoba went on, "and tell me to not waste a single second of this time."

She unstrapped her sandals, kicked them off, and leaned back on the bed, bringing one knee up and letting it fall to the side and sliding her dress up over her bare, brown thighs.

"Come here, Damastes," she murmured. "I always listened to my mother's advice."

* * *

Sometimes we had our meals sent to the cabin, sometimes we went to the dining room, so Jacoba could evaluate the wares of her competitors and, she added, "steal any ideas worth the thieving." I used the excuse of letting my wound heal, although, thanks mostly to Tenedos's magic, my leg was nearly completely mended.

Seer Tenedos also held to his cabin for most of the journey, and when he did appear his three women danced close attendance on him. I was amused—they behaved like pheasant hens doting on their cock at the start of mating season.

I did encounter him alone late one night.

He was leaning on the top deck's railing, staring back at our wake. I could tell he had been drinking, although his speech was unslurred.

We talked of this and that, then, without preamble, he said, "Are you ready to go back?"

"Back where?"

"Into Kait. But not as a legate, and not at the head of a single troop of cavalry."

I looked at him curiously. Perhaps part of me never wanted to see that country again, not its sere peaks, not its dry deserts, and above all not its treacherous, deadly people. But I knew that was where my duty lay, and most likely the rest of my career would be spun out in the Border States.

"Of course, sir."

Tenedos nodded once, as if that was the answer he'd expected, and walked off, without saying good night.

I stared after him. Suddenly I had questions that I'd not be able to ask him on the morrow when he was sober, and I'd missed my chance now.

How would he be able to decide what rank I might gain, let alone what commands I might have?

I wondered then, and have wondered many times since, if being a seer does allow a slight glimpse into the future. Or was Tenedos merely speaking from his own soaring ambition?

* * *

"I don't think I can come anymore," Jacoba whispered.

"I *know* I can't."

"Where'd the pillow go?"

"It's right over . . . no. It got kicked to the floor. With the blankets. Here."

I kissed her soft wetness once more, then turned end for end and lay beside her. She put her head on my shoulder. I stroked her back sleepily.

"What happens," I said, after a time, "when we reach Nicias?"

Jacoba moved away, and rolled onto her stomach.

"You mean with us?"

"Yes."

Jacoba took a deep breath. "Don't misunderstand me, Damastes, but 'us' stops when we get to the city."

I was suddenly completely awake, feeling the world shudder around me, although to be honest I'd wondered how our affair would continue. Having little money, I wouldn't be able to afford to find her apartments during my stay in Nicias. When I returned to the Lancers, there'd be no place for her, and I doubted she'd want to leave the capital for a staid, sleepy garrison town. Even if I wished to wed, which I certainly did not at this time, legates are not permitted to marry save under the most extraordinary circumstances. And I could hardly expect her to find living quarters on Rotten Row as a poverty-stricken officer's mistress.

"Can I ask why?"

"There's not anyone else," she said. "There hasn't been since before I took the job with Tenedos. And it's not that I don't . . . care about you. Maybe I even love you, although I'm not sure what the word means, really."

"Then where's the problem?"

"The problem is Seer Tenedos," she said. "Let me tell you something about myself. I'm not very adventurous."

"Of *course* you aren't," I said. "That's why you took a nice, safe job making sweets for a magician in the Border States."

"There was a bad time in my life then. Something . . . somebody that meant a lot to me turned out to be different than I thought. And I'd been cooking in the same damned place for almost three years, working for a pig who'd never teach me his secrets and ordered me around like I was his bonded slave.

"I heard about the position and applied for it. I guess I thought there'd be something glamorous, going to a faraway land, living in a mansion, and making the daintiest of morsels for noblemen and diplomats. Instead . . ." She laughed ruefully. "No. This has been enough adventure for the rest of my life.

"Let me tell you what my dream is, Damastes. I want, someday, to own my own restaurant. Not a big one, and not in the center of a city. Somewhere on the outskirts, near some rich estates.

"I'll have customers who don't mind paying for the best, but whose palates aren't sophisticated enough to tell when the meringue's a little scorched.

"As for a man, I'd want someone who's steady. Loyal. Good enough in bed. A nice man who won't get tired of me, or mind if I get a little fat.

"Children, maybe three or four.

"A nice quiet life, where the biggest dramas are whether the oysters are delivered on time, or if the melon has gone bad, or stopping little Fredrik from pushing his sister into the water barrel.

"Is that the life you want, Damastes?"

I was silent.

"Of course not," she went on. "I can *feel* greatness. Laish Tenedos will be a great man, greater than he is today. Whether he accomplishes all his dreams . . . I don't know. I'm not sure there *are* any limits to what he wants.

"As for you, well, I can see you tall, dignified, perhaps a bit of gray at your temples. A general of cavalry, respected by his country. Perhaps a count, with great estates and a beautiful lady waiting for you at one of your mansions.

"Perhaps you would go for a ride one day, with your staff, and stop by a humble inn for your midday meal.

"I wonder if we would recognize each other?"

"That makes me feel very sad," I said quietly.

"Why should it? We are as Umar made us, we strive to fulfill what Irisu wishes us to become, and we fight as best we can against Saionji as she destroys us. Then, at the end, we welcome her embrace, return to the Wheel, and she grants us rebirth.

"What can be sad about that?"

The right words took a while to form.

"It's sad," I said finally, "because I want to think we're more than small helpless beings on a treadmill."

"Of course you do," she said. "And that's why you'll be a general, and I'll be an innkeeper.

"But enough of that. We've still almost a week before we reach Nicias." She yawned. "Do me a favor. Get the oil from that stand, and rub it into my back before we go to sleep. My skin's terribly dry."

I obeyed, poured some of the oil, which smelled of orange blossoms, onto my hand, and slowly, gently, began rubbing it across her shoulder blades and then lower and lower still.

After a time she said, "You have a very loose idea of just where my back is." Her breath caught sharply. "That is *certainly* not my back."

"Do you want me to stop?"

"No. Oh no. Put another finger in me. No. Back there. Yes. Deeper. Oh gods. Oh, Jaen."

She moaned. I rubbed oil on my cock, rose to my knees, slipped the pillow from under her head, rolled it into a cylinder and slipped it just under her pelvis. I moved between her thighs, as she opened them. I caressed her sex with the head of my cock from its beginnings to where it ended, once, twice, three times, then slipped it between her buttocks and touched her tight rosebud.

"There," I whispered. "Do you want me there?"

"Oh yes," she said. "Yes. There. In me. Now, Damastes, now!"

I pushed, and there was resistance, then her ring relaxed, then clenched firm as I slipped into warmth. I cared nothing more about Nicias, generals, or anything else as we spun higher and higher into the heavens.

Every boat that had ever been built came to meet us as the *Tauler* thrashed its way up to the flag-bedecked dock. People were cheering, blowing whistles and horns, beating on drums. There were more organized bands ashore, each playing a different melody, although as we neared shore they reached some kind of agreement and broke into the Numantian anthem. Unfortunately none of them began at the same moment nor in the same key, so the cheery cacophony continued.

All of Nicias was behind the rope barricades at the end of the dock, barely held back by a cordon of brightly uniformed cavalrymen. These were the Golden Helms of Nicias, parade soldiers whose panoply was reserved for the greatest events.

The twin gangplanks banged down, and the crowd bellowed. I thought the line of soldiers would give way, and wondered if our fate was to be trampled in reverent honor.

Jacoba stood beside me, her two cases at her feet.

"Well," I began, looking for exactly the right words.

Jacoba put her arms around me, kissed me once, then pulled free from my embrace.

She picked up her cases and ran swiftly up the gangway to the dock. She glanced back, then vanished in the crowd.

A piece of my soul went with her.

FOURTEEN

THE RULE
OF TEN

I f I'd thought being a hero in Sayana was overwhelming, now we were drowned. The cheering crowd swept down on us and caught Seer Tenedos and myself up in their arms. They began carrying us off, where I knew not. I think we were lugged through every street in the capital, whether boulevard or alley, and everyone wished to touch us, throw flowers at us, or shout offers to pleasure us in as many ways as existed, from food to bed.

I managed to keep a smile on my face, and to pretend as if I were greeting people, although in the hubbub I couldn't be heard and was able to save my voice.

Tenedos bowed, waved, gestured as if he were a priest instead of a seer. His eyes gleamed with pleasure.

For a moment, the naked adulation was seductive, but then the thought came, What would it be like if next time the crowd hated you? These same loving hands would tear you apart in seconds.

Eventually we were brought to the bridge that crosses a branch of the Latane River to the moat-surrounded Rule of Ten's palace. The crowd would have carried us over the bridge, but there were three lines of dismounted Golden Helms blocking them, and two lines of the city's wardens in front of them. We were grudgingly let down. Tenedos waved for silence, and eventually the yammering died away a bit.

"Great people of Numantia and Nicias," he shouted, and then the crowd bellowed its pleasure, and I heard no more, although his lips kept moving. He motioned—back away, toward the bridge—and I obeyed. When we reached the wardens I sagged in relief, and realized I'd been terrified of what could have happened in that crowd. They swiftly escorted us through the cavalrymen and across the square to the broad steps that led into the palace.

Waiting for us was a man in robes faced with multicolored embroidery, who carried a staff of gold and ivory. "I bid you welcome," he shouted so the crowd behind could hear. "I am Olynthus, chamberlain for the Rule of Ten. In their name, I grant you the freedom of the city and the gratitude of all Numantia. We shall see you are properly honored." His voice went down to normal. "The journey and your, er, most tumultuous reception by our citizenry must have been tiring." He waved the staff, and two bowing servitors appeared. "Since you are high in the esteem of the Rule, we wish to offer you our own hospitality, and bid you follow these men to rooms which I trust will not disappoint."

I saluted, and Tenedos bowed. Hidden trumpets blared, and the two servants beckoned.

I wondered what sort of quarters we would be lodged in. Since this was the third palace I'd guested in, I felt I was becoming a bit of a connoisseur. I'd expected this to be the grandest of them all.

I was somewhat disappointed. I noted that the carpet we walked on, while still magnificent, was beginning to show a bit of threads at the center. The paintings on the walls had begun to fade somewhat, and the inlaid wallpaper was stained here and there. I saw that the uniforms of the various palace servants we passed were immaculate, but just a little shabby.

The Palace of the Rule of Ten, in short, looked like the residence of a respected uncle, someone who'd gotten rich years earlier, arranged his manse to please himself, and then let things slide quietly downhill.

But most of these perceptions came later, when I thought about what had happened. Now my nerves were on edge, waiting to see what the morrow would bring.

It was even more disastrous than I'd feared.

The hearing on "The Recent Regrettable Incidents in the Border States, called by Its People the Kingdom of Kait" began after midday. We were told the Rule of Ten little liked to conduct public business in the morning, devoting that to their own private concerns.

"Which means," Tenedos muttered, "making money or sleeping late."

We waited outside the audience chamber in full regalia. I wore the full-dress uniform of the Lancers, as did Lances Karjan, Svalbard, and Curti. Legate Yonge wore his best civilian garb, but with the sash of a legate in the Numantian Army wound around his waist. None of us were armed except Yonge, even though custom dictated that Lancers wear arms with any uniform. But we'd been told by the palace's head guard that no one, absolutely no one, was permitted to carry instruments of death into the presence of the Rule of Ten. Yonge had growled and given up his saber, but when a guard reached for his dagger he'd clapped his hand on its hilt and said no one could touch that and live. The guard began to object, looked into Yonge's cold eyes and hard features, and decided he never saw the blade.

Tenedos was garbed not as a Numantian resident-general, but in seer's robes, as if disdaining any part of the Rule of Ten's policies.

We were ushered into a large room, its walls paneled in dark wood. There was a railing near one end of it, and behind it the long raised dais where the Rule of Ten would sit. There were benches for those who would speak to the rulers of Numantia, a place for a note-taker, and seats for spectators. It looked more like a trial chamber than anything else.

The room had little room for the merely curious; every Numantian broadsheet that could find a writer in Nicias had sent a representative. The other observers were richly dressed, obvious members of the government. Some of them, I found later, were from the city's own rulers, the Nicias Council. It was generally considered as rock-bound as the Rule of Ten.

After half an hour's wait, we were ordered to rise and the Rule of Ten entered. They wore black ceremonial robes and dignified expressions. A priest blessed the gathering, and invoked Irisu and Panoan. As he did, Tenedos prayed briefly to himself in a low whisper, and I caught the name of the Destroyer and Creator, the goddess few had the courage to invoke, Saionji.

The speaker, a man in his early sixties named Barthou, welcomed us in a cordial tone, asked if we had been treated acceptably since our return to Numantia, and if we wished anything.

Tenedos rose and said we did not—we had been treated most cordially.

"I hope so," Barthou said, his voice drenched in sincerity, "even though nothing can compensate for those terrible events I now wish you to tell us about."

Tenedos began his tale.

I watched the Rule carefully. Tenedos had cast a Square of Silence spell—four identical objects at the corners, then words I couldn't understand, and it would take an experienced seer some time to break the spell and listen to what was being said—and told me much about who we'd be facing. The two members of the Rule whom Tenedos counted as in his camp I readily recognized from his descriptions. The first, quite old, was Mahal. Tenedos had said he was less convinced of the seer's philosophy than his new, very young and beautiful wife from a shopkeeper's family who was, like most of her class, intensely patriotic. She also prided herself on keeping current with every new idea that came to Nicias, "so," Tenedos said, "perforce Mahal must be dragged along with her into the embrace of the new, untried, and radical."

Our second friend was Scopas. He was middle-aged, and enormous. He was hardly a jolly fat man; his face showed the hard lines of intelligence and hard ambition.

Only the speaker, Barthou, and two others were worth worrying about, Tenedos had said. Those two, Farel and Chare, were young, in their late thirties, and had only been on the Rule for a few years. Tenedos warned me not to misjudge them by their years; they were as hidebound and reactionary as the most doddering ancient.

The other five would be counted on to vote whichever way they thought safest, which gave Barthou a solid majority.

"All we can hope to do is shame them into taking some action," Tenedos said. "Now is when I'd prefer to have more of the talents of the demagogue than the magician.

"I wish to several demons-haunted hells I *did* know some spells to warp the Rule's vote. But even if I did, they have the palace so surrounded by protective spells I'd never be able to finish the casting. And that would mean my death—it's the ax for anyone attempting to use sorcery against our leaders."

Tenedos's testimony was peppered with constant questions from the Rule, which were more to make sure the questioner appeared alert and interested than actually seeking knowledge, so the seer had just reached the point of our meeting at the ford and the ensuing skirmish when the meeting was adjourned.

Of course Tenedos said nothing about why he thought my orders to join him had come as late as they had, nor did he make any mention of the safe-conduct that didn't exist, nor why he believed the Rule of Ten had actually sent him to Kait.

The broadsheets that night were filled with the day's testimony, and accompanied by sketches of Tenedos and myself.

"Quite impossibly good-looking," Tenedos said, looking at one. "No doubt the morrow will find several marriage proposals, my young friend."

So it did, but more than several, and only a few of them were concerned with matrimony, but rather more immediate pastimes. There were nearly fifty, and they came from everyone from grandmothers who certainly should have known better to passionate scrawls from girls just out of the nursery. A number of women enclosed small gifts with their missives, mostly sketches or miniatures of themselves. Some of them were surprisingly good-looking. I puzzled over three letters: Each of them contained a tiny tuft of curly hair, and I blushed and felt like a fool when Tenedos dryly explained their obvious origin.

"So what do I do with these letters, sir?"

"You could answer them."

"I don't think so."

"Not even this one?"

I looked at the intaglio. "She's certainly pretty," I agreed. "With nothing to hide. But I've got to wonder—if she was so suddenly taken with me, as this letter says, and I must bed her this very night in the spirit of Jaen . . . when did she have time to get the engraving made?"

"Hmm," Tenedos said, gravely. He picked up the metal plate and pretended to examine its blank reverse closely. "Ah yes. You have a much sharper perception than I. On its back this says it's number forty-seven of a set of three hundred."

"Should I return the letters?"

"Damastes, sometimes your brain fails you. Why bring heartache? How many of these fair women have husbands, lovers, fathers? Not to remind you that some of them might think it was *your* fault their loved ones were so suddenly stricken with lust."

Yonge wanted to read them, but I fed them into the fire that night.

On the second day, we were able to move more swiftly, and I was asked to narrate some incidents as well. Once more, the broadsheets screamed of the monstrosities of Achim Fergana, and the horrors of Kait, and there were twice as many proposals.

But after the third day's appearance, by which time we'd reached the point of Achim Fergana's victory banquet, the defection of *Jask* Irshad, and the killer fog, there was nothing whatsoever, except a brief mention that the hearing was continuing.

"This bodes very poorly," Tenedos said. "The Rule of Ten strictly control the broadsheets. I suppose they've decided we've become entirely too popular, or what we're saying is likely to so inflame the populace they'll be forced to take strong action against Kait.

"I fear we're doomed, Damastes."

The next, the fourth, day, the broadsheet writers were still in attendance, although I saw that none of them were writing down our testimony. The members of the Nicias Council weren't present, and had allowed underlings to appear in their place for amusement. Then Tenedos mentioned the Tovieti. Instantly Barthou was standing, the rod of office held before him.

"This has now entered the realm of state secrets," he said. "Resident-General Tenedos, please cease speaking until the chamber is cleared."

Guards hastily hustled the audience out.

Tenedos, looking very unhappy, continued his tale. When he'd finished, there were no questions or comments, and Barthou adjourned the session.

Three more days went the same, and we were finished. During our story of the final retreat from Sayana, Barthou and his lackeys had urged Tenedos and myself to speak more succinctly—there were other matters requiring their immediate attendance.

Then we were done.

The Rule of Ten said they would announce what action they planned to take as soon as possible, and thanked us once more for appearing.

We'd barely returned to our rooms when we were summoned by the guards. Before I met Tenedos, and was still innocent about the ways of government, I would have thought this meant their ire had been righteously roused, and there'd be an immediate declaration of war against Kait. But now I knew better.

And so it was. The room was empty except for the recorder, ourselves, and the Rule of Ten. Mahal would not look at Tenedos, and Scopas's expression was completely unreadable.

In smooth, measured tones Barthou said that Kait had erred

most grievously, and there would be a most harsh diplomatic note sent to Sayana, "as soon as circumstances permitted its transmission." That meant they weren't even brave enough to send a full regiment of cavalry down the Sulem Pass and shove the note down Achim Fergana's throat.

Anger grew within me.

"We further proclaim mercantile sanctions against Kait," Barthou went on. "These, which will be announced within a week, will be maintained until Baber Achim Fergana makes appropriate restitution to the victims of the Sulem Pass horror."

Mercantile sanctions? What punishment was that? The men of the Border States took what they wanted at swordpoint, or traded surreptitiously in remote villages.

"Finally," Barthou said, "it is our decision that the matter of the Border States and their dissident natives has been ignored too long. Therefore, we are summoning a Great Conference, to be attended by the rulers of all states who touch on their lands, to be held in the Tenth Day of the Time of Births to discuss the matter.

"The Rule of Ten has spoken! Proclaim this word throughout all Numantia!" He started to set the rod of office down.

Tenedos was on his feet, speaking even before he was recognized: "But what of Thak? What of the Tovieti?"

Two of the Ten looked at each other.

"Local phenomenon," Chare said. "Not worth concerning ourselves about."

"Then why was I ordered to report on them when I first went to Kait? You seemed most concerned about the matter then."

"We were unaware of the nature of the . . . phenomenon," Chare said. "Now we are satisfied it is of little consequence."

"I declare this meeting over," Barthou said hastily, before Tenedos could challenge them any further.

Now rage took me like a mastiff shakes a kitten, and I was standing. All that I could see was that stormy pass, and hear Captain Mellet's last words: "Tell them there are still men on the Frontiers who know how to die!"

"Are you all cowards that—" I managed, then gasped as

Tenedos kicked me on the ankle, hard enough to make me stumble back against the bench. Before I could recover, the Rule of Ten had stood and swept out, so many crows walking a limb.

I almost went after them, and I saw alarmed guards start toward us. Tenedos and then Karjan had me by the arms, and were moving me out of the chamber as quickly as the Rule of Ten had fled.

I found enough self-control not to break away, or snarl at my two friends, and I let myself be taken to my rooms. I paced back and forth like a caged tiger, staring at the door, wishing one of those cowardly bastards would come through it.

But the only one who did, and that after two hours, was Laish Tenedos, who tapped softly, then entered without waiting for an invitation.

He held two ornate crystal goblets and a great decanter of brandy.

"This is seventy-five years old," he said. "It's supposedly good for soothing wrath. At any rate the palace's vintner says it will make you amazingly drunk and free of worries."

"I'll be blasted if I want anything from them, especially not their damned drink!"

"Tut, tut," soothed Tenedos. "Never turn down a chance to drink an enemy's liquor. It can be the sweetest of all, while you plan for the future."

He poured the goblets quite full and handed me one.

I took it, started to drain it, then stopped. I took two deep breaths, then pulled the stopper from the decanter and began pouring the liquor back. If you drink, it should only be when times are good.

But before the glass was emptied, I had a second thought, and left a single swallow.

I lifted it in a toast.

"To Captain Mellet," I said. "I, at least, shall not forget him."

Tenedos looked at me in surprise, then nodded agreement.

"To Captain Mellet." We drained our glasses.

"Thank you, Seer. I think it is time I sleep."

"As you wish, my friend. For me, sleep may require some assistance." He picked up the decanter. "I shall see you in the morning."

But in spite of my words, the world was gray outside before I was able to sleep.

Later that day, Seer Tenedos and I were called to the Rule of Ten's chamber. I expected to be disciplined for my outburst, and resolved to take whatever punishment those fools had come up with stoically.

There were only two of the Rule of Ten in the chamber: Farel, one of Barthou's contingent, and Scopas. He sat in Barthou's seat.

"Legate Damastes á Cimabue," he began, "it is the decision of the Rule of Ten that you have served us well.

"In recognition of this, we have ordered you promoted to captain of the Lower Half, this promotion to become effective immediately."

I was damned if I would give either of them the satisfaction of gaping, and managed to keep my face still. My outburst had been ignored, and instead my sash of office would now carry a single black band, a promotion I would not have expected in peacetime for ten years, and that after only the most meritorious service.

"We also think that your standards are worthy of note, and therefore are reassigning you from the Frontiers to our capital. You are hereby given a new posting to Numantia's proudest formation, the Golden Helms of Nicias."

Fuck!

"There is another reason we made this decision," Scopas went on. "We may wish to hear more details of your harrowing experience in the Border States when the Border Conference assembles, and wish you to remain close at hand."

He fell silent. I knew what I was supposed to do, but hated doing it. But a soldier must accept the harsh as readily as the soft, and so I came to attention, clapped my chest in salute, wheeled, and marched out, followed by Yonge and Karjan.

I started for my quarters, feeling, as one of my lycee instructors would have put it, shit and sugar, but mostly shit. But the guard stopped me, and said I was to wait for Resident-General Tenedos.

It was about half an hour later when the seer emerged, a tight smile on his face.

"We have great reason to thank the Rule of Ten," he said in a clear voice. "They have done us a boon, and we are in their debt."

When he and I were alone in his rooms, and his Square of Silence spell in place, he started to explain, but saw my expression first.

"Will it be that bad?" he asked.

I started to find some polite military lie, then decided to tell the truth.

"It won't be the best, sir. All I'll be doing is polishing brass, riding up and down, and holding the door open for fat-ass diplomats, begging your pardon, sir. It'll be a year, maybe more, before I'll be able to put in to transfer to some unit where there's likely to be some action. Hells, I don't even know if the Lancers will be willing to take me back."

"Legate," Tenedos said, "I was not speaking for unseen ears when I said we had been granted a boon. I'm very glad you're being stationed here in Nicias, for purely selfish reasons.

"I'll make a bet with you. Within a year . . . no, two at the outside, I'll have need of your service, and not to open any doors for me, either."

"What do you mean?"

"Time will answer that question," he said. "I shall not, because I can't tell how the future shall twist. But I know this course cannot run true much longer."

At the moment I had little patience for his theories about how the days of Numantia's rulers were numbered, but I said nothing. Then my natural curiosity took me.

"What reward did you receive, sir? I hope one more satisfactory than mine."

"Most definitely. Scopas praised me to the heavens, then

said I could either remain in government service or return to civilian life. If I chose the former, he had a list of some eight posts I could pick from.

"I scanned them quickly, and found them to be just as I'd expected—places where I would be absent from the public eye, and unhappy enough to resign in a short time.

"So I picked the worst of all—in their minds.

"Congratulate me, Legate. I am now the head of the Military Sorcery Department for the Lycee of Command."

That academy was intended to train hand-picked dominas for the highest rank in the army. An officer chosen for that school was guaranteed he'd see general rank before retiring unless he committed some unimaginable error.

"Now," he went on, "I knew full well before you told me just how low an opinion the army has of magic, which we've discussed. So now, in the bowels of the beast, I'm expected to be digested and shat out into the darkness, and my radical theories heard no more.

"But this shall be where I prove my ideals. Prove them and find the disciples I'll need. If I cannot, well then, Saionji has picked a weak vessel for her message. But I doubt that.

"Yes," he said. "Yes, indeed. The Rule of Ten will bitterly rue this day."

I was glad one of us was content.

As for me, in spite of Tenedos's reassurances, I was trapped in Nicias.

FIFTEEN

THE CITY
OF LIGHTS

I wasted no more time in the palace, but swiftly packed my gear and prepared to move to the barracks of the Golden Helms. Tenedos said he'd see that Yonge fell into as little mischief as possible, and took him into his employ, "always needing," Tenedos said, "the duties of a good serviceable murderer in these unsettled times.

"I hope," he went on, "the next time we serve together it shall be in happier times and circumstances. Assuming you do wish that to happen."

I thought about it for a moment, then grinned. I'd chosen a life of adventure, and certainly being around the seer had granted that. I was still sound in limb, and had learned an infinite amount in the year or so we'd been together.

"Seer," I said formally, "you have but to call. I'll follow your orders again."

And so I swore my first oath of fealty to Laish Tenedos. It was the least ceremonious of them all, but the most important, remembering our family motto:

We Hold True.

I bade Tenedos farewell, and promised to look him up at the lycee as soon as I settled into my new post.

I asked Lancer Karjan if he wished to remain my servant,

which I knew would be permitted, or return to the Lancers. He thought hard, then grunted and said, "I'll see this un through. F'r a while at least. Sir."

We were offered a carriage, but didn't need it, tying what little gear we had behind to Lucan's and Rabbit's saddles. Rabbit by now was used to riders other than myself, so he snorted only once when Karjan climbed into the saddle, and we set off to join the Golden Helms.

The Rule of Ten may have been complacent, but it did not show from the way they had positioned the military about Nicias. The army's main elements were just to the north of the Palace of the Rule of Ten, as were two other regimental headquarters, guarding their masters from a bare five minutes' distance. I wondered how much real trust the Rule of Ten had in their own people.

A branch of the River Latane was about half a mile to our west as it curved through the city, and there was one of Nicias's huge parks, named Hyder Park, between us and the palace.

Even though it was still winter, the weather was quite pleasant, as it generally is in Nicias, the farthest north and closest to the equator of all Numantia's cities, so our ride was quite pleasant. We admired the park's bridle paths, gazebos, openair taverns, and swan-decorated lakes. I thought it most curious that all the people I saw were well dressed and comfortable looking, a far cry from most of the city's populace. I wondered if the general populace was kept out by order, or if it was a matter of custom as was so much in this ancient city.

The Golden Helms' brick barracks sprawled among rolling lawns, graveled parade grounds, and manicured röl fields. Even though I knew I would hate this assignment, a half-smile touched my lips as we rode under the arching entrance to the cantonment, a smile of familiarity. Here a punishment squad under the snarling guidance of a lance-major spaded fertilizer around trees with their trunks uniformly painted white for three feet above the ground; there another warrant bawled orders at the awkward squad riding back and forth on a parade ground; an anxious officer hurried down one of the twisting stone paths, intent on a private errand and barely noticing the salute of a passing lance.

Familiar . . . but not really, for I realized at this time of day, early afternoon, the area should be filled with soldiers drilling, at sport, being lectured to, or practicing their tactics.

We asked our way to the regiment's headquarters, and I reported to the adjutant, a captain of the Upper Half named Lardier, and inquired when it would be convenient for me to present myself to the unit's domina.

"Perhaps tomorrow." The adjutant yawned. "Domina Lehar may have returned from his estate. Or perhaps not. Certainly he'll be back by the Twenty-Sixth Day, for there's an important parade, in honor of the Prince of Hermonassa, then.

"But don't worry, Captain á Cimabue. He's aware of you. We've all heard of your coming.

"By the way. Congratulations on your promotion. I'm *sure* you deserve it, and hope that a combat veteran such as yourself encounters no difficulties with the customs of the Golden Helms."

He turned and looked at a chart. "Mm. Yes. I think I'll put you in charge of B Troop. They call themselves the Silver Centaurs. Legate Nexo was in temporary command of the troop, but you have rank on him. Perhaps he'd be willing to serve on under you, although I doubt it."

I'd known this would happen, even in a line regiment. My rapid promotion over who knows how many thousand young legates would rouse resentment not only in the hearts of those I overleaped, but from my superiors as well. I would have to soldier well to find approval in their eyes.

"I'll have a word with the legate," I said. "Who is my troop guide?"

"At the moment . . . well, you don't have one. He bought himself out of the army a month or so ago, and Domina Lehar hasn't gotten around to promoting one yet. See what you think of your men, and offer some suggestions, there's a good man."

I saluted, and turned to leave.

"One more thing, Captain. Are those your horses outside? I thought so. Well, you can certainly keep them for off-duty mounts. But all the men of B Troop ride blacks. I'll notify the remount officer you'll be needing a new charger. You can select one at your leisure." I withdrew, somewhat shaken at my more-than-casual welcome, and went to my troop area.

Each troop had a separate building, with the regimental headquarters at the center of the cluster, and behind that the necessary shops for the unit's support. When I arrived the barracks were nearly deserted, and the only warrant in the orderly room was a junior lance-major. He sprang to attention, and I noted that his uniform was immaculate, as was everything else I'd seen.

I told him who I was, and asked where Legate Nexo was. He said in the city, visiting friends.

I made no comment, but thought this was the most social unit I'd ever seen. Where were the men of my troop? A few on detail, some in the stables, but most of them, since B Troop was standby troop this week, on pass in Nicias.

"Standby, eh? What are we on standby for?"

"Well, sir, in the event of any emergency."

"How would they be summoned, if they're all farting about in taverns?"

The lance-major looked perplexed. "Well, sir, there's never been an occasion like that in the six years I've been with the regiment. But I suppose we'd have to wait until they reported back. Maybe send messengers to the taverns the troop usually drinks in."

I began to growl an opinion, but caught myself in time. There is no bigger military fool than the one who joins a new formation and instantly knows what must be changed. I politely thanked the lance-major, and had him show me to my quarters.

As a troop commander and captain, I'd expected a room to myself, but I was quite pleased with how large it was, including not only a bedroom and separate office, but also a bathroom and small chamber for Karjan. I ordered Karjan to take Lucan and Rabbit to the stables. He saluted, started to leave, then hesitated.

"What's the problem, Lance? You may speak freely."

"Beggin' th' leg—captain's pardon, sir, but what the *hells* kind of army have we went an' joined?"

It was a good question, and became a better one in the next several days. First came Legate Nexo, a rather effete young man who affected a lisp. No, he'd rather not remain with B Troop, but wished to transfer where he'd be, er, among friends of his own sort. I could probably have put him in hack—sentenced to quarters—for a week for insolence. But I would rather have taken him back of the barracks, stripped off my sash, and invited him to discuss the matter in a more direct manner. But I knew an officer of his ilk would never, ever stoop to striking someone with his bare hands, and would have immediately reported me.

As for the 120 men I had under my charge: On the surface, it appeared I was in command of a unit an officer dreams of. I was only five men short of a full troop's strength, which is always a miracle. Almost all of my men had at least a year's service, and about half of them were career soldiers. They were all good-sized, the smallest being only five inches short of six feet, and a few even towered over me. They were in the best of health—no one could complain about the quality of our rations, nor the manner in which they were prepared and served.

Our horses were groomed twice a day, well exercised, and fed properly. The harness was always freshly soaped and polished, and the brightwork shone like a mirror.

The men's turnout was equally spectacular. I ordered a series of inspections, and the biggest offense I could find was a man who hadn't completely cleaned the blanco off the inside of his helm, where the strap was riveted. I did not chastise him. Even the soles of their boots were blackened before they fell out for parade.

They maneuvered perfectly, and every parade-ground evolution was done precisely, from "Squad . . . Assemble" to "Pass in Review." They could raise a cheer and charge past dignitaries without their line wavering more than a foot.

They could . . . enough!

They were the shittiest group of soldiers I've ever had the misfortune to command. Even now, all these years later, I find it impossible to refer to them as "mine," or "we," but only "they." If, Irisu forbid, they had ever been forced to fight a single squad of my sometimes-scruffy, sometimes-underfed, mostly undersized Lancers, the skirmish wouldn't have been remembered by the men of the Seventeenth.

These "Silver Centaurs" knew nothing of how to fight with their weapons, although they did wonderfully pretty pirouettes when they paraded through the streets of Nicias. Sabers were to be presented, lances were to hang pennons on, and daggers were for ornament.

They stood guard in front of the government buildings in Nicias, but if a mob had charged, they would have screeched and run in dismay, not having the slightest idea of what to do next.

As far as tactics, if I'd ordered them to dismount and advance with bare saber using all cover, I might have been speaking Kaiti. Camouflage, scouting, skirmishes, courier service, flank guard—all the real duties of a cavalryman in war were unknown. The only regimental charge they could manage was across a flat, well-groomed parade field for the approval of diplomats and cheering citizens on holiday.

There was nothing intrinsically wrong with these men. Almost all soldiers are the same; it is their leaders who make the difference. These same men, well and hard trained, could have been as good or better than any Lancers.

But the Golden Helms were as rotten as the Rule of Ten. Domina Lehar was more interested in the mansions and rice fields he owned a day and a half's journey beyond Nicias to the west, in the delta. The rest of the officers were the same sort of popinjays, fools, and idle gentlemen I'd seen at the lycee, of various ages, ranks, and states of disrepair, and in the Helms there was no one to bring them back to reality.

I've heard that in some puffed-chest regiments like the Helms it's forbidden to discuss business, that is soldiering, in the mess. There was no such ban with the Helms, nor was it necessary. If any of us had talked about our day's duties, we would have sounded like housewives discussing which brand of polish did the best job on our silver, or else horsedealers nattering on about what someone's mount might do in the furlong.

The sole exception was a rather disheveled legate three years older than I, who seemed completely uninterested in the latest gossip or horse-breeding, did not drink, did not gamble, and seemed to have little interest in women. Instead he buried himself in history, mostly military, and in the few broadsheets specializing in the military. He'd been eagerly and mistakenly drafted by the Helms because he was the top graduate at his lycee. They didn't find out until he reported that he'd achieved the position completely on ability in the field or classroom, with never a pin's notice mentioned about his appearance or failure to suck up to his superiors.

His name was Mercia Petre. Yes, *that* Petre, for the most part no different as a legate than when he held a tribune's baton not very long afterward.

I can't say we became friends—with one exception, I doubt if Petre ever had what conventional people call a friend. But I spent long nights in the shambles he called quarters, sipping tea, studying old battles, re-laying them out so the outcome might be different, and reading all we could find on the Border States, on Kallio, and even Maisir. Part of me may have been bored cross-eyed by the dryness of the books, but this was a necessary part of my trade. I was never bored by Petre's company, although others were, since he had but one interest, and that was serving the war god Isa.

He was the only pleasure I found in that cantonment during those long, drear months with the Helms.

This situation is a favorite in the romances. It's a great tale, of a staid, pigheaded formation, and how a brave, stubborn young officer stands true for what he knows to be right, and in spite of hostility hammers his own small part of the unit into fighting order, and then is vindicated when war comes and they all ride out and do something terribly heroic.

Reality, however, was that if I'd tried to behave like that young officer I would have had my head handed to me, most likely on the silver salver the domina had his first brandy of the afternoon served on. I could not chance that. Not after Captain of the Lower Half Banim Lanett and the röl match with the Lancers.

So I followed soldiering's oldest commandment: "Shut up and soldier, soldier!" I used the few hours allotted for Commander's Time to try to teach the men some tactical sense, but because we were never allowed out of the city to practice these tactics, nor was there anywhere to learn city-fighting techniques, I fear my talks only provided the men a chance to learn that most soldierly of all skills—to sleep with your eyes open.

All I could do was wait for the year or so to pass until I was forgotten, and then attempt to transfer back to the Frontiers.

That, and explore the world beyond the barracks, beyond the regiment—the wonders of the City of Lights.

I have never thought of myself as a city man, nor do I especially enjoy a metropolis. But Nicias is a city to fall in love with.

Its most remarkable feature is responsible for its name. When the first men were created by Umar and sent down to this earth, before he withdrew into silence and let the world be ruled by Irisu and Saionji, they found a roaring pillar of flame, flame from a gas that poured from a spring in the rock. Centuries later, that fire was somehow extinguished, and the gas channeled into pipes that were first laid beside and then beneath the streets of the city. When the fire was relit every house, from mansion to shack, and the streets themselves had and have free light that also provides a measure of heat. Nicias has more fires than other cities, but the citizens count that the price to be paid and especially venerate Shahriya. The supply of gas has never slackened, never run out. There is a legend that the day it does is the end of Numantia and perhaps the world itself.

It's easy to numb the mind with figures about Nicias—capital of Dara Province as well as of Numantia, sitting on the eastern edge of the Latane River's great delta, forty-five square miles, perhaps a million people, although I doubt if the bravest census taker has ever ventured into the towering, rickety slums of the eastern side or the evil streets of the northern docks that jut into the Great Ocean, nor has anyone numbered the people of the streets who sleep where sundown catches them, wrapped in their single garment.

There are half a hundred parks, from those no bigger than a city square that are owned and maintained by those living around it to the great expanses like Hyder Park or, to the north on the outskirts of the sprawling city, Manco Heath. There are at least twelve branches and who knows how many tributaries of the Latane River that twist through the city. Some of them, like the main navigable branch the ships use, are untamed. Others are channeled into stone banks like canals. Still others run underground, and are used to hurry the city's sewage to the sea.

I cannot conceive of anyone becoming tired of Nicias. Someone once said that a man could dine at a different restaurant every meal of his life and die before seeing them all. I could cynically add he might die of surfeit or, remembering some of the street vendors I grabbed a hasty snack from, stomach poisoning, instead of old age, but I'll accept the saying as truth.

Nicias has everything, from cool, quiet streets where the rich have their townhouses to the poorest garrets; shopping areas from twisting alleys with the strangest tiny shops imaginable to stalls to market squares to great emporiums that will sell you anything from a needle to a funeral. But enough—if you wish to know more, purchase a guidebook or, better yet, journey to Nicias and experience its splendor for yourself.

Sometimes I went out on my own, sometimes, when I felt like chancing the riskier parts of the town, I asked Karjan if he wished to accompany me. If he found no other pleasure, he could at least drink enough so I wouldn't be sneered at for my temperance, and he had an amazingly good bass voice that made him popular in the minstrel bars.

I called on Seer Tenedos, and found him honestly delighted to see me. That became a bit of a habit. If I didn't have night duty, which only fell once every three weeks in the Helms, and had no other plans, I would drop by the Lycee of Command, which was ten minutes distant, to see if he had any ideas for the evening.

He'd ask how my day went, of which the telling took but boring seconds, and then tell me of his. I assumed he had a Square of Silence cast around his office, since his comments on some of the high-ranking officers he was teaching, or on the staff of the lycee, were scathing.

He'd sacked the other two instructors in the Military Sorcery Department, one for senility, the other for incompetence, and replaced them with young, eager seers as convinced as he was that sorcery must become the third branch of the army, along with the infantry and cavalry.

At first it was the two of us, but in a few weeks there were other officers, students, younger captains of the Upper Half or dominas, clustering around. At this point, his dissection of his students ceased, obviously. Besides, his pupils were more interested in elaborations of his classroom lectures, accompanied as frequently as not by illustrations on a large sand-table he'd had installed.

I stayed well to the rear of the crowd, listening intently. I was fascinated. On the surface, it seemed all he was talking about was bygone battles, demonstrating how a skilled mage might have changed their outcome with a spell of darkness here, a weather spell there, and so forth.

But there was more to Seer Tenedos's speeches than just history, and it took me a while to realize it. I think that if I'd not known of his hatred for the Rule of Ten and his absolute conviction that Numantia must be ruled by a king or face doom, I might not have noticed. He'd slyly put in a dig about those who live in the past being strangled by its dead hand in the future or, if one of the battles had occurred during the time of the Rule of Ten, how the commander on the ground was the man who saved the day, not the panicked babblers in the rear.

Tenedos was building a corps of disciples to his philosophy. There was certainly no sign of his being rejected and cast into outer darkness. The Rule of Ten had erred badly in making this appointment, as he'd foreseen.

Since the students all out-ranked me, I was beginning to feel most out of place, when Tenedos announced a new schedule. He would only be available for extra sessions twice a week. The other nights he wished to himself.

"One of them at least," he said, "I promise you I'll spend with you, Damastes, assuming you're not tired of the company of a growling magician. I can feel myself getting stale in this damned office. I want to get out, in the streets, among the people."

It was well he made his plan firm, because he became a favorite of the lecture halls. One interesting thing about Nicians: They would rather go to a hall and listen to one man spiel his ideas or, better, two flail each other as incompetent, barren-minded baboons than visit a gallery or attend a concert.

A side benefit of being the season's pet philosopher was the number of women who wished to have a private interchange to, as one lovely said, "make sure I properly understand what you're saying." That person must have required considerable explanation, because when I saw Tenedos the next afternoon he was exhausted, and begged off our planned outing for the chance for some sleep.

But that was about the only time I saw him tired. He had vast wellsprings of energy, and never seemed to falter.

When we went out of an evening, there was no telling where we would go, nor whose company we would be in. Sometimes it was an invitation to a party that Tenedos had gotten, or, not infrequently, one that came to the "Lion of Sulem Pass" as one broadsheet had called me, which Yonge never let me forget. We were as likely to dine in the halls of the mighty as in some dockside shanty that happened to have the best oysters in Nicias, or to sit listening to four stringed instruments in a hall as watch naked dancers prance around a single man with a guitar and a voice that could move the dead in a wineshop where we carefully sat with our backs to the wall.

Nicias was a beautiful city, but it was not a happy one. There was something wrong, something amiss. Rich people did not go about without an armed guard or two. The populace openly sneered at the wardens and, in the poorer sections where the men of the law went in squads, were as likely to hurl a cobble at their backs and run as not.

Soldiers were not respected, either, but were the subject of imprecations and sometimes, if the Nician was bold and the soldier drunk enough, waylaid, robbed, and stripped.

This isn't to say injustice was only on one hand. Every street corner held a shouting orator, as likely to be howling obscene stories of whose beds the Rule of Ten slept in as condemnation of the entire system. They were certainly harmless, even if their numbers were worrisome. But the wardens seemed to single out these blowhards as desperate enemies of the state, and smashed them into momentary silence with their truncheons. And the wardens believed that anyone arrested was automatically guilty, and deserved a merciless hiding on the way to prison.

The beauty of Nicias was there, but no one seemed to want to take care of it. The streets needed sweeping, the sidewalks were generally blocked with trash, and too many of the buildings, public as well as private, needed painting and upkeep.

I remembered what Tenedos had said as we rode through Sulem Pass the previous year: "I can *feel* the unrest in Nicias, in Dara. The people are without leaders, without direction, and they know it."

I, too, felt this tension, felt as if the city were a great, dry wheatfield, parched by drought, waiting only for a single man with a torch. And I was beginning to believe I rode the streets with that very man.

But very seldom did my thoughts follow those grim tracks.

Laish Tenedos was excellent company. Frequently when he went out he changed into mufti, since, as he said, "wizard's robes can be off-putting as often as they gain an advantage. I might advise you to follow the same practice."

Against regulations, I purchased civilian garb, and kept it in Tenedos's apartments, although I wore my uniform more often than not.

The two of us, sometimes accompanied by Karjan and Yonge, found ourselves in strange byways.

I remember . . .

. . . paying a boatman a few coppers to give us a tour of the sewers under the city, roaring along as if caught by rapids in his tiny boat, the curved overhead bricks dank and dripping, rats hissing at us from corners. Yonge got the boatman drunk and we almost lost ourselves for good before discovering an open grating to pry up and get our bearings.

. . . There was an evening that began quietly, a visit to a small tavern along the river where the first barrel of the famous sweet wine of Varan was available for tasting. Somehow tasting became drinking became guzzling and we ended up in a long snake dance down the riverbank, the Seer Tenedos, in full regalia, roaring drunk at its head, I just behind him drunk only on the laughter and singing, the wardens standing bewildered nearby, hardly stupid enough to club down a magician for being drunk and disorderly.

. . . We were at a formal dinner party. I was seated next to a pretty, if rather cold-looking, woman about ten years my senior who'd been introduced as the Marchioness Fenelon. Between courses we'd chatted of this and that—I was actually becoming able to make small talk. Then she turned to me, and I saw for the first time the pin she wore on her breast.

It was a solid gold casting of a long cord.

Time froze for me, and I remembered the cavern, another,

real, yellow cord of silk around my neck, and the murderous beauty named Palikao.

"What," I said, my voice as harsh as if I'd been reprimanding one of my men, "is that you're wearing?"

She started, glanced down at the pin. Then she looked up at me, but her eyes moved away rapidly.

"Oh," she said, "it's just . . . something I saw in a shop and thought looked smart. Just a bauble."

I knew she was lying.

. . . We organized an impromptu race among the carriage drivers of Hyder Park, and combed through nearby taverns to find enough passengers to fill them.

The two sleepy wardens screamed and ran as they saw, pelting down on them, a cavalry charge of cabs, filled with drunk noblemen and -women.

By the time the wardens had called out reinforcements we'd done two laps, awarded first prize, which I remember as an enormous stuffed toy, and vanished into the night.

. . . It was late and I'd gotten lost trying to find the party, riding Lucan up and down the lanes of an expensive part of Nicias, with walled mansions on either side of the road. Finally, I'd found the place described on the ivory card, and rode into its grounds.

I wasn't that late, I decided with relief, because the drive was still lined with carriages and there were a dozen or more horses being held by grooms. I dismounted, tossed the reins to a retainer, and went up the steps to the main house.

I didn't know the people who lived there, not even their name, but the card that'd come to me had promised an evening such as "I'd never forget," and so I took the chance.

A solemn-faced man opened the door, bowed me in, and shut it behind me. I thought it a bit odd for a servitor to remain outside, but shrugged and looked for a cloakroom.

I went through a curtained entranceway into a large room, decorated only in pillows and a rich carpet with the thickest nap I have ever seen. It was well that it was so comfortable, because all of the bodies squirming on it were very naked.

Man-woman, man-man, woman-woman, man-woman-man: It appeared as if every possible combination was being tried.

A very small blond, as nude as the others, came to her feet and came toward me, walking as if she expected the floor to slip away from her. She had milky skin, curly hair, the face of an innocent child, and the perfect body of a young harlot.

"Good evening," she said. "Would you like to come between my tits?"

I had no idea what the proper response was then, nor do I now.

"Welcome to my party," she said. "We're having a *lot* of fun. You look like a big one. Come join us. It's always good to find a new . . . face." She giggled.

"Yes," I said. "Certainly. In just a moment. But . . . let me go find a place to hang my cloak."

"I'll be waiting," she said, and began massaging her nipples with her thumbs, moving her breasts against each other in a manner she thought inviting.

I backed through the curtain and went out the door.

"Leaving already, sir?" the retainer asked, his voice completely neutral. I nodded, and started toward my horse, then turned back.

"Excuse me. But whose house is this?"

"This is the residence of Lord Mahal of the Rule of Ten and his wife, sir."

I mounted and rode off.

When Tenedos said Lord Mahal's wife embraced the new, untried, and radical, he knew not how well he'd chosen the word.

Then everything changed.

Seer Tenedos had suggested I attend a gathering in his place, since he had suddenly been invited to attend Lord Scopas on a matter of some urgency. He said I might enjoy it, since it was a regular event most popular among the radical thinkers of Nicias. He said he'd already sent his apologies, and a note that I'd most likely be attending in his stead, so his "suggestion" was, not unusually, more of an order.

"Do I keep my clothes on, sir?"

He colored—I'd told him of the orgy at Lord Mahal's.

"You'll no doubt meet some people far stranger than any of those satyrs and nymphs," he said. "But they'll keep their clothes on there. Or most of them will, anyway."

"Who's sponsoring it?"

"A young woman. Countess Agramónte and Lavedan. The Agramóntes are a very old, very rich family. It's said they own enough land to have their own state.

"She married well a bit more than a year ago. Count Lavedan has almost as much gold as she does, but she insisted on keeping the family name, and the Lavedans know better than to argue with an Agramónte.

"These are people well worth the knowing, Damastes. Please give them my apologies, although I doubt if you'll meet Count Lavedan. He's more interested in his family's shipping than politics or philosophy.

"Enjoy yourself."

The house sat on the waterfront, a huge rectangle, five floors high, lit with gas flares at each side of the entrance gates through a tall, wrought-iron fence that was wonderfully sculpted. I dismounted and went inside.

I gave helmet and dolman to a doorman, and went toward the sound of conversation and occasional laughter.

I passed a huge, high-ceilinged ballroom that was empty and dark, and found the party. It was in a circular room, comfortably and expensively decorated. A silver punch bowl sat on a sideboard.

There were possibly thirty or so people inside, and I saw what Tenedos meant. They were dressed in every style imaginable, including at least two I hoped stayed original with the owner, and their wearers came from every class from the richest to the most humble. They were all happily arguing, listening, or waiting to rebut the speaker as an oaf.

"Ah," a voice came from behind me. "This must be the Lion of the Sulem Pass. Will you growl tonight, O Lion?"

I turned, a smile on my face, ready to comply with the joking request. Then the world shimmered around me as if a god had suddenly changed it to gold.

The woman was quite young, barely eighteen, I found later. She was just five and a half feet tall, her hair was dark blond, worn fashionably long and pulled to fall to one side of her face, ending just above her small, pert breasts. She wore a stylish, daringly filmy gown with thin neckstraps that crossed over her breasts, leaving visible their saucy curves.

Her face was rounded, her eyes sparkled with intelligence, and she had small but sensuous lips. She, too, was smiling.

Our eyes met, and the smile disappeared.

"I . . . I am Countess Agramónte and Lavedan," she said, sounding suddenly a bit confused, her voice dropping to a throaty murmur.

I managed to come to some sort of attention, reached out, and took her hand and lifted it, bowing over it.

"Captain Damastes á Cimabue, Countess."

"You may call me Marán," she said.

I released her hand, and once more looked into her eyes.

I drowned in them for a million years.

SIXTEEN

MARÁN

Suddenly her expression changed, and I can only compare it to that of a puppy who's done something wrong and expects to be whipped.

"I am sorry, Countess, I mean Marán," I said quickly. "I did not mean to stare."

"No, no," she said, and her expression returned to normal. "You did nothing wrong. I was just a bit intimidated, Captain. I seldom have soldiers to my salons."

"I can understand that," I said, trying a feeble joke. "Most of us don't know where to put our sabers when we enter polite company."

A wicked grin came and went. "That is not what *I* heard," she said.

"I don't understand," I said, pretending innocence.

She chose not to answer, but led me to the punch bowl and poured a cup.

"You have a choice," she said. "You may join the throng, and listen to former Count Komroff hold forth on why we must all renounce our titles, move to the slums, and exist on clotted milk if there's any hope for the world—"

"Or?" I interrupted hastily.

"Or you may get the grand tour, since this is the first time you've been in my house."

"Lead on," I said. "Having no title, and little taste for farmer's cheese, I put myself in your hands."

I admired the paintings, sculptures, gold inlays, cleverly carved wood etchings on the lower floor, including that great ballroom. When we came to the kitchen, Marán merely opened the door, told me what was on the other side, and passed on. I would have liked to have seen the mechanism necessary to feed such a great household, but was content to do whatever she wished, comfortable just being in her company.

As we went up the curving stairs to the second level, I asked, "Pardon, but since this house sits on the water, I'd assumed it belonged to your husband. But you said—"

"This was my wedding gift to him. And to me."

"You have no other residence in the city?"

"I don't know what you know of the Agramónte family," she said. "But we are country lords, not happy unless we can open any window and sniff pig shit and hay. I'm afraid I'm the sport of the clan, since to me green pastures and lowing cattle are about as interesting as watching rocks turn into sand."

"That's a pity," I said. "For I'm but a country lad and can think of nothing better."

"Perhaps," she said softly, "perhaps I never saw it through the right eyes. Or . . . with the right person."

Her hand touched my wrist, then was away.

"Now, on this level," she said, mimicking a palace guide, "we have such horribly interesting rooms as the sewing room, which I refuse to enter, the nursery, which is vacant for the moment, the library, here, which I love dearly."

The double doors opened into a great room lined with shelves, all dark wood, expensive quiet carpeting, and oak furniture. There were maps of our world and even a globe, one of the newer imaginings of the cartographers.

One of my most private fantasies was that somehow I'd manage to survive my military career and, even more improbably, amass enough of a fortune to build a great house somewhere in the country. Even though I'm not a reader, I'm not a barbarian, so of course part of the mansion would include a library. Here my friends and I could gather, and talk of old campaigns and long-dead comrades, while a great fire flickered and a winter storm roared, unheeded, outside.

Even though the books did not draw me, the maps certainly did, since I can sit over a map and dream of what country and terrain it represents by the hour, one of the few nonoutdoor pastimes, besides music, I enjoy.

I wondered what it would be like to have this library, and envied Count Lavedan again.

I admired the next room even more, a large room hung with curtains, with a podium at one side. This was their music chamber, Marán explained. "Once a month or so, we have a quartet or perhaps even a small orchestra in. We haven't done it of late, since music is something my dear husband finds deadly dull."

At the end of the corridor were arcing double doors that were open a few inches.

"This is my husband's study. Since he's not present, it would hardly be—"

"Marán? Is that you?"

"I *thought*," she said, "he was out." She raised her voice. "Yes, Hernad. I'm merely showing one of our guests around."

The door opened, and Count Lavedan emerged. He was about five or six years older than I, a big man, going a bit of fat. It was ironic—he looked every inch and pound the bluff country lord, yet his background was shipping, while his country wife appeared the city sophisticate.

"I came back from the docks an hour ago, and did not wish to disturb you, my dear. Good evening, sir," he said, cordially. "It's rare indeed to see a soldier attend one of Marán's little parties. I assume you've come up with some new and vital scheme to reinvent the military?"

"No," Marán said. "This is Captain á Cimabue. You know, the one who saved all those people down in the Border States."

"No. Can't say as I have. Don't pay much attention to things that don't pertain. But congratulations, Captain." He snickered. "A Cimabuan, eh? I wager you're tired of hearing jokes about your province."

"Not at all," I said. "There's little fighting with real enemies to be had these days, so I must make do with jesters."

The smile vanished, and he looked at me carefully.

"My apologies, Captain. But you need not be so touchy."

"I am sorry, Count Lavedan. But such tales are more than wearisome."

"I suppose so," he said, indifferently. "But if my state were the butt of such japes, I think I'd just learn to ignore them. Words are nothing but air, anyway."

I thought I knew a seer who would disagree, but said nothing. I had no idea why we were bristling in such a manner; certainly my attraction to his wife could not have been noticed, and I surely had no right having any feelings about him.

"Would you like to see my study, Captain?" he said, changing the subject. I said I would.

It was quite a chamber, cluttered with ship models, charts, bills of lading, and the big table in its center overflowed with samples, letters, and packages. The prize, though, he saved for last. It was a small glass case. In it was the model of a ship, one like I'd seen moored at one of Nicias's landings. I saw it appeared to be floating in water, then I looked more closely. It was a marvel: The ship was animated, each sail, each rope moving, as it was driven by an invisible wind. I looked more closely, and saw tiny men on its decks, busy with their tasks. The water it floated in changed as well, waves curling from the ship's bows and a smooth wake at its stern.

"That cost a sum," Count Lavedan said. "The wife bought it for me for our second anniversary last month. It took five seers to come up with it. It's a model of my most recently launched vessel, and it makes a real voyage, from Nicias to foreign landfalls." He grinned fondly down at Marán. "The little woman knows how to please, she does."

Again that look of the puppy waiting for punishment came and went on Marán's face.

"Are you coming downstairs, Hernad?"

"Of course not," he said. "I'm busy, and besides, I have no interest in whatever's being prattled by your latest charlatan. You'll see, Captain, that while my Marán's got a sensible head to her, at least for a woman, she really has no thought of how foolish all these clowns appear to men of real sense."

Marán reddened, but said nothing.

"At any rate, if you'll forgive me, I've got some letters to compose," he said.

"Shall I knock when I come up for bed?" Marán said.

"You needn't bother. I'll probably be up most of the night." He brushed a kiss across her forehead. "Nice meeting you, Captain."

He went back inside his study and closed the doors.

Marán looked closely at me, as if waiting for me to say or show an opinion. I showed none.

"So this finishes off the second floor," I said. I indicated stairs. "Up there is . . ."

"Third floor, my bedroom and Hernad's. Nothing of interest."

"As someone who's spent too many nights trying to believe a rock can make a pillow, I certainly disagree with that. Only two bedrooms for the entire floor? What else do you do up there besides sleep? Have a small rōl field? A swimming pool?"

Marán giggled. "No. There's dressing rooms, bathrooms, reception areas." Her smile vanished, and she said, almost to herself, "but we *don't* do much besides sleep up there." She went on, quickly, "Above that, servants' quarters, then the solarium, plant rooms, and such. All the areas we rich and foolish people need to occupy our lives." She brightened, stepped back and curtsied. "*Là*, sir, there you have it. The residence of Count and Countess Agramónte and Lavedan.

"Your opinion?"

I complimented her and we started back downstairs. This is most strange, I thought. Married two years and each with a separate bedroom. But perhaps that was how the very rich lived. As to Count Lavedan's mockery of his wife's pastimes, I hardly thought that a courtly thing to do. As we returned to the ground level a wistful thought came: If *I* were married to this Marán, I certainly would have better use for my nights than correspondence. That, too, was improper, and I tried to put the matter out of my head, merely assigning Count Lavedan to the list of assholes I'd met.

It seemed no one had missed us in the round room, and the party had broken down into a handful of hard-arguing knots, each defending or attacking a different problem. Marán poured me another cup of punch.

"While I'm delighted to have met you, Captain," she said, "I was frankly looking forward to meeting your friend, the Seer Tenedos." She motioned to the people around us. "Hernad may have been too . . . forceful, but he does have a point. Sometimes the people I invite here are very long on theory, but haven't much in the way of experience." Her face became serious. "But I'm hardly one to talk. All I've done is be born and grow up rich."

A strange woman, I decided. Most mercurial in her moods. But she would certainly never be boring.

Once again I found myself looking into her eyes, and once more the vortex drew me. I pulled back with an almost physical effort.

"Perhaps you can convince your friend to come to another of my evenings," she said. "Of course, I wish you would come as well."

"I could do better than that," I said, thinking quickly. It was wrong, but I wanted very much to see this married woman again. "I don't know if this is proper to ask a married woman, but the seer is speaking two nights hence, three hours after sunset, at the Morathian Hall. I would be happy to escort you there and ensure you arrive safely home."

"Escort, my good Damastes, if you do not mind me calling you that? That word is *most* improper, unless you mean it in the military sense."

"What other way *could* I mean it?"

She smiled. "Since you have such a pure mind, sir, then I accept the invitation. Shall I have my carriage pick you up?"

I bowed acceptance, and then one of the servants came up with a problem for her to deal with. I drifted through the throng, never hearing any of the earnest proposals being touted.

I was, in short, as dreamy-minded as any bumpkin who's just had an invitation to a harvest celebration accepted by a lass.

The next two days swam past in a haze. I paid but little attention to my duties, and even the dullness of my Tin Centaurs, as I'd privately dubbed them, couldn't rouse my ire.

Half an hour before the time she'd said her coach would arrive, I was waiting outside the mess, in dress uniform. Eagerness played apart, but I also did not wish any of the wagging mouths in the Helms to see us, although there was nothing particularly irregular about the matter.

Her brougham was luxurious, red enameled wood, with gold leaf covering it, and panels representing mythological events. There were four matched bays, and the driver and an outrider sat atop, and there was a stand for two more at the rear.

Marán opened the door and greeted me. She wore baggy pantaloons, which I'd learned were the latest style, a red-and-black silk blouse that buttoned demurely around her neck, and a hooded fur jacket against the chill. Her face was a bit flushed, even though she had the window rolled shut.

I bowed, kissed her hand, and climbed in. She shut the door and we rolled smoothly away. The inside of the coach was silk and comfortably padded upholstery.

"I am delighted to see you, Countess," I said formally.

"And I you, Captain." She smiled. "May I tell you something shocking?"

"You may tell me anything, shocking or no."

"Here we are, on our way to a probably boring lecture, yet I feel like I could be a character in a romance, wickedly eluding her husband to meet with a dashing lover."

I started to make a jest out of it, but changed my mind.

"Thank you, Marán. I am honored at the thought."

I could not see her expression in the dimness, and she remained silent for a moment. I broke the stillness:

"I am curious about something you said the other night. You came to Nicias out of boredom?"

Marán considered her words for a few moments. "That is what I tell people," she said. "But there's more than that. My family, as no doubt you know, is very old, and feels that all Numantia should revolve around their best interests."

"Most of us do, even if we don't admit to it."

"Not as intensely as the Agramóntes," she said. "My father, for instance, found me reading a book called *The Duties of Man* a few years back. Are you familiar with it? Well, it's a long essay that holds all men have a duty to each other, that a man who owns slaves must take care of them and, in the end, the Wheel will return him to a better position if he is willing to free someone from bondage for performing extraordinary services. We Agramóntes, by the way, have not manumitted a slave for at least five generations that I know of.

"The book also says the rulers of Man have a duty to rule wisely, firmly, and well, or else they forfeit their right to the throne. It says that a benevolent, but staunch, monarchy is the best of all possible rulers.

"Since my father is close friends with most of the Rule of Ten, this is heresy. The book, by the way, while not quite proscribed, is not in wide circulation.

"My family thinks that all is set, all is regulated, Irisu is the best of gods and Umar was well to abdicate to him. They frankly disbelieve in the merits of the Wheel, and while they'll grudgingly concede a bad man might be taken down a few levels in his next life, most of us return on the same level we died on."

"So a lord is always a lord, a peasant always a peasant," I said.

"Just so, from now until the ending of the world."

"What do you think?"

Marán considered.

"I know what they believe is foolish. I know that Man, and this world, must change, just like the seasons do. I don't think our rulers are the wisest. But what would be better?

"To be frank, that is the real reason I invite people with new and different ideas to my home.

"Women are not given much chance to learn," she said. "I think that, too, is wrong."

I couldn't but agree, and always had. Why was it accepted that my father could have gone to a lycee if he could have afforded it, but if my mother had wished to learn more than a tutor could have taught, there would have been cries of horror? So, too, my sisters had no chance of learning beyond the traveling teachers my father could convince to stay on for a time, able to pay them little but sustenance.

I chose my next words carefully.

"I guess, then, marrying Count Lavedan and being able to get away from your family's conservatism was a great stroke of good fortune."

Silence dropped around us, and there was nothing but the creak of the wood and the clatter of the wheels on cobblestones.

"Yes," she said, and her voice was flat. "Of course it was."

"What you are saying, sir, is nothing but high treason," the man sputtered.

"Not at all," Seer Tenedos said calmly. "I said nothing about overthrowing the Rule of Ten. They are our rightful rulers, and I have served them faithfully, as you should know. Were I a man of temper, I might take offense at your words. Instead, let me reiterate the point of my lecture.

"I'll try to put it more simply. The Wheel turns. We agree on this. It brings change, it brings new life. It dictates to all of us how we must live.

"We Numantians must learn to obey this. We must change as the years change. Once we had a firm, fair king, or so the legends tell us.

"The Rule of Ten took the throne during a time of great crisis, vowing to hold it only as long as necessary.

"This is what I am calling for. Is it not time for the Rule of Ten to take a hard look at what they are, at what they have done, and perhaps hear the sound of the Wheel for themselves?

"Imagine this, sir. Wouldn't you agree that the Rule of Ten are forced to spend too much time in useless meetings?"

"Of course," the man who'd leaped to his feet grudged.

"Isn't it also true they must spend too much time in neverending debate before a decision is reached?"

"I'll accept that point as well."

"Then isn't it logical, and hardly seditious, to wonder if perhaps their rule might be more efficient if, instead of ten, it were perhaps five?"

"But that is the way it has always been!"

Now there was a bit of laughter here and there in the crowded auditorium as the audience saw how Tenedos was leading the man.

"Now we go back to my earlier point. *Why* does it always, always, always have to be that way? Why is it treason to conceive of a Rule of Five? Of course, it isn't—there've been times when disease reduced their ranks and until new men were selected, the Rule performed its duties and the world did not come to an end.

"Consider further. Be bold, sir. What about a Rule of Four? Or even . . . Three?"

"Or even One, sir?"the man bristled.

"You offered the thought, my friend." Tenedos smiled benevolently. "So let's take a look at one."

"Who are you recommending," another voice asked. "Barthou? Scopas? Mahal?" There was more laughter at this last.

"I am no politician, Lady," Tenedos answered. "I'm a sorcerer who wishes to become a philosopher. So let us consider something else, since we're talking about a single ruler.

"Let us consider *none* of the men who currently serve. Let us imagine new, stronger blood.

"Let us talk about a man who comes from outside, a man who hopefully has traveled all of Numantia, from the jungles of Cimabue to the forests and farmlands of Kallio, not someone who's spent his entire life in Dara or, worse, in Nicias.

"Let us consider a man who might consider himself a Numantian, not merely a Nician or Daran or Kallian. Let us consider a man who wishes to offer that vision to all the people of Numantia, who wants them to look beyond their narrow horizons, and see the greatness that is before them.

"I tell you, men and women, Numantia *is* great. We have our problems now, problems most severe. But this is a passing thing, something that could be, to history, no more than an unfortunate note.

"If Numantia can be given a direction, its natural energy driven, this nation could truly be the greatest of them all, and shine proud in the heavens."

"We sure as hells ain't gonna get it from the Rule of Ten," someone shouted.

"Now, sir, be careful of your words. I respect your righteous anger at today's situation. But there is nothing to say it cannot change. Perhaps the Rule of Ten may wake on the morrow and take a firm hold of the reins."

There was a buzz of scorn.

"That is your opinion," Tenedos went on carefully. "Let us return to this mythical Rule of One. Imagine such a man who is not afraid to make the hard decisions, who has a vision of the future, who can lead from the front, not vacillate and waver from the rear. Imagine the battle standard of Numantia going forward . . . and all of us going forward, into the future, under it!"

I looked at Marán. Her eyes were shining, her lips slightly parted, all her attention fixed on the man on the stage. Tenedos's words were ringing true to her, going straight into her heart such as all the preachings in her salons had obviously not accomplished.

I myself had heard most of what Tenedos was saying before, and agreed with a great deal of it, although I certainly wasn't convinced that a Rule of One, a king, although he'd never use that word unless he wished the Rule of Ten's wardens to arrest him for sedition, was the only solution. I marveled at how carefully he was able to skirt the very edge of treasonous speech without ever crossing over.

I wondered if he'd cast a Spell of Persuasion on the room, but felt no unnatural working of my emotions, so eloquence rather than magic was holding the crowd.

"Umar created, then withdrew," Tenedos said. "Then it was Irisu's turn. But perhaps his rule is growing old, perhaps he is growing tired. Aren't even gods permitted to rest?"

"Then the future will be Saionji's," someone said, and I heard fear in the tone.

"Change is not always bad, my friend," Tenedos said gently. "And to create it is sometimes necessary to do some destruction. Perhaps you are right and it is to be the time of Saionji.

"Think of it," and his voice rose. "If the goddess smiles on Numantia, sees our lands as the hope of man, and chooses us for her spearhead, what golden times would we live in after the change?

"I am a seer, and I can tell you, when the gods and demons let me peep toward tomorrow, I see two visions. One is dark, a once-great kingdom lying in ruins and ruled by the harsh hand of outsiders. The other . . . the other is the dream I have held close, the dream I have shared with you this evening.

"Thank you." He bowed and stepped away from the podium. The crowd cheered, and boiled around Tenedos. Marán sat as if she'd been hypnotized.

"Well?" I said.

She shook herself out of her daze.

"Thank you, Damastes. Oh, thank you for bringing me here."

"Come on," I said, a little uncomfortably. "I'll introduce you to the oracle."

I took her elbow and led her around the throng to one side, waiting until the congratulators and fawners grew fewer. Tenedos waved me to him.

Standing beside him was a very beautiful woman, about his age. She had brown hair, cut close, wore a green gown with a matching head scarf. Her lips were full, lush, as was her body. She seemed to see no one but Tenedos.

"Baroness Rasenna," Marán greeted, her tone formal.

The woman noticed Marán, and looked surprised.

"Countess Agramónte and Lavedan. I never imagined I'd find you listening to the seer."

"Why not?" Marán said. "I listen to many. And the seer's words make perfect sense to me."

"Yes," Rasenna said, almost in a sigh. "Perfect sense indeed."

Tenedos looked at her, and now it was my turn for astonishment. His gaze was tender, loving. I wondered who this woman was who had evidently, if only for a moment, managed to calm the tiger of many bedrooms. Then he turned his attention to me.

"Captain á Cimabue," he said formally. "Thank you for bringing the Countess Agramónte and Lavedan." He bowed low over Marán's hand. "I am delighted to meet you. You must forgive me for missing your assembly."

"Only if you promise not to miss the next one."

"You have my vow. May I bring Rasenna?"

"Of course," Marán said, but I sensed her response was only out of politeness. "She's been too long a stranger at our house."

Tenedos turned to me.

"Damastes, there is someone you must meet." He indicated a small man just behind him. "This is Kutulu. He is a warden who came to see what perfidy I was preaching, and I'm afraid I've corrupted him."

I would never have picked Kutulu for a man of the law. In fact, from the gleam in his eye, I might have thought him to be one of the crazed anarchists the wardens were always chasing after. He was small, already balding. He wore dark clothing and would be completely unnoticeable in a crowd. His eyes ran me up, then down, and I felt as if I'd been reduced to a single card and that card filed with others, never to be forgotten and easily retrievable.

"Captain Damastes á Cimabue," he said, in a voice surprisingly melodious. "I have wanted to meet you for some time now. We shall serve together well."

I blinked. Tenedos moved his head slightly—this was not the time to question.

"I must return to my duties," Kutulu said. "Thank you, Seer. I shall see you in the morning."

He might have been a magician himself for the ease with which he vanished. Tenedos saw my puzzlement and pulled me aside.

"Kutulu came to spy, as I said, and listened to my words. Now he is one of us."

Us? I started to say something, then stopped. Was I one of Tenedos's men? At that moment, I realized I was, although I'd sworn no oath.

"Kutulu is interesting," Tenedos said. "He always wanted to be a warden, but the gods did not give him a bruiser's body. He chose to use his mind, but as yet the wardens of Nicias little respect intelligence." Tenedos added, softly, "That is another matter that shall change. He shall be most useful in the future. It is good to have a man who can . . . keep track of things."

As we rode back to my barracks, Marán told me who the baroness was. At one time she had a fairly lurid reputation for taking and discarding lovers, but her wealth had kept her from being blacklisted, although the best families were reluctant to invite her to their doings. Then she'd married, and her ways had changed. She'd been, as far as anyone knew, completely loyal to her husband. He'd died in a boating accident about eight months earlier, and everyone in Nicias's high social circles had begun watching Rasenna to see if she'd return to her old ways.

"But from the way she was talking," Marán said, "it appears she's completely taken with the seer."

"Good," I said. "He could use someone beside him. I just hope she realizes what he is. He'll never be a conventional person like I am."

"Are you, Damastes?" Marán murmured. "I think you might be selling yourself most short."

The coach pulled to a halt, and I pulled the window's drawn shade aside. We were in front of the regimental area.

"Thank you for the evening, Marán," I said, and reached across her to open the door.

Her perfume swept out like that fog in faraway Sayana, and took me. Our faces were about a foot apart.

Again I swam in the pool of her eyes, then they slowly closed and her lips parted.

I kissed her softly, just brushing her mouth, then my arm went around her shoulders and she came to me, our lips crushed together, her tongue moving deep in my mouth.

I don't remember the embrace ending, or stepping out of the coach or walking back to my quarters.

SEVENTEEN

CHARDIN SHER

Now I wanted my life to be calm, while I tried to work out this new and most vexing development. I had no idea what to do about Marán. I didn't know if I was falling in love, still not sure what that feeling might be, but I knew I cared more for her than any woman I could remember.

I knew I should never see her again. I had bedded married women before, certainly, but it had been for a single night, a momentary fling, and somehow I realized this was not in either of our hearts. Was I prepared to assume the responsibilities of an affair? I knew my father would growl and remind me of our motto, and that its corollary was that we must also respect the vows of others. I was a Cimabuan, not a Nician, who have the reputation of always carrying their cocks low and ready, like a water witch's wand, ready to stick them into anything that doesn't move fast enough.

Practically, seeing Marán again was also absurd. If we did have an affair, and word reached her husband, he could ruin me with a single word or a note to one of his friends in the government.

I needed time to think. But Saionji, who I was starting to believe *was* intervening in Numantia's affairs, did not grant my wish.

The day after Laish Tenedos's speech, Domina Lehar told us the Great Conference on the Border States would be held in Nicias within two weeks. In fact, Chardin Sher, prime minister of Kallio, had already crossed the border into Dara with his retinue, and other state heads would be arriving shortly. But their importance was secondary, not only because they represented smaller states—Dara and Kallio were the two largest in Numantia—but because Kallio had always been Dara's rival for the real power in the kingdom. This was especially true now, since Chardin Sher had taken the post of prime minister five years ago and had shown himself an independent-minded ruler of great strength, who only paid heed to the Rule of Ten when it suited him.

The Golden Helms were ordered to full readiness for the conference, to provide security and glitter. Two of the city's other parade units, the Nineteenth Foot and the Second Heavy Cavalry, also had leaves canceled and all men ordered to stand by.

We would be spread most thinly, even so. The people of Nicias pride themselves on never being surprised by anything. But this appearance of Chardin Sher, the first time he had deigned to visit the capital, set the populace atremble. His route from the docks to the palace he'd been assigned by the Rule of Ten was laid out in the broadsides, and every window along the procession sold for a good price in silver. The streets would be jammed on that day with spectators. Nicias planned to give itself a holiday when the Kallian arrived.

"Is it not interesting," Tenedos observed, "how the masses will flock around a man they know to be strong, even though he could well be their enemy in a month or a year." He then added that he himself hoped to meet Chardin Sher. When I asked him if this didn't mean he was no different from the rest of us, he looked angry for a moment, then chuckled. "That is why I like you, Damastes. You serve to remind me I'm just as prone to the passions and angers of the moment as anyone."

Now I was very busy, and Marán almost, but not quite, was put to the back of my mind. I had B Troop out half a dozen times riding the back streets that paralleled Chardin Sher's route—we were to be the reaction element if there were any problems. Fortunately, none were anticipated, except what could happen if the crowd pressed too hard in its enthusiasm. We received no word from the wardens of plots or anyone intending harm to the Kallian. But to make sure of his safety we would have the Nineteenth Foot along the parade route, and the cavalry units standing by.

During the conference we would also be called to add glamour to the various social events planned for Chardin Sher and the others in every capacity from door openers to escorts. I felt less soldier than body servant, and was reminded just how different the Helms were from the Lancers by the fact my fellow officers and soldiers were delighted by what was going on.

The two biggest events were a great masked ball, to be held shortly after his arrival, and a banquet the night the conference was scheduled to end.

The day before Chardin Sher's arrival, while I was busy grooming that misbegotten vile-tempered black my duties insisted I ride, while Lucan whickered jealously in the background, a uniformed equerry delivered a sealed note.

> *To My Friend Damastes*
>
> *My husband and I have been invited to the Masked Ball at the Water Palace four nights hence. Of course, we accepted the invitation to meet Chardin Sher. Unfortunately, Hernad was called away this morning to deal with problems with our factor in Cicognara, and will not return for at least a week.*
>
> *Could I impose, and request you do me the honor of accompanying me to the event, if that would not be too onerous a task?*
>
> > *With fondest thoughts*
> > *Marán, Countess Agramónte and Lavedan*

I should have told the messenger to wait for a moment while I jotted a quick note of regret. This was not only the path of common sense, but what duty required.

Instead, I told the man I'd reply within the day, and, before the noon meal, asked the adjutant, Captain of the Upper Half Lardier, if there was a possibility I could be excused on the night in question.

He glowered at me. "Captain, if you were a fresh legate I might expect such a question. But from a troop commander? I hardly think—"

Before he could continue, I handed him the invitation. Instantly his manner changed.

"Ah. Forgive me. I see why you consulted me on the matter. Certainly the Agramónte and Lavedans are important families, and the last thing we would wish to do is give the slightest cause for offense. But I must consult the domina."

He disappeared toward Domina Lehar's office, and was back before we'd been called to the table. "The domina quite understands the matter, and gives his full approval. He would only ask you present his compliments to the Count Lavedan when next you see him."

I blandly assured Captain Lardier I would do just that the next time the count and I were socializing. I felt guilty, but only for about three seconds.

That night, in the mess, though, a complication arose. Captain Lardier, as I'd already learned, was a gossip of the first water, and so the fact that I had an exalted friend was known to my fellow officers.

I'd gotten myself my usual before-dinner drink, a glass of iced lime juice with a sprinkling of sugar, and was about to join Legate Petre where he sat reading, when I heard a burst of laughter and my name mentioned. I looked across the room, where stood Legate Nexo with a group of his friends, all equally snobbish in their attitudes.

"Captain á Cimabue," he said, noting he'd drawn my attention and smiling nastily, "I understand you've been most fortunate in being favored by a certain countess. Might I ask what . . . hidden talents you have, since none of us have even been granted a smile from the beautiful one."

I certainly did not need a rumor like *that* to begin spreading. I set my drink down, and walked over to the legate, my face set hard. He tried to keep his smile, but it slowly vanished the closer I got. There was some merit to the reputation Cimabuans have as impetuous brawlers, after all.

My hand shot out, and he flinched, no doubt expecting to be struck. Instead, I plucked the glass he was holding from his hand, and sniffed at it.

"Legate, I perceive you have been drinking. Otherwise, I know you would not have slandered one of this city's most reputable families."

This was an angle of attack he was not expecting.

"Captain, I—"

"And now you argue with me?" I turned and caught the attention of Nexo's troop commander, Captain of the Lower Half Abercorn, senior to me with more time in grade.

"Captain, if I may have a moment of your time?"

Abercorn walked over.

"Captain, this legate of yours had the temerity to insult a friend of mine, Countess Agramónte and Lavedan, in the presence of these other officers. He is either a fool or a drunkard. I cannot, of course, call this lower-ranking man to account for his words, nor would I sully my blade with his blood willingly.

"I could call for him to appear before a court of honor. But considering the legate's youth and foolishness, might I suggest you impose a more fitting penalty for a stupid boy?"

Nexo was purple with rage and fright. He knew better than to say anything. I was beginning to enjoy myself. Captain Abercorn, not known for being a swift thinker, stammered, then said, of course, of course, this could not be permitted, and did I have a thought as to what might be appropriate?

"I do indeed, sir. Perhaps you might bar him from the mess for a month, and, since he evidently has a problem with the grape, from drink for a suitably longer time. If nothing else, it will reduce his mess bills."

"So ordered, sir. Legate, you heard what the captain said. Begone with you, and I never wish to hear of another such incident as long as you care to remain with the Helms!"

That took care of Legate Nexo. The rumor might persist, but it would travel well underground.

I still would rather have smashed his face in, but this more subtle army way of punishing him would be satisfactory. The only reason it had worked was, of course, because of the fear all these social climbers who called themselves soldiers had of offending a powerful family like the Agramóntes or Lavedans.

So I was going to play the fool after all. I thought about what sort of costume the fool should wear, and, for the first time in my life, had to deal with the meaningless but worrisome trivia the very rich fill their lives with.

I could not attend in uniform, of course. I thought of Vachan, but that might trivialize the monkey god I revered. Legate Yonge had a simple solution: dig out the rags I'd used to disguise myself as a Kaiti and wear them. I considered that, but my skin crawled—they were my enemies, and I would not deign to ennoble them in any way. Lance Karjan, who was definitely rising above himself, suggested I go naked and back into the room.

"What would that represent?"

"Why, a breadroll, sir."

I sent him to the stables and went to Tenedos for advice. He was also going, with Rasenna. I'd spent a bit of time around her by then, and, since I never paid much mind to people's reputation in any area other than honesty, was beginning to like her. She had a well-honed wit, and specialized in skewering the pretensions of the nobility who swarmed in the capital.

Tenedos said his outfit had been decided on already by the baroness: They'd be wearing furs and carrying clubs as the First Man and Woman.

"Why don't you wear peasant rags," he said, "with a yellow silk cord around your neck? Then look to see how many people recognize the costume, and you'll know how much of a penetration the Tovieti have made." I'd told him, of course, about the Marchioness Fenelon and her golden bauble, and he said he wasn't surprised. I thought his suggestion interesting, but no more.

Other ideas were considered, but discarded as absurd, expensive, or impractical. I guess half of the nobility of Dara was going through the same pangs—the expensive dressmakers' shops were packed, and the carriages of their customers blocked the streets outside.

Finally, I settled on the role of a wandering begger-monk, which required no more costume than a baggy orange robe, a rope around the waist, a hood, and begging bowl with hook to hang on the rope. I added a half-mask and was content.

Marán came down the stairs toward me, and I forgot whatever weak witticism about needing but a bowl of rice before my prayers.

A sea monster's evil visage covered her head, except for nose and lips, and wide, dark lenses hid her eyes. There was a small hole at the back to allow her hair to fall free.

The mask flowed into the rest of her outfit, a shimmering light green fabric that might have been silk but was not that clung to her body from ankle to head. It was slit to her upper thigh, so every step she took showed silken skin.

It hugged her form so closely it was obvious she wore nothing under it. I could see her nipples under the garment, and I felt my blood race. My reaction was obvious, because I saw her nipples firm and rise slightly. I was grateful robes hid my own body's response.

The dress had a subtle pattern that suggested the scales of a serpent. The outfit was magical, and I mean that literally. With each step she took, the colors of the dress moved as a snake slithers, coils running up to her shoulders, then back down.

She stopped a few steps from me.

"Well?"

"Madam the Sea Serpent is the loveliest thing on all the oceans," I said. "Count Lavedan's sailors are very lucky real sea snakes aren't so intoxicating, or he would have a great number of ships drifting on the oceans after their crews jump overboard."

"I thank you, sir." Her expression became serious. "However, one request. I do not care to hear the name of the count my husband for the remainder of the evening."

That was certainly acceptable to *me*.

Marán pouted. "This damned business of his in Cicognara. He could have sent an agent, but he had to go see for himself. I think he didn't want me to be able to go to this ball.

"But there is always a way, isn't there?"

"As milady has said, we are not discussing a certain shipowner, so I cannot answer."

She laughed, a silver glissade of loveliness.

"Your imagination frightens me," I said, once more studying her costume.

"*Anyone* can imagine," she said. "*I* admire the two who were able to build it. First my seamstress, then the seer who put the motion spell on it.

"It will live but the evening," she went on. "Then it shall be nothing but another dress. Not that it'll matter—I'll probably tear the stitches getting out of it anyway."

I'd heard the expression being sewn into a garment, but never imagined it could be real. I did not want to know what that dress cost—no doubt my father could have bought an entire season's seeds for our estate and not spent as much. But the Agramóntes could afford any extravagance.

"Shall we go?" I suggested. "You might bring a wrap, although I hate to ruin the effect of your costume. Since we'll be out of doors it might be chilly."

"Already provided for as part of the spell," she said smugly. "Besides, if I get cold I'm sure there's room for two under those robes of yours, most reverend sir."

In those days the Water Palace belonged to the Rule of Ten, although it was only used for ceremonial occasions. Now I am very familiar with its every garden, pool, and room, since it became mine not long afterward. But this was the first time I'd been there, and so was in awe when we stepped out of Marán's brougham in its courtyard.

It sits on a hill about three miles from the center of Nicias, in a 100-acre park. One branch of the Latane River flows close to it, and water is pumped from the river up into an artificial lake above the palace, where it is filtered until it is as clear as a mountain stream. Then it's permitted to run down the hill in over a hundred different stone creeks that feed fountains, purl over small waterfalls or swirl in ponds where multicolored fish swim, and then flow back into the Latane. Other pools are heated by Nicias's omnipresent gas supply to various temperatures, and are intended for bathing.

The palace is actually a series of buildings cascading down this hill, each appearing separate but all connected through underground passageways.

There are open pavilions, gazebos, and hideaways; the palace is perfect for everything from a secret lovers' meeting to a Grand Ball such as the one we attended.

I was right when I thought all of Nicias's upper class would attend—they were all there that night, and their costumes dazzled. Marán was watched and commented on more than most, but then, she most likely would have stood out if she'd been wearing my monk's robes.

The affair was held in the palace's main ballroom, a great, glass-domed structure that could have held twice as many people. There was one orchestra here, and others scattered throughout the grounds. Either by clever communication or sorcery, all of them played the same tune at the same time, keeping in perfect time with each other.

At the center of the room was Chardin Sher, and a long receiving line snaked toward him. About halfway up it I saw the Seer Tenedos and his baroness. We joined them, after asking permission from those behind. Both Marán and I lifted our masks, as had the others in the line. After meeting Chardin Sher the mysteries could begin.

"What do you think of my ensemble, Damastes?" Tenedos wondered.

"You're quite the First Man, sir," I said. "I didn't know he was supposed to have been that hairy."

"I think my tailor became a bit carried away," Tenedos

explained. "Or else he thought I needed far more concealment than I allow for."

If Tenedos's furs were somewhat exaggerated, Baroness Rasenna compensated in quite the opposite direction. Her costume began as a fur collar around her neck that ruffed down just far enough to cover the middle of her breasts, although when she moved her nipples peeped into sight. Fur went from the back of the collar down her spine, between her legs and then up across her hips to rejoin the spinal covering. She wore a wolf-head for a headdress and short boots.

"I think the costumer believed that the First Man was set down in the icy south, and First Woman in the tropics, but Laish doesn't like my theory," Rasenna said.

"I didn't say that," Tenedos said. "I just said I didn't know how they ever came together if your theory's right."

"What Umar willed would happen."

"More likely the Man would've settled down with the first friendly sheep he encountered and there never would have been a Second Man," Tenedos said.

I was right—Rasenna was good for the seer. He was quite jovial this evening.

But as we drew closer to Chardin Sher, his cheerfulness vanished and he quit bantering. His gaze was fixed on the Kallian. I followed his example, and let the women talk between themselves.

Chardin Sher was tall, almost as tall as I am. He was thin, his clean-shaven face almost gaunt. His eyes were the palest, hardest gray I have ever seen. He was flanked by three retainers and a third small man, who whispered in his ear each time a Nician stepped forward to greet him. Two of the others were his bodyguards, men whose eyes never stopped sweeping the room, although their smiles and even laughter came mechanically as required.

The third man made me start. It was Elias Malebranche, the Kallian emissary to the court of Achim Baber Fergana, whose presence and even stranger disappearance had never been explained.

None of the Kallians wore costume, and Malebranche turned, and saw Tenedos and myself. I saw he still wore the fighting knife in its horizontal sheath. He, too, stiffened, his hand reflexively touching the knife.

At that moment I knew one of us would kill the other.

I tapped Tenedos's boot with my foot, but he was intent on studying the Kallian prime minister and not to be distracted.

Chardin Sher smiled, and said something to the couple in front of Tenedos that made them laugh as they walked away, then the seer was in front of him. The little man whispered a few words to Kallian. Tenedos stood motionless for a moment, and I wondered if he thought Chardin Sher should be the first to bow. Then he inclined his head no more than politeness dictated. Chardin Sher did the same, paying no attention to Rasenna.

"So," he said, his tone amused, "you are the wizard who thinks I am such a threat. Now you can see I am no more than any other man."

"You have excellent information, sire. Would that we had the same for all that happens in Kallio."

Chardin Sher frowned.

"What would that mean?"

Tenedos smiled and said, his voice an obvious lie, "Why, no more than we do not hear nearly enough of what it must be like to live in your state or in your capital of Polycittara, which I am sure provides a fascinating life."

"Very good, Seer. You use more than magic to turn away a thrust, I see. Now, let me ask you, in all honesty, why you have been preaching that I need bringing down?"

"I have never said that, sir," Tenedos said. "I have merely offered you as an example of ministers who seem to pay little attention to their rightful masters."

"That is not true," Chardin Sher. "I do everything I am ordered."

"Ordered, yes. But if I had a servant who did no more than just what he was told, ignoring my unspoken policies, I'd have him thrashed and driven from my service."

"So that is what you would have the Rule of Ten do with me?" The smile was gone from Chardin Sher's lips, and his stare was the coldest of rage.

"I will not dare to speak for my leaders. If I could, though, I would require certain things of you before you return to Kallio."

"What would *you* will?"

"That you formally renounce all of Kallio's claims to the Border States and agree to join with Dara in mounting a punitive expedition into Kait to finally reduce that country to proper obedience."

"That would mean war," he said.

"I do not call suppressing bandits who call themselves a nation war, but if you choose that term, so be it."

"And if I do not call for this crusade? The Rule of Ten haven't suggested that to me at all."

Tenedos looked unblinking into the Kallian's eyes, and said nothing whatsoever. To my surprise, Chardin Sher was the first to look away.

"Yes, well, I'm afraid our chat's holding up the line," he said. "Perhaps we should make arrangements to continue this discussion before I leave Nicias."

"My time is yours," Tenedos bowed and stepped away.

Again, the little man whispered information, and I bowed to the Kallian.

"You are the man who saved Seer Tenedos's life, eh?"

"And he mine."

"Guard him well, soldier," Chardin Sher said. "I have no magic, but I can predict a man such as him will always be courting danger."

"I thank you for that advice, sir," and I stepped away.

Chardin Sher's eyes gleamed as he took in Marán.

"Countess," he greeted after the briefing. "You are the most spectacular thing I've seen in Nicias thus far. Thank you for honoring me with your presence."

Marán curtsied, and we joined Tenedos, who stood a few feet away, waiting. Rasenna was positively glowing, and seemed to care nothing for not being spoken to.

"You see why I love him," she said, unasked. "My little magician will stand up to anything for what he believes."

Tenedos looked embarrassed at her words. I waited for a comment, but, instead, he stroked his chin thoughtfully. "You know, that small one that Chardin Sher has with him. A walking file. Interesting. Most valuable at times like this when you're meeting strangers but courtesy suggests you should know them."

"Perhaps you could train Kutulu," I said.

"No," Tenedos said. "He will have other, more important uses. Such a man as Chardin Sher has must have no identity, no soul, beyond what his master gives him."

He replaced his mask, and I remembered what he'd told me in Sayana about never finding a man so monstrous that nothing could be learned from him.

"Now the preliminary skirmishing is over," he said, "shall we enjoy ourselves, even though I dance but indifferently? Oh, yes. One thing, Damastes. I'll lay ten gold pieces against one of your collar buttons that I never am summoned for a talk with Chardin Sher."

I grinned. "Sir, just because I'm but a captain doesn't mean I'm a fool. No bet."

"Tsk. I do love an easy victory." Tenedos bowed to Marán and led Rasenna toward the dance floor.

I took Marán's arm and followed.

Marán, naturally, danced superbly. I am regarded as a decent stepper, but she knew all of the latest steps, whereas I had only familiarity with older standards. So we sat out some numbers, talking of this and that, thoroughly enjoying each other's company. I thought, wistfully, it was like the beginning of a courtship, when both parties are delighted over their lover-to-be's wit, charm, and beauty.

A simple dance I knew the steps to began, and I took her in my arms and we moved together to the music.

The material of her dress felt like silk, but where silk is cold this was warm, living in the brief spell the magician had given.

I let my hand slip down from Marán's shoulders to the small of her back, and could feel the beginning of her cleft. I longed to slide it down farther, and cup her buttocks, but knew better.

"You dance a bit closer than a chaperone might approve of, Damastes."

"I apologize to the invisible iron lady. But not to you."

"You are a shameful man, sir. Does the army teach you such behavior?"

"That and worse, my good Countess. For instance, there is a dance done by soldiers of my *real* regiment, in faraway Mehul, when they visit the sinful dens of Rotten Row, that requires the man to put both arms closely around his partner. Of course we officers would never partake of such an ostentatiously sexual pastime as that."

"Is the dance slow or fast?"

"It alternates, and I've seen women leap from the floor and wrap their legs around their accomplices, and then lean back until their hair brushes the floor."

"Sinful, perhaps," Marán said. "And definitely acrobatic." She laughed. "Wouldn't that shock the good people of Nicias if we suddenly began such a turn?"

"Possibly," I said, a bit drunk with the notion, "but I at least wouldn't notice their response."

"Careful, sir."

There was a touch on my shoulder, and I came back to earth and prepared to relinquish Marán reluctantly to an interloper. Standing there was Elias Malebranche.

"Good evening, Captain á Cimabue."

Anger just at his presence flashed through me, but I said nothing, and stepped back. Marán looked puzzled, but moved toward Malebranche, ready to dance away. She smiled at him—the landgrave was a not unhandsome man, I had to admit.

"No, Countess, I am not asking for the dance, but thank you for the honor," he said. "My master wishes to have further converse with you." He nodded at me. "We shall need the honor of the lady's presence for only a few moments. So if you'll excuse us . . ."

Marán's face reddened.

"Captain," she said to me, "I am not sure I understand what this man really wishes, but I am most shocked he would ask me to leave my chosen escort at his master's beckon, for some sort of dialogue he is afraid for you to overhear. I gather you know him?"

"Yes," I said, pushing my own rage back, and put an expression of puzzlement on my face. "Yes, now I think I do. Forgive me. Countess Agramónte and Lavedan, this is Elias Malebranche. I believe he has a title . . . ah yes. Landgrave."

Malebranche bowed, Marán barely inclined her head. Before Marán could respond to the insulting invitation, I said, in my smoothest courtier's tones, "My humblest apologies, Landgrave Malebranche. But I did not recognize you without your yellow silk cord."

Malebranche's eyes flashed rage, and he spun on me.

"What does that mean, sir?"

Instead of answering him directly, I spoke to Marán.

"The good landgrave has close friends in the hills and now elsewhere who have most unusual ideas on how to enrich themselves. I shall not speak their name here, but his associates are the sort of murderous scum you might expect a man who behaves as he does to associate with."

Malebranche's words came through gritted teeth.

"Your manners, sir, are exactly what I'd expect from a peasant foot soldier. My master merely thought the lady might enjoy the company of a gentleman, rather than a mercenary from a forgotten and barbaric state who's probably taken vows of celibacy to match his costume."

There could be but one response to that. I was about to explode, but saw Malebranche's hand unconsciously caressing the haft of his knife. If I struck him, he would be entitled to defend himself by any means necessary right here, and I was unarmed, though I feared him not in the slightest. If I called him out, it would be his choice of weapons, and obviously he was an expert with the knife. Marán, too, knew what must occur, and her anger had turned to fear.

I don't know where I found control—perhaps Tanis or my monkey god Vachan granted me a boon. But I did, and said, in a fairly calm tone, "Landgrave, I know what you wish me to do. But I cannot. A Numantian officer must not duel with his inferiors."

"How dare you! The Malebranche family can extend its heritage for a thousand years!"

"If that is so, which I doubt, then your ancestors would be hanging their heads, seeing their descendant no more than a false nobleman's pimp."

That did it.

Malebranche, his voice ice, said, "Very well. My response shall be on the Field of Honor. Is that agreeable with you?"

I bowed agreement, and he stalked away.

The red anger subsided, and I looked about. Fortunately no one seemed to have heard our exchange, and we were merely getting puzzled looks as to why we were standing still in the middle of the dance floor.

I took Marán in my arms and moved away, pretending to dance.

"Now what happens?" she whispered.

"Now I kill the bastard."

A few minutes later, Marán's temper roared back, and she wanted to go to Chardin Sher and tell him what a contemptible swine he was.

"If you wish," I said, choosing my words carefully. "I'll cheerfully accompany you."

"No you won't. I can take care of myself. Besides, you'd probably take that wretched man's dagger away from him and stab the shit, and then what would happen?"

"I'd be executed, of course. But I would die happy, and rise on the Wheel for having served such a beautiful woman."

"Stop trying to calm me down, dammit!"

"My apologies." I started to say something more, that I had

not been the one to insult her, but fortunately held my tongue. We were alone in one of the gardens. We'd gone out of the ballroom to calm ourselves down, and clearly it was not happening. Marán stared out into the night. After a time, she turned back.

"No, Damastes. It is for me to apologize. I'm foolish to think of going to Chardin Sher. He'll deny he said anything of the sort, and then I'll be the fool.

"Why in the hells is it always the man who's believed?"

"I don't know," I said. "Maybe it's because man makes the laws."

"Well, it's stupid and it's fucked!" Her rage was returning. Her dress seemed to respond to her anger, because the coils seethed up and down her body.

"It is," I agreed. I didn't know what to do—the evening was ruined. I supposed that we should just leave quietly. But instead of suggesting that, I took her gently in my arms, and held her close.

We stood in silence for a very long time, and her breathing came hard, then relaxed, then hard again, then gentled as she fought for, then found, control.

"I am not going to cry, either," she said against my chest. "I won't give that son of a bitch the price of one damned tear!"

She lifted her head to me, and her lips parted. I kissed her, and she kissed me back, fiercely. Then she pulled away.

"I suppose he would have said how taken he was with me, and perhaps I might be willing to meet him in his quarters later. He doesn't impress me as a man who spends much time wooing those he wants.

"But I've heard nastier suggestions," she said. "The sons of the rich think they can talk like stable hands when they're not granted their every desire, and have very strange ideas of what an unaccompanied young woman might wish." A bit of a smile came. "Although I've never had them from somebody as high-ranking as Chardin Sher. I suppose I should be honored."

She laughed then, and the laugh was genuine. "I wonder how Malebranche qualified as Chardin Sher's procurer."

"Probably sold him his mother and sister," I said. I did not tell her I knew Malebranche to be far more than just a pimp— I now realized he was the prime minister's specialist for any and all dirty work.

"I shall tell you what we are going to do," Marán said. "We are going back in there, and we are going to enjoy ourselves, and forget about Kallians. I was having far too good a time to allow them to ruin anything."

That was exactly what we did. Chardin Sher and his lackeys were gone, so it was not impossible. As the evening went on, it became easier and easier.

The ball would last all night, but it was only a bit past midnight when Marán suggested we leave.

"We have made our appearance, I've shown off my outfit, and we've discovered Kallians are pigs. What else is there to do? I'm afraid to eat anything or I'll burst out of this dress."

"Hmm," I said. "What an interesting thought. Have you examined that tray of eclairs over there? They look delicious."

"Come on, you lunatic Cimabuan!" She laughed, pulled the serpent's hood from her head, and her hair fell free about her shoulders. I unmasked as well and followed her.

On the ride to her house, Marán was quiet. I assumed she was brooding about Chardin Sher's insult, and so tried to keep a jolly conversation going.

I stepped out of the brougham when it pulled to a halt, and handed her down. I was about to bid her good night, and go to the stables for Lucan, when she said, "Captain, are you a gentleman?"

"I would hope so, Countess."

"Then I can invite you in, although I have little idea on what to serve a nonimbiber."

"In honor of the occasion, Madam, I will make an exception and allow you to pour me a small bit of your finest brandy."

"You *are* a gracious man, sir, ever ready to help a distressed and puzzled damsel."

* * *

The house was deserted, and there were no servants about, even though the gaslights blazed.

"I suppose everyone thought we'd be out till dawn, and went out to look for parties of their own." She frowned. "Very, very old, brandy. That would most likely be in . . . in *someone's* study."

She led me upstairs, and bade me wait.

I stood in the luxurious halls, feeling foolish in my orange robes. After a moment, she came out with a crystal decanter that shot reflections of the light around the room.

"Let's see. Oh, I know. You haven't seen the solarium yet. Come on." She took my hand and led me up the stairs to the roof.

It was a large room, with a glass roof curved like the top of a breadloaf. It was all done in white, wrought-iron chairs and tables, even the frames that held the glass window panes. There were doors that opened onto a deck.

I sat gingerly in an ornate chair, and Marán poured me brandy, then sat down in a thinly upholstered lounge that looked as if it would collapse if I had tried to use it.

"I wish to thank you," I said, "for inviting me to the ball. Otherwise I would have been one of those poor cavalrymen we saw in the streets, sitting my horse, trying to look noble and freezing my, my—"

"Balls is the word you are looking for."

"No it's not. But it'll do. By the way, I meant to compliment you on your language. I didn't know countesses could swear like you."

"You can if you grow up in the country and ride a lot. All my horses respond better to that sort of language than cooing and such."

"How odd," I said. "Army horses prefer soothing and gentleness. Perhaps it's the unfamiliar that makes them listen."

I smiled, and she hesitantly smiled back. For a second, her expression once more became that of the innocent expecting punishment. She rose and went to one of the doors. I picked up my glass and joined her.

Below was the river, and even at this late hour I saw the lights of barges and vessels. I thought I heard something, and opened the door. I was right. Soft music drifted up from the water. After a moment I saw where it came from: Far upriver a luxury ferry moved slowly toward us, and there must have been a band aboard.

I was standing very close behind Marán, and could smell, over her perfume that was making me far drunker than the bit of brandy I'd tasted, the clean scent of her hair.

She turned, and took the brandy glass from my hand, and sat it down. "Now, you arrant bluffer, we are far from prying eyes and we have a magically provided orchestra. I wish to see this Rotten Row dance, sir."

I hesitated, and the way her eyes boldly took me made the decision.

"The hells with being a gentleman," I muttered, and her arms slid around me, and she melted into my embrace. I slid my arms down around her back and, as I'd longed, cupped her buttocks. She caught her breath, slipped one leg between mine, and we moved as one. I began kneading my hands, and her breath came faster and I felt her nipples rise, even through my costume.

I felt my cock hard against her thigh, and she forced herself closer. We danced like that for an eternity, and then I suddenly realized the ship was long gone, and the only music we had was in our minds.

She pulled me down into a kiss. Our tongues flared together, and she moaned, moving her head from side to side, crushing her lips against mine.

Then she pulled away.

"Yes, Damastes. Now. Quickly. Come with me."

Almost running, she led me toward the stairs.

I did not notice what her bedroom looked like, except that the bed was wide, invitingly laid, and the sheets were silken, but as warm as her dress. The room was lit by a single candle-like flame from a lamp on a bedside table.

We embraced once more, then Marán pulled away. Her fingers fumbled at her neck. She muttered in frustration, and I hooked fingers inside her costume, and tore. The stitching ripped with a tiny shriek, and she was naked.

"You," she said. "Now you. Hurry. Please hurry."

I lifted my robes away and kicked off my sandals. I picked her up in my arms, and we fell across the bed. Her arms were moving up and down my back, and she was moaning, murmuring my name. Her leg lifted across the back of mine, caressing. My fingers slipped down her body, the softest, fairest skin I'd ever touched, shaven clean, and then I found waiting wetness.

Her thighs parted, and she pushed up, against my searching hand. There was no hesitation, no time or need for long foreplay as I moved between her legs.

I touched her clitoris with the head of my cock, and her body jerked. "Oh, gods," she said. "Oh, Damastes. Please. Please. Take me. Fuck me, fuck me hard, fuck me now!"

I found the wetness, pushed, met hard obstruction, felt a flash of amazement, then pushed once more, and Marán cried out, guttural, a moment of pain, and then the tissue gave way and I buried myself in her.

I lay motionless for a moment, then her legs lifted, and she wrapped them around my lower thighs, and thrust up against me, slowly at first, then stronger and stronger. My thrusts met hers, and her fingernails dug into my back. Our bodies crashed together, and then I broke and I could feel semen gush, and a moment later she cried out sharply and her body jerked against mine.

Slowly her throbs faded, and she was still, her breathing calming. But I was still hard, still inside her, and rolled her onto her side and began moving, and she moaned my name and once more we were swept away.

"I've never done this before," she said, "so you'll have to give me advice."

"Well, this isn't a good time to be biting. At least not very hard. Use your tongue. Yes. Mmm. Like that. Now, take me in your mouth. Try to swallow me." It was my turn to moan. "Now, move your head back and forth."

The world was her lips around me, and I moved, and she moved faster, and I lifted my buttocks off the bed, feeling her hair sweep across my stomach my hands stroking the back of her head, and Jaen took me in her embrace again.

She let my cock slip out of her mouth, and swallowed. "Thank you, my Damastes."

"For what?"

"We didn't have time for dinner. You taste good."

Her words sent another spasm of desire through me.

She got up once to use the bathroom, and I glanced down at the sheet. It was stained, but with more than love. There was a small bit of blood where we'd first joined. I wondered what sort of strange marriage she must have, then, guiltily, put the thought out of my mind as she came back toward me and started to lie down.

"No." I stood up, and turned her around so she faced me. "Lie back on the bed. No, don't move up on it. Let your hips touch the edge. Now, lift your legs until your heels are on the bed."

I touched her knees and they fell open, welcoming. I slipped between her thighs, and touched her sex, still wet with love. My cock rose, and I slid it into her.

"Now, put your feet back on the floor."

She hissed and arced her back as I began moving in her, my hands caressing her breasts, massaging her nipples gently.

We were never sleepy, never losing the savage desire to bury ourselves in the other's bodies.

The world was silk, that single candle, and her body moving under me.

Once, in a brief moment of sanity, I asked, "What of your servants? Don't any of them have big ears?"

"Don't worry about it," she said, her voice muffled by the pillow. "I'm not a stupid woman, even if I'm not experienced in adultery. I made sure they knew, when they were hired, the Agramóntes pay their salary."

"I was just asking. So what do I do now that I'm not worrying?"

"What I want you to do now is just what you did before. Except this time, slowly, very slowly, putting it all the way in me. I like it better that way. I want to feel you on my womb."

"Your wish is my command, Countess," and her buttocks rose against me.

It was gray when I slipped out the door. I found the stables, where Lucan was tied. He nickered a soft reproach at having been left saddled for so long, and I whispered a promise that he should have a meal of the best barley as my apology.

As besotted as any drunkard, I rode through the streets of the city as the dawn rose golden over Nicias.

EIGHTEEN

THE ISLE
OF BONES

I managed to avoid the duty roster for that day, but had slept only two hours when Lance Karjan awakened me. "I know you told me not t' bother you, sir. But there's a messenger, an' th' bastard insisted."

I groggily pulled on a robe, and found a plainly dressed man waiting for me. He handed me an envelope, and I tore it open. It read:

> *Dear Captain á Cimabue*
>
> *You will note I sent this letter in the hands of a commoner. I meant no disrespect, but I want to make sure we were able to satisfactorily resolve our differences without interference.*
>
> *While my lord, Chardin Sher, cares little about the death of an arrogant Numantian officer, I recognize that you are bound by certain conventions, from your Army's policies, to no doubt the cowardice of the Rule of Ten, which surely would frown on our meeting.*
>
> *Since I have no friends in Nicias of the necessary rank, I hope you will forgive this somewhat demeaning manner of conducting business, in sending this missive by a commoner rather than one of our equals and proposing the matter be dealt with directly.*

But you and I need no seconds to settle things. If this
arrangement is satisfactory, do me the honor of sending a
note with this man giving the proper arrangements.
    Landgrave Elias Malebranche

The Kallian had a point. I bade the servant wait, and
scratched a quick reply. I told him I agreed, and we could surely and honorably come to an agreement.

My arrangements were simple: We would fight at dawn,
four days hence; the location was the Isle of Bones, a certain
island three miles above the city and not the usual place for
gentlemen to settle their differences; and finally my choice of
weapons was sword and dagger, identical swords to be provided by me, and knives of our own choosing.

I knew this last would surprise and please him, since it
appeared to be playing into his strength. But I had a small
secret he wasn't aware of.

I sealed the note, gave it to the messenger, and he touched
his forehead and left.

I was suddenly very awake, and told Lance Karjan to
make tea and prepare a bath. As he worked, I could see him
casting curious eyes at me, and so I told him what was in
the offing. I told him nothing of the night with Marán, but
assumed he would draw the obvious conclusions. If a man is
never a hero to his body servant, it's equally impossible to
have a secret.

"Wi'out seconds, sir, or anyone else t'witness, what's
t'keep th' Kallian from pullin' some dirt?"

"Nothing. I've got to assume the landgrave is a gentleman."

"A'ter Kait, an' th' Tovieti, an' what happened in th' retreat,
you're still willin' t'give Malebranche th' doubt?"

"I don't have any other choice, now do I?"

Lance Karjan muttered something he refused to repeat
more loudly when I asked him, and asked to be excused after
he readied my bath.

I did not see Marán before the duel, and I avoided Tenedos
as well. I was fairly sure if he learned about the matter he'd try

to use it politically and somehow damage Malebranche and hopefully his master. In the process he would also save my life, but that was the least of my concerns. All I could feel was red hatred when I thought of the Kallian. I knew this was wrong, not morally—for anyone who would ally himself with the stranglers of Thak deserved no kindness—but because anger is no good way to fight. Finally I was able to reach a state of cool detachment, and felt proud.

I sent a polite note to Marán, thanking her for allowing me to escort her to the ball. I thought long and hard for some way of saying what I felt, but was afraid the note might pass into the hands of her husband. Finally I added that the night had provided memories that would never die. I wished I was more clever, but that was the best I could manage. I hoped she would understand.

I heard nothing for a day, then a messenger from her household brought me an envelope.

It was unsigned. All the note consisted of was a time and day and an address. The date was noon, one day after I was to meet Landgrave Malebranche, and a line at the bottom said to present this note. I managed to ride down that particular street while carrying a dispatch to Domina Lehar at the palace, who was dancing close attendance on the Great Conference, and saw we were to meet at one of Nicias's more exclusive restaurants, and didn't know whether to find good or bad fortune in that.

Now all I had to do was live through the encounter with Malebranche.

I suppose I should have tossed and turned the night before the duel, but I didn't. I ate lightly, for fear of a stomach wound, prayed briefly to Tanis and Panoan, since in an odd way I would be representing Nicias, and went to bed early. My mind wanted to insist on planning the morrow, but I refused it permission. My father had said one of the worst things a soldier can do is try to determine the course of a fight—he'll send premature messages to his body, which it'll try to obey even when the foe is doing something entirely unexpected.

I came fully awake when Lance Karjan touched my shoulder, and washed and dressed quickly. Lucan and Karjan's black were saddled out front, and Karjan had the case with the two swords I'd borrowed from the arms room, blades with a reach, weight, and balance similar to the weapon I preferred, which was another small advantage.

My knife was light-bladed and long, almost eleven inches in length, razor-sharpened on one side and about halfway along the upper edge. It had a false hilt, a small fingerhold just below the hilt so it would be far handier than its length suggested.

I'd noted Landgrave Malebranche's knife had a blade about eight inches long, which would give him the advantage—a shorter blade is always deadlier in a knife fight. But I didn't intend to fight as if I were a tavern bully.

The streets of the cantonment were deserted except for the sentries, and I answered their challenge and was passed through onto the city streets. I had the time calculated carefully, so we'd arrive at the dueling ground just at first light.

Lucan wanted to run, feeling the pure joy of being in the country, when we came out of Nicias, but I held him back. The near-dawn wind came off the river, carrying all the scents of the wild with it, and I let it fill my lungs. Even though the river we rode beside was mostly slough, it still smelled better than anything I could breathe in a city.

The Isle of Bones is so named because the river's current constantly washes driftwood up on its sandy beaches, driftwood that whitens and ages until the island's rim looks like it's lined with the skeletons of giants. It's only about a mile long, has a few trees and, in its center, an open, sandy area that's surrounded by bushes, perfect for two men who did not wish to be disturbed. The river is shallow enough to walk a horse across everywhere, so there's no need to search for a ford.

Lucan splashed over, and I bent low as we pushed through the brush into the clearing. Landgrave Elias Malebranche was already there, his horse tethered to a tree. He was alone, as we'd agreed.

I dismounted, tied up Lucan, and took the cased weapons from Karjan.

"You can wait on the road for me. If I've not returned within the hour, I've told you what to do."

Karjan wasn't looking at me, but at the Kallian. A queer smile touched his bearded lips.

"Aye, sir," he said. "Those *were* your orders." He saluted, wheeled his horse, and disappeared.

I walked to meet Malebranche.

"Good morning."

"It is that," he agreed.

I opened the case, set it on the ground, and stepped back. He picked up each blade in turn, hefted it, checked it for temper, and made a couple of short thrusts.

"I'll use this one."

I picked up the other and walked to the center of the clearing. Malebranche followed. I chose a good spot, and turned. Malebranche eyed the ground, and moved to my left, about ten feet distant.

"When the sun first shows, we'll fight," I said.

"Agreed."

It grew lighter by the second, and I tensed, breathing deeply, steadily, from the bottom of my lungs as I'd been trained.

I'd taken but three breaths when there was a sudden shout of surprise from the brush behind me, a clang of steel, and a scream and then three dull thunks, like an ax cutting rotten wood. Malebranche jumped in surprise, and his knife slipped into his hand.

From the cover, four horsemen burst out. I had a moment to think—betrayal! Then I saw the first man was Yonge. The other three I did not know.

Malebranche went on guard as the four rode toward us, but they pulled their horses in before they rode him down.

Raw anger filled me, not knowing what the hells had happened. Then I saw Yonge held a man's severed head by the hair. He threw it down in the sand at Malebranche's feet. Two others landed beside it, thrown by his henchmen.

A fifth horseman, Karjan, trotted out of the clearing's other side. "Sorry, sir," he said. "But some orders come before others."

I saw the sun's arc through the trees, but no one, including myself, paid any mind. I was completely befuddled, but then saw Malebranche's face, dark with anger . . . and something else.

"Your friends should learn to watch their back," Yonge said. "They'd live but an hour if they were in my hills."

"I warned you, sir," Karjan put in.

Now it was clear. That I'd ever expected the Kallian, a man of shadows and dark deceit, to be honorable in any manner was stupid. His letter of concern that we should keep our meeting a secret was the setup for a trap. I recognized two of the heads: They were the men who'd served as Chardin Sher's bodyguards at the ball, no doubt ruffians under Malebranche's command.

The Kallian cursed, lifted his blade, and two of Yonge's friends had short bows up, arrows pulled to the head.

"You tell us, Captain á Cimabue, when we are to kill him," Yonge said.

I should have told them to loose then and there. It would have saved some lives and me a certain amount of grief. But I did not. Even now, a far older and more hardened man, I don't think I would have given that order.

"No!" I ordered. "He is mine! Landgrave Malebranche, the sun has risen. We had an agreement. Ready yourself, sir."

Malebranche grinned, and started toward me.

"If he kills me," I snapped over my shoulder, "he's yours."

Malebranche's grin tightened, and became the fixed snarl of a trapped jackal.

I noted how he came at me, sword in a conventional fighting stance, but his knife was held blade down against his hip. Very good, I thought. As I hoped. He does fight like a wineshop bravo. Now we shall see what we shall see.

My small secret was that one of the ways I'd been trained to fight was with sword and dagger, which is a fairly esoteric discipline. In this style the dagger is used as a parrying weapon, and only serves to strike if the two combatants close, to take advantage of a slip or to finish the battle.

Malebranche struck, a feint, and, as I parried, he jumped sideways and his knife shot forward. He was quick, very quick, but that was pretty much the attack I'd expected, and so I slashed at his wrist with my dagger and we were both back on guard.

He circled to his right, trying to get to the outside of my guard, and I turned with him, then sidestepped and flicked my blade for his throat. He jerked his head back, but my sword's keen edge gashed his cheek open, and his blond beard reddened.

He grunted in pain, and struck at me, a slash I barely evaded that cut through my tunic.

Without recovering, he came at me in a continuous attack, and our swords were hilt to hilt, and I blocked his knife away with my dagger. He tried to knee me in the groin, but I turned, smashing his shoulder muscle with the butt of my dagger, leaping away, but not quite quickly enough, as his knife seared along my ribs.

Then sand between us cycloned, and spattered at the Kallian. He shouted in pain, stumbled, and fell, momentarily blinded.

I heard Karjan shout, "Kill the fughpig!" but I did not move. I somehow sensed that wind's sending.

Malebranche rubbed his eyes, trying to come to his feet, and a voice came:

"Do not move, Kallian, and set your weapons down. If you do not, I shall slay you where you lie. Obey me, and you shall see no harm." The voice, of course, was that of Seer Tenedos.

Malebranche gaped, and obeyed. He scuttled backward, and his eyes were wide with fear.

"There is only one reason you are permitted to live, Landgrave Elias Malebranche, and that is I wish no stain on the reputation of Captain Damastes á Cimabue.

"He is not only a friend, but important to me and soon shall be equally vital to all Numantians.

"Believe me, you, and your dog of a master, will rue that your villains were not able to murder him, because Kallio will run deep with blood, yours part of that river, because of his doings in the near future, a future I see most plain.

"Now rise, leaving your weapons where they are, go to your horse, and ride away. Do not look back, or your doom shall not be delayed even a moment longer."

Malebranche, his face as pale as his skin, paying no mind to the blood pouring from his face, scrambled to his feet, ran for his horse, fumbled its reins free, flung himself into the saddle, and galloped away.

Tenedos's voice came once more, but this as no more than a whisper: "Captain á Cimabue, when you return to the city, and your cut is bandaged, come immediately to my quarters!"

"You are an idiot!"

"Yes, sir."

"An utter moron!"

"Yes, sir!"

"I thought the tales about Cimabuans being thicker than bricks were falsehoods, but now I wonder!" Tenedos stormed.

"Yes, sir." I was at rigid attention.

"I only heard of this matter last midnight, from Yonge, so all I had time to prepare was a spell to hopefully save you from your foolishness.

"What in the name of any god you choose were you thinking? Did you imagine you could kill Chardin Sher's assistant, who, as you probably do not know, was yesterday named as envoy to stay on in Nicias after the conference ends, without your own head rolling in the gutter?"

"Sir, he deliberately sought a fight."

"Do you *always* have to do what people always want you to?"

"It was a matter of honor."

"Honor can be easily redeemed without swordplay, sir!" Tenedos snapped.

"It was not mine, but . . . someone else's."

Tenedos stopped his pacing and stared at me.

"Mayhap the Countess Agramónte and Lavedan?"

I did not answer.

Tenedos's anger vanished.

"I see," he said thoughtfully. "Since you are a gentleman, and would not answer me, I shall not inquire as to how far this matter has gone, even though my question would be fueled less by prurience than politics. Nor will I make any suggestions as what you should do nor not do regarding the countess. I assume you well know how powerful her husband is.

"By the gods, Damastes, it's hard to keep you alive long enough to fulfill my promises to you!"

"Yes, sir. But I was not the one who pulled on Chardin Sher's beard that he doesn't have."

"No. No you weren't. But that was calculated, unlike . . . unlike some other matters." Tenedos sat down, rubbing his forehead, thinking. Then he rose.

"I have a seminar to instruct some dominas in how weather magic can help them win battles in fifteen minutes, so you'll excuse me. Oh yes." He went to a desk, and took out a leather bag. "Here's gold enough to get some very good friends of yours very drunk to repay a very large debt."

"No thank you, sir," I said. "I have money of my own. And if it's not enough, I'll sell my sword for more."

"Very good. Consider this somewhat regrettable episode set aside. But don't wander into dark places to meet men with disreputable reputations any more than you have to. I don't know where I'd find your replacement."

I wanted to ask Tenedos exactly what place he saw for me, but then doubted if I'd want the answer, even if he knew it. I saluted and left. I had to find a tavern to rent.

Yonge grabbed me by the back of the head and pulled me close. His words were slurred, since he was very drunk. I was not much better. Although I'd held myself to only a handful of brandies, my normally sober ways were not helping matters at all. Karjan was trying to convince the tavern lass she really didn't want to sleep alone, and Yonge's three associates, disreputable and dangerous friends he'd made in his whoring about Nicias, were singing a ballad—three ballads, actually, none of them capable of understanding the others' bellows.

"Y'know, Numantian," Yonge said, "I think I'll stick close with you."

"You've fallen in love, then?"

"Don't try to be witty. I'm serious."

"All right. Be serious."

"Do you know why?"

"I do not."

" 'Cause you're bound to be a gen'ral, and I've never been around a real gen'ral."

"May Vachan bless your words."

"I don't know if that's a blesh . . . blessing. But you didn't let me finish. You'll either be a gen'ral . . . or else you'll get dead doing some fool thing that'll prob'ly end up being a legend or something.

"Either way, I want to see what comes next."

He refilled our glasses until they overflowed onto the table.

"Now, put this away neat. You're not drinking the way a gen'ral should."

I shuddered and obeyed.

The next morning I wished Malebranche had killed me. Lance Karjan was in little better shape, but the hells with him. He didn't have to meet a beautiful countess at noon. Fortunately I had arranged with the adjutant to have the day off to keep my appointment with Marán.

I drank half a gallon of water, pulled myself into my sports uniform, and staggered out to the athletic field. I threw up three times in four laps, went to the troop's bathing area and steamed for half an hour, then leaped into the coldest pool in the building.

I went to the mess, and sweet-talked the cooks into a glass of sharp fruit juice and three eggs beaten into an omelet made with the sharpest of spices. That and a pot of herbal tea, and there was a slight chance I would live long enough to greet Marán.

I handed Lucan's reins to a serving man, and entered the restaurant. I thought it was best to come in mufti; the uniform of the Helms was far too distinguishable for my purposes. I handed Marán's note to the greeter, and he bowed.

"Upstairs, sir. Third door. Here is the key."

I went up the stairs, realizing that at no time had I been seen by any of the restaurant's patrons. I began to suspect this eating establishment's reputation was founded on more than culinary skills.

I tapped at the door, inserted the key, and entered as laughter tinkled within.

The room was small for a dining area, no more than twenty feet by twelve feet, and high-ceilinged, with another door at its far end. There was a table set for two in the center of the room. Along both walls were couches wide enough to be beds and next to one a sideboard with an assortment of bottles. The rug beneath my boots was soft and thick enough to serve as a mattress.

Sitting on one couch, an open bottle of wine in an ice bucket between them, were Marán and a woman I did not know. They both stood.

"Ah, so this is the brave captain," the stranger said. I bowed.

"Damastes," Marán said, "this is my very best friend, Lady Amiel Kalvedon."

Lady Kalvedon was, even to my prejudiced eye, as lovely as Marán. She was taller, and while slender, had larger breasts that jutted from a very low-cut peasant's smock in silk that ended at midthigh. She had the perfect legs of a dancer. Her black hair came down to her shoulders in curling waves.

"Amiel has volunteered to do us a great service."

"Oh?"

"I am your apron," she said. Her voice was sultry. She was looking at me carefully, and I almost felt like blushing, knowing, for the first time, how a pretty woman feels entering a roomful of men. I thought she was about to take out a tape, ask me to lower my trousers, and measure the length of my cock.

"Damastes," she went on. "Damastes the Fair, I think I shall call you."

"I thank you, Lady."

"Considering what I am doing for you, and the terrible cost to my reputation, you should call me Amiel." She picked up her wineglass, while I stood there, puzzled, drained it, bent and kissed Marán on the lips, picked up a shoulder bag, and went to the other door. "I shall be invisible until four, children. So have fun."

She left.

Marán giggled. I saw that the wine bottle was about half-empty, and her cheeks were a bit flushed. She was dressed conservatively, in riding tights with a short flared skirt over them and a loose blouse. She'd taken off her boots and they lay on the floor, with her jacket and scarf beside them.

"Do you want to explain?"

"After you kiss me."

I picked her up in my arms, and our lips slid together, her tongue slipping around mine. It lasted a very long time.

Finally, I broke away. "If that goes on any longer," I said, a bit breathlessly, "I'll never hear an explanation. What is an apron? And what are we doing to Lady . . . to Amiel's reputation?"

"Nothing, really. Here. Take off your jacket, get yourself some wine, and sit down. Over here, on the couch. Lean back, and let me take your boots off."

I obeyed. "But what will the waiter say? I assume there will be a waiter."

"When I pull that bell-cord, but not before. And for what I am paying to rent this room, we could be doing anything and he wouldn't say a word."

"You still haven't told me what an apron is."

"An apron is a woman who keeps another woman company, who covers her when she's having an affair, so the first woman's husband won't suspect anything. Amiel, who's very close and the first woman I met when I came to Nicias, is doing more than that. She's allowing word to spread that she is terribly smitten with a certain young army officer, so smitten she wishes to spend every minute in his company."

"Suddenly she is my friend as well. But as she said, what of her reputation?"

"She doesn't worry about that . . . nor does her husband. They each live separate lives, and seem quite happy doing it." I'd heard this was common in the upper levels of Nicias, but this was the first proof I'd had.

"I see. Now, what was this affair to which you were referring? I mean, what about *my* reputation?"

Marán laughed. "I've read about cavalrymen, so do not try that one."

She leaned back on the couch, and stretched, voluptuously, arching her back so her breasts rose proud.

"This restaurant prides itself on not only its privacy, but on being able to fix almost any dish that could be desired. And there's a menu on the table."

"I already know what I want to eat."

"Yes?"

I lifted her leg over my head and set it on the couch, then slipped both fingers under her blouse, found the tie of her tights, and undid it.

"You," I whispered.

I slid her tights down, and she lifted her hips as I did. I cast the tights aside, then pushed her blouse up until her breasts were bare.

"Are you going to let me get undressed?" she murmured.

"Maybe later," I said, and I teased her nipples with my teeth, then ran my tongue down her flat belly to where her skirt was bunched, then over her shaven smoothness and into her as her legs embraced my shoulders.

We ate no midday meal that day, and it was just four when we left.

I had made an interesting discovery that day. I held little use then, and less now, for alcohol in any form. But I'd found out that a hangover can make a man able to, in a rather indelicate expression, fuck like a mink.

* * *

So our affair began in earnest, Marán plunging into it as eagerly as I did. Before, I'd been slowly going mad with boredom, but now I was very grateful for the lack of real duties. I'm afraid the training I had been trying to give my Silver Centaurs, my Leaden Lummoxes, was nearly nonexistent. Not that the men objected—they gladly returned to their slothful ways. I should have been and should be now, I suppose, ashamed of my slacking. But with the Helms, it didn't seem to matter at all.

I was deeply grateful for Amiel's help, because I'd never been in this situation before, and now realized how few places a married noblewoman who wished to keep her reputation and her lover could be alone or even innocently together with him without talk starting.

I grew to like Amiel, and found that she was indeed a loyal friend of Marán's, even though every now and then she eyed me carefully as she had on first meeting, even though she never said anything even slightly suggestive. She had little use for Marán's husband, and sometimes referred to him as Old Copperbottom, after the sheathing his freighters were given. She treated Marán as if she were her younger sister, still unexposed to the world, and me almost as her own lover and coconspirator. She also kept referring to me as Damastes the Fair, and it was annoying when other people began using it. Marán, however, thought it very funny.

But even with Amiel being an "apron," we could only expect her to cover us so often. We became expert at finding restaurants or taverns like the one we'd trysted in that first day. But even better, since we were well into the Time of Births, and the spring was gentle that year, was riding out of the city separately and meeting at a prearranged spot.

We found wonderful places to be alone, from riverside shanties to an abandoned castle so deeply buried in a small forest that its existence had been forgotten, to mossy, secluded glens. There were even places within the city, including a beautiful tiny rose garden in the middle of Manco Heath no one but us seemed to know of.

Mostly we met during the day, because it was harder to meet at night. Even though Count Lavedan was frequently absent, I was loath to visit their mansion, in spite of Marán's reassurance that the servants would never talk. Of course she could not come to me in the barracks ever, since that was not only against orders but the jabbermouths who thought themselves army officers would have broadcast her appearance across Nicias within the hour.

It was a golden time, a time of honey, a time I wished could have a stop and be forever.

But both of us knew it must come to an end.

We had barely begun our intrigue when the Great Conference collapsed. The broadsheets said valuable matters had been discussed and there would be another meeting "in the near future." The states' leaders held their final banquet and then went separate, supposedly cordial ways.

But the word on the street was that the conference had been acrimonious and a disaster.

Tenedos had fuller details, which I assumed he'd gotten from either Mahal or Scopas. As expected, the problem had been Chardin Sher, who behaved as if he were a full member of the Rule of Ten rather than their subordinate.

Matters came to a head when Mahal, no doubt at Tenedos's prodding, insisted the matter of the Border States' sovereignty be brought up. Chardin Sher said since there was strong historical precedent for the areas to be annexed to Kallio, that would be his suggestion to improve the situation.

"That would certainly," he added, "be a way of pacifying them for good and all."

Barthou had fallen into the trap, and asked why that should be.

"Because, with a strong man who's willing to provide law to those savages, backing it up with the full force he is capable of, these damnable hillmen would no longer be the thorn in Numantia's side as they have been for many generations."

Chardin Sher put emphasis on the last, and Barthou began growling in anger.

Then Chardin Sher had said the Rule of Ten should think about what the other states had been concerned about for years: Why was this great country ruled only by men who came from Nicias?

Farel had acidly wondered if Chardin Sher had a better idea, and Chardin Sher said he had, and it was quite simple: The Rule of Ten should be immediately changed, so its representatives came from all Numantia. That tore it.

Tenedos said there'd been a screaming match, with very ill-chosen words being used on both sides, from *weaklings* to *traitor.*

"So what does it mean?" I asked.

"It means Chardin Sher will return home to the cheers of his countrymen. He stood up to those fools in Nicias, in their eyes. He'll then start quietly building up his armies, and possibly making alliances with some of the other states who little like Nicias or the Rule of Ten."

"War?"

"Not for a while. But there will be border incidents that justify Chardin Sher having a bigger and bigger army. Then . . . then he'll think about marching west."

But Tenedos was wrong. Chardin Sher was a far more subtle strategist than that.

I glanced at the large painting, and was about to pass on, when Marán said, "Well?"

I studied the picture more carefully, not sure what I was supposed to say. It showed a great house, more a castle, actually, sitting on the rocks above a river. The house was of stone, and I counted five stories, then the machicolated roof. On the river side jutted four-sided towers and on the one landward one I could see was a smaller round tower.

To the right was a wooded park, with horsemen, and on the left smoke rising from the roofs of a small village. The river in front of the house was calm, and there was a small boat on it, with a liveried man at the sweep and, in the bows, a young girl wearing pink. I attempted a joke.

"The king who built that had a *very* guilty conscience. Or else some very powerful enemies."

Marán giggled. "Both, actually. But be careful of your words, sirrah. Look closely at the plate."

I did, and winced, once again having spoken before I knew what was going on. The brass plate read:

IRRIGON, SEAT OF THE AGRAMÓNTE FAMILY.
A LOAN

It's one thing the idea of how rich someone is, and another seeing the reality. Even though I knew of the Agramóntes' vast wealth, and had seen Marán's house here in Nicias, it still was staggering to see a building of this enormity and realize it belonged to one family.

Marán touched the girl in the boat. "That is my mother. The painting was done just after she and my father married. She was only fourteen."

"That was where you grew up?"

"There, mostly, although I spent time at some of our other estates."

I marveled once again, and wondered how many people it took to manage such a monstrosity. "It must have been interesting growing up there. Any family ghosts in particular?"

Marán, in one of those sudden mood changes I was still learning to accept, was instantly very serious. "Interesting? Maybe that's the word to use among polite company.

"I thought it was mostly hell."

She stared at the painting. "Yes," she repeated. "Mostly hell."

An hour later, we were finishing the remains of our picnic in the park that stretched behind the museum. I'd made another discovery—no one ever thinks of illicit liaisons in the palaces of culture. So we'd sometimes meet in museums, galleries, or concerts. After we were assured we hadn't been followed, we could go elsewhere to be alone. Even though I was hardly interested in my surroundings, little by little I was picking up a bit of polish.

We'd made passionate love in her carriage on the way to the museum, and I wanted her again, but sensed this was not the time to suggest it. She'd always been reluctant to talk about her family, and after her words in the huge building behind us, I understood why. But I wanted to know more.

She looked at me quizzically after I repacked the basket.

"You have been quiet. Are you mad at me?"

"Now why would I be that?"

"I don't know. Maybe because of what I said?"

"About your home?"

She nodded.

"Not mad, my love," I said. "You can do anything, feel anything you want about your family, including having murderous intent. But if you want to tell me more, I'll gladly listen."

She hesitated, then began, without preamble.

"Everyone seems to think living in a castle is some kind of dream. But it's not. It's cold, and the stone walls echo, and all the rooms have to have fireplaces.

"That's what I remember most. Being cold." Her voice lowered. "Inside and out." She looked away from me, perhaps hoping I'd stop her from going on. But I remained silent.

"I'm the last-born, and my three brothers are all quite a few years older than I am. I guess my parents thought they were through with children, although they never said anything.

"My father . . . well, he's *the* Agramónte. Very severe, very righteous, always aware of what he's saying to make sure he doesn't present an untoward image to outsiders. He was always kindly to me, but remote, and became nervous if he spent very long with me, and quickly called for one of my nursemaids on the pretext that he was boring me.

"My brothers were, well, brothers. I always wanted to tag along with them, and for a while, when I was a baby, they'd tolerate me. But pretty soon I got older, and they had their own interests, and so they'd go to a lot of trouble to avoid me.

"In some ways, that didn't matter, because all they like are hunting, and auctions and talking about crops and how the government is incompetent and taxes are too high and all slaves are lazy spoilers." She shrugged. "Typical country lords, in other words. When I turned thirteen, all their friends realized I existed and came flocking around, trying to get into my knickers."

"What about your mother?"

"She died," Marán said shortly. "About three months after I married. I think it was out of pure happiness for the marriage she'd help make for me."

I kept silent, and reluctantly Marán went on.

"She was the daughter of another noble family, of course. They weren't rich, but they weren't poor. The reason my grandfather wanted her to marry my father was because her family owned a strip of land between two of our estates.

"So that was the dowry she brought to her wedding bed.

"But she was quite happy, having married into the Agramóntes. Indeed, she became the social arbiter for the family—who were our equals, our inferiors, our superiors. Fortunately for her, there weren't many of the latter. Like my father, she always worried about our role in society.

"When suitors started calling on me, she would barely greet them before looking them up in one of the peerage books, to make sure they were noble enough to be able to put their hand up my dress." She made a wry face,

"In the country, at first they try to fuck you, then, if they can't do that, they decide you should become their bride. Then they fuck your lights out until you're flabby with a dozen children and they get bored and start spending nights in the servants' quarters or in the city with a mistress." She gloomed in silence for a bit.

"That was your introduction to love?"

"Not quite. I'd read romances, and frankly dreamed of the day I'd have swains dancing around me. I just didn't realize what the acceptable ones would be like.

"Maybe I should have run off with the first boy I fell in love with."

"Thank Irisu you didn't," I said.

"Poor fellow," she said, paying no attention to me. "He was the son of my father's coachman, and I still remember his grin, and his curly hair. He had green eyes, and smelled most marvelously of horses.

"I was half in love with horses, then," she explained, "sometimes wishing I was one, and if I couldn't find a centaur, I would settle for him."

"What happened?"

"My mother found out about it, and within the day the family was sent away. Later, after I was married, I tried to find out what happened to him . . . them. All I could learn was they came to Nicias, and that was all."

Marán peered at me. "You don't mind me telling you this? Nobody but Amiel's ever heard my silly little tale."

"Why should I mind?" I wondered. "Should I be jealous of a schoolgirl infatuation?"

"Why not," she said, her good humor returning for an instant. "I'm jealous of every girl *you've* been with."

"Ah, but there weren't any," I said, looking pious. "I was a complete virgin until I met you."

"Right." Marán thought for a moment. "I guess, growing up, I was like some kind of doll. Everybody got to dress me up like they wanted, and show me off here and there, but what I wanted . . . well, that didn't matter. My father wanted me to look like this, my mother wanted me to act like that, and nobody ever asked what did Marán want. Not then, not ever.

"I was cold . . . and I was lonely. I never really had anyone to play with. When I was very little, I could romp with the children of our retainers or slaves, but I found out quickly they always made me queen or commander or whatever in every game we played, and made sure it was a game *I* wanted to play. Then, when I got older, there was no one, although once a month or so we'd visit some other noble family, and I'd get a chance to play with their children, if they had any."

She looked at me wistfully.

"I wish I was more like you."

I'd told her a bit of growing up in Cimabue, and of my love for solitary wanderings in the jungle.

"So I read all I could," she went on, "especially about cities, and dreamed of the day I could come to Nicias. I remember reading a poem once, about a man who came from the black forests, and even though the city had become his home, the coldness of those dark woods would be with him until his dying day. I wondered if that was me."

"I will loudly testify there is nothing cold about you, Countess." At least that elicited a bit of a smile.

"You know," she continued, "I never thought I'd be married when I did."

"What did you want to do?"

"Don't laugh. But at one time I wanted to be a courtesan. I'd be young, and beautiful, and all my noble lovers would pay for a night with me with a carriage full of gold, and they'd want to leave their nasty wives, but I'd just laugh and dance away."

"It's a good thing you didn't actually do that," I said. "Else you would have found most whores' customers are fat, old, unbathed, and have, shall we say, unusual tastes."

She stared at me, and her face was hard. Now it was my turn to apologize.

"Never mind," she said. "I just thought of something that . . . that wasn't very nice. Anyway, if I wasn't going to be a courtesan, I'd be some kind of very intelligent woman, and help philosophers and kings reach mighty decisions.

"That's the real reason for my salons. I guess I'm trying to give something to that poor lonely little girl that doesn't exist anymore." She turned away, but I saw her eyes fill. I reached out for her hand, but she pulled it away from me.

"But then, as I said, I got older, and then the wooing began. There was one boy I liked, who always made me laugh, and I looked forward to his visits. He was noble enough, but his family didn't have any gold, and so one day he, too, vanished.

"One of my brothers told me later his father had been given a goodly sum to keep him from calling again.

"You see what it was like?"

This time she let me take her hand.

"When I was sixteen the whole thing became a frenzy. There were balls, riding events, social evenings, and I had never a moment to be alone.

"I might have liked it, if I hadn't known all of this had but one purpose: to see me married to the most suitable man my family could find. Suitable to them.

"That went on for a year, and then my father brought Hernad home. Lord Lavedan. I thought my mother would expire in joy, finally having someone 'of the proper station' calling on her only daughter. As I said, not much later, she did just that.

"Somehow everyone, all of these sparkling young men, knew the issue was settled, and instantly found other flames to flit around.

"When my father introduced me to him, it was over, and my life was determined for all time."

I waited for her to go on, but she remained silent. Then she looked at me.

"I guess you think this is all shit. Poor little rich girl, and she should maybe have been born in a hovel and learn what real misery's about."

"No," I said truthfully. "I've known people who were poorer than poor, and were happy. Please, Marán, stop belittling yourself."

She kept staring into my eyes, as if unsure of whether to believe me or not. Suddenly she jumped to her feet.

"Come on, Damastes. I want to go home. I've ruined this day for the both of us."

I protested nothing was ruined, that it was important she tell me these things, but she would have none of it, and so we returned to the carriage and she took me back to the stables where I'd left Lucan. She just pecked my lips when we kissed good-bye, and I desperately wished there was something I could say or do to make her feel better. But there wasn't, and so her carriage rolled away.

As I rode back to the Helms' cantonment, I thought again

and again of what she'd told me. It was odd, with the exception of her wealth, how similar our childhoods were. But one produced a woman who was, I was learning, desperately unhappy, and the other a man who was quite the opposite.

That night, waiting for tardy sleep, I thought again on the matter. I suddenly recognized one difference: I did what I did out of choice, whereas she was never consulted about anything. Then I thought this happened—happens—to almost all women I've known. Everything they were permitted to do was decided by a man. By a man or, like Marán's mother, someone who delighted in doing men's every bidding.

I wondered how Numantian thinkers could rail on about the injustices done to slaves, or the poor or the benighted hill tribes, and never look across the pillow and see an even greater, omnipresent evil.

I set that out of my mind; if a soldier could barely hope to influence the course of a single skirmish, how could he hope to change what appeared to be immutable custom? Perhaps the only way things could change was if Tenedos's goddess, Saionji, was given her head and allowed to tumble society until it was entirely different. But that made me shudder—who was to say the goddess preferred things different?

Then another insight came. The biggest real difference between Marán and myself was that I grew up in a house of love, even though it wasn't spoken aloud that much. I was forever being given a hug by my mother, a loving pinch from one of my sisters, at least when they weren't angry with me, and a smile from my father when he passed.

But poor Marán? At no time in her story had I ever heard her use that word, and wondered if she knew what it was.

As I drifted off, a single clear thought came, and I don't think I realized exactly what it actually meant: Perhaps she didn't. But by the gods, I was going to do all I could to teach her.

We were lying naked in the sun, our horses tied a few yards away. I was slowly rubbing a soothing antiburn balm on the backs of Marán's thighs. She purred contentment, and slid her legs apart.

I dipped my finger into the oil, ran it up the center of her buttocks, and slid it into her. It met no resistance, but her body jolted, stiffened as if I'd hurt her.

"Don't do that," she said, her voice hard, cold.

I stopped, and said I was very sorry.

"Never mind. Just . . . just don't do that. I really don't like it."

I apologized again, and began stroking her shoulders.

She lay with her head turned away from me. After a while, she said something very strange.

"The morning after I was married," she said, in a completely toneless voice, "I walked into my dressing room, and saw the face of a stranger."

"I'm not sure I understand."

"I looked like a little girl," she said, almost in a whisper. "A little girl who's gotten lost, and can't figure out why, or what she could do to find herself."

Now began a bad time for Nicias, and other cities in Dara. It was as if Chardin Sher were some sort of wizard, and had cast a curse on us.

The Rule of Ten seemed almost invisible, and the few decrees they handed down had little to do with our problems.

Prices for staples, supposedly regulated, rose and fell like the tide. People began hoarding, especially the middle class who could afford it. There were shortages in oil, rice, butter in the poor sections of the city.

There were many more street speakers, each with a different solution to the woes of the times.

They had to fight for sidewalk room with a new plague: Nicias was inundated with magicians, and it felt as if we were back in Sayana, seeing everything from fortune-tellers to palmists to conjurers to those who would sell you anything from a love-philter to a poison.

Tenedos said this was truly a sign of evil. "Without insulting my own profession, not even these charlatans, when a populace feels change ahead, feels that the very ground under its feet may be quicksand, it seeks out those who claim to have answers." He smiled wryly. "Although perhaps I shouldn't complain, since now the auditoriums I speak in are always packed. I just wish I knew if anybody is actually listening, or if they're jumping from seer to seer like bees crazed on pollen."

I also noted that the temples were full, not only the great shrines to our principal gods, but also the smaller ones that worshiped their separate aspects or even for lesser godlets. Aharhel, chief of those aspects and the minor gods, who can speak to kings, was particularly popular, although I saw processions for everything from Elyot to many-headed animal gods I'd never heard of before. I even saw two or three parades whose members were loudly chanting Saionji's name.

When I reported this to Tenedos, he nodded in satisfaction. "As I told you, her time is coming round."

There seemed to be more crime, both casual robberies and thefts, but also horribly vile and senseless atrocities, committed not only by the desperate poor, but by some of the city's supposed best citizens.

I imagined Nicias as a beautiful silken garment that a thousand thousand hands were pulling at, and slowly, very slowly, the garment was beginning to rend.

I received a note from Marán, brought by one of her personal servants, asking me to meet her on the morrow at the restaurant we'd begun our affair at. Her note said *Important*, and the word was underlined twice.

Once again, I had to beseech the adjutant to let me have the day off, and he frowned, said something about young captains needing to pay more attention to their duties, but granted my wish.

I wondered what had happened, if Hernad had discovered our affair. I even wondered if she'd become pregnant—our affair had lasted for four months now. I'd tried to take precautions after that first mad night, but she'd refused to allow it.

But it wasn't Marán's problem, but rather her friend's.

Amiel sat sobbing on one couch, and Marán was trying to comfort her. She calmed, and told me what had happened.

About five years ago, she and her husband had taken a couple, the Tansens, into their service.They'd been perfect in every way, so much so that Lord Kalvedon asked the couple to move into one of the cottages on their estate. The couple had performed almost every service for the family, from groundskeeping to shopping to simply keeping their masters company. They'd had two children, "babes like I'd want," Amiel said, "if I ever wanted children. Beautiful little ones."

The woman had been supposed to go with Amiel that morning to visit her milliner. But she had not come up to the Kalvedans' mansion when she was supposed to, and so Amiel went to see what was the matter.

"I thought maybe one of their children was feeling poorly, and I'd tell her to forget it. I'm a big girl, and could buy ribbons by myself."

The cottage door was unlocked, and Amiel pushed it open, then screamed.

Sprawled on the floor was the woman, and beside her one of the children. In another room lay her husband. All three of then were dead, strangled with a yellow silk cord.

"But that wasn't the worst," Amiel said, and started crying again. "I went into the little room they used as a nursery. The baby . . . she was dead too. Killed like the others!

"What kind of a monster could do something like that?"

I knew what sort. Tovieti. So the yellow cord was now more in Nicias than whispers and a bauble worn by a foolish rich woman.

But what did this have to do with me? Hadn't she reported it to the wardens?

She had, but it seemed as if they didn't care. Either that, she went on, or else they were afraid.

"Probably."

"More than that," Amiel went on, thinking aloud. "They acted like . . . like this was just some sort of horrible routine. I know the Tansens weren't rich like I am . . . but they were my friends!"

"What should she do?" Marán asked. "I called you because my husband said something once, back when you and the seer were testifying before the Rule of Ten, that you'd encountered a cult of stranglers in the Border States that the councilors closed the room to hear about."

I said I didn't think I could discuss that, but that there had been some truth to what her husband had heard. I knew of these people, and how dangerous they were.

"If they came into our estate, past the guards, over the walls without anyone crying the alarm . . . they could come back," Amiel said. "Do they want me? Do they want my husband next? What should I do?"

Privately I thought that if the Tovieti wanted you, you would probably not be safe in the middle of an army camp. Instead, I said that they kept apartments in town, did they not? They should move into them this very night. As for being secure, I suddenly remembered a man, no, four men, very unlikely to be Thak's stranglers.

"Write the address down," I told her. "I shall have this man call on you this evening. Pay him well, he and any associates he brings, and obey his orders exactly. You can trust him, even though he looks a bit disreputable. He's held my own life in his hands.

"His name is Yonge."

I finished telling my story about the slaughter of Amiel's servants, and how the wardens treated it as commonplace, and was silent. Tenedos made no response, but turned to the young warden.

"Kutulu?"

"Routine is exactly what it is," he said. "There have been four hundred and sixteen such murders within our jurisdiction within the last two months. Rich, poor, it does not seem to matter. Sometimes the place is looted, sometimes not. It seems that the murderers' campaign is less for gold than to create chaos and dread."

"Yet there's no outcry," I said.

"We are doing our very best to keep the matter hushed," Kutulu said.

"Why?" Tenedos asked.

"Those are the specific orders of the Rule of Ten."

"What the hells good does that do?" I said angrily. "Ignoring it won't make them go away. What the hells will it take— Thak dancing on their gods-damned skulls?"

"Thak?" Kutulu looked puzzled. Evidently the Rule of Ten didn't even trust their lawmen with all the facts.

Tenedos looked at me.

"Go ahead, Damastes. We can't follow the Rule of Ten's orders anymore. The times are far more perilous than any of them . . . and perhaps we, as well . . . realize. Tell him everything."

The next evening, I was riding to meet Marán when I saw a rider coming toward me. I recognized him before he saw me, and pulled Lucan behind a high-piled produce cart.

It was Elias Malebranche. He wore a hooded cloak, the hood pulled back. He rode close, but didn't recognize me, since I'd slipped from the saddle and was pretending to examine one of Lucan's hooves.

As he passed I chanced a look, and saw, above his beard and burying itself into it, the savage redness of a half-healed scar. I'd marked him well.

I wondered where Malebranche was going. We were in a shabby section of Nicias, a route I habitually took to make sure I had no followers. I wondered what devious business he had in this district.

As much as I wanted to see Marán, I knew what my duty must be, remounted, and rode after the Kallian. Of course there'd been several times we'd not been able to meet—the price of a clandestine affair. We'd even developed a device for such an eventuality, and would meet in the same place the following night unless advised otherwise.

His route twisted and turned, but eventually led to the river. We were almost to the ocean docks, as bad a part of the city as existed. I loosened my sword in its sheath, and my eyes darted around the shadows.

The cobbles were loose, and I had to walk Lucan, afraid of making a noise.

Malebranche turned his horse down a narrow alley. I counted fifteen, then went after him.

I could see clearly down the narrow way all the way to the water. But there was no sign whatsoever of the landgrave.

I rode all the way down and out onto the pier at the foot of the hill and back, but the Kallian had completely vanished. I looked for hidden passageways that would permit a horse to enter, but saw none. There was nothing but solid brick and then the dark water.

I was a failure as a spy. I looked up at the rising moon, and my disappointment fell away. I still had more than enough time to meet Marán.

I held Marán's ankles stretched apart as we drove together, her body curled up, lifting from the bed, feeling the power of that great warm avalanche growing inside me. She moaned, pulled at me, and I released her legs and lowered myself onto her, her breasts flattened against my chest as her heels pushed against my buttocks, forcing me deeper and deeper into her.

My breath rasped as her body shuddered, shuddered again.

I opened my eyes and looked down into hers, staring at me, staring beyond me, her wet mouth gasping for air, head thrown back in sweet agony.

"Damastes, oh gods, Damastes," she groaned as her hips thrust, "I . . . I . . ."

"Say it," I said. "Say it!"

"I . . . oh gods, I love you! I love you!"

"And . . . and I love you," I said, the truth as naked as our sweating bodies as the stars exploded in our roaring cry of ecstasy.

Now there could be no turning back.

*   *   *

"Interesting," Kutulu mused. "Something I did not know about the good landgrave."

"So you keep track of him as well?"

"Of course. I keep track of everyone that I . . . or the Seer Tenedos . . . thinks worthy of concern."

"But what," I said, trying a small jest, seeing if there was anything in this precise little man resembling humanity, "do you do for pleasure?"

"Why," Kutulu said, "that *is* my pleasure." He made a note on a small yellow card. His shambles of an office was already filled with a thousand of them.

"I'll let you know what your friend is about. Assuming, of course, Tenedos approves."

At first the city looked as it always had at dawn, but then, as the sun's rays struck it, I saw it was terribly different. Now each building, each cobblestone, and—most horrible—each tree sent the sun's reflection flashing back, and I realized the city had changed, had become a monstrous crystal, where nothing human could live.

But then I saw movement in the streets, and there were people, but they, too, had transformed, and the sun sent its rays bouncing from them into my eyes.

Each of them, man, woman, child, carried something stretched between his hands, and when I peered more closely I saw they all carried yellow silk cords.

As I saw them, they saw me.

At that moment, the lake in the center of Hyder Park boiled, and up from it rose Thak!

He saw what his people were looking at, and raised his head and "saw" me. The air shrilled as when a wet finger is rubbed around the rim of a crystal wineglass, but far louder, and I saw the crystal trees shake and the city itself tremble.

Thak took a giant step and another, coming toward me, and his arms lifted.

I woke, shaking. I don't dream very often, and when I do, it's almost never unpleasant.

I had to light a lamp, get out of bed, and go look out, across the deserted barracks square for almost an hour, composing myself, before sleep came back.

I knew this dream was more than a dream.

Thak was in Nicias.

And he remembered me.

"Your Kallian is not behaving as a diplomat should," Kutulu said. "He has business with people, and in places, no proper envoy should."

"Have him sent home," I suggested. "Or, better yet, seized and tried as a traitor."

"Ah, but then he would be replaced by someone who we didn't know, and I'd have to start all over again trying to identify Charin Sher's new agent.

"The practice is for us to let him run his course and then we'll take appropriate action at the appropriate time." Kutulu frowned. "That's assuming, of course, my superiors will listen to me, and the Rule of Ten will listen to *them*."

"So that is the way of police work," I mused. "I'd never be suited for it."

"Of course not," Kutulu said. "Until you learn that no man does what he does for the reasons he says he is doing it, and then find there's frequently yet another, *real* motive behind even his most closely held beliefs . . . you'd best remain a soldier."

I looked closely at the small man to see if he was attempting a jest, but he was perfectly serious.

"At any rate, I've discovered where Landgrave Malebranche goes when he visits the docks," Kutulu went on, "although I haven't yet followed him all the way to his lair.

"I plan to do so this evening, since he's not that devious a person, and holds to far too close a schedule. Tsk. He should know better.

"Would you wish to accompany me?"

"I'd like nothing better," I said. "But won't I stand out?"

"Not by the time I finish with you," Kutulu said, and that was how I learned a bit about disguise.

First was finding me the proper clothes. Kutulu sent for a subordinate, and gave him orders. In a few minutes the man returned with a rather soiled uniform from one of the lesser infantry regiments.

"Since you are stamped a soldier, a soldier you'll remain. But not an officer. No more than . . . oh, a sergeant. The best mask is a partial one, Captain. No one would ever think a captain would appear as a warrant."

" 'Damastes' from my friends sounds better to my ears than 'Captain.' "

Kutulu looked uncomfortable. "Very well. Damastes. Next, we need to alter the way you walk. Man remembers man in strange ways, by his walk, speech, even smell, as much as appearance, but he is never aware of that. So someone will look at you, the sergeant, but somehow 'know' it isn't Damastes the Fair."

I grinned at that last.

"Do you know everything?"

Kutulu sighed. "No, and there'll never be time enough to learn it. Worse, I won't even be able to learn what I should be learning.

"We'll further fool your friends," he said, rummaging in a drawer. "Here. Stick this on your nose with some plaster you'll find over there, under that skull with the ax blade in it."

He'd given me a beautifully realistic duplicate of a boil. I stuck it into place, looked in a hand glass he gave me, and shuddered. Kutulu examined it, and nodded approval. "Anyone who sees your face will see Man with Terrible Boil, and be completely unable to distinguish or remember the rest of your features.

"Now for the final touch." He picked up a spray bottle, and misted its contents over me. I curled my nostrils—now I smelled like a soldier who'd not been bathed in a month.

"A dirty, smelly warrant from a line unit who's probably in trouble with his superiors," Kutulu approved. "Exactly what we want. Just the sort who'd be skulking around the docks looking for trouble. And with your size, they'll never notice the small mouse who's creeping beside you."

So I was going to be Kutulu's "apron." I grinned, then remembered my dream of Thak.

"We may need more than physical disguise," I said. "I'll bet there'll be magic about."

"Probably not a concern," Kutulu said. "Wizards are as prone to let their eyes fool them as any common man. However . . . I take your point. I think we'll drop by the Seer Tenedos and see if he can't provide a bit of a foggy counterspell. There is no gain in being overconfident.

"Now, for arms," he said, "although if we need to use much force it's likely we're doomed."

"I have my sword."

"Where we are going will not call for gentlemen's tools, but those of a footpad or worse. Can you use a knife?"

"I can."

"Here." He passed me a flat-handled blade in a sheath. "Strap this to your forearm. You can shave with it—I had it sharpened this morning. What else? Ah. It's chilly down by the water, so no one will question these."

He handed me a pair of rather shabby gloves. I almost dropped them because of their unexpected weight.

"There's a quarter-weight of sand sewn across the knuckles and an eighth in the palm," he said briskly. "Slap someone and they shall stay slapped."

He picked up a murderous-looking double-edged dagger whose sheath hung down the back of his neck along his spine, and we went looking for Elias Malebranche.

This time I was ready for Seer Tenedos when he said he wished to accompany us. Kutulu looked horrified, not yet familiar with the seer's admirable habit of leading from the front.

"You are *not* going," I said firmly. "You are *not* expendable, especially when all we intend to do is peer about. Don't you think your face is well known to most of Nicias by now? Don't you imagine Malebranche would be delighted to meet you in some dark alleyway? Don't you think Chardin Sher would reward him well to have your pelt in front of his fire, sir?"

"You pick amazingly picturesque imagery, Damastes," Tenedos grumbled. "Very well. I see your point. But can you tell me one reason why I shouldn't try to use sorcery to spy out where the Kallian goes and what his business is?"

"Thak," was all I said, and Tenedos's shoulders tensed involuntarily as he remembered how the demon had almost risen out of the mercury pool to take both of us.

"Very well." Tenedos sighed. "As Captain Mellet once said, I'll stay and tend the home fires. But as for some sort of spell to protect you. Hmm. I'll give you that, and something for emergencies."

He dusted us with a powder, said unfamiliar words, while his hands moved in strange figures in the air.

"You don't want to show up reeking of magic, but this is a simple spell that will encourage a sorcerous sentry to overlook you, without ever quite realizing why. Now for the other device."

He went to one of his trunks and fished through it until he found a rather ornately carved box made of several different-colored woods. Inside I saw what appeared to be tiny, perfectly sculptured animals, animals such as I'd never dreamed of.

"Here," he said, handing me one. It was like a tortoise, but with the edges of its shell spiked, and it stood clear of the ground on four stocky, clawed legs. Its tail was an armored mace, and its head was fanged and malevolent looking.

"What is it, a model of some sort of demon?" Kutulu asked.

"It's not a model at all, but rather the creature itself, perhaps a demon, I was able to fetch from another world and then shrink and put into a suspended state. I think I'm the only sorcerer who's come up with a series of spells that can do this. I call it, and the others I made, animunculi. I'd never found a use for them until now, although I suppose it would be possible to shrink a guard dog, carry it as a charm on a woman's bracelet, and she would be quite safe from any attack. So too with your small creature. In its normal state it is about ten feet long, plus the tail, and it has the temperament of a rabid bear.

"It will be activated by the slightest contact with water, so I'd suggest you keep it in this." He handed me a bottle with a stopper, and I gingerly inserted the tiny figurine in it. "Please try to return it to me undamaged," he said wistfully. "A great deal of probably wasted time went into creating it."

"If we have to, er, activate it," Kutulu wondered, "how do we render it safe?"

"You don't. You can't. Run like demons are after you, which they may well be. It will return to its own world after a few moments." Tenedos thought about what he'd said and smiled a bit sheepishly. "It might be well to provide you with a weapon against your weapon, I just realized. Put the creature away safely first, since I am giving you a spell of water."

He found herbs, and added them to a beaker of water. He took an oddly carved wand that more resembled a twisted bit of driftwood from a shelf, and stirred the mixture. He began chanting in another tongue, then his words became understandable:

"Water, guard
Water, help
Seek water
Find safety.
Varum take heed
These are now yours
Guard them
Help them
Now they are thine."

As he spoke, he sprinkled the mixture on us. Then, in a normal tone, he said, "this should be a bit of help, I should think. Again, it's a simple spell, and requires a bit of work on your part. If this creature, animal, demon, or whatever it is, does come after you, cross water. Any water will stop it. If the spell works as it should, you should be momentarily safe."

"Momentarily," I said. "That's a fairly imprecise time."

"You're both in good health. As I said, run like you've never run before, and you'll escape handily. I'm fairly sure of that."

Kutulu was looking rather skeptically at Tenedos. I suspected this was the first time he'd ever realized his hero might not be able to do all things perfectly. I took the warden by the arm.

"Come on," I said. "That's but his way of making sure the hayseed can't complain about the philter he purchased if it doesn't work. Thank you, Seer."

"Captain," Tenedos said, "has anyone ever suggested you're impertinent?"

"Frequently, sir. And they're always right. We'll report back to you as soon as possible."

Tenedos turned serious. "Please do that, regardless of the hour. Be most careful. I do not know what you might encounter."

"This is another trick of the police," Kutulu explained. "If you are following someone, someone who seems to have a regular route, and you lose him or he becomes suspicious, go to the last point you were able to track him, wait for his next appearance, then continue following."

We were hidden behind barrels on the very edge of a wharf. About twenty yards away was the end of the alley I'd followed Malebranche down to find nothing.

The night was quiet, no sound except the splash of small waves as the river flowed past behind and below us, and the occasional hoot of a ship's horn.

How much, I mused, of a soldier's time is spent waiting in perfect silence, from peacetime formations to wartime ambushes, yet no one ever considers it a part of his lot.

I heard muffled hoofbeats, and crouched lower.

A dark figure rode swiftly out of the alley, and I thought for a moment that it was about to ride straight off into the water. But the rider dismounted, knelt, and suddenly, noiselessly, part of the pier lifted, a hatch, and the rider, who must be Malebranche, led his horse down an unseen ramp. As rapidly as it had opened the trapdoor closed, and all was as before.

"Interesting," Kutulu said. "Shall we follow?"

It took a few minutes of close examination to find the round metal-lined socket in the wooden pier. It was made to accommodate some sort of tool, which we did not have, but I pried carefully with the haft of my dagger and suddenly the portal yawned open.

Kutulu took a tiny dark lantern from his cloak, lit it, and opened one shutter enough to illuminate the ramp. I spotted the closing lever not far along. He latched the shutter and we crept down the incline, closing the hatch, and darkness closed around us.

I started onward, but Kutulu felt my movement, and held me still. I obeyed. I thought my eyes were already night-familiar, and we would be forced to move by feel, but in a few moments realized they weren't. We weren't in total blackness, but there was enough light from the end of the tunnel to see dimly.

Kutulu tugged me onward. I made sure my knife was loose in its sheath and we went down the tunnel. About twenty yards along, we found an alcove, and here the rider's horse was tethered. The tunnel leveled, and turned, away from the river, back under the hill.

I wondered how the conspirators had been able to dig such an elaborate work without being seen, but when I brushed against the tunnel's walls, which were heavily nitered brick, I realized they'd merely happened on it. Perhaps this had been a smuggler or pirate's lair in the distant past, abandoned or forgotten.

I heard a rat chitter, then we came around a curve, and saw light. At the same time, we heard a voice booming, for all the world like that of a priest in a temple.

The tunnel mouth was a low arch, and I saw the outline of a figure, a man with a sword in one hand. But his back was turned to us, and he was intent on whatever was going on in the chamber inside.

I looked at Kutulu, and he gestured me back around the bend.

"So there's more than one entrance," he whispered. "That isn't Malebranche's voice, so whoever's speaking must have come in some other way. Either that, or people live down here. I think we should see more." I was impressed with the little man. There was not the slightest sign of fear in his voice.

"Now," he went on calmly, "I think a bit of your soldierly skills are needed. Can you take out that guard without raising the alarm?"

I thought so, and also thought that Kutulu was talking too much. I touched my finger to my lips, pointed to the ground—stay here. Stay silent. I considered various possibilities, then crept around the corner. I held close to the wall, and moved forward. I was relatively unworried. Unless I stumbled over something, there would be no way the sentry could be alerted—he would be night-blind and unable to see me.

I kept my eyes on the cobbles in front of me, and never looked directly at the man in front of me. I refuse to accept any senses beyond the normal, except those seers might develop, but it's a fact that if you stare at the back of someone's head long and hard enough, he will turn.

I'd thought of taking him down with my knife, but in spite of my assurances to Kutulu I was not really an artist with the small blade. The leaded gloves were a better solution. A few feet from the guard I went into a crouch, then went forward, not fast, but very smoothly, rising to my full height, and smashing the back of my fisted hand against his neck. His body contorted, I grabbed his sword before it could fall and clatter on the cobbles, and I eased him to the ground. I don't know if he was dead, but if he was not he'd be out for a very long time and very sick if he came to.

I went back to Kutulu, and we slipped to the mouth of the tunnel.

The chamber inside was rectangular, fairly large, with an arching brick roof. I saw two other entrances, both with large wooden doors. It did, indeed, resemble a temple, since there were benches from front to back and a low dais in the front.

The man speaking did have the rolling, sonorous speech of a priest, but he certainly didn't look imposing. Rather, he looked like the jolly fat grover in the market, complete with a small fringe of a beard.

And his words were anything but religious:

". . . but it isn't the gold which we must be thinking of at this most important time, Brother."

There were about sixty men and women sitting on the benches, all cleanly dressed and sober-appearing, paying no attention to anything but the speaker. Among them I saw the Marchioness Fenelon and some other noblemen and -women I'd seen around Nicias. I spotted Count—or rather former Count—Komroff, whom I'd seen holding forth the evening I first met Marán. But nobles were in the minority—most of the people in the audience were poor or working class in their desperately scrubbed best outfits.

I saw Kutulu's head swiveling from man to woman to man, creating new entries for his file.

The man whom the priest, for so I kept thinking him to be, had been addressing frowned, not satisfied.

"I know, Brother. But when a loyal Sister tells me she must have food for her babies, it's hard to tell her not to reap the spoils she's entitled, the spoils Thak promised us."

A man sitting with his back to me rose, and I recognized Malebranche.

"Sir . . . since I'm not a member of your order, I cannot call you Brother . . . let me repeat what I've said before. My master has more than enough gold to provide for all."

Son of a bitch! Quite suddenly it was obvious why Elias Malebranche had been in Sayana. It wasn't merely to stir up trouble and attempt to make an alliance with Achim Baber Fergana, but also to work with the Tovieti. Now, from what Malebranche was saying, the Kallian was bankrolling them as well. It was apparent we'd come on the Inner council, or whatever they called it, of the stranglers.

Kutulu's eyes widened briefly, probably as much surprise as the lawman could show.

The fat "priest" nodded.

"Thank you, sir. Brother, tell that woman in your band what our friend said, and tell her also to have faith in our coming victory. We cannot name who our friend's master is, although I'm sure many of you know. Also tell your woman why we must not linger over our kills.

"We have the wardens in a frenzy, the commoners quaking, nobility fleeing their estates for safe havens that don't exist, and even the Rule of Ten must be beginning to tremble. Think what it must be, when you do not know your enemy, nor where the silken cord may come from at any time, day or night, but know it is coming, as inexorably as the Wheel turns.

"Even the old gray gods must be shuddering at the new day we are about to bring.

"The minute one of us is caught, a bit of the mystery, the fear, the darkness that is the blanket we love, vanishes.

"Thak is content; Thak has his blood and a chance to play with the souls of those we kill before they return to the Wheel. Our day will be here very soon."

There was a murmur of pleasure. A woman stood.

"Brother, p'rhaps everything you're sayin' is true. But why're we listenin' to this man, this nobleman, one of the bastards we've given our lives to send into th' Darkness? He ain't joinin' us, he's made that clear. But we're willin' to take his gold. What's his stake? What's his master's stake?

"An' Brother, I don't need any fine words. I want answers."

"You'll find out when the time comes," Malebranche snarled. "Until then, you've no right to ask my business."

"Stop!" The fat man snapped, and I heard raw power in his tone. "Never address any of us in such a tone again, or be prepared to face our wrath. She has all the right to speak she wishes, sir. Let me remind you that the Sister is right. We are dedicated to bringing you, and all you now represent, down.

"Your master is helping us assist him in bringing down the Rule of Ten. Very well, very good. We are not fools, so we know he intends to return to the old days and old ways and sit the throne as king of all Numantia.

"That may happen, that may not happen. Thak has allowed us to work together thus far. But do not ever think we are your servants. If your master reneges on his promises to create a society of equals, to distribute the lands, the gold, and the women of the rich pigs of Dara among us . . . our war can always continue, sir.

"Our war can continue until the Wheel is choked with the corpses of those who do not follow Thak, and yours may well be one of them! Be warned, sir, and be aware, as should your master, that our alliance is but of the moment, and can be shattered with a single word or a single dream sent by Thak, who even now sits just Beyond, watching all we say and do."

We'd heard enough. We stole back into darkness. I pulled at the lever and the hatch rose, and we went out into the clean night.

Neither Kutulu nor I said a word—this vast conspiracy, stretching from Kallio to the Border States to Nicias itself, was too enormous, and shocked us both to our cores. Seer Tenedos must learn what was going on and then plans could be made.

We went up the alleyway at a fast walk, still worried that there might be some outside sentries. I could not believe the arrogance of the Tovieti in holding a meeting with no more than one guard, but then realized they truly did believe they owned the night, and were comfortable in its blanket. We were halfway up the alley when the ground shook and I heard a scraping, grating roar—a tremblor! But when I turned and looked back the river was undisturbed, nor did any building sway.

The street itself was turning, cobbles being churned away, a ridge snaking toward us as if some enormous, not-yet-visible mole were tunneling toward us, moving faster than a man could run, or a horse could trot!

We ran for our lives, out of the alley and onto the street.

But that was no sanctuary. The unseen digger raced on us, and then the stones of the street rained away and a dark, slime-gleaming shape reared out of the ground.

The demon, worm, mole, slime-dripping slug, whatever it was, screeched, a mouth in the center of its body opening to engulf us, as long tentacles snaked out.

The Tovieti did not need sentries.

Thak had his own minions posted.

NINETEEN

THE COLLAPSE

The demon struck at Kutulu, and he tried to duck away, but was too slow, and a tentacle had him by the ankle. Yet he did not scream, or panic, but somehow pulled his knife, slashed at the tentacle, and fell free.

Again came that scraping roar, and the monster's mouth was reaching for me. I hurled my own knife, a truly worthless defense, and it pinwheeled end for end, bouncing harmlessly off the creature's hide. The tentacles swept out, and I rolled underneath them, kept moving while my fingers found that tiny bottle. I yanked the stopper free with my teeth, spat inside, then tossed the bottle at the demon.

There was a flash of light that nearly blinded me, than a howl of rage as Tenedos's captive exploded to its full size.

Demon-roar, monster-growl, and I dimly heard shouts from the houses around us as people awoke. The demon's head snaked out, and took on the creature, then Thak's guardian bellowed pain as its jaws closed on spikes and the beast's tail swung and its mace smashed into the monster's slimy sides. It rolled, still in the demon's jaws, bent its head, and, snarling like a pack of lions over a kill, ripped and tore at the demon with its own fangs. The two nightmares, each blind in its own rage, rolled and ripped at each other, mere humans forgotten for the moment.

"The water!" I shouted, and Kutulu stumbled to his feet and we went back down that alley, running across the pier as the trapdoor yawned open. I did not look to see who was coming out, but flat-dove straight out into darkness. I hit the water cleanly, surfaced, and began swimming away.

I heard a shout for help. Kutulu! "I . . . I can't swim!" I saw floundering arms above the dark water, and swam for them as they went under, then had him. Kutulu clutched at me, and I banged the heel of my hand into his forehead to stun him, pulled away, dove under, and came up behind him.

I had his chin in my arm, his groping, panicked arms flailing without effect, and was swimming hard, a strong side-stroke, once more.

I let the current carry us down toward the waiting sea. Kutulu went limp, and I wondered if he was drowning.

I saw a dark bulk, swam toward it, and reached a drifting log, uprooted somewhere far south in the uplands and now on the final stages of its journey to the sea. I pulled Kutulu across it, and then lifted myself aboard our rescuing raft.

The warden started coughing, and I thumped his back. He vomited water twice, then gasped for air. His breathing became normal after a while.

"Thank you," he managed. "Now you *are* my friend, Damastes."

"The hells with it," I said. "You would have done the same for me if you were a swimmer."

He thought, seriously. "Yes," he said. "Yes, you're right. I would have." He looked about him. "Now what shall we do?"

"Since I've no plans to go avoyaging on this somewhat uncertain craft, we'll be swimming again, as soon as I see something to swim for."

A few seconds later I saw a long pier jutting toward us. The current swept us close, and when we were a few yards away I took Kutulu in the rescuer's hold, and we abandoned ship. There was a rickety ladder that extended down into the water, and we made our way up it.

We were in the worst part of Nicias, a part of the city where the wardens patrolled in squads, so, once Kutulu had his bearings, we went directly to the nearest warden's post and he ordered a team to escort us out of the area. They looked curiously at our sodden clothes, and wanted to ask questions, but Kutulu told them nothing. Thank several gods my boil had come unstuck during the swim and the spray-on smell had been washed away, so I wasn't as disreputable as before.

As to what happened to Thak's demon, and Tenedos's animunculi, I have no idea and less curiosity, other than that I heard no reports of monsters abroad the next day. I hope they dragged each other down into some inescapable dark hell.

We reached Tenedos's apartments only to find them deserted, even though it was only a few hours before dawn.

"Could he have gone to see Rasenna?" I wondered, then realized my question was foolish—he'd promised to wait, and he was a man of his word. We decided to do the same.

While we waited, we used Tenedos's bath to wash and, in my case, change, since I'd been keeping a couple of sets of somewhat forbidden civilian clothes at his place. Kutulu toweled himself off and started to pull on his wet clothes again.

"If the seer were here," I said, "it'd be a simple matter for him to cast some sort of clothes-line spell and they'd be dry as toast." I went to one of Tenedos's closets, and hunted through it until I found a dark set of pants and overshirt I thought suited the warden. "Put these on," I said and tossed them to Kutulu.

"But—" Kutulu looked appalled.

The warden had the worst case of hero worship I'd ever seen. It would be some incredible breach of his private ethics to dream of touching, let alone wearing without permission, something of his idol's. But I did not josh him about the matter.

"Don't be absurd," I said. "He'd tell you the same thing if he were here. You'll probably have to find a belt and punch a new hole in it. Our esteemed sorcerer is a bit more fond of the dining table than you."

Reluctantly, Kutulu obeyed. In the kitchen I found canisters with tea leaves, and made hot drinks for us, although I wondered if I'd gotten the wrong container and created a concoction to change us into frogs or something.

Two hours before dawn, an angry and worried Tenedos returned.

"My apologies," he said. "But I was summoned not an hour after you left by the Rule of Ten. Or, perhaps, I should now call them the Rule of Nine. Farel and his mistress were found dead late yesterday afternoon. Strangled by the Tovieti."

"Shit!" I said. I couldn't remember when one of the Rule of Ten had died by anything other than sickness, accident, or old age, let alone murder.

"Naturally, the Rule of Ten wanted to hear, immediately, everything that I knew about the stranglers, as if they'd paid no attention when we testified last year. Incidentally, the Nician Council sat in on the meeting, and provided leadership fully as thrilling and competent.

"Now, did you two uncover anything as shattering?"

"We did," I said. "I'll let Kutulu tell it, since he's more experienced at precise reporting than I am."

Kutulu told Tenedos exactly what had occurred, adding nothing, leaving nothing out. He made no judgments, but provided a perfect image of events. He even told Tenedos, unemotionally, as if it had happened to someone else, how he'd panicked in the water. He was about to continue when Tenedos held up his hand.

"Enough, my friend. Does your tale include anything more of either the monsters or the Tovieti?"

"No, sir."

Tenedos nodded, and Kutulu obediently said no more. He got up and paced back and forth for a while.

"I will return to the Rule of Ten, and inform them of what happened," he said. "But I do not think it will make a difference."

"What?" I was incredulous.

"Let me repeat what they said after I finished telling them

what we know of the Tovieti. They admitted the Tovieti *are* probably a threat. But we have a very efficient force of wardens, who can deal with the situation. Perhaps we should consider giving them some emergency powers."

It was Kutulu's turn for surprise.

"May I interrupt, Seer? How can they think that? We've yet to take one single Tovieti to prison. But what powers are they speaking of?"

"Setting up teams of crack officers to go after the menace, which of course they believe is quartered in the slums where our foreign workers live. No true Nician would listen to such garbage, or so Farel's ex-harness-mate Rask said. A magistrate to accompany the teams, so the proper orders can be issued on the spot for searching any house or business immediately.

"The Tovieti are to be added to the list of forbidden organizations.

"Scopas suggested that mere membership in the organization should be cause for the death penalty. But since they don't appear to have convenient tattoos, uniforms, nor membership tokens, how this would be proven went unmentioned. At any rate, the measure went undiscussed and therefore was forgotten. No doubt too radical.

"Those were the only specifics. But, my good Kutulu, you can rest assured the Rule of Ten hold you wardens in the *highest* esteem."

Kutulu's lips worked.

"You may say anything you wish here," Tenedos said. "Even if it borders on the treasonous."

"This is nothing! They can't just sit there and wait for the threat to vanish! Chardin Sher will be marching into Nicias and they'll still be talking. Or else all of us will be lying dead with silk nooses cutting into our gullets! Those men," the little warden spat, "are fools! Fools and worse!"

"Such is what I've been saying for some years now," Tenedos said.

"What else?" I wanted to know. "What about the army? We heard no details about the Tovieti's future plans, but I assume they'll be escalating their murder campaign. Are we, too, going to just sit with our thumbs in our bums?"

"The army is to be ordered to full alertness, although the Rule of Ten did not think it necessary to declare martial law.

"All mention of this matter is to be kept from the public, so there'll be nothing in the broadsheets. Instead, rumor will be permitted to run riot.

"Some other, smaller things, might amuse you.

"I was appointed to a special position, privy adviser to the Rule on the Present Emergency. I was ordered to use all of the magical powers I have to determine whether there is sorcery behind this organization."

"What the hells do they think Thak is? A wisp of sewer gas?"

"I'm not sure they believe Thak even exists."

"What was your response, sir?" Kutulu said. I could see how angry he was, and how hard he was trying to hold it back.

"Like you, I lost my temper. I'm afraid I shouted at this point that we don't need sorcery, we need order.

"Again, I was told that the wardens could handle the matter.

"After all, Nicians will instinctively obey the law. There is no cause for panic." Tenedos shook his head sorrowfully. "Now you see why I'm not at all convinced reporting the small matter of a country-wide conspiracy bankrolled by one of their own subrulers would matter a beggar's fart?"

"So what do *we* do?" I asked.

Tenedos started to say something flippant, then turned serious. "First, we must guard ourselves carefully, and ensure we aren't the next victims of the Tovieti. If Thak knows of us, and of course he does, then he'll communicate that knowledge to the Tovieti leaders.

"I'd assume that means we'll be at the top of their murder list.

"Second, try to ensure that anyone either of you holds close finds a place of safety. I'm not sure what that might be, but suggest somewhere beyond the city, perhaps even outside Dara."

"I've no such person," Kutulu said, and there wasn't even a touch of regret in his voice.

I was wondering how I'd tell Marán, and how she would convince her husband.

"The final thing I'd suggest is keep a war bag packed and your weapons handy. Be ready for anything. Anything at all."

Tenedos got up and went to the sideboard and unstoppered a brandy decanter. Then he looked out the window at the lightening sky.

"No. I'm afraid that's another weakness to be set aside until better times," and he restoppered the container.

"That's all, gentlemen." We got up to go.

"Thank you," Tenedos said. "You've not only proven yourselves worthy servants of mine, but Numantians of the most noble sort."

His words meant more than a medal.

Bugles were sounding the troops awake as I rode into the cantonment. I shouted down a lance, threw Lucan's reins to him, and told him to take my horse to the stables and feed and water him.

I ran for my quarters, and hastily changed into uniform in time to be at the head of my troop for the reveille formation.

After roll was taken, the day's orders given out by Captain Lardier, and Domina Lehar had taken the salute and dismissed us for breakfast, the adjutant called my name. I marched up, and saluted him. He handed me a small envelope.

"This was delivered late last night to the officer of the watch, with a request it be given to you personally. Since you weren't to be found in the cantonment, he gave it to me when I relieved him this morning."

I saluted him once more and walked off.

Inside the envelope was a second one, this one with my name on it. The handwriting was Marán's. Inside that, a brief note:

My dearest

I wish I could tell you this in person, for it might give me a chance to hold you and to feel you in me. But my husband came to me only this noon, and told me that due to the present unsettlements, he feels it best if we leave Nicias until the situation clears.

We will be sailing aboard his yacht this morning, before dawn. He told me we'll be cruising in the Outer Islands and off the Seer's home island of Palmeras for at least a month, most likely longer.

I am so sorry, and wish that you could take me in your arms and make me stop crying. But I shall be brave, and think of you every minute of every hour.

O My Damastes, you cannot know how much I love you and want to be with you, even though the times are dangerous. Be good, be well, and dream of me as I shall dream of you.

I love you
Marán

Marán would not have been pleased; the first feeling that came was overwhelming relief. She was out of the line of fire. Yes, I'd dream of her, and yes I'd think of her, when duty did not demand full attention. But I'd have few spare minutes in the near future.

I changed into fatigue uniform, went to the stables, and was currying Lucan when the gong clanged alarm across the parade ground. Like everyone else, I dropped what I was doing, as the emergency alert sent me, and everyone else in the Helms, scurrying for our battle gear.

The standby troop should have been formed up and ready to ride out in ten minutes, the rest of the regiment in an hour.

I was ready in that time, as was Lance Karjan, but we were two of a handful.

I heard shouts, curses, and saw confusion as men went here, there, and everywhere looking for their fighting gear, which should have been instantly at hand but instead was "turned in to Supply for fixing," "loaned to a friend a mine, I think," "I dunno, sir," "Guess it don't fit right," "th' straps broke an' th' saddler never give it back t' me," "I was never issued that item, sir." Battle garb had been ignored for polished leather and shiny brass.

It was two and a half hours before the Golden Helms of Nicias were in formation.

Perhaps if we'd ridden out when we should have the catastrophe wouldn't have happened. But I doubt it.

There'd been a brawl in Chicherin, one of the city's poorer districts, that began when three shops on a single street simultaneously doubled their price for flour. As it turned out, the three shop owners had formed a syndicate to prevent competition. There'd been an argument with some outraged customers that became pushing and shoving, and then blows were exchanged.

Someone pulled a knife and there was a body in the street. Moments later, rocks pelted one of the shop owners and he, too, went down. His shop was looted, and the mob had the scent.

They milled about, then decided to punish the other two shops as well. In one the owner fought back with a spear and was killed, but both stores were ripped apart.

The lunacy spread to other streets and other stores that hadn't the slightest involvement, until half the district was a raging madhouse.

At that point someone in authority panicked and sent for the army.

This was not the proper response. Squads of wardens should have moved into the district, isolated the ringleaders, and arrested them. If that couldn't have been done, solid walls of law officers should have gone down the streets and by a combination of fear and brute force the mob would have been quelled in this early stage.

Instead the wardens in the area were dispatched in ones and twos. A few of them were attacked, others fled, and the mob had control.

The army should have been used only to seal Chicherin off, and wardens used to calm the district. Armed soldiers in the streets signify to everyone, passersby as well as madmen, that order has broken down and the state itself feels threatened.

But someone overreacted at some headquarters. Whether this was deliberate or not, I do not know. Later it was claimed the Tovieti were responsible for the events, which I doubt, but if there were any of the stranglers involved I would believe it to be that unknown official.

Also, the Golden Helms should not have been the unit called out, for several reasons. Its incompetence at soldiering can be ignored, since no one was aware of that until far too late. But cavalry should not be sent into crowded streets against massed civilians. Not only can panic erupt, and cause more deaths than the worst riot, but it's entirely too easy to maim a horse or pull a rider out of his saddle. Foot soldiers should have been used instead, or else added as reinforcement to our horsemen, but that did not happen.

Instead, C Troop, under the command of Captain Abercorn, was sent in. They weren't even given proper weapons, but rode in with lances held high and their sabers sheathed. The point column was led by Legate Nexo.

They rode into a square filled with shouting Nicians. About half the civilians were drunk on wine, the other on the rage they not incorrectly felt about the mismanagement of politicians. The mob slowly formed an idea: They wanted to meet with someone from the Nician Council, to meet immediately, and air their grievances. They were hungry, they were destitute, their children were in rags, and it was time the city helped them. All of their plaints were certainly true.

The square had only three entrances. One of them had been barricaded by the mob against the wardens, the second was very narrow, and Legate Nexo's column blocked the last.

The highest-ranking survivor, a very junior lance-major, said Captain Abercorn had been working his way to the head of the column when Legate Nexo took it upon himself to proclaim that the gathering was illegal, forbidden by the Rule of Ten, and the people in the square were ordered to disperse immediately or face the wrath of the Golden Helms. Why Captain Abercorn wasn't at the front of his troop, and why the legate, even though he was the next-highest-ranking officer, chose to usurp authority, is unknown. I believe that Nexo, an arrogant and foolish man from a very wealthy family, was appalled that working swine—peasants—would dare demand anything from their superiors, and should have fallen on their knees or at least stood respectfully out of the way when the famous Golden Helms appeared.

Suddenly the front ranks of the mob wanted to get out of the way of the solid line of cavalry, and a shouting struggle began. But there were other, braver men in the throng, and rocks and filth pelted the soldiery.

That was enough for Legate Nexo. He ordered lances lowered and the Helms to attack at the walk.

That was almost the last coherent observation the lance-major was able to make. No sooner had Nexo cried out his orders than a rock, which the lance-major thought sling-launched, caught him below the rim of our famous helmet, crushing his face and probably killing him instantly.

The mob screamed triumph. Well-trained troops would have paid no mind to the loss of their officer, but would have automatically obeyed his last command. But the Helms were anything but well trained, and hesitated.

In that fatal moment the Helms were struck hard. Missiles rained, some sling-fired, some thrown hard and accurately. People appeared on the roofs and in the upper stories of the tenements, carrying cobblestones, bricks, anything heavy, and a rain of death came down, sending soldiers spinning from their mounts, their horses rearing crazily, lashing out in their own pain and rage.

Instead of the mob breaking, the Helms broke, turned their horses, and kicked them into a gallop, back the way they'd come, straight into the other three columns, and as the chaos spread the mob charged.

Sometime during this, Captain Abercorn was pulled from his horse and beaten nearly to death. Two years later, he was discharged from hospital a broken cripple, with no memory of anything that happened that day.

There were men in that rabble who knew what they were doing—or possibly had been trained by the Tovieti. Men with knives darted close to horses, cutting hamstrings, slicing into bellies, slashing at animals' throats, and finishing their riders when they came off.

The lance-major who told the story had been knocked from his horse by a well-thrown bottle that shattered and took out an eye. He'd had sense enough to roll into an open doorway and play dead in his gore until the melee was over.

C Troop would almost certainly have been wiped out to the last man if someone hadn't "seen" army reinforcements coming from behind, the single other open street in the square, and screamed a warning. Now it was the mob's turn to panic, and in an instant it was no more than hundreds of fear-crazed commoners, each looking to save his own skin. The irony is there were no reinforcements—whoever'd called for the Helms hadn't thought that more than a single column was needed, and our own commanders didn't think of providing backup. By the time word of the disaster came to our cantonment, it was all over, and there was nothing for me, and the others, to do but rage impotently.

Of the 119 men who rode out of the Golden Helms' barracks that morning, thirty-two returned. Forty-six were dead or dying, and forty-one others were wounded.

And this was just the beginning.

The regiment exploded in blind wrath, wanting to ride into Chicherin and kill everyone in sight. Then came fear, as the men thought an entire city had turned against its favorite gilded toy, the Golden Helms. That fear was almost paralytic. We had five men go absent, which was a rarity. Several legates began talking about transferring to other, more distant posts, or perhaps applying for long leave with their families.

Domina Lehar and too many of the other officers seemed helpless, not sure what should be done.

I requested an audience with the domina, even before the funerals of the men of C Troop, and as politely as I could, which was not very, reminded him that I'd seen real fighting on the Frontiers, as had Lance Karjan and a sprinkling of others. I told him I had personal knowledge that this was not an isolated incident, but he could expect more and most likely bloodier things to happen.

He looked haplessly about his office, found no suggestions in the statues, plaques, and awards various dignitaries had sent the Golden Helms for dazzling them on parade, and said perhaps I was right.

I should immediately begin drawing up a training program for the Helms. He'd approve it instantly, and we could begin schooling the men in the practical aspects of soldiery.

"Sir," I said. "Can't we just start teaching? Does everything have to be on paper before it's done?" I might as well have suggested we all grow wings and become cavalry of the sky. I saluted, and was about to leave.

"Please hurry," the domina said. "We'll need your expertise soon, I know. And one other thing. That lance you named . . . Kirgle or Kurtile?"

"Karjan, sir."

"Since he's seen fighting, I want him promoted. Make him a lance-major. No. I want him listened to. Troop guide."

That was Domina Lehar's idea of desperate action.

I told Karjan about his sudden rise in fortune, and he refused to believe me. I showed him the written order from Domina Lehar, and his face clouded in anger.

"I turned down th' rank slashes when y' offered 'em back in Sayana, sir, an' there's naught that's happened t'change my mind."

"You don't have a choice this time, Karjan. The domina spoke, and by the lance of Isa you'll sew the damned slashes on!"

"I'll not!"

I was losing my temper; one of the few competent men I knew was refusing promotion, while all these morons about me were clamoring for greater and greater rank, even though the idea of actual responsibility horrified them.

"You shall!"

Karjan glowered at me and I back. He was the first to look away.

"Ver' well. I'll wear 'em, sir. But I give you m'word I'll go on a bender th' first day we're off an' wreak enough havoc t' lose 'em for good an' all."

"The hells you will!" I bellowed, and a vase on the table beside me tumbled and shattered. Karjan looked stubborn.

"Let me put it like this. You *will* sew on the badges of rank, showing proper respect for the army you joined. You *will* do your duty as a senior warrant until I tell you otherwise. You will *not* go on any drunk and you will certainly *not* tear up any bars, is that clear?

"You won't for one reason. Because if you do not obey my orders, obey them just as I've told you, I will take you out behind these barracks and only one of us will walk back. I promise you two other things: The one who stays on the ground shall not be me, and you shall certainly need a good time in the hospital before you rejoin the troop. And the minute you're healed we'll go back out and I'll hammer your sorry fool ass again!"

Karjan stared at me, and a look of grudging admiration spread.

"I b'lieve you would do just that. An' I b'lieve you might win."

"Sir."

"Sir."

"Now go get your gods-damned sewing kit out and stop bothering me, Troop Guide. I have a stupid damned training schedule to write!"

But I got no work done on it that day.

The orderly messenger knocked on my office door an hour later. I bade him enter, and he told me, eyes wide in awe, that with Domina Lehar's compliments, I was to report to the Palace of War in full uniform, two hours hence.

I thought of asking why, but of course the boy, just a fresh recruit, would not have known. I, too, was shocked. The Palace of War was the headquarters for the entire Numantian Army.

"Thank the domina, and I of course shall obey," I said formally. The messenger started to leave.

"Wait. Did the domina tell you who I was to report to?"

"Oh. Yessir. Sorry, sir. I was . . . too excited, sir."

"Dammit, lad, the only thing that'll keep you alive in war is repeating your orders just as they're given. Now, tell me the rest of what the domina said."

The boy gulped and told me I was to report directly to General of the Armies Urso Protogenes.

Then it was my turn to goggle. What could *he* want from a lowly captain?

I couldn't even imagine, but I had less than two hours. I shouted for Troop Guide Karjan to get his ass back in here and help me.

I was at a complete loss.

Not quite two hours later, in dress uniform with an armband of black, which all men of the Golden Helms were wearing after Chicherin, I was ushered into the antechamber of General Protogenes's office.

Waiting for me was Seer Tenedos, which provided a likely explanation as to why I had been summoned. I'd expected the room to be filled with waiting officers, but Tenedos and I were the only occupants, other than an aide who greeted us, asked if we wished anything to drink, then returned to his work.

Tenedos's dress surprised me. I would have expected him to wear elaborate robes such as most seers put on for formal occasions. Instead, he wore breeches and a tunic of light gray, and knee-boots, and a cloak in darker gray with a red silk lining lay on a chair beside him.

"I asked for you to assist me," Tenedos said, "because I certainly didn't wish to offend someone as important as the general, and thought someone more familiar with military matters such as yourself would keep me from making any mistakes." He spoke in a quiet tone, but one that could be overheard by the aide, and I knew he was lying. Tenedos wanted me there for some other reason, and I set my mind to trying to puzzle it out.

But I didn't have the time, because precisely at the time ordered the aide rose and conducted us into General Protogenes's office.

It was exactly what you would expect a long-serving soldier, commander of the armies, a man of great honor, to have. The room was large, with bookcases full of military books. There were maps, swords, countless mementos of battle hanging on the walls. General Protogenes's desk was to one side, and it was small and bare, little more than an officer's field table, clearly showing that this room was occupied by a man of action.

The chamber was well illuminated by a glass dome in the ceiling, and directly under it was a long conference table. Sitting at its head were two generals: Protogenes and Rechin Turbery. This was to be a very important meeting indeed. Turbery held the title of commander of the Nician Army District, which meant he was the second most important man in our army.

Tenedos bowed respectfully, and I saluted and the generals got to their feet.

"Seer Tenedos," General Protogenes's voice rumbled, "I am delighted you could find the time." He gazed at me. "And this is the captain your note said we'd derive great benefits from meeting, eh?"

"I am pleased to meet the both of you," General Turbery said simply, and reseated himself, his eyes coldly measuring us.

General Protogenes was not only the most senior officer in army, but he may have been the most beloved. He returned that love wholeheartedly, always finding time for the complaints of the lowliest soldier. In that love and in his deep affection for Nicias would be his doom. He was a big man, only an inch shorter than I am, but far heavier. His face was cheerily reddened, showing that he appreciated good living and saw no reason others shouldn't do the same.

He was an example to all soldiers, in that he'd come from Wakhijr, a poor desert state, a herder's son with no friends and less money. He'd risen steadily through the ranks and then been given a field commission, quite a rarity at the time. Protogenes was not only a good, brave soldier, but also a lucky one. He was wounded many times, never badly, but that was not what made him lucky. Most heroes go unnoticed, with no one of proper rank to witness their bravery. Not so with Protogenes. Without his ever seeking favor, glory and recognition always came.

He had served in every state of Numantia, in all of its skirmishes and little wars, from the Border States to fighting pirates in the Outer Islands to quelling savages in the mountainous jungles of the East.

His rise to the top had been accelerated when he met Rechin Turbery, after he'd taken over a regiment in the Border States. Protogenes would have been the first to admit he was no cunning tactician—once an enemy was found, he'd have the bugles sound the charge and it was be up and at them with a cheer and the sword, lads.

Turbery was more cunning, and looked it, never attacking a position frontally, not taking heavy casualties when he could outflank or outmaneuver the enemy and bring his troops home safely. He was in his late forties, some twenty years younger than Protogenes. He was slender, balding, sharp-faced, and his gaze seemed to expose your every secret.

The two had made a perfect team, and became fast friends. When Protogenes was promoted to the army's staff, Turbery was promoted to domina and given a regiment of his own on the border between Kallio and Dara. He achieved fame not only for keeping the peace between our two states, but also for leading daring raids against the hill bandits. It was well known and admired by officers that he seemed always to know, and have the correct response, when these "bandits" were mere ruffians, and when they were disguised members of the Kallian Army, who delighted in probing the army they were supposedly a part of to find its weaknesses.

When Protogenes was chosen to head the army, it was quite natural that he'd call for Turbery to join him.

"I asked you here," Protogenes said, "because of this damnable trouble. I'm afraid I wasn't able to attend the Rule of Ten's hearings on these Tovieti. My sincere apologies.

"Would it be possible for you to briefly summarize what you told them? And perhaps the captain could add anything you might have overlooked?"

"I would be delighted," Tenedos said, and began talking.

After a few moments, I noted that the two generals didn't seem to be paying close attention to what Tenedos was saying. It was as if they already knew what he was telling them. If so, why were we here? I determined to watch my words very closely.

To the broadsheets Tenedos might have glorified our exploits, but now he briefly and exactly summarized the physical facts of what had happened in Sayana and, the week before, along the docks of Nicias. I noticed he did not mention Kutulu by name, but merely referred to him as a responsible officer of the wardens. He finished, and asked if I had anything to add. I said I did not, that he'd done a complete job, and clamped my mouth shut, waiting for the real reason we were here.

It came in seconds, from General Turbery.

"What we are about to discuss must be held under the rose. If that condition is not acceptable, Seer, Captain, then our business is finished. Frankly, the only reason we considered this meeting is because of how highly certain well-thought-of senior officers, who've been impressed by the job you're doing at the lycee, speak of your tact, integrity, and perception."

I looked at Tenedos for guidance. He nodded, and I sat

back. "I think I can speak for Captain á Cimabue as well as myself," he said. "You have our vows, on any god you wish, that what is said here will not be repeated until you give us leave."

The two generals exchanged glances, as if reluctant to begin. Turbery stood after a moment, and began pacing back and forth.

"Our leaders, the Rule of Ten," he began, "seem to feel that this . . . trouble, will be swiftly ended, and require no more action than what they've already ordered.

"I hope they are right, as does General Protogenes."

"Of course," the older man growled. "Damned if anyone wants to think his masters aren't on top of it."

"But I'm of the opinion they might have all their arrows in a single quiver," Turbery went on. "You've given us the facts, sir. Now I ask for your opinion, and your honest assessment of the threat."

Tenedos took a deep breath.

"Very well, and I know I am going to shock you. But as you said, this meeting is under the rose, and I would wish you to respect that condition as well.

"Briefly, the Tovieti are but a symptom of what's going on. Our country is near collapse, our people floundering around without guidance, without direction. The Rule of Ten are not ruling wisely nor well, and as they stumble about they are sucking all the other institutions of Numantia into the morass with them."

"Harsh words, sir."

"Harsh words, yes. But these are harsh days, and the time is well past for dancing hearts and flowers around a nasty subject," Tenedos retorted.

"Go on," Turbery said, listening intently. General Protogenes looked most uncomfortable.

"Add to this the Tovieti, who are being financed by Chardin Sher. I don't know what other mischiefs he's been causing, but I assume that his agents are causing as much trouble as possible throughout Numantia."

"Like father, like son," the old man rumbled. "The old Sher was a pain in the ass as well."

"But Chardin is worse," Turbery said. "Because he's got brains, something his father fortunately—for Numantia and for peace—managed to live without.

"I'm not sure," he went on, "the situation is as serious as you believe, Seer. But there's no harm in preparing for certain eventualities. So let me ask you what must be done right now?"

"Declare martial law," Tenedos said promptly.

"We cannot do that," Protogenes said. "That's a prerogative of the Rule of Ten."

"Is there any reason you can't do everything short of the actual declaration?" Tenedos asked. "By this I mean mobilize the army immediately. Put small roving patrols under the command of battle-experienced officers, in the streets. Move the men out of the cantonments, sir. Put them in, as emergency reinforcements, at the wardens' posts. The people already fear the worst, so seeing the army about, ready for action, should reassure the faithful and perhaps make the wicked rethink their plans.

"Sometimes a show of force is enough. But that should not be all. You should . . . sirs, you *must* reinforce the army, here in Numantia, and you must reinforce them with the best."

"You mean the frontier forces," Turbery said.

"Just that. Pull Captain á Cimabue's regiment, the Ureyan Lancers, plus the other two Ureyan units . . ."

"The Twentieth Heavy Cavalry and the Tenth Hussars," I put in.

"Pull them down here at once. Commandeer swift steamers and have them sail south as soon as possible. If I were in your chair, sir, I'd have a dispatch out within the hour with the order. I'd further bring another ten regiments of the best in, keeping them hidden outside the city to see if the situation worsens."

"That would leave the borders undefended," Protogenes objected.

"What does a finger, a hand, a foot, mean if the heart is

about to be impaled?" Tenedos said, his voice heated. "When the present emergency is over, even if the worst happens, we'll be able to retake the Frontiers. But if Nicias goes down in chaos . . . we might as well turn those lands over to Achim Fergana and the other bandits. They'd be no worse off.

"Another thing that must be done immediately, although it is nearly too late. All food supplies must be commandeered and moved to a central location, where they can be well guarded. We can strike at the mob through its stomach, if it's forced to come to us for rations.

"We must also put out foraging parties into the outlying districts, and send word to all cities on the river that we are prepared to pay, in hard gold, for any supplies that can be brought in and given to the proper authorities. If thievish merchants take too great an advantage, we'll simply commandeer what they have at swordpoint.

"The people who stand by us must and shall be fed. Only then will they stand firm behind us."

"You are a man of strong measures, indeed," Turbery said. "Yet . . ."

"Sir," Tenedos said, "this is an action that *must* be taken. We serve Numantia. Now is the time to serve her well, not with half-measures or no measures at all."

He knew when to shut up, and silence hung in the large chamber for a long, long time. I dared not move, hardly dared breathe, for fear of breaking the mood he'd created.

"General," Turbery said to his superior, "what the seer is telling us isn't altogether fresh information."

"Dammit, it isn't," the old man said. "But he doesn't have to sound so damned gleeful about it!" They were talking as if neither of us were in the chamber.

"As he said, these are harsh days," Turbery said. "I'm of a mind to do as he suggests. After all, the Rule of Ten have seldom expressed much interest when we move our soldiers about, so long as they themselves are well-guarded."

Protogenes nodded, like a great, wise bear.

"Yes," he said. "I despise judgments of the moment, fearing them to be based on the heart's summons. But I sense the seer is telling something very close to the truth, General Turbery. We shall follow his suggestions."

Tenedos only smiled a bit, but knowing him as I did, I could feel the pure joy radiate.

"Still further," Protogenes went on. "I am of a mind that this seer, whether he's using magic or just common sense, is giving us far better insights than our other advisers and staff.

"Seer, I would like you to give up your teaching duties, at least until the present situation clarifies itself, and work directly under myself and General Turbery. I don't know what the position might be called, but I'll give you full powers, in writing, to do whatever you think is necessary, and I mean *anything*. Just one favor: Before you start moving my whole damned army about, at least do me the favor of telling us." He chuckled, but there wasn't much humor in the laugh. "I'm not sure what else to order, but as the days pass I'm certain there'll be changes made. Will you serve us, sir?"

Tenedos rose.

"There could be no greater pleasure or honor, sir, than to serve you . . . and all Numantia."

"Very well. Is there anything you need?"

"Yes," Tenedos said. "I'd like to have Captain á Cimabue detached from his regiment and assigned to me."

"Done. Captain, will you need anything?"

"No, sir." Then I thought. "Or, rather, yes, sir. Not for me, but for the seer."

Tenedos frowned, but I continued.

"Sir, I've served under the seer for more than two years, and I think he's a great man. I shouldn't be saying this in front of him, I suppose, for it sounds like I'm sucking up. But it's the truth. He has one monstrous flaw, though. He won't see when he's in jeopardy, and I know, right now, he is in the greatest danger of his life, as great a one as Numantia herself."

I don't know where these words were coming from—I was not generally gifted with the ability to make speeches. But now they flowed easily.

"I think that's a reasonable assumption," Turbery said. "So what would you have us do?"

"Order him to find safe living quarters, sir. Right now it'd take no more than one or two Tovieti, creeping in at night, and . . ." I stopped.

"The captain exaggerates," Tenedos said. "I'm sure my magic would warn me." I felt like responding that at least twice before he hadn't been able to foresee an action of Thak's, but kept my mouth closed.

"Your suggestion is excellent," Turbery said. "As it happens, we have just the place, not half a mile from this palace. It was used to house hostages who were in fact prisoners, and is hence easy to guard and hold. Seer Tenedos, I order you to move into these quarters."

"Very well, sir."

Protogenes was studying me closely.

"Seer Tenedos," he said, "is this man to be trusted?"

"Absolutely, sir."

"It strikes me," the old man said, "remembering my own days as a junior officer, how hellish hard it was to get anything done if it didn't coincide with the interests of my superiors.

"The easiest solution would be to promote you, Captain á Cimabue. Just as it'd be easier for you, Seer, if you held the rank of, say, general. But I'm not prepared to do that, at least not yet. General Turbery, when you have Seer Tenedos's orders drawn up, also include the captain's name in that.

"You, sir, are now empowered to do anything you think necessary to not only save Numantia, but to keep the seer alive."

"Yes, sir. Thank you, sir." I saluted.

"That's all," General Protogenes said. "We shall be in almost daily contact, I'm sure. Now, we have set ourselves a task. It is time to go to work."

"Thank you, sir," I said as Tenedos and I rode away from the palace.

"I'm not sure I was right in asking for you to attend this

meeting, which I did not only because I wished you to share the honor, but because I shall need your clearheadedness in the days to come."

"Why not?"

"Now it would appear I have acquired a nursemaid. Hmmph."

I laughed, then asked, "Sir. Your opinion. Will this save the day?"

Tenedos considered for a long time before he answered.

"I don't know. Certainly the generals said all the right words and supposedly gave me complete powers. But they are as much a part of the system as the Rule of Ten. They rose to their present positions under it, so I wonder if they're able to question things as deeply as they should."

"I noted you said nothing about it being time for the Rule of Ten to be replaced."

"Of course not." Tenedos snorted. "I'm mad . . . but I'm hardly a fool."

Three hours later a messenger from the Palace of War came to report that the "orders in question" had been dispatched, and that the *Tauler* and six of the other fast packets had been requisitioned by the army for "special purposes."

Now all we had to do was hang on until some real soldiers arrived, and we could move to the next step: going into the warrens of Nicias and winkling out the Tovieti.

Domina Lehar liked it little when I told him of my new assignment. He said he'd been counting on me to help rebuild the regiment, and I almost felt sorry for him. But what the hells did he think his badges of rank were given him for—to impress the other rice planters at a formal ball? I'm sure he was even less happy when I informed him I'd be stealing certain of his warrants. The Golden Helms may have been a useless formation in my eyes, but there were certain men I'd noted as being worthwhile.

The first, after Troop Guide Karjan, was Legate Petre, of

course. He grumbled that he'd not joined the army to be a warden, but when I told him how important it was, and would he rather be teaching his men just why the inside of their buckles should be polished when they went on parade, he gave in.

Quite joyously I put away the Helms' dress uniform for a simpler fighting dress of a helmet with plain roached crest, nosepiece, and cheek plates; mail waistcoat over a flaring silk blouse; tight pants; boots with sideplates; and a cloak. Instead of a shield I laced a steel guard to my left forearm. I ignored the normal cavalry lance and saber, and carried a plain straight sword of the style I preferred, a dagger shorter than the one I'd dueled Malebranche with, and, unstrung and kept in a saddle-carrier with war-arrows, a short compound bow.

My first task was to make sure Seer Tenedos's new quarters were completely secure. The building was just as Turbery had said, a four-story circular tower with a moat on the outside and a small keep on the inside. It had sat disused for years, so the first order of business was getting it cleaned. As one of my last duties with the Helms, I'd set my own troop to the task. The "Silver Centaurs" howled complaints about being no better than housemaids when I turned them out with brooms, mops, and orders to clean the building until it shone like their helmets. I refrained from agreeing that was about the limit of their abilities.

I wished I'd not been so cavalier as to loan Legate Yonge to Marán's friend. I could have used him and his friends, but my word had been given. When I thought of Amiel, Marán's face and body crashed into my mind, and I was swept away for an instant, thinking of her. But then I came back, and hoped she was lying tanned, lithe, and lazy on the deck of her husband's yacht. I also, idiotically, hoped she was celibate, and that her husband had acquired an acute shrinking disease in his private parts.

I fought my mind back to duty and the job of protecting Tenedos. I wished the Lancers would hurry and arrive—I planned to loot them thoroughly for Tenedos's bodyguard.

The best I could manage at present was to select men from

the units around the capital, not accepting volunteers for obvious reasons, and then assign them to their details randomly. Even if there were Tovieti among them, and I assumed there were, they would have little time to plan an attack and, since I teamed up the soldiers arbitrarily, the chances of everyone on a detail being conspirators was unlikely. Each day I reshuffled the details as well, and once a week returned the men to their units to be replaced with fresh soldiery.

As senior warrants I used Karjan and the other warrants I'd stolen from the Helms. Karjan, even though he gave me a dark look from time to time, proved an excellent leader, and I found myself depending more and more on him.

But all this was no more than putting a plaster on a scratch while the patient was bleeding to death from a hundred wounds. I wondered what would come next, how this unrest in Nicias would be permanently ended.

Kutulu was also reassigned to Tenedos, and with him came his stacks and boxes of cards. He also brought some assistants. I don't know what duties Tenedos put them to, but when I asked the warden if I could borrow a few of his men to instruct my guards in the fine art of security, he snapped that I could not—he was casting for far greater fish.

I saw little of Tenedos during this time. He was closely guarded in his travels by specially picked guards who worked directly for the Palace of War. I didn't trust them entirely, but could do little until my own escorts were chosen and ready.

He came back to the tower late one night, and came into my quarters.

"I would dearly appreciate a small brandy," he sighed, "and the hells with the state of emergency. There are times you've got to cheat on yourself."

I kept a flask for exactly these times, and poured him a drink. He sipped at it. "In case you have ever wondered, the singularly most stubborn, selfish, thickheaded people who walk this earth are magicians."

I said I was already *very* well aware of that, thank you.

"Have you heard of the Chares Brethren?"

I had not. He explained they were a group of the most influential magicians in Nicias. They weren't a secret order, but were quite comfortable with few people knowing of their existence.

"They were created," Tenedos went on, "as a sort of mutual aid society. They've also become a very powerful political group in Nicias. I've been trying to woo them and I'd just as soon try to seduce ten temple virgins at once, or herd a flock of rabid sheep."

"Might I ask why?"

"I won't be specific, Damastes, because my idea might be a foolish one. Perhaps you know that magic is the most selfish of all the arts."

I did not.

"A magician works a spell to benefit himself or, grudgingly, a client, for which he expects to be richly rewarded. The more selfish the deed, the more likely it is to be granted, or so it seems to me. Perhaps that's why there's more talk of black magic than white. Certainly spells that have been tried, altruistically trying to spread a blanket of peace over the world, or ending famine, seldom seem to take.

"Or perhaps the gods are happy seeing us squirm in misery.

"At any rate, I had a thought on the matter, and am trying to get these raving fountains of all knowledge to help me test it.

"But so far all they're doing is talking, and don't seem to notice that the world is in flames around them."

I was wandering around the outside of the tower, trying to think like a Tovieti intent on breaking in and how I could thwart the villain, when the messenger found me. He was a Golden Helm, and with the adjutant's compliments, could I find the time to return to the Helms' cantonment on what I might consider personal business?

I couldn't imagine how I had any personal business at all

these days, but grudged the time, telling Petre where I was going.

Sitting outside the regimental headquarters was a for-hire pony trap. I dismounted, pulled off my helmet, and entered.

Marán was sitting on a bench, just inside the door. She came to her feet as I entered, and gladness lit her face. Then it vanished, and I saw that look of an innocent who'd somehow sinned without knowing it and expected to be punished.

She rushed into my arms and I held her, my helmet clanging to the floor unnoticed. I did not know what to say or do. Looking over her shoulder I saw a leather valise sitting by the bench.

We stood in silence for a space. Then she said, her voice a bit muffled against my shoulder. "This is the first time I've ever hugged anybody wearing armor."

"I hope not the last," I managed.

She stepped back, and we looked at each other wordlessly.

"I left him," she said.

"When?"

"Three days ago. We docked at some island, and we were supposed to have a big banquet with its governor. And . . . and I couldn't do it. I couldn't do any of it. Not anymore.

"I threw some things in that bag, found a sailor who had a fast boat, offered him gold, and he took me back to Nicias." She smiled a little. "He was old enough to be my grandfather, but I still think he hoped I'd think him young and lusty."

"Idiot," I said fondly. "You could have been sold to the pirates."

"Would you have come looking for me if I had?"

Of course the notion was quite absurd—I had a far more serious duty here. But I knew enough to lie, and as the words came I knew they weren't lies at all, but the raw truth.

"Always and forever."

I kissed her, and out of the corner of my eye I saw Captain Lardier peer out of his office, look shocked, and vanish.

"Are you sure of what you've done?" I asked her.

She nodded. "I'll never go back to him. Not even if you and I . . . not ever." She stepped away from me.

"I came here as soon as we landed. Now . . . I guess I'll go to our . . . my house. I'll have his things moved out, I suppose. My family will be too busy screaming for a while for me to go near them." She looked wistful. "I wish I could stay with you. But I guess that'd be scandalous."

"Worse than that," I agreed. "Forbidden by law." I didn't like the idea of her going back to that house, even if every sign of Count Lavedan was stripped away. Also, more logically, I assumed that others might know of our affair, and see Marán as a way to me, and through me to Seer Tenedos.

But there was no other choice.

Then the idea struck. For the first time, and one of the few times thereafter, I used a trust dishonestly. And by the gods I'm glad I was brave enough to do it. I felt that then, and I feel it now, even knowing what came later. If I had unlimited powers, by Jaen I was now going to use, or rather misuse, them.

"But you aren't going back to that mansion," I said firmly.

"Then where?"

"You are going to live in a nice, safe tower, surrounded by men who'll do anything to ensure you're safe. With me. That is, if you wish."

Marán looked at me, and again I fell into the dark, warm depths of her eyes.

"I wish," she whispered. "Oh, Damastes, how I wish."

"This is most irregular," Tenedos said. "But I can see your point. I don't think you could be blackmailed even if the countess were a hostage, but there is no point in taking the chance."

"Thank you, sir." I was vastly relieved.

Tenedos shrugged.

"Since it's already done, it would look even stranger if I countermanded your orders."

"Might I suggest you consider doing the same with Baroness Rasenna? There's more than enough room."

"No," Tenedos said firmly. "First, because at the moment I

have no time for anything personal. Secondly, she is in no danger whatsoever."

"Are you sure?"

"If it makes you feel better, know that I cast a certain spell using, among other things, some of my own blood. Rasenna is very safe, very invisible, even if Thak himself came seeking her. Now, please remove your long Cimabuan nose from my business!"

"Yes, sir."

Two weeks passed, and we'd heard no word about the reinforcing units upriver. Worse, the Palace of War informed us that heliograph stations along the river were not answering signals.

Where was the army?

It was ugly riding the streets of Nicias. There was no more open violence, but only because no soldier or member of the government rode alone, but with a full escort. Bodies were still found in the streets at dawn.

It looked as if there were only two classes left in the capital: the commoners, who held the streets in sullen anger, and the gentry, who huddled in their enclaves. The merchants, clerks, traders—all the middle levels of Nicias—seemed to have either vanished or joined the lower classes, waiting for something to happen.

I started awake, hearing the chanting of many voices. Torchlight flared into my open window, and I rolled out of bed, naked, fully awake, reaching for the sword hanging from its sheath on the bedstead.

Marán sat up, sleep-dazed.

"What is it?"

I didn't know, but I hurried to the window and peered out. Our rooms were on the third level of the tower, looking toward the city, away from the Palace of War.

The night was a sea of bobbing torches, the streets alive

with marching men and women. I could hear bits of what they were chanting, but no more than a word here, a word there: "Bread ... peace ... down with the Rule ... voice of ... people ... Numantia ... burn or live ..." and through it a thin chorus: "Saionji ... Saionji ... Saionji ..."

Marán was beside me, wearing only the thin shift she'd been wearing when I came to bed, exhausted from work, hours after she'd retired. She leaned out the window, elbows on the sill, fascinated.

"Can you feel it, Damastes?" she whispered. "Can you feel it? The goddess is calling."

It was just the roar of the crowd, but then it came to me, *she* came to me, the goddess, the destroyer, the Creator calling to my blood, and it stirred.

Powerful magic was abroad this night, and it moved me, and I wanted to go out, to be down there, amid the crowd, ready to rend and tear, then, from the ashes, to build a new realm, a realm of absolute freedom, where all that could be wanted was there for the taking.

Marán turned, and I saw her eyes gleam in the torchlight.

"It's like Tenedos said," she whispered. "A new world. A new time. I can feel it, Damastes, I can feel it like the Wheel turns. Can't you?"

I could indeed, and it gripped me, seized me by the throat, and all the dark passions rose high, and now there might have been drums out there in the night, or it might have been my pulse, but then it changed, and it was not Saionji's manifestation of Isa, six-headed war god, but rather Jaen, and my cock rose hard, throbbing, painful.

I was behind Marán, pulling her shift up above her waist, forcing her legs apart, and then I impaled her on my cock, burying it in one thrust, and she whimpered and Jaen took her as well, and she thrust back against me and cried out.

I pulled back, until the head of my cock was at her inner lips, then rammed forward, my hands finding her breasts, pulling her against me, and she screamed, scream buried in the crowd-roar outside, and again and again, each time thrusting deeper, reaching, tearing deeper into her body, into her soul, and I shouted as I came, gushing hot, hot as the fires inside the earth that made Thak.

After a time, time came back, and I realized I was lying half-out the window across Marán, crushing her against the sill.

"I'm sorry," I said.

"Don't apologize," she said. "Just . . . give me a little warning next time. So I can put a pillow down."

I slipped out of her, took her in my arms, and we stumbled back to the bed.

"I have the feeling," she murmured, after we'd calmed, "I'll be a little sore tomorrow."

She stroked my chest.

"I think, my love, that what we just did is what I've heard called sex-magic. Amiel loaned me a book about it once."

Darkness touched me for a second. "Sex-magic for who?" I asked. "Who called it?"

"I don't know," she said. "But I've never felt anything like it. And I don't know if I want to ever again. I feel like . . . like we were, not used, but part of somebody that's not us. No, maybe I'm wrong. Maybe we were no more than someone's vassal."

The Tovieti's sorcerers? Thak himself?

Or—and the thought made me shudder—Saionji herself? Was the goddess of destruction out there, hanging over Nicias, smiling as she saw the order that had always been tremble?

I don't know if sex-magic was cast that night, if others were grabbed and shaken by a spell, or if it was just Marán's and my own sudden lust.

But the next day Nicias shattered into chaos.

TWENTY

THE FIRES OF NICIAS

There are many tales of what caused the riots. Some say a peasant's child was ridden down by a nobleman's carriage, others that a young girl was brutally beaten by the wardens, others that it began in a drunken bar fight between some government clerks and some carters.

I don't doubt any of them, but I don't believe the city erupted over a single incident—the madness spread too rapidly. There'd been too many years of the poor being neglected and downtrodden, too many years with their leaders not leading, too many years of instability, and so the city was like a pile of dry wood that a burning ember is touched to there . . . there . . . there . . . and the wildfire explodes.

The commoners ran rampant, burning, looting, beating, killing, and raping when they encountered an enemy, or simply someone who looked better off than they were.

The wardens fled to their stations and barricaded themselves in; the soldiers hid in the barracks; the rich cowered in their mansions; while the Rule of Ten and the Nicias Council met in emergency session and did nothing.

Again the disorders struck home. Rask, one of the Rule of Ten, Farel's comrade, simply disappeared, and no one knows what became of him to this day. A mob sacked the Council Hall, happened on four of the city councilors, and tore them apart.

Scopas came to the tower to consult with Tenedos, and the seer told me what their conversation had been. Tenedos made the same suggestions he had before, and once again Scopas weaseled on taking such drastic steps. Perhaps, he said, since the commoners are mostly looting their own quarters, they should be let alone until their frenzy dies away.

Surprisingly, Tenedos agreed with what was happening, at least partially. "Let the poor burn their tenements and slums," he told me. "When this is over, we'll be able to rebuild Nicias as it is supposed to look." That callousness shocked me, but I think I was able to hide my reaction. "But anyone who thinks this rising will run out of combustibles is a fool. The Tovieti, and Chardin Sher's agents, will make sure that will not happen."

The insanity grew worse and worse.

Days passed, and there was still no sign, nor word, of the soldiers who'd been summoned from the Frontiers. Tenedos tried casting a spell, but said nothing happened. It was, he said, like trying to peer through a dense fog. He said this could mean only one thing—sorcery, which meant the Tovieti were keeping the troops from the capital.

I'd had Tenedos use his emergency powers to move the Golden Helms, the Nineteenth Foot, and two other of the parade regiments into tents in Hyder Park, equidistant from our tower, the Palace of War, and the Rule of Ten's palace, for security and as an immediate reaction force. They whined about having to forsake their comfortable brick barracks. I suspected if the rioters left them alone, they'd be quite content to sit there polishing brass and practicing empty roundelays on the parade ground until all Nicias was ashes around them. Instead, they rode, and walked, guard; and made short patrols through the city's major thoroughfares, complaining all the while. Terrible soldiers, but they were the only game in town. At least, I wryly thought, I probably didn't have to worry about any of the complainers being Tovieti—those would be most grateful for any chance to get close to Tenedos, the Rule of Ten, or the army staff.

It was a terrible time, and there were terrible sights.

I saw a screaming, drunken woman run into the middle of a square just as a column of the Helms rode into it. She was waving something I couldn't distinguish. But another soldier could, and a horseman spurred his horse into a gallop, his lance dropped into position, and the woman went spinning away, blood spattering the cobbles.

The soldier pulled his lance free, and came back to us, and by that time I had my sword out, and at his throat.

"Tell me one reason," I said, "you should not die for murder, you bastard!"

"Sir . . . you didn't see what she had in her hand. Sir, it was a man's jewels . . . cock an' all!" Paying no heed to my blade, he vomited suddenly. I could not kill him, but at least I told Troop Guide Karjan to deal with him later. Perhaps I should have slain the man. I don't know.

I told Marán some of what I saw in my daily rounds, but not about the emasculator. No woman of her youth should know about such evil. I just considered that thought, and realize how foolish it is. No one of *any* age or *any* sex should be subjected to what we went through in those days.

After a week, the city was paralyzed. But that was not enough. Now the Tovieti moved out, smoothly taking command of the mob.

They didn't burn their own hovels anymore, but rather sent raiding expeditions into the rich parts of Nicias. Stores miles from the slums were ripped apart and fired. There was no doubt as to who was leading the rabble—bodies would be carefully left for the patrols to find, always with the yellow silk cord around their throats.

Next signs appeared, scrawled huge on walls demarcating certain districts like Chicherin. Sometimes they held messages:

NO ARMY
WARDENS DIE FROM HERE ON
NO RULE OF TEN BEYOND THIS SIGN
FREE CHICHERIN

Or sometimes it was simpler, just a scrawled, twisting line in yellow.

"Quite interesting," Tenedos observed. "The Tovieti's progress would make an excellent case study. First chaos, then strike directly against the enemy, then delineate your own territory, where you'll make the laws and customs. They'll keep the pressure on us, making sure the Rule of Ten never have a chance to take a deep breath, let alone think or listen to what I'm trying to tell them. As the days pass the Tovieti will gain recruits, since all mankind flocks to join a winner. When they think they're strong enough, then they'll come for us. Fascinating.

"What puzzles me is who was the mastermind of this plan? It isn't Thak—no demon, no matter how powerful, could be expected to understand the affairs of man so closely. Nor would it be Chardin Sher or his errand boy Malebranche.

"It could only be that unknown being who first summoned Thak to carry out his dreams for mankind.

"It is a pity Thak slew him, for now I know that must be the case, or he would have resurfaced and tried to bring his juggernaut under control.

"I wish I'd known the man, for his ideas are most interesting."

I rather hoped Thak had spent a long time enjoying himself with his master before letting him return to the Wheel, and that it would be many turnings before Irisu allowed him to reincarnate as anything above a slime-worm.

The nobility were almost as insane with terror as the mob was with blood lust. They would hire, and pay any amount, for the services of a man who owned a sword and promised to keep them alive. Naturally, some of these men, and I heard of a few women as well, were phonies or, worse, thieves who used this trust for opportunity. And some of them were Tovieti.

Mahal, hurrying home to his lustful young wife, was pulled from his carriage and strangled by his own bodyguard. The man was cut down by Mahal's driver, but the Rule of Ten was now seven strong.

No one had much time to mourn Mahal. In the predawn hours of the next morning the rabble formed around the barracks of the Second Heavy Cavalry, whose domina had refused to deploy them closer to the palace. The sentries were silenced, and men with torches, pikes, and strangling cords slid into the compound.

The unit woke to screams, flame, and death. Perhaps one or two of the 700 men of the Second Cavalry managed to escape. If so, none of them ever returned to the army. In less than three hours, an entire regiment of the Numantian Army was obliterated. This had never happened in all the army's proud history, at least not for the last thousand years records had been kept.

At noon that day General Urso Protogenes rode out to the still-flaming ruins of the Second's barracks. He'd refused a heavy escort, saying he'd be gone only a few minutes, hardly time enough for any of "those villains" to put together an ambush.

The legate in charge of the five-man party said General Protogenes had taken a look at the sprawled bodies of what he sincerely believed had been fine soldiers, and heavy sobs had shaken his chest. He kept shaking his head in disbelief, but his eyes could find no ease.

"My people," the legate heard him whisper, and no one knows if he was talking about Nicians or his soldiers.

He bade the legate wait a moment; he wished to step inside the regimental office, which was no longer aflame. There was something he hoped to find there.

Ten minutes later, when the general had not reemerged, the alarmed young officer went looking for him.

The general had evidently gone out the back door of the office, across the rear of the compound, and out into the city.

He was another who was never seen again, nor did his murderers ever claim credit for helping a sad old man find the death he sought.

By now we were so hardened that the next deaths almost made us smile. Another of the Rule of Ten's councilors, notorious for preferring the most brutal of bedpartners, couldn't restrain his lust. He, along with the mealymouthed chamberlain, Olynthus, went looking for satisfaction one night.

Their bodies were found sprawled in front of the Rule of Ten's palace the next morning. The cords that strangled them would have come as a blessing, from the savage wounds on the corpses.

This was finally enough for the Rule of Ten. They determined to negotiate with the mob, with the Tovieti, even though there'd been no leaders show themselves, nor any demands made.

The Rule of Ten's speaker, Barthou, managed to convince five of Nicias's smoothest-tongued diplomats to take on this vital mission. Tenedos said he'd been asked if he wished to accompany them, and he'd told Barthou he thought the speaker was mad.

With a full troop of the Helms, who actually were beginning to shape into something vaguely resembling soldiers, I escorted the five to the edges of the Chicherin district, where the riots had first broken out, and where the Rule of Ten had somehow decided the heart of the rebellion was.

The negotiators had white flags tied to staves, and, holding them high overhead, the five walked down the winding street into the slum.

Half an hour later, I heard a single scream, a scream that reflected all of the pain the world could hold.

Then silence. We waited for another hour, until rooftops began bristling with slingers and even a few archers, then wheeled our horses and rode back to the tower.

General Turbery took over command of the army, and ordered all troops to withdraw into a ring around the Rule of Ten's palace. We would hold, and then strike back from there.

With them came those wardens who'd faithfully tried to hold their outlying stations. The regiments were ordered to loot as they came, so every granary and warehouse was stripped bare.

As the troops marched or rose into the parks around the palace, the rich, the noble, all those who were the Tovieti's or the mob's targets, came with them. Makeshift camps were set up everywhere.

Among them were Amiel and her husband, Pelso, still loyally guarded by Legate Yonge and his three scoundrels. I wished I could find a way to move the count and countess into the tower, but knew there wasn't one. Rasenna had also arrived inside the perimeter from wherever Tenedos had been keeping her hidden, and at least she was allowed to be with the seer.

I took Yonge aside, and told the hillman his charges were now safe in the bosom of the army, his responsibility was over, and I needed him and his friends desperately.

Yonge looked sly. "Ah, Captain Damastes, but I cannot. You remember what I told you once, how impressed I was with your way of honor and loyalty, even unto death?"

"I do."

"Then I must hold to my oath and still serve the Lord and Lady Kalvedon." He looked most pious.

"Besides," I said dryly, "I wouldn't be paying you in good red gold."

"There is that," Yonge said, brown teeth flashing. "There is that, indeed."

I went to Tenedos and asked him how long would we have to prepare for the attack.

"I'm not sure," he said. "I've been having better luck with my magic, and whatever spells Thak has been spreading are wearing thin. I can *feel* it building, feel them readying their weapons. I'd say, oh, three days. Five at the outside."

"What do you think our chances are?"

"Well, let's count, or guess, really, since I haven't counted noses. Let's think as small as we can. We have four regiments around us, two thousand men. A thousand wardens. Another six or eight thousand fugitives, let us imagine, although I'll wager there's twice that many. Then there's the government clerks, diplomats, hangers-on, magicians . . . other useless types.

"Against us, what? Half a million? A million?"

"Sir, aren't you supposed to be a pillar of inspiration?"

"Only to legates and below. Captains can keep their own lips stiff. Besides, I'm certain with truth and justice on our side we'll win through," he said bitterly.

"Oh. One other thing." He reached in his pocket, took out a small ornate metal case, and handed it to me. "There are two tablets inside. If the gods don't find it in them to change our luck, you and the countess are welcome to these.

"They're painless and shall return you to the Wheel in seconds."

I left his cheerful company and started detailing men to dig trenches.

When the sun rose the next morning, welcome warmth cutting through the mists, the Latane River was a cacophony of ships' bells and whistles.

The army had finally arrived.

TWENTY-ONE

RETRIBUTION

The whistles and bells sounded the mob's doom as well as our salvation, and they and the Tovieti knew it. A group of them charged the docks, but were broken against the arrows coming in from the transports and from the welcoming force I'd quickly assembled.

The riverboats moved to the docks then, and gangplanks dropped and long lines of men snaked across them, carrying their weapons with the ease of long familiarity. They paid no mind to the jeers and chants coming from other parts of the waterfront, but keenly looked about, evaluating a new battlefield, and, as like, what loot might present itself.

There was no singing, no flashing display, and I wanted to grab each of the surviving Helms by the throat and say, "See, this is what soldiers are, not your empty bullshit of trumpets, parades, and banners."

General Turbery and Tenedos arrived just as the formation's de facto commander, normally head of the Varan Guard, was disembarking. He was a tall, rawboned man, cleanshaven, with short hair and a scar-seamed face, Domina Myrus Le Balafre. I knew him by reputation, a brawler, a swordsman, a duelist who'd killed more than his share, and a supremely confident and able battle commander.

He saluted General Turbery.

"I thought you might never come," the general said.

"I thought the same," the domina said. "We should have expected opposition the minute we put out down the river. But we didn't . . . and paid hard for our confidence. But no matter now.

"Sir. I have the honor to present the relief force for Nicias, thirteen regiments strong, six of horse, seven of foot. We await your orders."

General Turbery hesitated, thinking. Tenedos stepped forward.

"Sir, may I offer a suggestion?"

Domina Le Balafre scowled at him.

"Who the blazes are you, sir, if I might ask?"

"Seer Laish Tenedos, special adviser to the general of the armies. Sir."

The two men stared hard at each other. Domina Le Balafre was the first to lower his gaze, but I felt the clash of wills had just begun. General Turbery turned to the seer.

"Go ahead, sir. You've always been the first with an idea."

"Sir," Tenedos said, "I think we should not wait, not develop a firm plan. Let us move immediately. Put the regiments into the parks, break them down into battle formation, and move them out into the city at first light. The Tovieti will never expect that."

General Turbery blinked, then turned to Le Balafre.

"Can that be done?"

The domina was as startled as the general. Then he considered, and smiled tightly.

"Yes. We can manage that. Yes, indeed. That would be a short, sharp shock for the rabble. Sir, I can guarantee the Varan Guard will be ready, and . . . let me think . . . at least half, most likely more of the regiments. Maybe all of them," he thought aloud. "I'd suggest you only hold one of them back. The Seventeenth Ureyan Lancers won't be ready to fight."

My own regiment! A pang touched me. What had happened? Le Balafre went on to explain, and now we found why the army was so late. They'd not been able to move downriver as fast as they should, because the supplies and new driving belts for the *Tauler*-type transports "somehow" weren't waiting at dockside as had been arranged. But things had not come to real grief until they entered the great delta, upstream from Nicias, just below the city of Cicognara. They'd encountered dense river fogs that forced them to tie up for days.

"Did you not recognize sorcery, sir?" Tenedos said.

"I pay little heed to magicians," Le Balafre said. "This time, it was my error."

General Veli, the expedition's commander, had realized time was running short, and so, in spite of the weather, had set out once more. The fleet had become lost in the delta, taking dead-ended passages or channels that shallowed uselessly. In one long, narrow strait they'd been attacked. The flagship had been hit by huge boulders, catapult-launched, "although how the hells the gods-damned rebels managed to build them, let alone wrangle them into position in those gods-damned swamps, is beyond me." The ship lost way, listed, and began sinking, and then archers came from hiding and volleyed arrows into the men trying to swim to shore.

"They killed General Veli then. And that's when the Lancers were crippled. They had their domina, uh . . ."

"Herstal," I put in, in spite of myself. Le Balafre gave me a dark look—captains don't interrupt dominas—but said nothing.

"Herstal, yes, that's it, plus their adjutant and about half of their senior captains had gone on the flagship for a conference. We only fished a handful of men from the water, none of them officers."

So my old enemy, Captain Lenett, was dead. Oddly, I was disappointed—I had been looking forward to a chance to show him he'd sadly misjudged me. Now, I'd never have the opportunity.

Three other riverboats had been sunk, but the fleet had rescued most of the men. Their attackers vanished into the swamps as rapidly as they'd emerged.

They went on, and found the main channel, then lost it again.

"It was then I had a bit of an idea," Le Balafre said, smiling grimly. "I'd heard, just rumors, y'know, about these scum and their strangling cords. They haven't come yet to Varan, where we'll give them a warm welcome.

"But I thought I'd have a peep into the gear of the riverboat pilots and officers. You'll never guess what I discovered in eight of them."

"What did you do with those Tovieti when you'd discovered them?"

"Why, hung them, of course. They made pretty decorations on the boat's cranes, dangling and kicking like pomegranates in a summer wind." He looked hard at Tenedos, probably expecting shock from the civilian.

"Good, sir," Tenedos said warmly. "Very good indeed. I promise you you'll have more strange fruit to admire before you leave Nicias."

Le Balafre nodded approval. "After that, we had no further trouble, and we came on Nicias late last night. We didn't dock because, frankly, we didn't know what our reception was. Glad you were able to hold out."

"Yes," General Turbery said. "Now, let's get the soldiery ashore. It'll be a long day preparing for the morrow."

"One thing before we move, sir," Tenedos said. "This matter of the Lancers?"

"Yes?"

"I had the pleasure of having a troop of them guard me when I was in Kait, and—"

"You're *that* Tenedos, eh?" Le Balafre interrupted. "My apologies for being rude before, sir. You did well, sir. Very well indeed."

"I thank you." Tenedos turned back to Turbery. "As I was saying, I found them to be excellent soldiers. I think it would be a pity to lose their services now."

"You have a suggestion?"

"I do. Name Captain á Cimabue their domina. He's from the regiment, and has served well."

Both the domina and the general gazed at me intently.

"Irregular," General Turbery said. "Most irregular . . . hmm."

He thought for a moment. "Jumping a man two full grades . . . that'll not sit well with the army's list keepers, now will it?"

"And the hells with them," Le Balafre snapped. "As if you and I haven't spent most of our careers battling those shit-heads, always carrying on about who's senior to whom, and who's in the Upper Half and who's in the Lower Half and who gets to sit ahead of whom at the banquet.

"Balls to them all. I hope the Tovieti killed more than their share down here."

General Turbery smiled a bit. "I'd forgotten how subtle and diplomatic you were in your speech until now, Myrus." Once more he considered. "You know, General Protogenes *had* said that, when this emergency was over he wished to reward the captain if he lived."

He looked at me closely. "Captain, do you think you can handle the task?"

"Sir, I *know* I can." And I did. Hadn't I been ordering around, even if indirectly, dominas and regiments lately? Maybe I was arrogant, but I felt a swell of confidence.

"Then, sir, I take great honor in naming you, Captain . . . ?"

"Damastes, sir."

"Damastes á Cimabue, domina of the Seventeenth Ureyan Lancers. Now, sir, take charge of your regiment!"

I came to attention. Domina Le Balafre looked about. "Hell of a place to be promoted. No bands, no speeches, no pretty women to kiss. Here, boy." He untied his own sash of rank and tied it about my waist.

And so, on a greasy riverside dock, witnessed by one sorcerer, one general, and one domina, I received my first regimental command.

I was proud . . . and I was humble, remembering the faith of all those, from my father to the brass-lunged instructors at the lycee to the lances and warrants who'd taught me how to really soldier, and knew I had to prove to their memory I'd been worth the trouble.

Now I had to justify that faith.

* * *

I was determined the Lancers would march out with the rest in the morning if I personally had to be behind them with a whip.

First I found Regimental Guide Evatt, who looked most guilty, remembering the way I'd been set for a fall by the late Captain Lanett back in Nehul. I told him we had no time for the past. I wanted him to take charge of disembarking the horses and making them ready for the morrow. He hesitated, thinking of the enormity of the task, and I told him bluntly if he wished to hold his rank slashes he'd see it was done, no matter how. He had to call on the entire regiment to make sure it was done, especially the men of Sun Bear Troop, the regiment's support element.

I sent messengers to hunt down Legate Yonge, Legate Petre, and Troop Guide Karjan.

I had Troop Guide Bikaner report to me immediately, and informed him I was commissioning him legate. He looked startled, then pleased. At least he wasn't another like Karjan. I told him to take charge of the regiment's enlisted men and see they were marched to the assembly area I pointed out on the map, just on the shores of one of the lakes in Hyder Park. I told him to clean out any civilians camped in the area, but to do it politely, for they'd almost certainly be nobility, no matter how shabbily dressed, and they'd have good aim at his ass if he lived through the days to come, when normality, civility, and nitpicking returned to the capital.

I had the regiment's surviving officers assemble, and introduced myself. Most of them remembered me, if just as the young legate who'd supposedly done something uncalled for at a rõl match, then redeemed himself in the Border States. My address was simple and short. I told them there would be changes made, some involving promotions over their heads, and they were to keep their resentments hidden until later, or else I'd be most displeased and take the extreme measures these extreme times seemed to warrant.

I told them I'd admired the late Domina Herstal, which was

mostly the truth, and hoped to be worthy of commanding the regiment he'd built. I finished by saying there were terrible days ahead, and they'd need all of their courage and intelligence just to survive.

"But survive you must, for I won't be able to finish the task without you. Lead your troops as best you can, gallop always to the sound of clashing steel, and you'll find no disfavor in my eyes.

"Lastly, you'll be facing a cunning, evil, duplicitous enemy. Hold in your mind the skills of our troops. I want you to show the caution of the sambar, the cunning of the tiger, the courage of the lion, the stealth of the leopard, the speed of the cheetah, and, when we're in battle, the tenacity of the sun bear.

"Now, go to your men and lead them as you've done in the past!"

A trifle pompous, perhaps, especially coming from a twenty-two-year-old talking to older men, some in their late forties, but not as bad as some inspirational speeches I've heard . . . or made, come to think of it. At any rate the officers raised a ragged cheer before they dispersed. But I knew their opinion of me was yet unformed, and would be made the first time we met the enemy.

Liking the comparison to the animals our troops were named after, I used the same analogy when I spoke to the regiment, drawn up on the shores of the lake. I told them they must think of me as new to the unit, so I had no grudges, no favorites, as yet. Each of them and all of them were given a clean slate and a fresh opportunity.

"Soldier hard, soldier well—and stay alive! Let the other bastard die for his cause!"

The warrants raised a cheer, and the men set to.

Yonge and Petre had arrived as I was finishing, and I waved them to me.

"Congratulations, my Captain," Yonge said. "I said you would become a general one day, and now you are well on the way."

"Thank you, but save your admiration. You're through

guarding the Kalvedons. You're promoted to captain, and I want you to take over Sambar Troop. Their captain drowned coming downriver. They're the regimental scouts, but I'm sure you can teach them things about skulking."

Yonge grinned.

"I cannot argue with that. But how will these Numantians take being led by a despised Man of the Hills?"

"They'll like it," I said shortly. "Because there's always room in the rear rank for horsemen who used to have higher rank."

"Very good, Domina. I shall go and inspect my new command. One thing more, sir. I have a message for you."

"Give it to me."

"I have but to show it." He pointed. Across the park, on the far side of the regimental area, I saw Marán, sitting on a horse. I waved, although I suppose a domina is supposed to be more dignified. She waved back, then turned her horse and galloped back toward the tower. I felt a glow of love and pride; she knew I'd have no time for anything but the Lancers now.

It was Petre's turn. "Take Tiger Troop," I said briefly. "You should have no troubles—I remember them as the best of the regiment. I'd make you my adjutant, but you're too damned valuable for that. And you're now a captain as well, Mercia."

It was as if I'd given him the throne of Maisir.

"Thank you, Damastes . . . I mean, Domina. Now we can show them what we can do, can't we?" We grinned at each other like fellow conspirators who'd just won their cause, then he saluted and hurried off.

Finally, I spotted Troop Guide Karjan. I told him that he'd be serving as my right hand. I couldn't promote him, because there could be but one regimental guide, but expected him to serve in that capacity. I guess he was becoming used to sudden change, because he just grunted, and said he'd be making sure our horses were ready for the morrow.

And so the Seventeenth Lancers set to work on our impossible task.

* * *

Three hours before dawn, I was feeling a bit of satisfaction that perhaps we'd be ready as promised, when a messenger came and asked me, with General Turbery's compliments, to report to the tower for briefing.

The large dining room had been cleared of furniture, and large maps of Nicias hung around the walls. One by one the regimental commanders who'd freshly arrived in the capital reported. Already there were the dominas and captains of the four home regiments, including my former commander in the Golden Helms, Domina Lehar.

I was interested to see Kutulu and several of his assistants conferring with Tenedos, each of them with a large box of files.

The general called us to attention, then told us we'd be given our tasks by the seer.

Tenedos went to the map and, without notes or ever pausing, told each of us our missions and what part of the city we'd be moving into. He said that each domina would be given two aides: one an officer from a Nician regiment, the other a warden who, in Tenedos's words, "has specialized in the Tovieti. Take heed of what they tell you, gentlemen, because their information is exact. There'll be other wardens accompanying you who have been set their own tasks." He paused for a moment.

"I wish you well," he said. "This day we fight for Numantia and the future."

I noted several of the ranking officers exchange looks, and could easily read what they were thinking from expressions— this was no creaking pedant, far removed from the harsh realities of war. Perhaps the Seer Tenedos deserved the respect he was getting from the army's commanders.

General Turbery called us to attention and dismissed us after a few encouraging words, and we streamed back out to our commands.

Tenedos told me a week later that General Turbery had offered him a direct commission as a general that afternoon, but he'd turned it down. I asked why, and he said, "Truthfully, because I wish no trace of the old order soiling the hem of my garments. But I didn't tell the general that, but rather that I felt I could be of more service observing from the outside."

I'd been astonished, having an idea of Tenedos's goals, and wearing a general's red diagonal sash would have been a long step toward achieving them. But the seer always preferred the long shot that would strike directly home.

It was still dark when the troops moved out into Nicias. Company by company the army moved into the assigned districts. Wardens trotted behind them.

The first to go were the signs. They were ripped down or white paint was splashed over them. Then the soldiers went in, street by street, moving carefully, methodically, as we'd been ordered:

First the four corners of a block would be taken, and outposts set. Then the troops smashed into the buildings, house by house, never less than in squad strength. Each store, each residence, was ransacked. Women screamed, babies wept, men tried to fight back, but without effect. If obvious loot was found, the residents were rousted into the street. If the items were minor, their names were taken by the wardens and they were released with a warning. Bigger items, gold, piled delicacies, too many garments, and all adults were turned over to the wardens, to be escorted to prison pens being hammered together outside the Rule of Ten's palace.

If a yellow silk cord was found, or if there was evidence someone had committed a serious crime, for instance if a warden's sword or truncheon or bloodstained clothes were found, the men and women of that apartment were told to stand aside and were well guarded.

The search went on, house by house, tenement by tenement, until the block was completely taken apart.

The ropes were tossed over the lamp standards and the Tovieti and other men and women of violence were hanged unceremoniously.

The soldiers would re-form and march to the next block,

the bodies dangling behind them and the wail of mourners keening loud into the summer air.

Those were the orders that'd been given us, signed by the Rule of Ten. I knew those weaklings wouldn't have the guts to order such ruthlessness, and that the policy had been created by Seer Tenedos.

The mob and the Tovieti were shocked into immobility by our brutal and immediate tactics. All through that day and the next there were outbursts of violence, quickly suppressed by the soldiers, who did not use batons or blunted lances, but the sword and spear.

It was not just civilians who died. Small, desperate bands of men made sudden attacks, and squads went down screaming, and there was always the silent archer who'd loose a single arrow and flee. It was a man here, two men there, but the army was bleeding badly, more than a hundred casualties each day.

This pacification went on day after day. I grew sick with slaughter, but grimly kept on. There were things that happened at least as bad as, and possibly worse than, in the riots, but at least the rioters had the excuse of wine and rage to lessen the blame. We did not.

I'll give but one example: I was riding with Lion Troop toward a new district, passing through an area being cleared by the Varan Guards. I saw the soldiers rush a tenement, and the screams began. A window smashed open on an upper floor, and I saw a warrant hurl something out. It spun down and thudded limply in the street, not far from where I rode past. It was the body of a boy, no more than ten.

I found the officer commanding that company, and raged at him. He looked at me without expression until I'd finished, then said, flatly, as if I weren't his superior, "Sorry, sir. But I have my orders." I thought of smashing him down, but was too weary with blood to do it. I turned back toward Lucan. "Besides," he said to my back, "there's no great harm done. Nits grow up to be lice."

I determined to pursue the matter, but instead of complaining to his domina, Le Balafre, I went to Tenedos.

I found him in the tower, supervising six men who were maneuvering a large, somewhat battered marble statue toward his rooms on the floor above mine. I took him aside, told him what had happened, and said it was hardly the only atrocity I'd seen committed by our soldiery. Someone needed to rein the army in, before we all became no more than a murderous mob ourselves.

"Domina á Cimabue," he said, "I have no sympathy for you. Perhaps you need a bit more iron in your soul. The Tovieti, and those who fought with them, had no sympathy for us, neither man, woman, or child. They declared utter war.

"We are fighting by their rules, and it's far too late to change them. A ten-year-old is more than old enough to carry a cobblestone to a roof and use it to crush a soldier's skull. We've both seen that happen, seen boys and girls younger than that even with blood on their hands.

"We can find people to mourn for the innocent once we've tracked down the last of the guilty.

"We are in a state of war. You and the rest of the army have been given lawful orders by the rulers of Numantia. Now carry them out, sir."

That night, by chance, the Lancers were rotated back to the perimeter to be given a full night's rest and a chance to clean up. I took the opportunity to see Marán.

I was still so gripped by the sight of that dead child that I felt no lust, no passion. I told Marán what had happened, and she was as shocked as I'd been. After a time, she said, "I don't know what to tell you, my love. Is there anything you can do?"

"I don't even know if there's anything I *should* do," I said honestly. "I feel like I've been thrown into a pool of filth, and the harder I struggle to get out of it, the dirtier I get."

I got up and went to the window, looking out at the city. Marán joined me.

"Maybe this sounds stupid," she said. "But remember how it was last week? All we could see was fires and darkness. Look now."

From this distance, and in the darkness, the city did appear to be returning to normal. The heights, where the rich lived, now twinkled with occasional lights as the braver nobility found the courage to return to their homes. The gas had been relit on the boulevards around the palace, and it, too, looked almost as it had been, although there were far too many splotches of darkness and ruin.

"Come, my Damastes," she said softly. "I don't know any answers, and neither do you. We have each other, and we can sleep, and it may be less painful in the morning."

She was right. I took her in my arms and gently stroked the softness of her hair.

From the floor above me, from Tenedos's rooms, I heard an explosion, a crash. I yanked my sword from its sheath, tore out the door and up the stairs. The bastards had found a way to get at the seer!

I hammered at the door, and Tenedos pulled it open.

"You're all right?"

"Yes. I'm fine," he said. He looked over my shoulder and I turned and saw other men crowding the landing, weapons at hand. "An experiment of mine got out of hand," he explained. "There is nothing to worry about. My apologies."

There were grumbles, and some laughter about the various stages of undress the rescuers were in, and they filtered away toward their rooms. But I remained behind, looking over his shoulder through the door. His workroom was a shambles, fragments of marble littering every square foot of the floor.

"Great gods," I said. "What happened?"

"I attempted a certain spell, which in fact didn't go awry, as I told the others, but quite the contrary. Thank Saionji I gave Rasenna a strong sleeping potion, since I thought there might be some excitement. Not like this, however."

There was an elongated triangle etched into the top of a round table, with symbols carved around it. In the center of the triangle was a circle, and in that what I thought to be piled gems. I looked more carefully, and saw that the flashing reflections from the fire came from nothing more than shards of broken glass.

"What is it?"

"It is, or rather I think it is, exactly what I have been seeking."

"Which means?"

"Which means I'm evoking a wizard's privilege of mystery, and will tell you more when I choose to . . . or when the spell is put into service, which I hope will be in no more than a day or two.

"Thank you for responding so swiftly, Damastes. Now, good night."

I shrugged and left. If Tenedos would not tell me, there'd be nothing I could do to cozen anything from him. I told Marán what had happened as I undressed. Then the sight of that boy lying dead in the street came back.

I shuddered, and climbed into bed. Marán looked into my eyes.

"Do you want to make love?"

"No. I don't think so. I don't think I could."

She blew out the lamp.

"Do you want me to hold you?" she whispered in the silence.

"More than anything," I said. She put her arms around me and her head on my shoulder. I caressed the softness of her cheek. After some time, her breathing gentled and she slept.

I lay for a long time, staring up into the darkness.

The Tovieti were broken. All districts were secured, although of course no one with any degree of sense traveled by night or in groups of less than a dozen.

The Tovieti were broken, but not destroyed, and so the army and the wardens began drum patrols.

Snares would rattle as a platoon of soldiers, backed by a team of wardens, marched up to an address, generally at dawn. The senior lawman would shout names from his list, and sleepy men and women would stumble out.

These were known Tovieti, on the long lists that Kutulu and his agents had gathered.

A yellow silk cord was tied around their necks, and the death sentence read. Kutulu and his wardens had stacks of them, signed by one or another of the Rule of Ten. All that was needed was to fill in the name, toss a rope over a standard or pole, and the sentence was carried out.

It was like currying a horse. The army had been the coarse comb, now the fine-toothed one swept the capital.

Not only the poor died. I saw a face I recognized, blackened as it was. Count Komroff, the man who'd renounced his title and thought everyone should live in poverty and on milk, had evidently found a more dynamic philosophy, since the yellow silk cord dangled from his elongated neck.

Nicias, even in ruins, was close to normal. Only the docks were still deadly. We had not even been able to send full-size units into these warrens without taking heavy casualties. But we—and they—knew the end was only a few days away.

Tenedos summoned me to the tower late one afternoon.

"Tomorrow night we shall end this nightmare," he announced. "Kutulu's agents have discovered that the last elements of the Tovieti, their leaders and their most fanatical, plan a last stand, taking down as many soldiers as they can, when we assault the docks. I suppose they think such a blood sacrifice will bring Thak to life."

"Why hasn't he already made an appearance? Surely the massacre of his disciples can't be pleasing."

"Why shouldn't it be? He's but a demon, hardly capable of real reasoning, at least not as we know it. I'd imagine that death, any death, even those of his own people, gives him drink and meat. I doubt if he'd feel any personal threat until the last of his believers faces doom.

"Perhaps he's even abandoned this city and returned to the Border States, or other places where he's worshiped. Not that I plan on taking any chances.

"I cast some careful spells, and found that the Tovieti are still using that smuggler's den you and Kutulu found as their headquarters."

"I can't believe that, sir," I said. "That's completely foolish. That hideout was exposed. Wouldn't they find another?"

"I agree they're hardly showing much intelligence, at least from our viewpoint. Perhaps they think Thak killed the intruders, or perhaps that the invader was nothing but my animunculi, under sorcerous command. Or, just as likely, they're as arrogant about our faults as the Rule of Ten were about them before the murders started.

"At any rate, I'd like a raiding party made up from your regiment. Perhaps some of those stalwarts who were with us on the retreat from Sayana might wish to put a bit of adventure in their lives.

"No more than twenty men. And yes, I'll be accompanying the raid, which is an absolute necessity, not adventurism, Domina.

"Let me show you why."

He took out a box, and opened it. Inside were the fragments of shattered glass I'd seen a few nights earlier.

"You remember how angry I was trying to get those idiots in the Chare Brethren to work together and produce a single Great Spell? Well, I ran out of time, although I still think it's a possibility. Instead, I had glass bottles blown from a single vat of molten glass, and given to each member of the brotherhood. I had each of them cast a single, identical spell. When they'd succeeded, I broke the bottles, then took a bit of this glass, which was the results of the spell.

"I already had the Law of Association working for me, and I created another spell, using the Law of Contagion, and overlaid a third incantation on top of that."

"And the result is?"

"Damastes, I'm a bit ashamed of you. I shall not tell you, not out of any desire to be mysterious, but out of personal pique that you're not assembling the evidence your own eyes have gathered.

"If you haven't figured it out by tomorrow night, then perhaps you'll get a chance to see it being cast for real."

I had one final question: "What about Kutulu? Will he be coming with us?"

"Why should he?" Tenedos said. "His work will begin after the raid. Until then, there's no need to risk his abilities.

"Now, go prepare your troops. I've several other spells to prepare for emergencies."

Of course there were more than twenty men from the Lancers who wished to volunteer—there were twice that many just from the men of Cheetah Troop who'd recovered from their injuries and sicknesses gained in the retreat from Kait and returned to the regiment.

Every officer in the Lancers volunteered, and I'm afraid I made the party rank-heavy, since I took Captain Yonge and Legate Bikaner as well as myself. Captain Petre gave me a dark look when I refused him, but I wanted at least one officer I knew well to remain with the Lancers.

At dusk I kissed Marán good-bye, went upstairs to get Seer Tenedos. I approved of his dress: dark, tight-fitting tunic and pants, a matching watch cap, and boots that laced to midcalf. He had a belt-pouch with magical supplies in it. Like the rest of us, he was armed with a dagger as his primary weapon. He also carried a shallow wooden box about two feet by one foot, closed with a clasp. Fortunately, it weighed less than five pounds. I assumed this contained the elements of this special spell he was so proud of.

He'd also devised a plan on how we would reach the waterfront undetected. It was a bit elaborate, involving a diversion from the ring of soldiers sealing the docks off from the rest of the city and using that excitement to mask our party's moving through the lines.

"Have you already asked the army for the diversion?"

"I have. It'll be the Tenth Hussars, and I've given the domina a duplicate of this." He held up a hand, and showed me a rather ugly brass ring. "When I rub it, he'll feel a tingling on his own ring, and know it's time to begin his feint. We'll move forward from the lines of the Humayan Foot."

"I think I have a better idea . . . although your idea of the diversionary attack is good."

"Go ahead," Tenedos said, with just a bit of frost, "I'm still learning to be a tactician."

"Sir, I think you missed the easy way."

"Which is?"

I pointed, and he swore at himself. "Of course! I should have seen it for myself. I'll summon a courier and tell the Humayan Foot not to expect us."

I'd pointed to the Latane River, gleaming in the setting sun, and had already procured five flat-bottomed boats whose sides barely stuck up above the waterline. We loaded into them, untied the moorings, and let the current take us into the heart of the enemy. All of us were dressed in dark clothing, wore daggers on our belts, and carried small packs with the other tools necessary for our strike.

There was enough light so we were never in doubt of where we were. I had the men stay low in the boats. When we neared the Tovieti headquarters, I whispered to Tenedos to rub his ring. In a few moments, I heard the screech of battle as the Hussars launched the diversion, and we brought out oars, rowed to a ramshackle pier, and moored our boats.

We made sure we hadn't been spotted, then went straight toward the pier. The warehouses around us were fire-blackened, and I could smell the stench of unburied bodies.

The Tovieti may have been foolish about not abandoning their burrow, but at least they'd set human sentries out this time. There were three, and I almost felt sympathy for the poor, untrained fools. One actually whistled to himself in boredom, and the other moved back and forth in a regular manner, and the third stood close to the edge of the dock, staring fixedly across the river.

I touched sleeves—Yonge . . . Karjan . . . Svalbard—and they went forward, knives out. All I heard was one quiet splash as the third sentry's body was dropped into the river. The other two corpses were eased to the wood, and my three assassins were back beside me.

We found the hole where the lever should be inserted. Tenedos held up a hand: Wait. He touched his temples, touched the wood, and nodded. I should proceed. He'd sensed no magical alarms. Once more I felt with the butt of my dagger, found the socket and pried, and the hatch lifted noiselessly.

I still could not believe this wasn't a trap, but after a few seconds, when nothing happened, I started toward the ramp. Tenedos stopped me, and shook his head. He handed me his case, and went down the ramp first. For a moment I thought this was mere bravado, but then I realized, seeing him move so carefully, arms spread in front of him like a drunk trying to keep the world steady as he walks, that he was the right one to lead, the only one with a counterspell to stop any waiting Tovieti sorcery.

He stopped twice, each time taking something from his pouch and whispering a spell. The first time I saw nothing, but the second time the darkness glowed purple for just an instant, or perhaps it was an illusion.

The Tovieti masters had done a better job of guarding themselves than before.

We moved down the tunnel, then saw light and heard voices. There was no sentry at the mouth as before. Evidently the Tovieti felt that magic was a more reliable guardian than steel. Tenedos took the case, and I crawled forward a few feet until I could peer into the chamber.

I counted seventeen men and women. They were gathered around a sand-table they'd used to model the dockyard area, talking in low tones, and pointing to various locations, obviously laying out the final attack, completely lost in their work. There were maps everywhere. If the seventeen had been in uniform, male, and a bit less disheveled, it would have looked exactly like any army planning session.

I slid back a few feet to my men, and held up a curled forefinger, thumb atop it. Everything was as it should be. The men drew their weapons. In one hand each of us had a knife, in the other a canvas tube full of sand. We'd kill if we must, but had hoped we wouldn't have to—corpses would be of no use.

We crowded together at the mouth of the tunnel. The men's

eyes were on me. Breathe . . . breathe . . . breathe . . . my hand
dropped and we charged into the room!

The Tovieti turned, saw us. There was a scream or two, and
then we were on them, sandbags swinging. Only a few of them
had time to draw weapons, and they were either cut or clubbed
down before making more than a couple of wild slashes. Two
women ran for an exit. Accurately thrown sandbags dropped
them.

Then there was no one left standing in the room except
Lancers. I saw only one of my men down, unconscious or
dead; another in trouble, on his knees, gasping for air where a
chance kick had winded him. A few others had minor wounds,
swiftly bound by their mates.

Scattered around us were the dead, unconscious, or wounded bodies of seventeen Tovieti leaders. We'd been amazingly
successful, and so far I hadn't heard a hue and cry. But we had
made some noise, and could have only a few more lucky
moments.

The men were already taking precut lengths of rope from
their packs, binding the hands and feet and gagging the twelve
Tovieti who we thought would live. Of the others two were
dead and the other three unlikely to survive. That was as Tenedos had ordered: Kill only if you have to. We wanted as many
as possible able to talk.

The raid was, thus far, outstandingly successful, more so as
the prone men groaned back to life and sat up. I was privately
less content—I'd hoped the Kallian Malebranche would be
among the Tovieti, but he was absent. But then I saw the fat,
bearded man who was the Nician leader of the sect lying
bound on the floor, and next to him the Marchioness Fenelon,
who glared hatred at us all.

I thought Tenedos would be happy, but he was looking
about, worried. "Hurry," he said. "I sense something. Something coming."

We needed no urging, and in seconds had the bound men
and women carried over-shoulder, and our own casualties
were assisted back up the tunnel.

Then the ground rumbled and shook, as it had before, and I looked about, for signs of that fearsome mole-monster. I saw nothing, but the ground rumbled harder, bricks groaned and shrieked, and I heard the gush of water as the passageway was torn open and river water began to pour into it.

We went up the ramp at a run, the roaring torrent just behind us, and burst out into the night and safety, nothing behind us to show signs of the smuggler's cave but a dark, swirling pool.

The ground kept shaking, the wooden dock creaking, about to tear apart.

I looked downriver, toward the sea, and saw Thak!

I don't know where he'd hidden himself—underwater, in some warehouse or burrow or perhaps there was a door into his world somewhere out there.

On he came, clawed hands stretching for us, ready to crush, ready to tear, as he had in my nightmare, and I heard that screeching of unoiled metal and high shrilling I'd heard before in the Tovieti cavern in the Border States.

Now he was not orange and sun colors, but darkness and moonlight. Thak gathered enough light from the stars and sliver of moon to send darting slashes of illumination across the water and buildings as he crashed toward us. I heard cries of terror and joy as men and women saw their god, their destroyer.

A few of my men, those who hadn't been in the cavern and seen the demon before, were wavering, about to flee.

"Stand fast!" I shouted, and my shout brought them back into the chains of discipline, and they dropped our captives and made ready to fight, pinprick knives against a monster.

Tenedos was busy opening that case. Flashing bits of light revealed those bits of glass, held somehow within the confines of a smaller circle and triangle.

Tenedos took a fragment in each hand, and stood, holding his arms toward Thak, who was now no more than a hundred yards distant, his hellish keening louder in expectant triumph. Tenedos began chanting, and his voice boomed across the river, louder even than the demon's death song:

"Little voices
    Little spells
    Spells that broke
    Spells that smashed.
You are an echo
    An echo of another
    Who in turn
    Reflects another's voice.
Now come
    Come together.
Touch your brother.
    Feel your brother.
You are one
    You are mine
    Mine to hold
    Mind to send.
You are mine
    I fathered thee
Now you must obey.

"Ahela, Mahela, Lehander

"I hold you
    I order you
    I send you.
Seek your target
    Seek your enemy.
Seek it out
    As you were taught.
Strike now
    Strike hard
    Strike as one."

I don't quite know how to explain what I saw, but something rose from that case, just as I belatedly understood what the spell was, that each of those bits of glass had been the result of a shattering spell cast by one of the Chare Brethren, combined by Tenedos as symbols to create one enormously powerful incantation, which had smashed that marble statue in its test.

What I saw was barely visible, shimmering like heat above a fire, but this had a form, a shape, a rough V. I saw it, then I saw it not, but felt a wind rush, and barrels on the dock between us and Thak were bowled aside as the spell rushed toward its target.

Thak must have seen or sensed doom rushing upon him, for he reared back, holding up his hands in front of him. But the spell struck true, the crystalline "singing" crashed into discordance, like a million, million goblets crashing onto stone, and then it cut suddenly, and Thak exploded, exploded like a huge stone that had been cut by a master jeweler, examined and found flawed, and smashed with a great hammer in a fit of rage.

There was a rain of fragments, fragments that vanished even as they fell, and then Thak was gone.

"Now it is over," Tenedos said in the stillness.

TWENTY-TWO

CIVIL WAR

But it wasn't over. Not yet. There were still Tovieti to hunt down and destroy. Once again, Elias Malebranche had slipped away. Kutulu could find no traces of him in Nicias. Tenedos shrugged. "He's fled to his last bolt-hole. He . . . and his master . . . don't realize it, but their time has run out."

It was still cruel, still nasty—the Tovieti who refused to vanish fought as bitterly as any fanged beast does when tracked to its lair. But we found them, and we killed them, although more soldiers died in the process. In these final days, Tenedos's hellhound Kutulu was given his own nickname by the broadsheets: The Serpent Who Never Sleeps. The fear his name brought was to grow and grow.

Nicias, a city half in ruins, was at peace once more. Now would come retribution and blame. I privately expected the people of the city to turn against the army and especially Seer Tenedos after the brutal suppression. But they didn't. He was once more a hero, a great man. I puzzled, but Marán, who I was learning was far more perceptive than her age might suggest, said she wasn't surprised. "The people did things they don't want to remember doing, so whoever *really* did what happened, well, they're someone else, someone different. All the seer did was destroy those horrible, different people so the common people can be happy again." I realized that yes, people did think, or rather not think, like that. So I merely shook my head when the army was cheered every time it rode out, and once again I was Damastes the Hero.

The Rule of Ten proclaimed a "time of healing," and no doubt would have gotten on with rebuilding with never a finger-point of blame, a convenient policy since they were far guiltier for the riots than any Tovieti or Kallian. But Tenedos would have none of that. He called for a tribunal, but the Rule of Ten quickly responded that they'd have hearings on whether or not that should be allowed.

Perhaps the matter might have ended there, but once again the Rule of Ten's ineptness showed.

Nicias was starving to death, even though food was coming into the city by the day in great barge-loads. The rice, the meat, the fruit were being off-loaded into warehouses . . . and there it sat. Unless, of course, you had the right amount of gold. The rich, as always, ate well.

Once more the city rumbled with disquiet. This time, Tenedos didn't wait for the Rule of Ten to fumble with a response. No one had rescinded his special orders, and so he sent out elements of the Frontier divisions with orders to smash into the warehouses and take the food. He set up distribution centers throughout the city, manned by other soldiers, and the city ate—for free. Tenedos was no longer a hero, but a demigod.

Nicias's profiteers whined loudly to the Rule of Ten, but they were frightened to stand against Tenedos.

Again Tenedos called for the tribunal, and the Rule of Ten was forced to give in. They took the opportunity to let him hopefully hang himself, and named him head inquirer, supposing, I guess, he'd muck up matters and show his incompetence. How they imagined a man who'd spent as much time in public debate as he had would ruin things was beyond me.

Their second weapon, calling for the tribunal to meet in camera, was blunted; Tenedos announced the hearings would be held in the city's greatest amphitheater. All would be welcome to come and see, and judge for themselves.

The Rule of Ten fumed but could do little. Their utter incompetence was very clear now—they still hadn't been able to name replacements, but buried themselves in bickering, with Barthou determined to find acolytes even more toadying than the ones slain in the riots. Scopas, according to Tenedos, tried to stand up to Barthou, less, the seer thought, from patriotism than from the desire to make sure his own powers weren't lessened.

But the date of the tribunal was set, less than a week distant. Two things of interest happened during that time.

Marán had returned to her home beside the river. One morning, I received a note, asking if I could attend her at a certain hour. Unusually, she asked me to leave my horse at the public stables a block away, and come to the rear of the estate, where there was a small back entrance. A servant would be waiting.

There was but one door in the huge blank expanse behind her mansion. I tapped on it, and the door swung open. A rather plain-faced woman I thought I'd seen serving tidbits at Marán's salon told me to follow her. I saw, in front of the house, a long line of freight wagons, and heard men shouting.

The woman led me in a circuitous path through the gardens of the house, to a rear entrance, and through the kitchens. The scullery workers and cooks were very busy, too busy about their work to pay me the slightest mind. The woman bade me wait for a moment, peered through a door, then said, "Hurry," and we scurried across a bare corridor and up curving back stairs to the solarium where Marán and I had danced to the secret music of our hearts.

Marán was the only one in the room, and the woman bowed once more and left. I started to embrace her, but something in the way she was standing said I should not.

"Come here," she said. "Look down there."

I gazed down on that line of wagons, piled high with books, tables, wardrobes, and other furniture. Teamsters busied themselves packing the vehicles, and there was a man supervising them. It took a moment, for I'd met him but once, then I recognized Marán's husband, Count Hernad Lavedan.

"He returned four days ago, and attempted to enter. I had my servants drive him away, and ordered him to have all his possessions out of here by this day or else I would have them piled in the drive and burnt.

"The last is being loaded at this moment."

I saw that Lavedan was holding a small case in his hand, and remembered the small ship model he'd been so proud of. He handed it to one driver, who put it carefully on the floor of the wagon. The other teamsters were climbing into the wagons, and I faintly heard the cracking of whips. The wagons snaked out of the driveway and drove away down the street.

Count Lavedan walked to his horse, stopped, and looked up at the house. For a long moment he stared, and I fancied he could see me. Ironically, I felt like flinching, even though I didn't fear him. I suppose it was because I still felt it was his wife I was in love with, and I was a trespasser. Then he mounted, and rode off, not looking back.

Marán stared after him, until he turned a corner and was gone.

"Now I live alone," she said, her tone flat. I couldn't see her face, but knew it held that strange expression of a puppy awaiting punishment.

After a while, I said, carefully, "You don't have to—unless you wish it."

She turned to me.

"Damastes, are you sure of what you are saying? If you move in here, you'll be revealed as the cause of my husband's shame. He knows I'm having an affair—he told me so—but I don't think he knows with who yet.

"The Lavedans are a powerful family, and I know he'll go after you with every device he can imagine, and try to destroy you and your career.

"Am I worth that?" Her expression suggested she didn't think she was.

I could have answered reasonably, saying I'd already

reached a far greater rank than I had dreamed of and was content. I could have said, after the acclaim the rabble showered on me, that I doubted if the count, a man who had cut and run during the crisis, would, at least for the near future, be a danger. Even later, what could he do at the worst, but have me reduced to my former rank of captain and sent to one of the Frontier regiments, my constant dream? I could have answered logically, but, instead I said, "In a soldier's words, fuck him and the horse he rode in on."

A tiny smile touched Marán's lips, then vanished.

"You might make another, more dangerous enemy," she went on. "I don't know what my family will think of all this—I sent a long letter to Irrigon after I'd returned, not naming you, of course. I don't know if it was received, and am about to compose another one, since I've had no reply.

"I'm sure they'll feel the Agramónte name is disgraced by my behavior, and may well seek revenge on the evil cocksman who brought me down. Are you prepared for that? I must add the Agramóntes are vastly more powerful than the Lavedans have ever dreamed."

I made no answer, but took her hand, and led her to the side of the room, where a thick rug lay. My eyes never left hers as my fingers undressed her, very slowly. I removed my own clothes. I kissed her lips gently, then bent farther and kissed her nipples. Her breath tickled the back of my neck.

I laid her down gently on the rug, knelt over her, and she brought her knees up and apart. I kissed her clitoris, and ran my tongue into her. She shuddered, and her hands moved in my long hair as it fell across her thighs. I moved upward, and my cock glided into her, as if of its own will. We moved together, both of us with our eyes open, slowly, the wave lifting us gently, then breaking and I felt her throbbing around me.

"I guess," she said, after our breathing slowed, "that's an answer, isn't it?"

It was more than an answer, it was the beginning of a pact. We lay comfortably together.

"I'm having carpenters and painters in tomorrow," she said.

"There'll be no traces left of him when they're finished. Do you wish to have anything to say about the redecorating?"

"How can I? This is your house, not mine."

"If you live here, my Damastes, it is ours."

I kissed her. "Very well. I have but one request. We should have but a single bedroom. Make it this one, if you would, here where we danced. I love the sun on our bodies."

"I was hoping for that," she whispered. "I never understood why he never wanted to just sleep with me. To hold me. I didn't understand that and . . . and some other things." She shuddered and turned the subject slightly. "What of *his* office? What do you wish done about that?"

"I don't care. Turn it into a nursery."

Her eyes widened in surprise, then she giggled. "*Là*, sir, you *do* presume."

"Do I?" I murmured, my cock suddenly rigid. I thrust hard, deep, and she gasped and her hands pulled at my back. I lifted her knees against my chest, and laid hard on her, my hands cupping her buttocks as we crashed together, both of us shouting aloud at the final moment.

The broadsheets may have been incompetent at reporting the actual events of Numantia unless the Rule of Ten dictated it, but they were most skilled at scandal.

I'd no sooner moved Lucan, Rabbit, and my few possessions into Marán's house . . . *our* house, as I kept reminding myself, without effect, being in fact the poorest as well as the youngest of all Numantia's dominas, yet resident in a great mansion not of my building, when our romance was trumpeted across the city. Now all knew me as Damastes the Fair, Damastes the Seducer, Damastes the Despoiler of Innocent Brides and Cuckolder of the Rich.

I heard snickers in the large tent the Lancers' officers used for a mess, which of course I could never acknowledge or challenge, even if I wished to. I know not who talked—possibly some sharp-eyed soldiers from the Helms, more likely a servant or two who wished some silver to add to his wages. I didn't seek the scalawag out; everyone lusts after scandal, and if it hadn't been leaked by one, it would have been by another.

Tenedos jested with me as well: "Damastes the Fair. Well, Domina, you certainly are amassing a reputation once more. Now the city's lovelies have testimony that you have *two* long swords at your disposal."

All of the lonelies and fame-seekers who'd importuned me before redoubled their efforts to woo me or at least have the pleasure of spending an afternoon with me, and now their suggestions and desires were most explicit.

"But don't they realize I'm happy with the woman I'm with? Otherwise, why the scandal?"

"If *they* don't mind a bit on the side, as most of them seem to suggest," Tenedos said, "why should you? You're just a man, aren't you? Don't all of us spend most of our time trying to fornicate with anything that moves?"

"I, sir, am no Nician."

"It's not a bad reputation to have," he said thoughtfully, although I noticed that, as far as I knew, he remained faithful to Rasenna in those days.

But that was not the second event of interest.

The demon was no larger than my thumb, and looked more like a tiger-fanged seal with four arms than any conventional fiend. It hissed when I came near.

"What is he?" I wondered.

"A useful little fiend," Tenedos said. "At the moment, he is about to be a miner for gold."

"It looks like quite a task for him," I said skeptically.

"He'll seek but one coin," Tenedos said. "I'll use that to obtain others. That is, if there's anything where I hope it to be." He bent over the tiny creature and chanted:

"Hararch
Felag
Meelash
M'rur."

The demon squeaked something in an equally incomprehensible language and dove into the water.

Tenedos had asked if I could take an hour to witness something I might find interesting, and bade me attend him at the dock where the Tovieti hideout had been.

The wooden hatch still yawned wide, exposing a dark, oily expanse of water that had filled the passage when Thak had shaken the earth.

When I arrived, the demon had already been summoned, and allowed outside his small pentagram. Beside that was a greater figure, an eight-pointed star almost the size of a freight wagon, with various-sized circles and symbols carved into the dock's wooden timbers. An open trunk with Tenedos's paraphernalia stood beside it, and, not far away, a squad of soldiers waited by a large wagon with eight bullocks hitched to it.

I asked what the hells was going on, and Tenedos said, "I have been considering our mutual embarrassment of wealth, my friend. Even though we keep company with the nobility, and our ladies are quite rich, neither you nor I has a pot to piss in nor a window to pour it out of."

That was certainly true of myself, but I doubted Tenedos was as poor.

"I propose to rectify this matter . . . I hope. Examine my logic, if you will. The Tovieti were . . . are a secret order, are they not?"

"Obvious."

"Have you ever heard of a secret order who didn't have vast riches?"

"No . . . but I never *saw* any order's wealth, either. Of course, the only such group I was ever around were the stranglers, so I can't generalize. But isn't anybody who's secretive rumored to be rich? I remember an old hermit who lived in the hills behind one of my father's farms. Everyone knew him to be fabulously wealthy, but when he died all they found was a scrap of silk, two brass coins, and a spoon."

"Ah, but we know the Tovieti amass wealth," Tenedos said.

"We have heard how they are encouraged to loot their victims and we saw great mounds of it in the cavern in Kait, did we not? Well, no such trove has been uncovered from the Nician stranglers, and I thought I'd take a few hours to show my greedy, mercenary self."

I realized we were both babbling a little, neither of our eyes leaving the surface of the murky water where the demon had vanished.

"I propose to share any of my findings with you, Damastes, since you were the first to discover this lair."

I was utterly astonished, and from the smile on Tenedos's face I knew I'd had the reaction he'd expected.

"I . . . I thank you, sir. But you owe me nothing."

"I owe you what I choose to owe you, sir. And by the way, this is in no way repayment of that debt, but rather my decision to simplify life for the both of us."

I stammered something, more thanks, then, "Actually, Kutulu found its entrance first," I managed. "Since you're being so generous, shouldn't he be included while we're gleefully dividing up all this so-far-invisible gold? He'd be welcome to half of my probably nonexistent half."

"I asked him," Tenedos said, suddenly turning sober, "and he said he had little use for money. I fear I know what he wants, and it's something no one, not even myself, will be able to grant. Ah . . . here's my sprite now."

The tiny monster surfaced, holding, clenched in its claw, a single gold coin!

"Come up, come up, my little friend," Tenedos said, and the spirit sprang from the water onto the wooden decking. Tenedos said something in that tongue, and the demon answered.

"Very good, very good, so there's much, much more down there, eh?" the wizard said. "Now, I am in your debt, which you may require the repayment of at any time." He said more in the demon's language, and it scuttled back into the pentangle, turned, spun, my eyes ached, and the pentangle was empty.

Tenedos was turning the coin in his fingers.

"Interesting. It's not a Numantian coin, or anyway not one which I've ever seen. Suddenly my conscience is lightened, because I'd worried that perhaps we'd have to be honorable, and make repayment to anyone who's heirs of the stranglers' victims.

"I could see the circular: 'Will the owner of a certain gold coin please form a line at the Palace of the Rule of Ten?' Perhaps this gold isn't even from Nician victims, but part of a general hoard Thak amassed. I doubt if we'll ever know, nor shall I make close inquiry.

"Now, we shall see what we shall see." He put the coin in the center of the star, and paced back and forth, muttering. "Woodruff for luck . . . pomegranate—prosperity . . . almond for the gods' blessing . . . and the two real herbs, clover and basil."

He took vials from his chest, and sprinkled herbs into the four braziers set around the star. He lit them, and fragrant fumes filled the air. I noted, not for the first time, that the tiny amount of spices used in a ceremony should not spread so widely, but they always did. It was if I were in a pomegranate grove, with almond trees nearby, and basil growing wild underfoot.

"This will be an interesting spell," Tenedos said, and began chanting:

"Gather my friends
Join your brother.
You're of the sun.
Rise now
Linger not.
Your tomb is dark
Your tomb is dank.
Join your brother
As I touched him
Let me touch you.
Rise now
Rise up.
The sun waits to caress you."

Nothing happened for some moments. "If I believed in the possibility of resurrecting the dead," Tenedos commented, "I'd worry about this spell working on the wrong matter. We did leave some corpses down there when we departed so hastily, and I imagine they would have fondled any riches. I'd hate to have *them* shamble out of the slime down there. But it looks as my spirit was either mistaken or mischievous, since nothing—"

Tenedos had spoken too soon, as the area above the star shimmered, and then gold cascaded out of nowhere. There were gems, gold bars, coins, statuettes. The pile grew and grew until it was nearly the height of a man. I heard shouts of amazement from the soldiers.

Tenedos stroked his chin thoughtfully.

"It would appear, my good Damastes," he said, "while we are tied to one Wheel for the nature and length of our lives, we have just freed ourselves from another, the Wheel of worry for our daily bread." He grinned, and I saw a flash of what the boy named Laish might have looked like before he chose to don the solemn robes of a sorcerer. "We're rich!"

And so we were.

Tenedos betrayed me later in many ways, but I still must remember this day. He could have called up the gold and kept it and I would never have thought anything else should have been done.

But he willingly chose to share it, and again I'm reminded the seer was perhaps the most complex man ever to be given life by Irisu.

Nothing to match the tribunal had occurred in Nicias, at least not within memory. For the first time the commoners were given a glimpse of how their rulers thought and talked, and of the decisions they made.

Tenedos ran the proceedings as if he were the judge, not Barthou and the Rule of Ten. Aided by Kutulu's wardens, he produced witness after witness, who described how the Tovieti had slowly entered Nicias, slipping into each layer of society as subtly as their stranglers slid the yellow silk cord around their victims' necks, precisely laying their plans for the uprising.

I saw with disgust that most of the prisoners were in sad shape. It was more than evident that Kutulu's interrogators had used more than words in their interrogations. I liked it little, but force is the custom with our wardens, which is foolish since a man under torture will confess to anything to make the pain stop.

What was not the custom was that *all* of them had been tortured, rich or poor. When the Marchioness Fenelon was put on the stand, she began what was obviously a rote confession, memorized at the coaching of her tormentors. She became more and more emotional, and suddenly broke.

"Counselor Barthou! You cannot believe what they did to me," she shrieked. "I was treated as dirt by these pigs, these wardens! Look what they did to me! Just look!" She held up clawed hands, and I saw where her fingernails had been torn out. "How could they do this? How *could* they?"

Barthou made no answer, but turned his head away, and two wardens dragged her from the stand. She never reappeared, and I am ignorant of her final fate. I made no inquiries, either, and it was as if the woman had never existed. A traitoress she was, but did she deserve this end? I do not know, and am grateful I've never sat the bench or had to apply anything other than the crudest, most immediate justice, following the clean, sharp laws of the military.

The tormented ones were not the most telling. That testimony came from the bearded, fat man I'd seen in the smuggler's den, who looked like a district grocer but was head of the entire Tovieti organization in Nicias. His name turned out to be Cui Garneau, as plain as his appearance. He told the inquirers absolutely everything, freely volunteering the most damaging information. He confessed to murder after murder, not only by others, but by his own hand, and spoke of his pleasure in serving Thak as he pulled taut the yellow silk cord. His tales went on and on, and even the bloodthirsty writers for the broadsheets sickened. It hadn't mattered to him; he told with equal relish of strangling a newborn infant and a doddering, senile beldam.

It appeared he'd undergone no torture, and I inquired of Tenedos why he was so cooperative. Wasn't he aware he was surely dooming himself, or didn't he care?

"No one has laid a finger on him," Tenedos verified. "In fact, he's living in a cell more luxurious than these apartments, although it matters not at all to him.

"You'll see this again, Damastes. He served one master passionately, so that nothing else existed. When I destroyed that master, Thak, his world was shattered. He turned for something to cling to, and found me. Since I had power enough to annihilate Thak, he now wishes to serve me. The best way he can do that is to tell everything.

"The odd thing is that he may well live to a ripe old age. I myself will vote to keep him alive, so future historians or even the curious can visit him and find that this great conspiracy wasn't a mad illusion, but something very real, very deadly.

"My only problem is turning his words away from an enemy who no longer exists, Thak, to one that must be confronted. Chardin Sher. I also wish he knew details of other Tovieti branches in Numantia, but he claims ignorance, saying that no one but Thak knew that."

As a matter of fact, Tenedos was partially correct, but only partially. When the trial was finished, Cui Garneau was sentenced to death, but the sentence immediately commuted, one of only four. But Garneau didn't live out the year. Walking outside the cell he'd been assigned to, his guards' attention diverted for a moment, three convicted murderers beat him to death with iron clubs they'd concealed under their rags. There are some crimes, and criminals, that even the most evil of men cannot tolerate, I suppose.

Having heard Tenedos's strategy, I began attending the tribunal more regularly, and little by little saw how he was leading all testimony toward that arch villain, Chardin Sher.

The Rule of Ten squirmed, not wanting to have such information known, fearing they'd actually be required to *do* something. But their wishes didn't matter. Day by day the evidence was presented: Malebranche attended such and so a meeting, gave out a certain amount of gold, gave encouraging speeches, on and on. Kutulu had ransacked Malebranche's apartments. The Kallian had burned his correspondence before fleeing, but hadn't bothered to crush or remove the ashes.

Seers cast spells, and little by little the ashes formed into burned paper, then what the fire had taken from them was given back, and they were as legible as the hour they'd been tossed into the flames. Chardin Sher had been careful in his letters—he'd hardly been fool enough to say, "I wish such and so number of people to be murdered on this and that a date," or "If enough die in Nicias the Rule of Ten will be forced to abdicate or call for a strong man to take the throne," but his treacherous desires and traitorous orders could be easily translated from the vague phrases he used.

I was waiting for a protest to arrive from Kallio, or, more likely, an outraged delegation. But none came. Instead, General Turbery reported, in secret session, that the Kallians were calling up their reserves and moving their armies toward the border. Units loyal to Numantia were broken up, or disarmed and confined to barracks. Those closest to the border managed to flee to safety, but that was no more than two regiments of foot.

I could no longer spend time at the tribunal. I knew what must come next, what my duties would be, unless something truly outrageous happened and once more the Rule of Ten were able to avoid responsibility.

The Rule of Ten writhed and squirmed, but Tenedos had the hook truly sunk.

The tribunal came to an end. All of the Tovieti, save four, were sentenced to die, and went to their fate within the week. That was as grisly a sight as Numantia had ever known—more than 300 men and women were hung on long gallows built to accommodate fifty at a time, and special executioners hired to work the drops. Grisly, and awful, because the hangmen, often as not, were ignorant and drunk. Instead of the quick drop and the dry snap of a neck breaking, the Tovieti kicked and fought their way out of their bodies and back to the Wheel, a slower death than they'd given their victims. But it was much worse when the rope was too long, or they were too heavy, so when the rope snapped taut their heads were ripped away as bloodily as a farmer pulls a chicken's head off.

When the thrashing had ended, the bodies were cut down, and taken to long common graves. They were covered with oil, and sorcerers cast fire spells so the bodies were utterly consumed, not only so there'd be no martyr's relics for the few Tovieti survivors, but also to keep the ashes, ropes, and such from being used for black magic by other evil ones.

Tenedos called a special meeting of the Rule of Ten the day after the last Tovieti died. Once more it was to be held in the amphitheater.

Tenedos was the only speaker, and he spoke for almost four hours. His speech was simple, and his point constantly reiterated: A decision must be reached. Now, in this coliseum, today. Today, or once more the wrath of the people might voice itself. Kallio, and Chardin Sher, must be brought to justice.

At this the packed arena roared, and the Rule of Ten knew the people had to drink blood that day. It would be theirs—or the Kallians'.

They acceded, sending a special message by heliograph to the Kallian capital of Polycittara. Chardin Sher was to surrender himself to the nearest Numantian Army post to be immediately conveyed to Nicias in chains, to answer for his terrible crimes.

There'd be but one answer.

Kutulu never appeared on the stand during the tribunal, nor was his name mentioned. I encountered him in Tenedos's office, sorting through yet another pile of files, and wondered why he hadn't made an appearance.

"There was no need, Damastes my friend," and to tell the

truth his feeling of friendship for me was a bit upsetting. This was the man who'd coldly, carefully, assembled files that sent several thousand people to their deaths, either by drum patrol or tribunal, yet appeared completely unchanged. But I supposed it was better to have him thinking well of me than otherwise, although I knew then if he ever thought I would break my still-unspoken oath to Tenedos he'd hunt me down and see me punished as callously as he'd seen to the butchery of the Tovieti.

"So what comes next?" I asked. "I can't see you returning to being just another warden."

"I shan't," he agreed. "Seer Tenedos has already requested my permanent reassignment to him, as one of his aides."

"But the rioting is over," I said. "What need does he have of a private lawman?"

"The rioting is over," Kutulu said, and his voice lowered. "But the greater task has only begun."

In spite of the summer heat, I felt a chill.

It was the custom of the rich of Nicias to lounge abed until everything, from bath to breakfast, was prepared for them. Then all that was necessary was to step out of the huge new bed and walk about, accepting robe, bath, scrub brush, clothes, food from servants who, Marán advised me, I was supposed to find invisible.

"At all times?" I complained once when one of them had walked in while I was taking a peaceful shit. I'd bellowed and chased her out—I hadn't had to suffer my privacy being invaded like this since I was a boy at the lycee or in the field on maneuvers.

"At all times," Marán said firmly. "It's one way we high-class sorts separate ourselves from you common swine."

"Even when we're doing something like this?" I growled, then rolled her over and bit her on the buttocks. She yelped and matters were about to proceed from there when there was a knock, and her personal maid entered.

She carried a tray, and there was an envelope on it. It was the long-awaited, much-feared letter from Marán's father.

Marán huddled next to me, staring at it.

"We'll never know what it says until we open it," I told her.

Reluctantly she ripped the seal off and took out the four pages. Marán began reading, and her eyes widened. I thought it was even worse than we'd prepared ourselves for. She finished and handed it to me.

"I do not believe it," she said.

I read it, and felt as she did.

I'd expected her father to write a scathing note, damning her for her behavior and rubbing her face in her shame. Instead, the letter was quite reasoned. He was sorry her marriage had come to an end, but was not surprised. In fact, he was quite pleased. He had never found the Count Lavedan to be truly worthy of the nobility. He said the only reason he'd agreed to the match—and he apologized for not telling his youngest daughter this before—was because of an old and large debt owed by the Agramóntes to the Lavedans.

"I knew about *that*," Marán murmured, rereading the letter over my shoulder. "Hernad boasted of it after we were married. He didn't say what it was . . . but I gather it involved something embarrassing."

"That's pretty damned awful," I said.

Marán shrugged. "The nobility marries for other reasons than love as often as not. I guess that's why so many of us take lovers. And why are you surprised? Doesn't a peasant marry his daughter to a man who owns a bullock so he's no longer forced to drag the plow himself?"

The letter went on. Marán could do exactly as she wished: stay in Nicias, even though her father thought that was far too dangerous, even though the mob seemed to have been put in its place by the army, or return home to Irrigon. He would have the family's bankers contact her immediately, and ensure she had full recourse to any gold she needed to properly maintain the Agramónte image, should she decide to stay in the capital. He said he knew she could well be depressed by events, so she was not to worry about money. She could spend like a wastrel until the day she died, and never cut into the Agramónte fortune.

The last lines really surprised me, coming from a man I envisioned as the most reactionary of country lords, a man who barely would admit to his own humanity, let alone anyone else's:

> *It's hard, my daughter, for an old man such as myself*
> *to say how much he loves you, and has always loved you.*
> *You came as a surprise in the autumn of my years, and*
> *perhaps I haven't cherished you as I should.*
>
> *You are the dearest in my heart, and I want you to*
> *know now, when times are bad, that I stand completely*
> *behind you. Our concern with the Lavedans has come to*
> *an end, and we shall have no further dealings with the*
> *family. I have already sent letters to our family's represen-*
> *tatives in Nicias, with orders your marriage is to be legal-*
> *ly annulled as rapidly as possible, with the minimum of*
> *notoriety. I don't care how or why things happened as*
> *they did, nor whose fault it was, although in my heart I*
> *wish to believe it was your former husband's. If any of the*
> *Lavedans attempt to make a scandal of that matter, rest*
> *assured I shall deal with them personally. I love you and*
> *will support you in everything you wish to do, without*
> *censure, without blame.*
>
> *Your father, Datus*

I put the letter down.

"So what do we do now?" Marán said, looking as shocked as if the letter had disowned her.

"You can keep on being the rich Countess Agramónte," I said. "And I could go back to biting you on the butt," I offered.

She grinned.

"You could do that . . . or anything else that comes to mind," and she laid back on the bed most invitingly.

I barely had time to spend every other night with Marán, being busy getting the Lancers ready for the months to come.

I'd not, in fact, even been able to attend Seer Tenedos's great speech in the amphitheater.

Troop Guide Karjan came to me and said he was fed up with being a warrant. He wanted to return to just serving me.

I told him to get the hell out of my office, I was busy.

"Sir," he said, "I so'jered like you wanted in th' 'mergency. Now there's no more riotin'. Everybody else is gettin' medals. Why can't I have th' one thing I want?"

I said there was no way in the world a troop guide would be permitted to be servant to a domina. I didn't think even generals could have servants of that high a rank.

He looked thoughtful, saluted, and left.

That night he found one of the bars the Golden Helms drank in, walked in, and announced none of them were fit to drink with a real soldier. Ten men charged him, and he managed to beat up six before they knocked him to the floor. The four survivors made the mistake of turning their backs and ordering a celebratory flagon of wine. Karjan rose up, seized a bench, and put all four of them in the infirmary.

Then he proceeded to destroy the wineshop.

Five army provosts showed up, and he piled them up with the shattered Helms, and two teams of wardens, four in each team after that. He was settling into a definite rhythm when the wineshop keeper's wife came up with a smile, a flask of wine . . . and a small club hidden behind her back.

Resignedly I paid Karjan's fine, took him out of prison, and, in front of the assembled Lancers, tore away his rank slashes and reduced him to horseman.

I don't think I'd seen a happier man in months. Karjan actually smiled, revealing he had taken some damage in the battle royal—there were a couple of gaps where teeth had been.

I sighed, told him to assemble his gear and report to my house. Once more I had a servant.

That night, at the mess, Legate Bikaner told me there'd been a pool set as to how long Karjan would hold his rank slashes. It wasn't the first time he'd been promoted, nor the first time he'd calculatedly done something to make sure he was reduced to the ranks.

"Anything higher than lance," Bikaner said, "and he gets upset."

"Who won the bet?"

"One of the new legates," Bikaner said. "It certainly wasn't me. I had my money on one week after being promoted. Guess he thinks a lot of you, sir."

"There," she said, slipping me out of her mouth. "Now we can go to the next step." She was breathing almost as hard as I was.

"Why can't you just keep doing what you were doing?"

"Because we're going to do something new, and it's always you showing me. Now it's my turn."

"Very well. What do I do? Before I get soft, I mean."

"You could drill holes in the wall with that thing," she said. She straddled me, and guided me into her, gasping as I lifted my hips and plunged farther into her body.

"Don't do that," she managed. "Now, sit up, and cross your legs behind me. Put your arms around me, so I don't fall. If you start laughing I swear I'll slay you."

Marán moved her legs around me until she sat as I was.

"Now what?" I wondered. "What do we do next?"

"We don't do anything, we just sit like this . . . no, don't move, dammit . . . and then we're supposed to come together."

"What is this, more of Amiel's sex-magic?"

"No," she said. "But it is from another book of hers I read once."

"Are you sure you took good notes? I mean, this is nice, but nothing's happening. Have you ever tried this before?"

"Shut up. That's none of your business. Of course I haven't! Who would I have to do it with, you bastard?

"You're supposed to concentrate. Pretend that all you are is cock, is what the book said."

We sat together in silence. I honestly tried to obey her orders, closing everything out of my mind, and feeling every inch of myself inside her. I honestly thought it was silly, but concentrated, and then I could feel my cock's head, just touching her womb opening, her inner lips curling around me, feel each inch of the shaft where it touched wet folds, felt my balls against her outer lips.

Marán gasped. "Don't move, I said!"

"I'm not! I didn't! Now you're moving."

"No I'm not," she said, "not down there." Now she was panting, and her legs pulled tight against my back. "Oh, gods," she moaned. I vow I was perfectly still, but I could feel blood roaring, and the world narrowed until all I knew was Marán's breasts mashed against my chest, my tongue in her mouth and her hot warmth pulling me deep into her and even that vanished in this strange, sudden gift of the gods.

It took me a long while to come back, and I found myself lying beside her. We were both drenched in sweat and I felt as helpless as a newborn kitten.

"You can borrow that book again if you want. That was kind of . . . interesting," I managed.

"Mmm," she mmmed, and we lay quietly, she pulling gently at the still-sparse hairs on my chest.

"Will there be war?" she said suddenly.

"That's a hell of a question at a time like this."

"Will there?"

I sighed.

"Yes. I'm afraid so."

"Afraid? Don't lie to me, Damastes. I know you're a soldier, and I know you'll go off to fight. That's what your life is, what it always will be, I guess."

"Yes."

"When you do," she said, "I hope I am carrying your baby."

I felt very proud, but very unsure as well. Before Marán I'd never considered children, feeling that I'd most likely marry when I retired from the service, if I lived that long, and would father the appropriate number of descendants as my father and grandfather had.

"I would love to have your son," she said.

"What's the matter with daughters?"

"Nothing. Later. First a boy."

"And you said *I* was forward," I complained. An idea came. I started to discard it as if not foolish, certainly sudden and premature. But my mouth was obeying its own laws, and I said, "But I can't see any of my children being bastards."

"Don't worry about *that*," Marán said. "No acknowledged child of an Agramónte is a bastard."

"That wasn't what I meant."

"You mean . . ."

"I mean. Countess Marán Agramónte, would you consent to wed a poor domina of cavalry who would do nothing more than adore you for as long as Irisu allows him foot on this earth? I love you, you know."

There was a long silence, and I realized Marán was crying. I felt monstrous, not knowing what I'd done wrong.

"I'm sorry, my love. I didn't mean to offend."

"You didn't, oh, Damastes, you didn't. You never can. But . . . did you know no one ever proposed to me? It just sort of became a given sort of thing I'd marry.

"Isn't it funny? I can't remember anybody, except my mother and maybe a nurse or two, saying they loved me, not ever. Hernad never did. Then you say it to me, and then my father says it. . . ." She began crying again.

I held her until the storm passed.

"You know," I said, "if it bothers you, I can withdraw the question. I mean, it's probably mad to even think about something like that. You've got all of the stuff to go through getting your marriage annulled, and I've heard that nobody is supposed to marry on the rebound, not for a while, at least, and—"

"Shut up, Damastes. The answer is yes. Of course I'll marry you."

As she spoke, I was one with the gods, almost crying, myself, in joy. She went on:

"You know it can't happen at once. No matter how skilled my father's factors are, it'll take time for the annulment," she said. "Since I'm an Agramónte, the matter will have to go before the Rule of Ten. I'm sorry."

"Don't," I said. "It'll give me a reason to fight hard, so I can come back to you."

"Not too hard," she said. "Because you *must* come back."

"Oh, I shall, I shall." I may have been young and full of foolish bravado, but I *knew* I'd come through the war unscathed, and I don't know how I knew it.

"So we are engaged," she said. "We should do something to celebrate."

"I know just the thing," I said.

"I know you do," she said throatily, lifting her legs around my waist as I grew within her. "I know you do."

If I could have reached out and stopped time just then, I would have, lying as we were, me still inside her, feeling the moisture of love on our thighs. I wish now it had been possible; pain, sorrow and betrayal would never have happened.

But I couldn't, and they did.

Three days later, the response came from Chardin Sher. The special envoy returned, on a stretcher. His tongue had been torn out.

Now it was civil war, and the declaration came within hours.

General Rechin Turbery, having experience fighting the Kallians, chose to lead the campaign personally. The elite units brought to Nicias would be sent against the Kallians, as well as all other regiments who were able to be moved from their area of responsibility.

This war would not be fought by bits and pieces, but as a mighty sledgehammer. It wasn't quite civil war, but close enough so it had to be settled quickly and harshly.

Everyone knew that our supposedly friendly neighbor, King Bairan of Maisir, would be very concerned with the course of events, and any weakness on the part of the Rule of Ten might well spark interest about our vulnerability.

But the best came last. Seer Laish Tenedos was named to a new post: sorcerer of the army. He would have as many staffers as he wished, and was responsible only to General Turbery.

Now, finally, he would have the chance to develop his strategies and tactics.

Now we might see a new kind of war.

It was a gray morning, not yet dawn, with cold mist blowing off the river. Horseman Karjan had both Lucan and Rabbit packed and ready. He politely sat his horse, looking away from the house as Marán and I came out.

I kissed her, and never wanted the kiss to end.

I wondered if this was all history, a man kissing a woman good-bye and going away to fight, and wondered why we so loved to kill each other.

I put the thought aside and kissed her once again.

Again, I saw that look of a hurt animal, and turned away.

I walked to Lucan and stepped up into the saddle.

Marán watched me, her face utter misery, her hands clasped in front of her.

I clucked to Lucan, and he moved off, Karjan behind us. I turned as we went out the gate, onto the street, and watched her never-moving form until it disappeared in the river mists.

And the war reached out and took me.

TWENTY-THREE

DISASTER AT THE IMRU RIVER

Geneneral Turbery had requisitioned every available craft to carry us upriver to Cicognara, at the head of the Latane River's delta. There, the army would assemble and march east toward the Kallian border.

I didn't see Tenedos—he was on the flagship with the general, but he told me later of his fumings at how terribly slow we moved.

I had little time to notice, because it took eight huge cattle lighters to transport the Lancers, and I was constantly shuttling back and forth between the ships with my new adjutant, Legate Bikaner, in a small sailing boat helmed by a villain whose politest speech reduced the most profane lance-major to respectful silence.

But once we disembarked at Cicognara, even I saw how glacial was our progress. For three weeks there was nothing but interminable staff meetings as to how we should move, in what order, which regiment belonged to which division, and so forth, further confused as more and more units trickled into the city.

Some of the snarl was understandable, since the Numantian Army hadn't moved in such a mass for generations.

Eventually there were over 100,000 soldiers camped in and

around the city, everyone in awe at the size of the host. This sounds laughable, since a few years later I'd be comfortable personally commanding many times that number, just one part of Emperor Tenedos's forces, but it's necessary to remember that the army had fought in no wars, only border skirmishes and internal disputes, for years.

The eventual order of battle was as follows: Each regiment, now augmented to about 1,000 men, was grouped with four others to form a division. Five divisions then formed a corps. These 25,000 men formed a wing, of which there were three: Left, Center, and Right.

The thirteen elite regiments that'd been called to Nicias to suppress the riots were built back up to strength, given additional support elements, and used as either forward or screening elements of these three wings.

On a blistering day, the second of the Time of Heat, we set off for Kallio, a long, multicolored snake curling along the road that leads to the border. I'd been angered before by how slowly the Khurram Light Infantry moved, but that pace was that of the cheetah compared to this cumbersome monster. I had learned that a good soldier could carry all his possessions on his back or on a packhorse. If that was true, I marched east with over 100,000 idiots. I include myself, because Marán had had new uniforms designed and made, and I hadn't had the heart to tell her no, nor to leave them in Nicias. In fact, to be truthful, I rather admired them, with their silk facings, their exact fit, their gold and silver embroidery.

I tried to rationalize this by thinking I'd provide better leadership since I was so easy to mark, and that soldiers always wished their leaders to stand out. But in fact, a previously unknown streak of vanity showed itself. I'm not that ashamed—has there ever been a cavalryman without more than a trace of vainglory?

I couldn't maintain the silly rationale for long, not after Karjan looked at my wardrobe, and asked, expressionlessly, where we'd cage the peacocks we'd need for replacement feathers.

So my personal gear filled two handsome leather wardrobes,

and I was by far the most conservative of the higher-ranking officers.

Soldiers had cases, warrants had trunks, legates had cabinets, dominas had private wagons, and generals had trains.

On the march I had something to keep me occupied other than duty, since the Lancers ran of their own accord, like a perfect clockwork mechanism, needing little attention. Marán had written at least once, sometimes twice, a day, and I savored each letter as it arrived, reading and rereading the small delights of peace. There were pleasant surprises: Her husband would not contest the annulment; she'd encountered surprisingly little rejection for being a scarlet woman; and, best of all, her monthly time had not occurred yet.

She was also surprisingly explicit about what she wished me to do to her, when and where, in bed, standing, or in the bath, when I came home. I rode around with a seemingly perpetual bulge in my breeches, and wondered if I'd have to find a convenient bush to shame myself behind before the campaign ended.

Two days into the march, when we could still see the not-terribly-tall buildings of Cicognara in the distance, I saw a young, and obviously rich, legate shaving. He had his own tent, a clever folding table, desk, chairs, a personal cook with his own stove making breakfast to one side, two servants attending him, and a canvas bathtub beside. As he finished, a rather attractive young woman came out of the tent, pulling on a silk robe.

He was not the only one to bring a mistress or wife—one general brought *three*. Since he was slightly older than Irisu, no one knew what he did with one, let alone all of them.

Camp followers, ration wagons, sutlers' carts, bullocks for the slaughter—we looked like a migrating nation, not a fighting force.

I found a new pastime as our horses plodded onward across the countryside. Captain Petre and I returned to one of our old amusements—designing the army we'd rather lead, rather fight with. I even took to keeping a notebook with schemes we thought particularly valuable. This is an odd thing for a domina and a captain to waste their time doing, and is rather the pastime of freshly commissioned legates. But it must be remembered I was only twenty-three and Petre a year older, so our foolishness can be understood. But considering what happened a few weeks later, it turned out not to be foolish at all.

I encountered Tenedos when we'd made camp, a week after we'd marched out of Cicognara and inquired as to how it was going. He looked around to make sure we couldn't be overheard.

"It is not going at all, as you should know," he said. "No one, not even General Turbery, seems to be aware that the Time of Heat will not last forever, and we must be across the border into Kallio and dealing with Chardin Sher before the monsoons begin. Instead, we stroll along at our leisurely pace, stopping to pick a flower here, investigate a byway there—" he broke off. "Damastes, is there anyone in your army who knows how to fight?"

"*My* army, sir?"

"My apologies. I mean no slur. I'm fresh from a conference with the general, and I seem to be speaking a different language than he does." He sighed heavily. "I just hope things will come right when they must.

"Oh. By the way, you may congratulate me. Turbery's given me general's rank."

I blinked. "Well, my heartiest, sir. But . . . you turned that down once before."

"That was before," Tenedos said. "And that was when I wished to keep some remove between me and the army. Now I must not. There is a time to watch, and then a time to swim with the current."

I wasn't sure what he meant, but congratulated him, saluted, and went back to the Lancers.

I told Mercia, Captain Petre, of my conversation. He made sounds I knew I was supposed to take for laughter.

"The seer general is quite right, I think. But he's hardly blameless."

"Why so?"

"Oh, you haven't heard? He's brought his lady along."

And so it was; not a day later I saw him riding with Rasenna. I waved, and they waved back. If it wouldn't have been a scandal, I almost wished I'd brought Marán. But an army on the campaign isn't the best place for gentlefolk unused to harshness, although the manner in which we traveled was, indeed, more like rich, happy wanderers on a vacation than hard soldiering.

Then the word came: Chardin Sher had crossed the border into Dara! Now it was open war.

Scouts and magic discovered that his army was waiting for us, in prepared positions along the Irmu River, not far from the small Daran city of Entoto.

Four days later, we came on them.

We were near the headwaters of the Imru River, so it wasn't particularly wide, no more than thirty yards. It runs south-southeast to eventually join the Latane. We were moving across rolling, fairly open countryside, scattered with groves of trees—open country ideal for warfare.

Chardin Sher's army held an excellent position, a choke point that we must pass through to reach the border between Kallio and Dara. The road we'd been following ran down to a ford, and across it was Chardin Sher's main force. Across the river to the west reared a heavily forested mountain, the Assab Heights. Downriver, past the ford, were Chardin Sher's reserves, and beyond them to the east the river forked and passed through a marsh.

We formed battle positions, and waited to see what would happen next. We estimated Chardin Sher's forces at about 50,000, surprisingly close to the exact number revealed after the war. Outnumbered, they made no move to attack, but waited for us.

I was surprised to see they'd prepared no fighting positions other than shallow trenches near the river, since they planned to be on the defensive.

I began to feel the fire build. This might well be a battle decided by the cavalry, and I would be in the forefront.

*   *   *

Mail reached us.

> *My darling, darling, darling*
> *I AM pregnant. A seer confirmed this only today. I*
> *asked her what else she could see about the child, as to*
> *its sex or its future, but she said nothing more came to*
> *her.*
> *But this is for certain, my love.*
> *This is beyond my happiest dream. I said I wished a*
> *boy, but if it's a girl, that is also perfect. All that matters*
> *is that he or she is yours, is ours.*
> *I wonder which time it was that our love so pleased*
> *Irisu he let our child-to-be leave the Wheel? Was it when*
> *we fucked on the balcony, and you managed to break the*
> *glass table? Or was it . . .*

But the rest doesn't matter.

So I was to be a father.

Now I hoped the campaign would be a very short one, or else I might have an interesting wedding ceremony, with my firstborn as ring-bearer.

Then it began to go wrong.

General Rechin Turbery called all regimental commanders with their adjutants for a briefing one morning. We would attack on the following day.

Such a major move required far more notice than the eighteen hours he'd given us.

He'd made no consultation with his corps or division commanders.

He'd sent no patrols to the far shore to make reconnaissance.

The size of the briefing guaranteed no one could ask anything but the most obvious question, let alone raise objections.

The soldiers would be ready to move at midnight, and the attack would begin at false dawn.

Too long a time would pass between assembly and battle.

The army was completely unpracticed at moving, let alone fighting, at night.

Each wing would attack frontally, crossing the river at once.

No soundings had been taken to see if the water was shallow across our entire front.

The Right Wing was to swing right after it reached the far bank and immobilize Chardin Sher's reserves to the east, near the swamp, while the Center and Left Wings were to close Chardin Sher's main force in a pincers.

The Numantian Army might have survived the other errors, but this last was the worst:

What was on the other side of the Assab Heights?

I was about to ask that question when the general laid the final stroke of the whip.

The cavalry was to be withdrawn to the rear of the Center Wing and take no part in the initial fighting. Once the Left and Center Wings had broken Chardin Sher's main force—this was an automatic assumption by Turbery—we would then charge across the Imru and settle the Kallians' hash for good, the so-called final moment of battle.

I reddened in anger and disbelief. It might have been a good idea to have a strong striking force ready to seize any opportunity, but *all* the cavalry? I barely knew the names of the other regimental commanders. That we were supposed to fight together as a team without plans, order of battle, rehearsal, without field exercises, was utterly absurd. If General Turbery had planned on using us in this manner, he should have had us practicing in Cicognara and on the march east, rather than letting us skylark about with no purpose. Turbery's plan would also leave the army without screening riders, flank security, or frontal scouts—in short, completely blind in its attack.

I glanced at Bikaner, and he was as aghast as I.

General Turbery went on to describe what was to be done with Chardin Sher when we captured him, although he'd not said anyone knew he was actually with the Kallians across the river, then closed with some inspiring remark about how Numantia would now prove its iron, its strength as a great nation. I was too angry to hear him.

I headed straight for Seer Tenedos's tent, which was not far from Turbery's headquarters. It was large, divided into two sections, one for an office, the other for the seer's bedchamber. I saw no sign of Rasenna. I started telling Tenedos what idiocy I'd just listened to and he held up his hand, stopping me.

"Did you notice I wasn't present?"

Of course I had, but idiotically had assigned no importance to it.

"The general informed me of his intentions last night. I objected strongly, as strongly as I could, but he insisted he knew better, so I refused to honor the farce with my presence.

"I'll tell you two things that you must not repeat to anyone, not even your adjutant, that will make you even angrier, and this is why I refused to take part in the briefing, because I know we face potential disaster.

"First is that there is great magic swirling around this place, magic such as I've never heard of before, never encountered."

"No one has told me anything about the Kallians having a great sorcerer," I said. "But considering the disregard the army still holds magic in, that means nothing. Can you detect who's casting these spells?"

"That's the unusual aspect, for I detect no single . . . signature might be the word, the sign that one man or woman is working these incantations. I almost fear Chardin Sher has a magician who's perfected a Great Spell, somehow getting others to work together with him.

"But I can't believe that. I'm prideful enough to think if I couldn't produce anything cohesive from those master magicians, arrogant fools that they are, of the Chare Brethren, no one else, using other wizards, can either."

"What's the other problem?" I asked.

"I brought half a dozen magicians with me, and we've been trying to cast searching spells across the river, since General

Turbery has refused to send scouts out, fearing to lose the element of surprise.

"All of our efforts have been turned back, as if we were but tin swords lunging at steel plates.

"This worries me more than the first."

"Is there anything that can be done?"

"Very little. Probably nothing. Try prayer—and not to Saionji. We do not need to encourage the Bringer of Chaos to even notice us on the morrow. Return to your regiment, and be very wary of the way you fight on the morrow. If you cross the river, be prepared for surprise. I'm going to try yet again to penetrate this veil of darkness, to see what Chardin Sher is up to."

"One question, sir. Have you, or any of your seers, been able to ascertain whether Chardin Sher is over there in person?"

"We tried, and were rebuffed. I tried another method, and sent a searching spell across the country, aimed toward Polycittara. I detected no sign of the prime minister, but that isn't certain. My spell could have failed, or he could be in yet another location, or have wards up to prevent my locating him.

"But I can tell you I feel his presence. I would wager, with nothing more than that feeling, that he is, indeed, over there, waiting to preside over our destruction."

"Sir," I said. "I mean no disrespect to our commander, but I thought General Turbery had experience; I thought he'd fought the Kallians."

"He has, Damastes. But with how many men? A regiment, perhaps two, against small probes by a company or two of their forces, both sides breaking off when real blood began to be shed, since neither side wished to acknowledge real enmity. I'm afraid General Turbery's reach has far exceeded his grasp.

"There might also be another problem: It's not uncommon for a man to achieve greatness so long as he isn't the final rung on the ladder. As long as General Turbery could fall back on a superior, such as General Protogenes, all was well and good.

"But now he stands alone, and will be judged."

No longer angry, but worried, I hurried back to the Lancers.

The various units were supposed to wait until dark to begin movement, and the Lancers obeyed orders. Others didn't—I saw dust clouds swirl as various foot units began, literally, stealing the march, dust clouds visible across the river to warn Chardin Sher something was in the offing.

Finally, the Lancers began moving, and if the morrow were not looming close, it might have been funny. Columns got lost, troops ended up riding with other regiments, men fell off their horses, men rode into tents, men rode into wagons, men rode into latrines . . . the list of mishaps was as various as the numbers of swearing cavalrymen wallowing around in the night.

But eventually we found a location approximately where we were to be, and waited for battle.

At false dawn, the havoc began.

The Battle of Imru River is correctly taught as one of the finest, least subtle, most complete catastrophes of war known. It should have been a great victory—we outnumbered the foe nearly two to one, it was a calm day, the heavy clouds overhead were unthreatening, and both sides could see each other perfectly.

Most combats, once joined, are a confusion of blood and screaming, where no one knows quite what's going on, and frequently the victor isn't sure he's won until the next day. Imru River was different. Since my role, until the end, was to sit fuming helplessly on a ridge, waiting for the grand opportunity that never happened, I can tell precisely and briefly of the disaster.

Just at false dawn, trumpets sounded, and the three Numantian wings marched toward the river. General Hern led the Left Wing, General Odoacer the Right, with General Turbery taking personal command of the Center.

They marched straight into the river, in closed battle order, and the floundering began. The water at the ford was a bit deeper than anyone had thought, and men struggled and yelled, the river's swift current catching their shields and sending them stumbling. General Turbery and the other high-rankers, on horseback, had noticed nothing.

In the Center, confusion began.

General Odoacer, on the right, was perhaps more eager than the others for his share of glory, and so he'd moved forward a bit faster than the other two elements.

Our right flank was therefore exposed.

On the left it was a debacle. The shallows did not extend that far west, and the river deepened to more than eight feet a few paces from the bank. Men toppled into water over their heads, flailed about, trying to swim in armor, and began drowning. The implacable press of the formation forced other men after them, and the water became a seething mass of helpless soldiery.

On the other bank, the Kallian forces rose out of their shallow pits, and a single man rode out in front of them—Chardin Sher, magnificent in silver armor astride a chestnut stallion, his standard-bearers behind him.

General Turbery was evidently not aware of the problems of the Left Wing, and, as he saw his foe in plain sight, he called for a charge, and the Center crashed forward, out of the water onto dry land.

Without even waiting until they were within arrow range, the Kallians began falling back. Perhaps Turbery thought they had panicked, seeing the determined Numantians come at them. But he should have known better, for they retired in an orderly manner, marching backward, line on line. The Numantian Center shouted exulting war cries and broke into a run, sucked even farther into the trap, for of course that's precisely what it was.

Our Right Wing was having a bit of trouble, the river being wider where they were crossing.

At this moment, Chardin Sher struck.

His sorcerers brought up a wall of water, like a sudden neap tide, and sent it rushing down on us from the west. It was no more than two feet high, but that was more than enough. It caught the men of the Left Wing and swept them along, but there were only a few ranks to be sent tumbling downriver.

It took the Right Wing in midcrossing, smashing into it as hard, and lethally, as if it'd been a blacksmith's sledge.

Kallian horns screamed, and Chardin Sher's center turned back and attacked, archers to either side volleying arrows into the massed Numantian Center.

General Turbery was killed in that first volley, and I saw, from my vantage point, the Numantian colors go down. The Center took the shock of the first wave, then stumbled back a bit.

Chardin Sher's forces must have rehearsed this battle over and over. Isa knows they'd had time enough, having held the ground for long days before our dilatory arrival. The Kallian Left Wing split its forces, sending half in against the Numantian Center, the other half across the river, on a hidden ford, to our side of the bank and striking against our Right Wing.

Then came the deathstroke. From their positions, which had been masked by sorcery and the Assab Heights, ran the rest of Chardin Sher's army. They were mostly cavalry or light infantry, and drove directly into the open flank of the Center Wing.

The battleground became swirling chaos, man fighting man, man killing man, no more tactics, no more grand design, just bloody slaughter.

I saw Numantian flags go down, and small knots of soldiers I knew to be ours make a last stand, then disappear, overrun by waves of Kallians.

I heard a cavalry general shouting, to whom I don't know, perhaps the god of war, for someone to unleash us.

But there was no one to give the command.

General Turbery was dead. General Odoacer was dead. General Hern was pinned under his fallen horse and had a broken leg. Three other generals died that day, ten dominas, and who knows how many lesser-ranking officers.

The Numantian Center Wing was obliterated, the Left mired in confusion, and the Right cut to ribbons. Chardin

Sher's forces reformed, and rolled toward the river, an indestructible force bent on our total destruction.

I sat on Lucan seeing this nightmare, the worst defeat imaginable, and something broke within me.

There were other dominas with the cavalry far senior to me, and two generals. But no one did anything.

I knew I must.

"Trumpeter," I shouted, "sound the advance!"

The horns blared, at first raggedly, surprised, but then strong, and the Seventeenth Ureyan Lancers, as they'd been taught, went down the hill at the walk to battle.

Shouts of surprise, possibly countermanding my orders, came from behind, around us, but I cared not. If other regiments joined us, well and good. But I could not see my country destroyed on this unknown ground by some dead fool's mistakes.

Marán, my child, my own life, all were swept away.

I heard other trumpets, glanced behind me, and saw other regiments, shamed by our action, start forward. Then they were all moving, perhaps 10,000 men, against five times their number.

Thunder rolled then, and a man walked down the slope in front of us, toward the water, toward the ford.

It was the Seer Tenedos, in half-armor, but without his helmet.

His voice was the thunder, and the thunder was his voice. I could not make out his words as the spell rolled and crashed from the hills around us.

Raindrops pattered, and I saw the clouds had suddenly changed, now dark, threatening as his ringing words took effect.

Archers came from nowhere, and war-shafts arched over the Imru, landing among the oncoming Kallians, and then the storm broke, a roaring cataclysm, so no one could see more than a few yards ahead of him.

The rain lessened for a second, and I saw the Kallians, still hesitating at the ford's far beginnings, seeing the Imru swirl up in flood, afraid to chance being stranded, and then the storm pulled a curtain across my view.

Men cannot, will not, fight when they cannot see, when their leaders cannot see beyond their horses' ears, and so the battle was over.

I would be permitted to live the day, and not to have to make the sacrifice I'd offered Isa and Numantia.

Sanity came back, and I remembered Marán, and breathed a prayer of thanks to my wise monkey god Vachan and my own godling Tanis. But the field was littered with more than 45,000 Numantian casualties.

The rain-roar slowed, and I could see across the Imru again, see the Kallians pulling back.

Tenedos still stood where I'd seen him last, but now his arms were at his sides. He tottered then, and fell, and I kicked Lucan into a trot through the mire, desperately afraid the seer had been hit.

I dismounted and ran to him, where he lay facedown. I turned him over, and his eyes came open.

"Damastes," he said. "Did the spell break them?"

"Yessir. They're pulling back."

"Good. Good. Took . . . took everything I had. You'll have to . . . help me up."

I lifted him, half-carried him to Lucan, and helped him into the saddle.

I led Lucan away, toward Tenedos's tent, the sorcerer swaying in the saddle, barely able to stay mounted. Karjan rode out of the murk, and caught Tenedos, not letting him fall.

I suddenly realized it was late afternoon, and growing dark. Somehow the day had gone without the hours being noticed.

Now there was nothing but the driving storm, the cries and moans of dying men and horses, and the bitter taste of utter defeat.

TWENTY-FOUR

THE BIRTH OF
AN ARMY

When we reached Tenedos's tent, a sobbing Rasenna helped me get the wizard inside. He told her to get a certain vial from a chest and shuddered the contents down.

I could see the mixture hit, see the gray pallor pass from his cheeks, see him straighten, see strength pour into his system.

"I shall pay for taking this," he said. "Nothing is for free, and these herbs call up my innermost energy, leaving no reserves. But there is no choice.

"Damastes, collect as much of your regiment as you can. I want them as messengers. Go to all the dominas and higher you can find, or whoever's left in charge of a formation, regardless of rank, and order them to report to the command tent as soon as possible."

"That'll take a while, sir, with the rain."

"The spell should break within the hour," he said, "and there'll be a quarter-moon to guide your riders."

"Can I tell them what the purpose of the meeting is?"

"Yes. Tell them General-Seer Laish Tenedos is taking command of the army, and will issue appropriate orders at this time. Failure to attend will be dealt with as disobedience of a direct order."

I saluted and turned away.

"One more thing. Send a small party to the river, and try to find out what the Kallians are doing, if you would."

I took approximate bearings, by guess and by Isa, where the Lancers might be, and started in that direction. So Tenedos was taking over the army, without orders or authority. But what of it? Someone must. As far as I knew then, there were no other generals on the field—General Hern still hadn't been found. Also, I'd learned that in an emergency the man who appears calmest, who can issue sensible orders, is most likely the man to obey.

I found elements of Cheetah Troop in about half an hour, and they helped me grope my way to the rest of the regiment. As I finished passing along Tenedos's orders, as Tenedos predicted, the storm cleared.

I found Legate Yonge, and, with five of the men of Sambar Troop, we rode cautiously down to the Imru, past the crawling bodies of the wounded, past the corpses, trying to ignore the pleas for help or even a merciful blade between the ribs.

I was waiting to be ambushed. Chardin Sher should have pushed pickets across the flood to keep in touch with our forces. But we encountered no one except Numantians. The moon was bright enough to see the far bank, and the raging waters of the storm-flushed Imru. All was quiet, and there was no sign of life nor of fires from an enemy camp.

Chardin Sher must have retreated, which in fact he had. Perhaps he'd not expected such a grand victory and frightened himself; perhaps he had made no plans beyond that day; or possibly he had no intent of taking the kingdom he so desired by the sword, but only by its threat, and now hoped the Rule of Ten would announce his majesty by proclamation. I do not know, but I do know better than to theorize about those who wish to sit a throne.

In fact, we found days later, when the river subsided and we were able to slip spies and small patrols across, that the Kallians had retreated all the way back to their own borders, where they began building strong defensive positions.

But that came later. The first task was to recover from the debacle of the battle.

Eventually the command tent was surrounded by exhausted, sometimes bleeding commanders. I was shocked—some formations were evidently led by legates and sergeants, since I saw many of those ranks shivering in the night.

Seer Tenedos mounted to the back of a wagon. His voice carried to us all, his magic drawing even more of his vital energy:

"I am General Tenedos," he said. "I have taken command of this army. We were beaten today, beaten hard. But there is always tomorrow.

"We shall not be attacked again, not this night, nor in the next few days. The Kallians have withdrawn in triumph.

"They shall rue their arrogance, rue that they did not finish us to the man.

"I promise you bitter revenge shall be taken for this defeat. Numantia has just begun its battle.

"Here are my orders. Return to your formations. Wait until sunrise. Then look about you. There are wounded men, there are lost men, to help.

"There are a few who wish to shirk further duty. Tell them to return to their formations or face punishment.

"All those fancy wagons we brought, carrying our luxuries? They'll carry our wounded.

"Strip them of the fripperies, and share those items among us all, a private having the same rights as the general who owned them before.

"There is to be no drunkenness, I warn you. If you cannot keep your men's hands from the wine bottle, smash it in front of them. I order that any man found drunk be given twenty lashes across a wagon wheel. Any officer will be given twice that and reduced to the ranks. Now is the time to pull together, not fall apart.

"When we are assembled, as an army, not a rabble, we shall fall back on Entoto.

"There, we shall build a new, greater army, an army that will destroy Chardin Sher's pretensions.

"And we shall build it this year, this season. I promise you, we shall be in the field once more, before the Time of Storms."

That sent a shock through us all, that Time being only a third of a year away, and I knew it would take a year, possibly two, to rebuild our forces.

"Now, go back to your units. You are given license to punish doom-criers, deserters, and the lazy as harshly as your units' policies permit. No one shall be judged for having obeyed my command to the fullest extent of the law.

"That is all. All of us shall leave this field . . . or none."

There was no cheering; none of us had the energy, nor could we feel any cause to rejoice. But the steel in Tenedos's words had struck common metal in most of us.

As bad as I dreamed the field would look, at dawn it was worse. But we'd gotten some momentum, and we were cleaning up and reforming. The hardest task for me was putting together a detail to kill the wounded, still-screaming horses, and I dreamed of a day when war could be fought with magically impervious mounts. Man might have a right to bring blood to his arguments, but he has none to slaughter the innocent beasts of the field in his disputes.

By morning of the next day we marched away from the blood-soaked Imru River. Behind us, a great funeral pyre sent flames and greasy smoke boiling to the gods, while black kites circled overhead, screaming disappointment at being denied their carrion reward.

The army swamped Entoto, taking over every public building for hospitals and quarters and sheltering healthy men among the population. Tenedos sent couriers to the river, to Cicognara, with a full report, and orders that the army needed all things immediately, from bandages to food to tents to replacements. He cobbled together a unit of signalers, and ordered them to build a heliograph line from Entoto to Cicognara, where it would tie into the main system that led downriver to Nicias.

The first to arrive from Nicias was what we needed least:

The *Tauler* churned up to Cicognara and unloaded Barthou, speaker for the Rule of Ten; Scopas, the only surviving member of the Rule of Ten who'd been occasionally on Tenedos's side; and a cadaverous-looking individual named Timgad, one of the new electees to the Rule of Ten. There was another man with them, a balding, pompous-looking sort wearing the sash of a general. He was named Indore, and was the Rule of Ten's hand-picked successor to General Turbery. I knew him not, but asked around, and learned he had an enviable reputation for always having been at the correct spot, politically, at the correct time. His only field experience was on various staffs, where he'd made sure never to contradict his superior, fail to praise him for his genius, and try to take over his position as rapidly as possible. "Indore is his name and Indoors is where he made it," was the bitter joke that went around.

The army, still wounded, still in shock, shuddered at what they knew was coming: The Rule of Ten would have some sort of plan, almost surely guaranteed to get us killed, and Indore would be the general to carry it out.

I was not present when the Rule of Ten representatives met with Tenedos, of course, nor was there any record made. But twice over the years Tenedos reminisced about the old days, and told me what had happened. Both times his accounts were precise, so I accept them as the truth, even if the tale is self-serving.

Barthou began by congratulating the seer on how brilliantly he'd served, helping the army retreat, although of course he suspected if General Turbery hadn't gone down "on the field of valor," he would have mounted a counterattack. Tenedos told me he refrained from asking "With what?" and listened, keeping a carefully polite, but blank, countenance.

Barthou had turned into a saber-rattler. Chardin Sher must be destroyed immediately. He didn't see why the army couldn't be reconstituted from surviving men, combining units to produce one single full-strength force. In fact, he was surprised that Seer Tenedos's report had been so gloomy—why, riding from Cicognara to this headquarters, he'd been amazed at how hale and hearty the soldiers were.

"I would think we could march out against that traitor tomorrow."

One half hour, and Barthou knew the army better than it knew itself.

Barthou went on to say the Rule of Ten had unanimously voted a title to Tenedos, and wished that he would stay on to assist General Indore until he had "the reins fully in his hands." Then, Barthou went on, no doubt there'd be other ways Tenedos could serve Numantia.

Barthou was about to slide into a smooth commending speech that was actually an eulogy for the wizard when Tenedos stood.

"Stop," he said calmly. Barthou gaped, a man not used to being told to shut up.

"You say the Rule of Ten voted unanimously to appoint the good general. Is that true, Scopas?"

The fat man shifted uncomfortably. "Well, yes," he said. "Not on the first ballot, but eventually."

"I see." He turned his attention to Barthou.

"Speaker, the answer is no." Now the politician was completely stunned.

"N—no? No to what?"

"No to you, no to your lapdog general, no to the Rule of Ten. There are no witnesses to this conversation, but you may walk out of this tent, and ask any of the men your stupidity sent against Chardin Sher. Ask them if they will follow me . . . or if they wish to follow you, or whoever you name to caper at your command."

"This is treason, sir!"

"Perhaps it is," Tenedos said, his voice rising. "If so, it is more than overdue. Let me tell you what shall happen. All of you, including this sorry excuse for a leader, are going to leave this tent, smiling politely, and we are going to walk to a convocation of officers I called when I heard you were on the outskirts of the city.

"You are going to name me as general of the army, and you are going to say the Rule of Ten has full confidence in my abilities to destroy Chardin Sher, end this civil war, and bring peace to Numantia."

"And if I don't?" Barthou said, his chin bulging red in anger.

"If you don't, I doubt if the army will permit you to leave Entoto alive," Tenedos said. "But I am willing to take my chances that I'm right. Are *you?* If you are, get on that platform and repeat what you told me.

"Are you so stupid you believe those riots we suffered through recently were completely brought about by the stranglers or by Chardin Sher?

"You did as much to create it with your stumbling excuse for ruling, you and the rest of the Rule of Ten.

"You created the morass, you ordered the army to march into it, and now you are trying to step on its fingers as it tries to claw its way out.

"No, sir. The army will not obey your command.

"I give you one turning of the glass to consider your choices. One choice could well mean an open revolt by the masses, and if there is one, the army will turn away from Chardin Sher, content to deal with him another time, to confront their real enemy who repeatedly stabs the only hope Numantia has in the back.

"That is your first choice.

"Your second is to do as I ordered. Then you can return to Nicias holding the power you arrived with, and be certain the Kallian shall be brought down and crushed in the dust. But you cannot make this choice and then renounce it once you reach safety. In Nicias, you will, you must, satisfy each and every demand I shall have for the army's rebuilding. I want that very clear in your minds.

"Consider your choices well, gentlemen. Your very lives may depend on it."

He set a small half-hour glass on the desk in front of him and stalked out.

Tenedos swore he had no magical eavesdropping devices in the tent, and I must believe him, but I would give a fair amount of gold to know what happened among those four men while the sands trickled.

Tenedos said there were angry shouts, and once or twice one or another of the Rule of Ten stormed out, only to be called back before he could get ten feet.

Time ran out, and Tenedos returned.

"I knew I held victory when I saw their faces. Scopas looked worried, but a little confident, sure that he had chosen right, and power would not be taken from him. Barthou and that other corpse-looking fellow, Timgad, well, they were like schoolboys who've been whipped and told by the master they must confess to stealing apples to the entire lycee, pouting, sulky-faced."

"What of that general, Indore?"

"Why, being what he was, he had the same politely interested expression as he did when he walked into the tent. That man could murder his parents and then ask mercy of the judge for being an orphan!"

Two hours after that, Speaker Barthou, flanked by his two fellows, Indore having conveniently absented himself, climbed to the platform and, holding out their hands to quell the cheers, named Seer Laish Tenedos general of the armies of Numantia.

That done, they fled to their carriage and drove it out of the city as if demons were after them, never pausing until they reached "safety" in the palace in Nicias.

Now the real work would commence.

All Numantia responded to the shock and shame of the defeat, and supplies, money, weapons, and recruits poured across the country, on foot, on horseback, by boat.

The recruiters we sent out had to turn men, and even a few hopeful women, away, some of them in tears.

Numantia had scented chaos in the riots, and feared the biggest monster of civil war still more.

Chardin Sher must be stopped.

* * *

Tenedos called a meeting of all senior officers.

"This shall be very short, gentlemen. I intend to make changes in this army, changes that shall turn it into a modern, sophisticated fighting force.

"There shall be no more Imru Rivers, not as long as I lead you.

"Obey me, and you'll find glory and riches. Disobey or hesitate, and I'll break you like sticks."

His gaze swept the room, and men looked down or away.

One man waved his cane enthusiastically. It was General Hern, sitting most uncomfortably in his plastered leg. "Sir, let me be the first to say I'll gladly march under your orders. I'm damned if I was comfortable following that garrison soldier Turbery. You lead, sir, and I'll follow. If this damned leg won't let me sit a horse I'll ride in a cart like a milkmaid!" There was a bit of laughter—Hern was highly thought of, and would certainly keep command of the Left Wing.

Tenedos's eyes continued sweeping the room. One man not only met his gaze, but stood, his pose defiant. It was that brawling swordsman, Domina Myrus Le Balafre, commander of the Varan Guards.

"I mean no offense," he said, meaning offense and waiting for a moment before adding the obligatory "sir," "but I follow those who can lead me.

"Even though you did well after the Imru, you're still a wizard, a politician, I've heard, a man who makes great speeches.

"Well, shit on speeches and those who make 'em! We're always the poor fuckers who have to clean up afterwards.

"So why should I follow you, Seer? I give not one damn if you tear away my sash of rank. I'll soldier on, for someone else, as I have before."

"No you won't," Tenedos said calmly. "For you're a Numantian."

"What does that mean?"

"It means the days when a freelance blade could find an army to fight in without regard to the colors he was under are gone.

"The time has come, sir, when you are either a Numantian, or an enemy.

"Stand with me, or stand against me. There is no other."

His gaze burned into Le Balafre's for long moments, a stare as harsh, as compelling, as the one he'd given me when we'd first met, in Sulem Pass.

The domina broke, and looked away.

"I'll . . . I'll stay. Sir. And serve well."

"I never doubted that, my friend. Not for an instant. You're too brave a man not to."

And with those simple words any grumbling among the commanders became impossible.

Not that there wasn't grumbling, in fact it was as loud and protracted as any I'd heard. Even beyond a soldier's gods-given privilege to complain, there was some reason.

Men who'd soldiered for years in a unit were suddenly transferred to a new, unknown formation. Experienced men were needed to give a backbone to those regiments shattered or obliterated in the battle or to brand-new units, which were daily being formed. Some of the complaints were muted because promotion went with these transfers, and not promotions of a single grade, but of two and even three ranks.

The only formations left unscathed were the thirteen elite units that'd been called to Nicias, including the Lancers. Tenedos would use us as his spearhead and his right bower until the rest of the army was completely trained. Then, he said, we could expect to be rewarded for our sacrifice by suffering the same fate as the others, and we'd be given promotion and command of new formations ourselves. "This is true for every man, private, lance, or officer. This preposterous distinction of class that keeps a good man from reaching the highest ranks is gone. Let those who think accents or background or wealth matters find some other arena to prance around in."

Tenedos said those who couldn't fulfill the responsibility would be quickly returned to their old ranks and old units if possible.

This scheme was going to cause problems, and some deaths, he knew. But we'd have to accept them. "There's a saying on Palmeras," he said, " 'The easier the birth the lazier the man.' "

That reminded me of my own life, and I grinned, and told Tenedos to never mind when he asked. I was evidently going to be the father of the laziest Numantian in history, for Marán's letters told of no troubles, no problems whatsoever, which reassured me, even though we were in the earliest stages of the pregnancy.

The second reason for complaints was the loss of discipline. The army before Imru, before Tenedos, had been strict, formal, tightly disciplined. That vanished, never to return, and it may sound odd, but I was glad, remembering all those stifling evenings in mess when I sat around forced to listen to boring men mutter on about events no one, not even they, cared about.

The new men changed all this.

I was outside my tent, not wearing my rank sash, and saw a formation, if that is what it was, shambling toward me. There were thirty or so of them, from the ages of fifteen to maybe thirty-five. Some of them were barefoot, even. Others wore tradesmen's clogs or shabby boots.

It looked like they'd outfitted themselves from the discard heap, wearing everything from peasant smocks to tattered jackets and pants that would have been fine three or four owners ago, to one proud lad wearing nothing but a loincloth and a battered dragoon's helmet without leather or horsehair.

What made them even more ragged-looking is that some of them thought they should arrive in uniform, and so wore bits and pieces of every sort of military wear, including one or two with Maisirian gear, which they'd gotten from gods-knew-where.

At their head was an average-looking man immaculately dressed in a sergeant's uniform that was the pattern some five years before. If it had been his originally, he'd had a comfortable existence since then, for the jacket wouldn't button, and the pants were kept decent by a patch of matching material to cover his comfortably successful gut.

He was calling a cadence, and the recruits were stumblingly trying to keep in step. He saw me, shouted attention, and saluted. Half of the yokels tried to follow, not yet having learned the only person who salutes is the senior member of a formation.

The uniformed man wore rank slashes.

"Sergeant," I called, and the man brought his formation to a stumbling halt.

"Yessir."

"How long have you been on the road?"

"Depends, sir. Some of us for a few days, some of us, like Cutch there, who comes from the far east, almost two weeks. But we're eager to serve, sir."

"Is that . . . was that your uniform?"

"Yessir. And so were the slashes, although I know I'll have to cut them off when I'm sworn in."

"Why'd you get out?"

The man hesitated.

"Go ahead."

"Didn't seem to be anything worth soldiering for, sir. So I got married. Settled down."

"In what trade?"

"Tradesman, sir. But really I was more a peddler. My wife, Gulana, ran the store, filled the orders, and I tramped the country. I must've seen this country end to end, sir. Including a lot of Kallio. Maybe that'll be useful."

"It will be. So why did you reenlist? Times get hard?"

"Nossir. Store's doing fine. Had to take over the two buildings on either side of it to make room for all the merchandise. I've got half a dozen assistants, five peddlers out on the road, and my wife and our boys can take care of matters until I come back.

"I joined up again for two reasons, sir, the same two as the other boys who're with me. That damned Kallian is one, and the other's the seer. Right, men?"

There was a rough cheer.

Now, here was a man who perfectly illustrated Seer Tenedos's words about the constricts of rank. He was well spoken enough to be an officer, but under the old rules the rank he held was the highest he could dream of. No wonder he chose to return to civilian life.

"We're glad to have you," I said truthfully. "Soldier well, and there'll be gold and fame for you all."

"Thank you, sir. Might I ask who you are, sir, if you don't mind my boldness?"

"Domina á Cimabue. Commanding Seventeenth Ureyan Lancers."

I heard a murmur go through the ranks—my name must have spread beyond the lonely women of Nicias. "And yours?"

"Linerges, sir. Cyrillos Linerges."

He saluted, and the men marched away into the never-satisfied belly of the army, to be ground up and turned into soldiers.

I tapped on the pole of Tenedos's tent.

"Enter," he said, and I pulled the flap aside. The seer sat at his field desk, reading.

"Sir, may I take some of your time?"

"Of course. Rasenna's already snoring, so she'll never know I'm not beside her. She's getting used to my hours anyway. Come on in. There's a flask of tea over there, and bring me a brandy. I think I deserve one."

"Yessir. Sir, I brought someone I think you should meet." I beckoned, and Mercia Petre entered rather shyly. I introduced him.

"So this, I assume, is to be more than social," the seer said. "Very well. Captain, do you drink, or are you a prune like the domina?"

"Nossir. I'm an abstainer, too. Promised my father."

"Gods," Tenedos moaned. "I'm surrounded by prigs." He appeared in a vastly good mood, and I was relieved.

"Sir, the reason we came here is because you're in the middle of reforming the army, and we have some ideas."

"Doesn't everyone?"

"Not like ours, sir," I said. "The captain and I've spent a lot of time working things out, ever since I met him when we first came back from Kait."

"Ah. Another set of conspirators against the Way Things Are. You are both to be commended, although Damastes, I admit to some surprise, since I thought you were a man of deeds, not words." He looked at Petre. "I call the domina by his first name since we've served together for quite a while. Don't think I hold him and what he says in any less regard because of it."

"Nossir," Petre said. "He already told me that." He was fumbling in his sabertache for the notebook containing our ideas we'd laboriously built up over the months. He started to hand it to Tenedos, who waved it away.

"Tell me first. Then, if there's merit to what you say, we can work from there.

"Where's the starting point for your army?"

"First, sir, we should abandon the baggage train. All it does is slow us down, like it did when I was riding into the Sulem Pass after you, or—" I shut up, because Tenedos was waving his hand at me.

"I'm not quite a fool, Damastes, and I'd already figured that out. It's already in my plans. But how, in your view, should the army resupply itself? Carry a limited amount of supplies and encamp when they run out, waiting for the victual-bearers to catch up?"

"Off the country," Petre said. "We put out quartermasters in wagons, cavalry to screen them, and we take what we need. From the rich, if possible, but from any enemy."

Tenedos looked a bit surprised. "That's interesting," he mused. "And it would certainly lessen the cost of a war, turning it onto the enemy's back. That will win vast approval from our cheeseparing masters in Nicias."

"We also leave the camp, uh—" and Petre broke off, involuntarily glancing at the inner part of the tent where Rasenna slept, since the next word was "followers."

But Tenedos had caught his meaning.

"No women, no laundresses, no candy butchers, eh? How deeply would you make the cut?"

"No one who isn't a soldier moves with the army. Period. No sutlers, no servants either. The only purpose for the wagons are for heavy gear and ambulances. And sir, that would mean everybody. There's no point in telling a sergeant he can't throw a trunk in the company wagon if he sees the general with a brougham and mistress."

Tenedos smiled. "Captain, I can see you made your rank on merit, not diplomacy. But how much faster would this change let us move?"

"We're not through," I said. "I want to put the infantry on horses, or mules anyway."

"Gods, that'd mean the biggest stableyard in history," Tenedos said.

"It'd be big, but not that big. One riding, one walking would be the way I'd set up these foot soldiers. Then, in time, let them all ride. Carry enough wheat to keep the animals from foundering on grass. Again, resupply off enemy granaries when we take them, not burn them to the ground as we do now. Let every mule have its own feedbag and saddlebags for provender."

"How would the men fight?" Tenedos asked, his interest now roused.

"They'd ride to battle, and fight as they always do, on foot. That way we don't have to take the time to train them to be cavalry," I said. "No lances, no sabers, but spears, javelins, swords, daggers."

"Arm some of them with bows," Petre put in. "We never have enough archers in a fight. Try to keep them out of hand-to-hand fighting. All it does is pin units and keep them from maneuvering. We'll lose less men if we can keep them out of a melee."

"But we're skirting the main point here, sir," I said, gathering all my courage. "First, I think we should form the cavalry into one single striking arm."

"But it is already, or should be when generals use it properly."

"No it *isn't,* sir," I said. "Look at what you yourself ordered the other night: Damastes, use the Lancers as messengers. That's the way it always is, sir. An officer sees a man on a horse and instantly finds a task for him, messengering, couriering, whatever, anything other than his true purpose, which is to strike hard when opportunity offers, then move quickly on to the next weak point. Messengers can't do that, sir. We can't even train to do it when we're running dispatches from General Poop to Domina Crud. Sir."

"The other night was an emergency," Tenedos said, frowning.

"Sir," I said earnestly, "it's *always* an emergency. If you need messengers, train a staff of them. But keep your hands off the cavalry."

"Thank you, *Domina,*" he said, putting emphasis on my rank. "No, no. Don't apologize. So what do I do with this cavalry, now that it's one great whinnying mass of warriors?"

"We strike for the enemy's heart," I said. "It's like playing rōl. You get the ball, you cut around the forwards, and go straight for the goal. Ignore everything else. In order, we go after his army, his capital, his leaders. Cut through the lines as fast as we can, don't worry about our flanks, and go for broke. Let the infantry take and hold the ground. Ignore their damned fortresses, unless we have to have them. Go around them. They'll surrender after we've killed their king or burnt their capital."

I realized how vehement I'd gotten, hearing a sleepy query from Rasenna as to what was going on, and subsided. Tenedos sat for a long time, thinking. Neither of us dared move, for fear of disturbing him.

"Interesting," he said. "Very interesting. But what happens if the cavalry is cut off?"

"Then it's their mistake, their responsibility to break free, or hold out until the infantry can relieve them. If the unit moves fast enough, and doesn't allow itself to be pinned down by superior forces, it should never happen."

"Is all of this down in that little book of yours?"

"It is, sir. And there's more," Petre put in eagerly. "For instance—"

"Captain, please stop. A man or a sponge can only absorb so much at a time. If your handwriting is legible, would you object to leaving it with me? I'll return it within a day or so, or perhaps have copies made."

"Gladly, sir, gladly."

"Now that you've ruined my quiet meditation, and probably my brandy-drinking as well, you may depart."

We stood, saluted, and went out.

"Camp followers indeed," I heard Tenedos mutter.

Petre looked at me questioningly. I shrugged. The seer was his own man, and impossible to read. All I knew was that, unlike other times I could think of, we'd not be punished for having our own thoughts.

That, in itself, made the army very new and wonderful.

Tenedos called me to headquarters a day later.

He waved over a short, stocky man who looked like he was better suited to be a hotel's concierge than an officer. "This is Captain Othman," he introduced. "I've chosen him as my new chief aide. He's quite remarkable, you'll find. He has an absolutely perfect memory, don't you, Captain?"

"I don't know about that, but thank you, sir." Othman looked uncomfortable.

"That's all, Captain. I intend to take a short walk with the domina, and shall return in a few minutes."

"Very well, sir."

We walked out of the tent. I expected . . . no, hoped, Tenedos would bring up what was in our notebook, but he didn't. Instead:

"I've discovered how Chardin Sher was able to fool me with his spell."

"What is it? And, if I may ask, how did you discover it?"

"I had the foresight to scoop up a bit of sand from the battleground, and I used that as the thinnest of aids to see if the Law of Contagion could help. It did, especially after I forced my mind to make full recollection of the few minutes I was able to spend with Chardin Sher, back in Nicias, then brought that memory into the present, and into reality with a spell.

"I sought his magic both in this world and in others, and I was able to find enough traces to be quite sure of his method, or rather the method he ordered to be used.

"The man is vastly more clever than I thought, and succeeded where I failed."

"He *was* able to convince many magicians to work together?"

"Indeed. His own master magician, a man whose name I haven't learned yet, assembled sorcerers, then sent them into trances, and while their individual wills were quiescent gave them instructions to work together. Since these orders didn't interfere with any of their own desires, or not seriously, it performed nearly perfectly."

"So now you'll be sending orders to Nicias, conscripting the Chare Brethren?" I shuddered. "I'd not wish to be the drill warrant ordered to teach *them* what foot to march off on."

"I don't think that will be necessary," Tenedos said. "But I do plan to send a secret message to Scopas suggesting that, and telling him to leak the idea. That should frighten those fat, lazy impostors into being cooperative with any favors I may need.

"No, Damastes. That is their spell, and I know they must have built in countermeasures. I'll use something different, something better, now that I know what their secret is." He smiled, and his smile wasn't pleasant. "Chardin Sher will have some surprises in the next few months."

But the next surprise was for the army—and for me.

Once again, Tenedos ordered the top-ranking officers of the army to assemble. My orders also said I was to bring Captain Petre. I knew this would have to do with our proposal, and began to hope, for Tenedos was not the kind of man who'd summon an underling to butcher him in public. I had some real evidence our ideas might be implemented: Two days earlier, without any fanfare, Rasenna left the camp, and returned to Nicias, and other mistresses or wives of high-ranking officers had followed her. Now it would be interesting to see what came next and if we were to learn how to become an army instead of a costume ball.

There were other officers there than just command-level. I was very surprised to see Legate Yonge, whom Tenedos had not mentioned in my orders. He grinned, half-waved, and then Tenedos came out of his tent.

He began without preamble.

"We are building a New Army, as you know. Well, my changes . . . our changes . . . will cut more deeply than originally outlined.

"Two of my officers have made an interesting proposal, one that I intend to implement even further than they suggested.

"There will be changes in tactics as well, but first we shall make organizational changes so our new way of combat may be possible."

He looked about the audience, and smiled, seeing the dominas and generals exchanging worried looks, terrified that this new amateur was about to shatter what little foundation the poor, battered Numantian Army had.

"Don't worry. The changes aren't as great as you think, at least not on the surface."

He then went on to outline them. First he announced plans to mount as many infantry regiments as possible, and said he'd already sent orders to requisition every mule that could be found and send them south.

Then he announced that the cavalry was to be organized into a separate branch of its own, much as if it were its own wing. This brought gasps of wonderment, but looks of sudden pleasure from cavalry officers who were tired of playing honor guard to their superiors. They would have a new mission, which was secret at present. But I knew what it was: When we went to battle next, we'd be striking directly for Chardin Sher.

"There is one other type of unit I propose to create, or rather take an existing group of units and redefine their mission. I am creating a Scouting Wing, and in it I will be placing all existing light infantry units, and creating new ones. They shall be the army's eyes and ears, replacing the cavalry, for whom I foresee a somewhat different mission, as I've said.

"These new wings will require new commanders.

"For the mounted infantry, I appoint Domina Myrus Le Balafre to general.

"For the Scouting Wing, a man you may not be familiar with, a man who's currently in a lesser rank than he should hold, more due to my inattention than anything else. I name Yonge to the rank of general." Tenedos had the grace not to say just how low-ranking the Kaiti was. The hillman stood, transfixed, then yelped like a schoolboy and leaped straight up in the air.

"A general," he yelped. "Me, a general! Hey, Damastes! I beat you. I'm there first!"

Some officers were looking scandalized, others laughed. I was one of the latter, and was about to call for a cheer for the hillman, when:

"Finally, heading the Cavalry Wing . . . Domina, now General, Damastes á Cimabue!"

The only person happier than I was Captain Mercia Petre. Tenedos named him the new domina for the Seventeenth Lancers.

The Time of Heat came to an end, and the Time of Rains began. We cursed and slipped, but the pace of our training never slackened.

Tenedos had promised we'd fight before the Time of Storms, and we were determined to keep that vow.

My most wonderful Damastes
I am writing this outside the Palace of the Rule of Ten,
and have hired a courier to carry it by the fastest means
possible, regardless of expense, to you.

I am free.

Not an hour ago, my annulment was granted by a special session of the Rule of Ten, at least a year before we thought the matter would be heard.

I do not know why this happened, why we are so lucky, but will make sacrifice to all the gods I know because it did.

Oh, my Damastes, now there is nothing that can come between us.

When this war is over, we can be married.

I am too happy, too excited to write more, but I am well, all is well, all is wonderful.

Your loving Marán

"My congratulations," Tenedos said. "Thank you for sharing your happiness with me."

"Uh, it's more than that, sir."

Tenedos lifted an eyebrow.

"Sir, I request your permission to have my bride-to-be come here, and also wish your permission for marriage."

"That is very irregular, Damastes. We are supposed to be preparing for war."

"I realize that, sir. But I would be a traitor to myself if I didn't ask."

"Ah. Yes, you would. I forget love can dictate louder than common sense. Well, now you've asked, so . . ." his voice trailed off.

"I understand, sir." I came to attention, and was about to salute and depart.

Tenedos shook his head.

"Wait. No, I don't think you do. Nor did I, until I heard the echo of my own words.

"Irregular such an event would be, I said, and I was right. But aren't we building an irregular army?

"Surely a cavalryman is expected to be full of vapors and impulses.

"Why not?" Tenedos mused aloud. "It would certainly give

the men something different to talk about. The idlers could complain about the privileges of rank, and the rest of us could envy you.

"You have my approval, General. Send off a letter immediately. Wait. I have a better idea."

The captain in charge of the heliograph unit scowled at the message I'd handed him.

"Impossible, General. I'm not supposed to send messages to any civilian. The seer-general's own orders."

I handed him the next piece of paper.

"Oh," and his manner changed. "Sorry, sir. I should have known you'd have the seer-general's permission. The weather's clear, for a change, so we can send it this very minute."

Seconds later, the light began flashing from atop the tower, carrying its simple message north:

Come at once. Bring your wedding gown.

TWENTY-FIVE

LOVE IN WAR

I bowed deeply over the hand of the Countess Agramónte, who curtsied and whispered, "It is permitted for the bridegroom-to-be to kiss the bride."

I needed no further encouragement, and pulled her into my arms. Behind me, soldiers cheered and on the riverboat I heard laughter, but paid no heed to either.

But my tongue barely moved between her lips before she pulled her head back.

"As I recall saying once before, sir, you *do* take advantages," she whispered.

"You have no idea the liberties I plan to take," I said.

"Here? On the dock?"

"Standing up with my boots on and a brass band playing. Gods, but I've missed you."

"And I you, my Damastes," Marán said. "I cannot believe that we've been so fortunate, and that a great general such as yourself is willing to have a poor soiled woman from the country as your bride." She laughed and gently removed herself from my arms. She was even more beautiful than I'd pictured her, even here, standing on a splintered wooden dock, wet from the first downpours of the Time of Rains. She wore a high-bodiced dark purple velvet dress that followed the lines of her body to midcalf. She wore laced boots and a teal green, shimmering jacket that matched her wide hat.

"Now, if you'll give me a hand with my baggage."

She needed more than a hand; she needed a working party, which I'd brought in the form of an escort—four men from each of the regiments I now commanded, plus a full column from the unit I'd always consider "mine," the Ureyan Lancers, all in full-dress uniform. Thank my personal godling Tanis I'd remembered to bring a couple of freight wagons as well, although they were high-piled by the time the detail had finished and her two retainers sat on the sprung seats in front of Marán's trunks.

"Are you planning to stay until next spring?" I wondered.

"This, darling, is the way nobility travels. Actually, most of the better sort in Nicias are *terribly* scandalized I didn't bring more than two maids, but was brave enough to travel into the hitherlands without a complete staff." She laughed. "Now do you see what you are letting yourself in for? Now we must do all things properly."

"I assume part of that 'properly' is that we shall be very proud to be the parents of a thirteen-month child?"

"No one will ever dream to wonder such a thing of an Agramónte," she said. I wanted to take her into my arms and feel our baby next to me, but I could not.

I was about to inquire, but noticed there were soldiers approaching, so chose my words delicately. "Is . . . everything all right?"

"You mean the heir?" Marán said, evidently not caring a bean for what anyone thought. "He's a perfect child, so far. Hasn't spoiled my figure, and I seldom get sick as the midwife I consulted warned me to expect."

Newly promoted Captain Bikaner, whom Domina Petre had made the Lancers' adjutant, saluted. "Sir. We await your pleasure."

I returned the salute, and took Marán's arm.

"The carriage awaits."

Her eyes widened as we left the dock, and she saw what I'd brought.

"It's gorgeous," she said. "But what is . . . was it?"

As we walked closer, I told Marán what little I had been able to find of its history. Sometime in the far past, some high nobleman or -woman had visited the tiny city of Entoto, and there'd been a special carriage built, which had been carefully maintained over the decades, which one of my staff legates, on a private scrounging mission, had discovered. Entoto's head of council had cheerfully loaned it to me, and I'd had men polishing, painting, and cleaning since the day I'd heard Marán was on the way. It was enormous, almost as big as the Numantian coronation coach I'd seen in a museum in Nicias. But where that was red and gold, this was black and silver. The coach body sat on two four-wheeled trucks, the wheels taller than I am, and there was room for outriders and guards atop. I'd managed to find eight white chargers to pull it, and they were curried as finely as if they were about to enter a show ring.

Horseman Karjan, whom I'd decided to promote back to lance, held the door open, and we climbed up the steps and he closed the door.

The inside was as large as the exterior suggested, with soft leather seats at the front and back, and servants' pull-down seats against the doors on either side. The windows were glassed, with curtains. There was almost enough room for me to stand, and there were four lanterns to give light, and, hidden in the floor, chests to hold wine and foodstuffs.

I pulled the speaking tube down from its clip in the ceiling, and whistled into it. I heard the snap of a whip, and the coach creaked into motion. In front of it rode fifty cavalrymen and behind us more. There were flanking outriders as well, fitting escort for one of Numantia's noblest countesses.

We moved through Cicognara on the road that led to Entoto and the army's headquarters.

Marán was looking about, wide-eyed. I took off my helmet, and laid it to one side.

"Now," I said, reaching out and pulling her to me. Her lips opened, and our mouths moved together. I slid my hand up under her dress, caressing the sweet curve of her buttocks through her silk undergarments. But it only lasted for a moment, and once more she pulled away.

"I suppose," she said, breathing hard, "you would like to fuck me, right here in this coach?"

"The thought had occurred."

"I have a surprise for you, my love," she said. She ran her hand down my chest, until it touched my erect cock, clearly outlined under the light fawn trousers I wore. She ran her fingernails up and down it. "We are going to pretend we have never made love before, and are not going to make love until our wedding night."

"Who decided that? Or is that another noble custom?"

"*I* decided it," she said, her fingers still caressing me. "I want you all at once, then, when we're both quite mad with passion."

"I already am," I protested.

"Then let me make it worse." She bent her head and kissed the head of my cock through the material, then bit it gently, once, twice and my body suddenly jerked.

She pulled back in surprise, seeing the stain spread. "Oh dear," she said. "You weren't jesting." Then she grinned. "At least there's no question you've been faithful.

"But maybe you'll wear dark-colored pants for the ceremony."

"But what about right now," I said, starting to laugh. "I'm too old to be showing off wet dreams."

"What do you care," Marán said. "You're a general aren't you? And about to be Count Agramónte. Tell everyone come stains are the required uniform."

I snorted.

Count Agramónte. That evening, as I was trying to sleep, alone, in my tent, I considered. A general. And a nobleman, although Marán had explained that it was by courtesy, and was not hereditary, except so long as I stayed married to her, which I told her I had every intention of doing until I returned to the Wheel.

I'd sent letters, of course, to my parents, and wished they could meet Marán, and be here for the occasion. But that was an impossibility—I doubted if my letters would even reach our jungle estate before the ceremony.

I mused once more how the gods play their game, and how so much had turned on a single game of rõl.

Our wedding was proclaimed a day of feasting and celebration for the army, and General Yonge's skirmishers had combed the country for delicacies, although I heard it grated for them to have to pay for what they purchased with gold rather than a sword-tip as they would in enemy territory.

Seer Tenedos had summoned me, and announced he would perform the ceremony, unless I wished otherwise, and named the site. I thanked him profusely, and said I could think of no greater honor. Neither Marán nor I had any particular religious bent, and cared little if a priest or a sage performed the ceremony.

"*You* do me the honor, my friend," Tenedos said. He smiled wryly, and said something odd: "Now you see how I use all those about me."

"Pardon me, sir?"

"Your marriage will be a great day for my army, something they'll talk about for the rest of their lives, how Damastes the Fair, General of Cavalry, married just before the army marched off to subdue the rebellious Kallians. You see?"

"No sir, I don't," I said honestly, although now I do understand what he was saying and possibly even warning.

All that was beyond me, and, besides, I wanted to ask *him* if he was sure he'd chosen the right location.

"I have, indeed."

"But—"

"You just show up, O Nervous Groom. The rest is in the capable hands of a wizard."

And so it was.

Tenedos had chosen the strangest of all spots for the ceremony. To the north of Entoto was an enormous ruined cathedral, almost a palace. No one knew to what god it had been built; in fact, there were even stories that it had been constructed by the gods themselves, in the days before, when they sometimes lived on this earth.

I'd looked at it when we first retreated to Entoto, in the hopes we might somehow use it for military purposes, but had abandoned the idea, less for fear of sacrilege to forgotten deities than because of its decay.

All that remained were huge stone steps leading up from the rutted dirt road, and the four stone walls that stretched toward the heavens for more than 100 feet, crumbling at the top, but with never a buttress or reinforcement to keep them from falling. The windows were arched, the glass long shattered, and the floor of the single chamber was covered with arcane scripts that men said were epitaphs for those buried underneath.

There were more than a thousand soldiers in formation around the church, and behind them cookfires for the feasting and barrels of wine and beer for the drinking to come. It was an unhappy trooper who found himself stuck with duty on this occasion.

It had stormed hard that night, but the rain stopped for a moment as I rode up to the ruin.

I dismounted and handed the reins of Lucan to a soldier—newly promoted Lance Karjan had been invited as my guest, and waited within. I was to one side of the steps, and Marán walked into view on the other.

She wore a white gown of silk with lace paneling, with a long train being carried by her maids. She'd curled her hair in ringlets that outlined her face, with a lace headcovering that fell around her shoulders.

She looked afraid, and somewhat lost. I felt pity for a moment—she was one of the only three women in the vast horde of men, far from home and family, and then felt a swell of pride at her courage in coming to me, in being willing to wed a mere soldier, far beneath her in class.

Tenedos appeared at the head of the stairs, spread out his

hands, and began chanting in an unknown tongue. As he spoke, thunder growled, and I felt the patter of rain.

From nowhere girls danced, young girls, wearing the white outfits of spring, and they had baskets of flowers that they cast in front of Marán and me as we walked toward each other. I do not know if they were apparitions called up by Tenedos or if they were the virgins of Entoto, although I'd seen no girls that fair in my visits to the town.

I saw no band, but music swelled as we met, turned, and started up the steps.

Over the music I heard commands being barked, and a saber guard marched out of the rain. The orders were shouted by General Le Balafre. The soldiers marched toward us, sabers shouldered, then, on command, crashed to a halt, turned, and their sabers flashed out to form an arch. Each man wore the sash of a general. The army was giving us its highest honor.

I swear it was raining, and the sky was gray, but from somewhere shot a beam of sunlight, and the polished blades shot facets of light about us as we entered the ruin.

Thunder crashed, and rain poured. It should have been chill and miserable in the roofless devastation, but it was not.

Tenedos's magic turned the raindrops into drifting flowers that spun and twisted as they floated toward the stone floor. I smelled their perfume as we walked forward.

Tiny braziers formed a corridor we walked up, and from each of them coiled a different-colored plume of sweet smoke, an army of hues far vaster than the burner could have conceivably produced.

Men and, yes, women filled the room. Some of them I knew, and had personally invited—Yonge, Karjan, Bikaner, Evatt, Curti—others I was proud to have served with. Others I knew not. Marán gasped inadvertently, recognizing someone who was in reality far distant, then I almost followed suit, because I saw, for only a few moments, Marán's friend Amiel, then the faces of my father, Cadalso, my mother, Serao, and my sisters.

Later I received letters from them, saying they'd dreamed they were at my wedding, and were able to describe it exactly.

Tenedos stood at the end of the chamber, and we stopped just before him.

He bent his head in prayer:

"I am the Seer Laish Tenedos," he said, and his voice boomed through the chamber, "asked by this man and this woman to join them in matrimony.

"I pray to the gods of Numantia their union be blessed. I pray to Umar"—his voice fell silent, and I wondered if he'd had the courage to silently call upon Saionji—"and Irisu. I call upon Aharhel to name these two with favor to her subjects. Let those gods who rule the elements, Varum for water; Shahriyas for fire; Jacini for earth; Elyot for air, bless them. May Isa, our own god of war, grant them safety from his fierceness. May Jaen give them the powers of love, both in ecstasy and in comfort. May our own god of Nicias, Panoan, bless them. Let their own gods smile, Vachan, wise monkey god of Cimabue; Tanis, who watches over the fate of Damastes and his family; Maskal, god of the Agramóntes, all, all, heed my prayer and grant your boons to these two.

"So we pray, so we all pray."

He lowered his hands, and there was silence. Then he spoke once more.

"This day is sacred as the day when a man and woman wed. These two are Marán, Countess of Agramónte, and General Damastes á Cimabue.

"They have sworn their love and devotion, and vow there shall be no others to come between them. They wish to join their lives together. . . ."

If I hadn't had exact instructions, I would have missed the turnoff from the main road. The rain came in drifting sheets as the white horse pulled our small carriage up the lane, winding through the thick forest. It was not yet the Time of Change, but the leaves around us had begun to change to reds, bronzes, yellows.

The lane ended in a clearing, with a great tree in its center whose branches were a perfect umbrella.

The cottage sat to one side, almost buried in the red ivy that curled around it. It was small, built of multishaded woods, and cleverly crafted, all corners rounded and curved, so it was almost like a small, furry animal's burrow.

I pulled the horse up, stepped out, and handed Marán down.

A man in Lancers' uniform appeared from nowhere and, without speaking, led the horse and carriage away. I barely noticed, having eyes only for Marán.

I took her hand, and we walked to the door, and pulled the latchstring.

The door swung open, and we entered. It was early afternoon, but the rain had made it dark enough for the two lamps to give welcome light, and the crackling fire warmth.

I do not know where Tenedos found this marvelous place, but we fell in love with it. There were only four rooms: this living room, a loft bedroom above it, a small kitchen, and, behind it, a very large bathroom, built over a rocky pool heated by unseen springs. But neither one of us noted these details.

We had but three days, but now I felt I had all the time in the world.

I lifted my helmet off, and cast it into a corner. Marán, her eyes solemn, never leaving mine, came close, and her fingers slowly unbuttoned my tunic, and I slid out of it, and pulled off my shirt.

There was a chair behind me, and I fell back into it. She pulled my boots off, then I stood as she unbuttoned my trousers and I stepped out of them.

Marán turned her back, and my fingers moved down the long line of buttons of her gown, and it fell in a pool about her feet. All she wore was a transparent white lace undergarment that began between her legs, ran vertically in the rear until it reached the base of her spine, then Y-ed out to reach over her shoulders and down to her sex, barely widening enough to conceal her nipples.

I ran a fingernail down the smoothness of her stomach, and she shuddered, her eyes closing.

I lifted her in my arms, and laid her down on the carpet, barely noticing another marvel, that it was as warm and soft as a comforter.

I kissed her eyelids, the edges of her lips, caressed the inside of her mouth with my tongue, the rims of her ears, her neck, slipped the straps of her undergarment, and teased her nipples with my teeth.

She lay with her hands together, above her head, as I moved my lips down over her stomach. Her hips lifted and I slipped the undergarment away. Her knees lifted and spread as I slipped between them, lips moving on her shaven satin, tongue sliding inside her, warmth meeting warmth.

"Oh, Damastes," she whispered. "Oh, my husband. Now we are one."

I rose to my knees, and guided my cock into her, measuring its length within her as her legs embraced me, her nails rasping on the rug above her head as we moved in the rhythms of love, little heeding the storm roaring outside.

"How does it feel to be doing this legitimately?" I asked.

"You know," Marán said, and I saw in the flickering fire-light that her expression was quite serious, "I never felt what we were doing was wrong.

"I just wish I'd met you when I was seventeen."

"Now what would the chances have been of me, a country legate of what, twenty, being able to woo the beautiful, virginal daughter of one of the richest families of Numantia? I would have been horsewhipped off your estates by one or maybe all of your brothers. Things like that happen only in the romances."

"I wonder," she said. "I'll always wonder."

"Do you know when I first fell in love with you?" Marán asked. We lay side by side.

"The first time I held your hand, and lifted my eyebrows?"

"Stop being lascivious! It was when Hernad . . . when a certain person who shall never be named told you that 'the little woman knows how to please,' the very first night we met, and the way you looked at him. I'd never seen such contempt before. Do you remember?"

"I do. But I thought I kept better control of my features."

"No, my Damastes. I fear you can be read like a book, at least by me. For instance, I can tell what you are thinking at this very moment."

"That's hardly much of a challenge," I said. "You can *feel* what I'm thinking, too." I lifted her thigh over mine, then came to my knees, pulling her legs over my thighs until her sex was close against me and I was fully inside her. She locked her legs around my back, and pulled herself back and forth, each time almost letting me come free. I slipped my thumb down, moving it gently across her clitoris, and her back arched as she moaned, then screamed aloud as her body spasmed.

I felt my own throbbing build, pulled out of her, and moved up over her, rubbing my cock between her breasts and then I came, gasping as I spattered across her body.

Marán smiled up at me, breath still coming hard, and began rubbing my semen over her nipples and breasts.

"A lotion to keep you forever mine," she murmured, and licked her finger.

"What do you want your son to be named?"

"I didn't know it was going to be a son. Or did you visit another mage without telling me?"

"I just know it will be a boy."

"Thank you, my wizardess. We can name him after your father."

"No."

"All right, then *my* father."

"Can't we give him a fresh beginning?"

"Marán, isn't this a little . . ." I stopped myself. "Very well. Let's name him Laish. That seems to be a very lucky name these days."

She considered.

"Yes," she said, finally. "Yes. That is a very good name."

* * *

She was lying on her stomach, staring at the dying embers of the fire. It must have not been far from dawn. I was lying on one elbow beside her, admiring the way the fire outlined her sleekness.

She got up and went into the bathroom. I heard her rummaging around in one of her cases, then she returned and lay back down.

"Can I ask you something?"

"I never knew you had to answer all these questions on your wedding night."

"You don't," she said, and her tone was strange. "Not if you're unlucky."

I grimaced, ashamed I'd accidentally led the conversation onto uncomfortable ground.

"You can ask anything, you can tell anything," I said, and hugged her around the hips.

"Once, when we were on a picnic, you started to do something, and I stopped you from going any further. Do you remember?"

Suddenly I did, and said so.

"Damastes . . . make love to me again. Please. Make love to me . . . that way."

I felt a chill. I was wondering what I should say, and she turned her head and looked at me.

"Please, my darling?" There was urgency in her tone. I nodded. She gave me what was in her hand, and I saw it was a tube of unguent.

I caressed her buttocks, and moved my finger between them, and she flinched.

"Marán," I whispered. "I don't think this is right. I don't want to hurt you." My cock was limp against my thighs.

"You *must* . . . and I know you'll never hurt me. Please. This is important."

I began caressing her back, then moved my hand between her legs, stroking her sex, feeling the wetness I'd left from our lovemaking. After a time, her breathing became faster, became panting. I responded, growing hard once more. I lifted her hips and slid a pillow under them, then moved her thighs apart and knelt over her. I slid gently into her.

She gasped. "Not there, I meant—"

"Hush!"

I moved slowly, long regular strokes, and her gasps became moans, her hands digging at the carpet. Now I put unguent on my finger, and put it in her, moving it in a circle, feeling my cock inside her body as it moved and my finger caressed. She cried out in pleasure, and I put another oiled finger beside the first, both moving, moving.

"Oh yes, oh now, oh Damastes, I'm ready," and I felt her pulse back and forth around my fingers.

"Ready for what?"

"Oh please, fuck me, oh fuck me where I want it, where I told you to, please, do it, do it back there, oh please, put it in me, I can't stand it any longer," and I pulled my cock free, touched her open ring with its head and pushed, and she screamed and bucked, ramming her buttocks hard against my thighs, swallowing me in her, her hands clawing at mine as I supported myself on them. I pulled back until I was almost free, then buried myself in her as she writhed in passion, no more than a dozen times and then I, too, shouted aloud as we came together and collapsed.

We may have laid like that for minutes, or forever. I don't know.

"I love you," she whispered.

"I love you."

"Thank you. It's over now."

I said nothing.

"I like feeling you . . . back there. We can do that again."

But we never did.

Three days . . . I think we ate a day or so, slept every now and then, and spent even more time in the hot spring. But mostly we loved, loved and laughed. Blood and winter lay just ahead, but our love made a strong fortress, and kept the wolves of doom away.

I remember those three days as one long orgasm, of gasping lust and slow, serious, rolling joy, and wondered if I would ever be as happy again.

Then it came to an end.

Marán went back to Nicias.

And I went back to war.

There weren't enough hours, there weren't enough days, for my men to be ready for battle in time. We drilled, trained, cursed, and drilled once more.

I'm sure no soldier felt anything but hatred for his warrants, they for my officers and my officers for me, but there would be no more disasters like the Imru River if I had anything to do with the matter.

Little by little, the new recruits were becoming soldiers, although they were hardly as good as my Lancers. But exercises can only do so much—the final test of a soldier is in blood.

We developed new tactics, officers learning as much as the new men. Of course the most serious grumbling was done by the old-timers, who'd "never seen an army run this way." The novices knew no better, and so found these new ideas no more or less perplexing than anything else.

Possibly the biggest change came from Tenedos himself. He'd vowed magic was as important a piece of the passage of arms as anything else, which Chardin Sher's cadre of wizards had proven. Now it would be our turn. He had recruiters out throughout Numantia, seeking out magi who wished to serve their country, and day by day they trickled into camp and were slowly, reluctantly, absorbed into the army. If we'd had more time, and if there weren't the charred corpses at the Imru River, it might have been amusing, to see all these sages, experienced with demons and spells, but having no more idea whether they should salute a private or a general than how to wind a crossbow. But they learned, and we learned the new tactics of sorcery Tenedos proposed to employ.

When the monsoon grew too fierce we moved under canvas, great umbrellas the men could crowd into and watch tiny battles being laid out on sand-tables. Then, when the storm abated slightly, they went into the field, to practice.

The Time of Rains came to an end, and the Time of Change began, and we were still not ready.

General-Seer Tenedos announced we'd march against Kallio in two weeks.

One of Laish Tenedos's most famous sayings, made years later when he was emperor, was "I don't care how skilled a soldier is. Is he *lucky*?"

He meant more than just being able to survive a battle unwounded—Myrus Le Balafre, for instance, rarely left the most minor engagement without some injury. He meant battle-luck, primarily, in which a warrior is able to be in exactly the right place—for him—and the wrong place—for his enemy—without ever planning the maneuver.

Tenedos said once I was the luckiest of all his tribunes. Perhaps so, although I wonder now. Perhaps I am the unluckiest, since I am the last survivor of those splendid, bloody days. But regardless of today, I have had much luck, in small things as well as great.

One such was what I chose to wear the morning I was summoned to the seer-general's tent. One of the hundreds of wedding presents I'd received was a handmade knife from General Yonge. Where, in this wilderness, he'd found a knifemaker of such great skill, I didn't know. But it was a beautiful blade of ondanique steel, about eight inches long, slightly curved, single-edged with its upper edge sharpened. Its hilt and pointed pommel were of worked silver, and its grip a wonderful mosaic of multicolored woods. Its sheath and belt were of patterned leather and silver as well. I buckled it about my waist as I left my tent, slinging my sword in a baldric over my shoulder.

It was blowing cold, but the army was alive with movement as the constant drills continued. I was just one more horseman, anonymous under a cloak, and no one paid me the slightest attention.

I reached Tenedos's tent, the guards recognized me, saluted, stepped back, and I tapped on the tent pole.

"Enter," Tenedos said, and I obeyed.

"I have a letter for you," he said, and for an instant I felt my stomach crawl—something had happened to Marán. "It was brought to the border under white flag yesterday morning. The outer envelope was addressed to me, with a note asking the inner one be given to you." He handed it over. It was addressed: To the Cimabuan named Damastes who styles himself a General.

It took a moment to recognize the handwriting, then I knew it to be Elias Malebranche. What the devils could the Kallian want with me? I tore it open, and took out the single page within. It was thick, heavy, and felt strange to the touch, like oilskin. I unfolded it and began reading:

> My spies have informed me that you have so fooled
> the charlatan Tenedos that he has promoted you to an
> absurd rank, far beyond what a bumpkin of your lineage
> could possibly manage. I look forward to meeting you on
> the field of battle and personally destroying you.
>
> I also understand you took a wife recently, which I
> found even more risible, since the slut was well-known in
> Nicias before your return for tumbling every long-dicked,
> unwashed nobleman within the city's reach—

I could read no more of Malebranche's lies. I crumpled the letter, threw it to the floor, and began to snarl an obscenity.

But before I could speak, the balled paper grew, turning, swelling, lengthening, and the parchment changed, and between the seer and myself was a huge snake, fifteen feet long, its body nearly as thick as my thigh, its fangs dripping, and a horrible hissing filled the tent.

Tenedos pulled back as it struck, then it turned on me, yellow eyes glaring, smoke pouring from its open mouth.

My sword was in my hand, and I slashed at the monster, but my blade passed harmlessly through the creature. Again I struck, as its head struck, lower jaw smashing into my arm, sending my sword spinning.

It threw a coil around Tenedos, and he gasped agony. Outside the tent, I heard shouts of alarm, but the guards would be far too late, as the snake drew back for its deathstroke, fangs oozing poison.

My dagger was in my hand and I flung myself on the serpent, my arm around it just below its head. Again I struck, and again I might have been stabbing air. But I'd at least enraged the beast, and it turned away from Tenedos, on me. I tried to block with the pommel of my knife, knowing death an instant away. But my blow struck true, thudding into cold muscle, not air, and the snake shrilled pain! I struck again, not knowing why the blade did no harm, but its butt seemed to agonize the apparition.

Its hiss became a scream, and it writhed, thrashing, smashing me against the tent's wooden flooring. But I held on, and then I heard Tenedos cry out, half-strangling, "Silver! Kill it with silver!"

The pommel of my dagger! Once more I bashed at it, and the creature whipped back and forth, sending me rolling away. I was about to dive back on the monster, then remembered my belt of worked silver, and, in desperation, tore it free and jumped toward the snake's head. Somehow I managed to loop it around the serpent, and began twisting, as if I could somehow strangle it.

The hissing scream grew louder, still louder, and the monster contorted, beating me against the floor, but I hung on grimly, nothing else in the world but my hands pulling at that belt, tighter, ever tighter, and then there came a final convulsion and the beast shuddered and was still.

I managed to get to my knees. Tenedos lay motionless, facedown, a few feet away. The tent door was ripped open, and there were soldiers there. Then Tenedos stirred, groaned, and pushed himself up to his knees.

"Ah gods," he moaned. An officer ran to him, but the seer waved him away. "No. Wait." He carefully felt down his rib cage as he gasped for air. "I . . . think . . . they're unbroken," he managed. He tottered to his feet, and came to me.

"Are you all right?" I managed to stand, and felt pain shoot through me. But I, too, had nothing broken, even though every inch of my body was bruised.

"That bastard," I said, as winded as Tenedos.

Tenedos turned to look at the snake's body, and I followed. My eyes widened: The great beast was vanishing, wisping away in vile-smelling green smoke as I watched.

"Quick, Damastes! Give me your dagger! And your sword!" I obeyed, finding my sword in a corner. Tenedos took them and hobbled to the fast-vanishing body of the serpent. He touched the two blades to it, and chanted:

"Steel remember
Remember defeat.
Learn from silver
Feel the foe.
Remember your shame
Another time
Another place.
Then remember
Then atone
Then strike
At the heart
At the man
At the disgrace."

By the time he finished, the monster's body had vanished completely, and there was nothing left but the fast-vanishing stench. The soldiers were babbling, and Tenedos shouted for silence.

"Your guardsmen are dismissed. You did no wrong—what came, came from outside. Return to your posts. I am well."

They obeyed. Tenedos touched his ribs and winced.

"I lied," he said. "I'll have a chirurgeon bind these for a few days." He bent and picked up a decanter of brandy. "Ah. At least the demon left us with two glassfuls. Will you alter your habits for the moment?"

I did, and he found unbroken glasses and poured.

"Most interesting," he mused, and he seemed completely undisturbed. "And very clever. I must meet this master sorcerer of Chardin Sher's, for he is a man to learn from.

"What a subtle way to attack me, through you. I could sense no spell, since it was dormant until you did what you did to the letter.

"Malebranche deliberately wrote it to anger you, knowing you'd destroy it. I imagine there were other variations if you'd, say, thrown it into a fire, to produce the monster.

"Very clever indeed."

"Maybe so, sir. But this is the second chance . . . third, if you count the fog-demons in Kait and allow for Malebranche's involvement, that shit-heel has had to kill me. I'd like a chance to be a little clever with him."

"You shall, Damastes, you shall, if the stars are right. Since Malebranche feels some special enmity toward you, I sealed your weapons to him. Perhaps, if you meet on the field of battle, that will give you a bit of an advantage."

"I don't want an advantage, I want his guts for a winding sheet!"

"General á Cimabue, calm down. Drink your brandy."

I did, and Tenedos took his own advice.

"Yes," he mused, "Chardin Sher is proving himself an excellent enemy. It's almost as if he had been listening to what you and Domina Petre said some time ago, about the need to strike for the enemy's heart. Except that he's taking it to its extreme.

"Very, very interesting. I think we should follow his fine example ourselves."

Another letter reached me that shook me even more deeply:

> *My dearest dearest*
> *I do not mean to worry you, but I've been advised by my midwife that our child in my womb is in delicate health. She has instructed me to keep my chambers, take*

no exercise, and to guard myself well for the months to come.

She says our son needs great care to ensure his birth will go well.

I asked her if my traveling up to see you and marry you could have anything to do with it, and she said she wasn't sure, but did not think so.

Since I love our son, whom I dream of daily, nearly as I love you, I shall obey her commands.

Forgive me, darling, if I write no more, as I'm quite upset by this. I shall send another letter on the morrow, when my spirits revive.

> *Your dearest wife*
> *Marán*

Three weeks later, halfway through the Time of Change, our soldiers still only half-trained, we marched west against Chardin Sher.

TWENTY-SIX

INTO KALLIO

We smashed over the border into Kallio an hour after dawn, scattering the light defenses like chaff. Seer-General Tenedos had found a new way of moving secretly.

The magicians he'd recruited had cast spells of normalcy, if that's the correct description, so it appeared that the army was still at Entoto. The plan, which worked perfectly, was that an army moving in "silence" was impossible, so therefore it wasn't happening.

Another thing in our favor was the time of year; no one ever, not ever, began a campaign halfway through autumn, for all the soldiers were busy building winter quarters, not intending to take the field until after the Time of Storms.

We moved fast, and our New Army showed its merits. Instead of taking sixteen days to reach the Imru River, we took four, moving in forced marches and abandoning those who could not keep up. Wagons that broke down or horses that gave out were turned over to the quartermasters bringing up the rear. They were to be repaired or stripped for parts, and the animals either healed or butchered for meat. As for the men who straggled, they were rounded up by provosts, informed they were no longer part of their units, and would join heavy work gangs, little better than slaves, until they proved their willingness or ability to march and fight.

This was the time for steel to be tempered.

The border between Kallio and Dara is no more than a creek, and their defenses were intended to do no more than give warning to Chardin Sher's main force a day's travel distant behind fortification.

We hit the border guards hard, but of course there were survivors who escaped to sound the warning. We didn't pause, but marched on, all through that day, and by night we'd come on the Kallians' camp.

As our magic and spies had told, Chardin Sher was building major fortifications. But he'd been doing it leisurely, not expecting our attack until spring, and so they were but half-finished. They would have been formidable, when complete. Pits and embedded stakes were used to cleverly divide the attacking force into separate elements. Once the attackers— our army—had been divided, then it would be led into killing zones where magic, archery, and spears would destroy us.

There were three defensive lines laid out. They began with a deep ditch, filled with brush to make the obstacle harder to cross. Just behind the ditch rose a steep earthen wall, about twenty-five feet tall. The wall was manned by the first line of defenders, then came the secondary ditch, wall, and its defenders; then a third, and then the army's camp. But only the first line was finished, the second was half-built, and only the ditch was dug for the third. To go out in front of the lines was through one of the six gates, but these were barricaded shut and well defended.

Chardin Sher, not being a fool, had realized he'd challenged the entire Numantian nation, and so ordered conscription throughout Kallio. He had, in total, about a million men under arms, most still training, of course, and had moved almost 150,000 of them to the border. Against him marched a quarter of a million Numantians, with a million more being trained or shipped to Entoto. His willingness to wage war, merely counting heads, seemed absurd. But he'd taken the measure, or so he thought, of his foe, and would hardly worry about troops as easy to fool and destroy as we'd been on the Imru. I suspect he thought, correctly, that all Numantia was tired of the Rule of Ten's ineptitude and ready for change. They may have been, but Imru, and Seer Tenedos, created a cause and a rallying point. Also, he no doubt intended to deal us a sharp defeat once more, and then negotiate or terrify the Rule of Ten into meeting his conditions.

Even seeing our army march toward his lines, Chardin Sher must have thought he still had time. Previously, we would have taken up battle positions that afternoon, then developed defensive lines over the next few days while each side decided its strategy, and only then would the two armies creak into battle.

Instead, we attacked at false dawn the next morning. Again, our new organization helped. Since we marched into battle order, with no supernumeraries and camp followers to shuffle aside, we were ready to move against the Kallian positions that had already been well scouted by Yonge's skirmishers. Tenedos, his devoted adjutant Captain Othman, and the generals had developed our attack as we closed on the Kallians.

As if fooled, we even attacked into those zones intended for our destruction, as Chardin Sher had hoped. But since we knew his intent, we broke our army into completely separate forces before battle, so there was no real division; rather, it was as if separate armies were moving against the same goal. In command of the Left was General Hern, the Right General Le Balafre, and Seer-General Tenedos himself ordered the Center.

My cavalry, once more, was held back, but no one was upset, knowing horsemen cannot attack entrenchments. We would exploit any openings when they developed.

The Kallians were surprised, but fought back bravely, stopping the Center Wing cold as they came out of the first deep trench. The lead regiment should have ignored its casualties, and fought on. But their domina and company commanders were dead, and so they milled around, easy targets for arrows and spears fired from the wall above. Among them was Cyrillos Linerges, and it was here that he first distinguished himself. As I'd thought, he'd done better than keep his old sergeant's strips when sworn in—there were far too few experienced soldiers for him to hold no higher rank. Instead, after a few days' probation, he was given a legate's sash and a half-company of infantry. Promotions, in peacetime, come slow and hard. But in war, they shower like the monsoon for the brave and the lucky.

Linerges shouted for the troops behind him, still on level ground, to rip the Kallian stakes out of the ground and tie them together in threes. He seized the fallen regimental colors and, holding them high, scrambled out of the ditch, standing just below the wall, heedless of the arrow-storm coming down at him, and shouted, "Men who fear not death . . . attack!" There were enough of those yet living to scramble up the dirt wall, paying no heed to the defenders' spear-shower, and fall on the Kallians with sword, dagger, and clawed hands, and then the enemy ramparts were a melee of confusion.

Then the tied stakes were thrown against the steep dirt walls and men of other regiments swarmed up them. Chardin Sher's men on the wall wavered, and just then Le Balafre's forces broke through on the right and, not much later, the Left Wing followed suit and the first wall was ours.

Other stakes were tied into bridges and thrown over the ditches, just as the storming foot soldiers tore away the barricades, smashed open the gates, and bugles sounded for the cavalry.

We went forward at the trot, long lines of horsemen moving toward the smoke and dust of battle, some streaming through the gates, other regiments flanking the entire battlefield.

Chardin Sher's army broke, but it had held long enough for Chardin Sher and his top command to flee east and south, into the heart of Kallio. Domina Petre took his Lancers around the right flank in pursuit, but didn't make contact, and, disappointed, turned back after an hour's pursuit.

The rest of us drove into the enemy camp. We carried flaming torches to set fires and slashed down tent ropes as we gal-loped. Those who had the bravery to stand against us were spitted on lances, or cut down with sabers. The Kallians cast weapons aside, and we heard cries of "Mercy," and saw impro-vised white flags flutter.

Now began the real nightmare of war. I've spoken of the blood of dying men, men wounded in every ghastly manner imaginable and beyond imagination. Worse was the fate of the poor animals, horses, and mules, who had no reason for quar-rel but suffered and died with their masters. But there were greater horrors, as the soldiers stormed through the army's camp. There was wine, and there were women. Willing or not, they found new masters that night. Men and boys who'd been free before the battle became slaves . . . or were murdered in the redness of slaughter.

Men who'd been the bravest of heroes an hour earlier sometimes now committed the most awful barbarities, and it was excused them as the "rights of soldiers in victory." This is what war has always been and what war will always be, and I wish those who are so quick to cry for bloodshed and soldiers could have walked among the flames and heard the screams.

It was terrible . . . but it was nothing compared to what I would see in other battles, other wars.

Officers allowed their men license until midnight, then with the soberest warrants went out and ended the rapine. Some-times a word was enough, sometimes a blow, even, a few times, a sword thrust, to break up a melee.

It was fortunate for our captives that we'd driven the army hard to reach the battlefield, because exhaustion struck the conquerors down before long, and then the field was quiet except for the crackle of flames and the whimpers of the wounded and torn.

At dawn, the army reformed. But other units, the thirteen elite, had for the most part held back from the license of the night, and were already on the move. In the old way of fight-ing, we would have marched back across our borders and sent envoys to Chardin Sher, asking if he had learned his lesson.

But this was new, this was Tenedos's manner of making war, and so by midday the entire army was moving east again, with only one objective:

Chardin Sher.

We would destroy anything that tried to stop us.

The light cavalry moved in front, acting as scouts. With the command elements of each cavalry regiment went sorcerers, and at regular stops they'd send their special senses out, seeking signs of the enemy.

Behind the light cavalry moved the new mounted infantrymen, dragoons on muleback. Interspersed with them were heavy cavalry, for support.

Then came Yonge's skirmishers and the rest of the army. Among them was a newly promoted domina, Cyrillos Linerges. Our attack on Chardin Sher's camp had caused far more casualties than we'd taken, and the swiftness of our assault had been far less bloody than if we'd laid siege to their lines, but there'd still been many, many corpses and cripples—gaps in the ranks to fill. Linerges was but one such lightning promotion.

We moved through the rich countryside like a plague of locusts, looting and laying waste as we went. The Rule of Ten would be well pleased, as Tenedos had predicted, at the way he waged war. Nicias's treasuries remained full, and we ate the beeves, fowl, and winter-stored supplies of the Kallian people, and found our remounts in their stables. Their leader had begun this civil war, and so they must bear the cost.

The Time of Change should have been harsher, colder, but it was quite mild, and I needed only a lined jacket under my mail most days, and was grateful for the warmth of my fur-lined sleeping roll at night. I wondered if Tenedos's goddess Saionji *was* favoring him, and holding back the winter.

Kallio was a beautiful land, not spectacular with great canyons, rivers, and peaks, but gentle, rolling countryside, ideal for farming or ranching. War had never come to this state within memory, and so the people were as fat and comfortable as their oxen.

Loud and long were the wails that went up as Yonge's skirmishers ranged far and wide to either side of the army, each party accompanied by a quartermaster's wagon. The army ate well as we marched on, always easting, and the days grew into weeks.

Tenedos's orders were that each farm was to be left enough for its people's survival during the winter, but I fear that command was honored more in the breach.

Any resistance was met with fire and sword, and the army's progress was marked by smoke pyres rising along our trail. Too often these were funeral pyres as well, as farmers decided to fight for what was in the pens and granaries.

We were moving too fast for the Kallians; they seemed bewildered at our speed. We encountered only scattered units as we rode, and their resistance was mostly brief—an ambush, a volley of arrows, and then they fled.

A few times, though, brave yeomen formed home-guard companies, partisans actually, and these fought bitterly, often to the last man, for their land and possessions. Their courage was admired, but admiration did not extend to mercy.

Sometimes their stand would be aided by a village or town witch or wizard, but just as audacious farmers were no match for Yonge's skirmishers or my cavalry, so a local sage's ploy would be discovered and turned against him by one of Tenedos's wizards.

Word spread that it was suicide to stand against the Numantians. The best way to stay alive was to flee, to surrender and cooperate. There was no third option.

It was brutal, but as Tenedos said, "The best, cleanest way to make war is total. Begin it quickly, end it the same, and there will be fewer deaths to mourn and misery to endure."

There were no battles worthy of the name, merely skirmishes, but each day gave our half-trained recruits more experience and confidence as the army shook itself out.

The image of our army that no doubt occurs is of brave riders, brass polished, armor shining, horses curried as if for the ring, as we rode through Kallio. Let me describe one cavalry troop:

There were perhaps seventy horsemen, far fewer than the 125 the rolls called for to be at full strength. The horses, while fat with grain, were no more than cursorily brushed, their winter coats shaggy, manes and tails matted and worn. The men's tack was scuffed and muddy, frequently hastily mended with rawhide. The soldiers' clothing was ragged, filthy, and not infrequently civilian or that of the enemy. Sometimes dirty or bloody bandages showed. Helmets were strapped to the saddle, not the head, and held eggs or perhaps some dried fruit. Wine bottles protruded from the saddle rolls, and perhaps a chicken, duck, or goose dangled from the saddle. Saddlebags bulged with looted riches that could be easily carried and traded for an even shinier bauble.

The only thing that gleamed about these men were their always-ready weapons—and their wary eyes. The gods should have had mercy on anyone who dared stand against my cavalrymen, but they did not.

> *My dearest Damastes*
>
> *Yesterday morning, our child, and it would have been a boy, died, in premature birth. The midwife did what she could, summoning the best chirurgeons and sorcerers of Nicias.*
>
> *I wish you could have been here. Perhaps if you were, this would not have happened. Perhaps my worry about you harmed our boy.*
>
> *Now, I mourn alone, and cry for you, for me, and for him.*
>
> *I am so very sorry, I swear to you, I did nothing wrong that I know of. Perhaps I did something to anger the gods. I do not know. But I cannot pray, cannot ask forgiveness.*
>
> *The world is empty for me.*
>
> *Marán*

Empty for me, empty for her. I knew not what to do. Tenedos must have heard, for he rode forward, and offered his sympathies. I hope I made the correct responses. I wrote a letter back, trying to soothe her, trying to reassure her that these things happened, that our child was spared the pain of life, but returned swiftly to the Wheel, where all was good and easy.

But I did not believe it for a moment.

I wanted to turn my duties over to another, and go to Nicias, and be with my wife. But that was impossible.

Nor could I allow this tragedy to affect me. I had too many others, men who also had wives and children, thousands of them, dependent on my being able to think clearly and move precisely.

A priest came, tried to offer condolences, saw the look on my face, and fled.

I walked out from the camp, ignoring the challenge of the sentries, and stared up at the skies where the gods supposedly lived.

I wished them all, each and every one of them, to be torn by demons and feel a bit of Marán's and my agony.

I shut off my soul then and let the killing fields welcome me.

A rider came from Domina Petre, requesting my presence, if possible. I did not have the time, but it was the Lancers, and so I rode forward.

The regiment was camped in the ruins of a village that had either stood against them, or else had been put to the match by looters. A grim Petre saluted me.

"General, this is highly irregular, but I thought you should be aware of what has occurred. One of my Lancers, a sergeant, has been found guilty of rape."

"What has that to do with me?" I said shortly. Even though I tried to watch myself, my pain made me short-tempered and capable of even greater anger than my Cimabuan temperament normally allowed.

"The sergeant is named Varvaro, sir," Petre said. "He was with you on the retreat from Kait."

I remembered the cunning climber from the mountains to

our north that bordered Dara and Kallio, the brave volunteer who'd been just behind Yonge on the rope when we went over the ridgeline to counterambush the Men of the Hills.

"Sorry, Mercia," I said. "I am grateful for your informing me. Summon the man."

In a few moments Varvaro was brought before me, guarded by two armed warrants. He looked at me, and then his gaze dropped.

"What happened?" I asked Petre.

"According to his column commander, Sergeant Varvaro was in charge of an advance scouting party. They found a farmhouse, actually a group of them, almost a village. They were checking the buildings for enemy stragglers or partisans, and came upon this woman. Girl, really, perhaps fourteen.

"One of Sergeant Varvaro's men said the girl was almost shaking in fear, but she smiled at the sergeant. He ordered his troopers out of the house, and told them to check the barns once more.

"They protested, but he said it was a direct order, and so they obeyed.

"A few minutes later, they heard screams, ran back inside, and found the girl naked, moaning, and the sergeant fastening his breeches together."

"How is the girl now?"

Domina Petre shrugged. "I can't say. Captain Dangom found a witch in another village, and we took the girl to her. The witch said she will recover."

"Varvaro, is this the truth?" I snapped.

"Sir, I thought th' bitch wanted it," he said, not lifting his eyes to meet me. "She was leadin' me on."

"What does that matter? No means no. Look at me, Sergeant."

Varvaro reluctantly raised his eyes.

"Do you have anything to say for yourself?"

There was a long pause. Finally: "Nossir. I guess not. But . . . but I ain't had none since Nicias, an' shit like that clouds th' mind."

"You knew the penalty for rape," I said, unwavering. "The people of the land are still Numantians, even though they gave fealty to Chardin Sher. Your duty as a soldier—as a warrant—is to protect the innocent, not ravish them."

"Yessir. But, sir . . . *please,* sir." Naked fear was in his stare. I met it, held it, and once more his gaze fell.

"Domina Petre, all is in order. Carry out the sentence!"

"Yes sir!"

An hour later what elements of the regiment that could be assembled were in formation in front of a tall oak, its branches bare against the gray autumn sky. Varvaro was led out, his hands tied behind him. He saw the dangling noose and began crying. They had to lift him onto his horse. The noose was draped about his neck, in spite of his efforts to duck, a hood drawn over his face, and a quirt lashed against the horses flanks.

The horse whinnied, leaped forward, and Varvaro was yanked from the saddle, the noose pulled taut. His untied legs flailed against the air, and he twisted, slowly strangling. Against orders a warrant ran forward, grabbed his legs, pulled, and I heard the snap of his neck breaking.

A hard death from a hard law in a hard war.

I rode back to my headquarters in silence, and Lance Karjan, riding behind me, was equally still.

A wonderful story ran round the army within a day of its occurrence:

A carriage had been stopped by skirmishers, a carriage that obviously belonged to someone wealthy. Inside was a very beautiful woman, in her early twenties, and several trunks of clothing.

She announced she was Sikri Jabneel, yes, *the* Sikri Jabneel, and was to be taken to the seer-general at once. None of the foot soldiers had heard of her, but they figured it was best to be gentle with anyone who looked to be as wealthy as she did. She was passed back through the lines, after both she and her belongings were thoroughly searched, to indignant squeals, and eventually taken to the Seer Tenedos's command area.

She was repeatedly asked what she wanted with Tenedos, and said her wishes were for his eyes only.

I suppose Tenedos's curiosity was roused—she was, and as far as I know still is, very gorgeous and most charming. I also suppose, after the letter from Landgrave Malebranche, that he put out all the sorcerous wards he could think of before going to her, to make sure she wasn't an assassin sent by Chardin Sher.

I do not know, and would very much like to, who was listening to what happened. Tenedos never told me of the incident, nor did Sikri, and Captain Othman never discussed his personal business. But someone's ears were close to the canvas wall of the tent that afternoon.

Tenedos introduced himself, and the woman did as well, expressing her pleasure at his giving her the time, and complimenting him liberally. He asked what she wished, and she pretended mock indignation that he'd never heard of her. She was the toast of Polycittara, indeed, of all Kallio, had even sung her songs in Nicias itself twice, and appeared in a masque before the Rule of Ten. Tenedos, always civil, apologized for his ignorance, and once more, a little wearily, inquired her business.

She giggled, and said that, well, she'd heard so much about him, even though that terrible Chardin Sher forbade any mention of the seer, and desired to see what he was made of for herself. "For," she said, and her words were always told exactly, "I fancy great men, and I have sensed, even though I have no more of the Talent than any of us who play the part of others for only a night, true greatness about you."

Tenedos ignored the compliment. "So Chardin Sher is still in Polycittara?"

"As far as I know," Sikri said, "although I care little about that man, nor about his piddly little city or his piddly little ambitions. I have renounced them, for I am no traitoress, but a true Numantian, and wish to do all I can to help the cause, and bind up the wounds of our poor country."

A good storyteller could relate this in ringing tones, and

suggest that Sikri may have been modifying a speech she'd learned sometime earlier for a stage role.

Tenedos wondered exactly what contributions she thought she could make.

"Why," she said, her voice now a purr, "I was told that you have no one to share your troubles with, no one to help you carry the burden of your duties."

"You mean," Tenedos said, "you want to sleep with me."

Sikri giggled. "Is that not the best way a woman can help a man?"

There came a *very* long silence, and the unnamed eavesdropper must have assumed the lewdest. But then Tenedos spoke:

"I am deeply honored, my lady. But you should be aware I plan on marriage when this campaign is over, and frankly consider myself affianced."

"What of it," Sikri said. "Is a prize stallion content with only one mare?"

Again, silence, and then a shout for Captain Othman. The singer started to become angry, but Tenedos told her to be silent. Within a few minutes the little adjutant bustled in.

"Captain, this is Sikri Jabneel."

"Pleased, my lady."

"She wished to help our cause to victory. I have accepted. Lady Jabneel, if you wish to remain with us, you may do so, as Captain Othman's leman, under his protection."

"But—"

"Either that, or you shall be escorted out of our lines within the hour and sent back to Polycittara. The choice is yours."

Tenedos left the tent, and the listener must have had to flee, because nothing was ever reported as to what next happened between Othman and the singer.

But an hour later her baggage was moved into the adjutant's tent, and when the army moved out the next day, she rode happily in his staff carriage, the only woman with the army.

It was against policy, against all the rules and regulations.

But the story was too delicious for her presence not to be permitted.

I am afraid I did not laugh when I heard the tale, for I was far too worried about Marán. I'd had no more than two letters, brief notes that said she was recovering since her miscarriage and there were no complications.

I tortured myself about what could be the matter, but somehow found the strength to drive the problem from my mind. It must wait until the war was over.

The ground rose steadily, and we marched across a wide plateau, the Kallian farms smaller and interspersed with woodlands. We moved more slowly, for now there were canyons and draws that required thorough scouting before we could move past them.

The weather grew colder as the Time of Storms began, and gales swept Kallio, the ground freezing at night, then thawing into mire during the day,

We were less than a week's journey from Polycittara, and wondering when the Kallian Army would come out to fight.

I was riding ahead, with the scouts, when we came on the great forest of Kallio. It covered the entire end of the plateau, and swept out like the wings of an enormous bat. We must pass through the center of the crescent, where the land had been cleared and planted, to follow the roads that led down to the Kallian capital.

Waiting in that crescent was Chardin Sher's army.

TWENTY-SEVEN

DEATH IN
THE FOREST

This battle would be Chardin Sher's triumph. He—or whoever his top general was—had an excellent eye for terrain. His forces held the inner part of the crescent, with what appeared to be impenetrable forest on either side to protect his flanks. He occupied higher ground, and the rising country between us offered little cover except for a few tree clumps, ditches, some farmlands, and the tiny village of Dabormida.

The Kallians had dug only hasty trenches for their lines. This didn't mean they'd just arrived at this battle site, nor that they were lazy, but almost certainly that they planned to wait for our attack, inflict as many casualties as possible, then fall back into the forest.

The map showed the woods were no more than three miles thick in the center, so they'd be able to pull back into clear ground on the far side and re-form. When our forces stumbled out of the dense trees in broken order, they'd counterattack and smash us.

So I read the enemy's plans, and Tenedos and other generals agreed.

"However," Tenedos said, a grim smile on his face, "this is where Chardin Sher is going to meet with another surprise.

"We will attack, but not in the manner they expect. Here is my plan."

He went to a table where a covered map lay. He pulled the cover away. "My thrust will be double-pronged," he said. "The first attack will break their careful arrangements and harry them until the second strikes at their throat." The officers considered his plan for long moments, and I heard murmurs of dismay. Tenedos noted them. "Are you generals saying it cannot be done?"

He looked at me first. I considered, then said, "No, sir. I think it can, at least my cavalry will be able to pull it off, assuming we've got enough hours to move, the forest isn't completely impossible and that you'll provide a feint of some sort."

"Good," Tenedos said. "What about the dragoons? General Taitu?"

"Impossible," their commander, an old regular, snapped. "Men'll lose sight of their goals, stumble about, make too much noise, and the Kallians'll have us for breakfast."

"I can provide an infallible guide," Tenedos said.

"I guess you're talking about magic, which never holds firm on the battlefield. Still impossible, in spite of what my young colleague dreams. Your plan's too exotic, anyways. It's one of those quick-fix ideas, and we'll lose a third of the army trying it."

"General, thank you for your opinion," Tenedos said, his voice suddenly hard. "Now, will you carry out my orders?"

There was a long silence, then the grizzled veteran shook his head. "No, sir, I will not. I cannot. Your scheme's doomed, and I'll not hazard my dragoons on such a wild plan."

There could be but one response.

"I am grateful for your honesty, General Taitu," Tenedos said. "You are relieved. I want you to turn over your command within the hour to the successor I'll name." He turned to the rest of us. "This was unexpected, so I must ask all of you to step outside for a moment. General á Cimabue, will you remain?"

I did. Tenedos's iron reserve broke as the tent flap closed behind the last commander.

"Bastard!" he swore. "What the hells do they think an army is for but to fight? I swear to Saionji I shall relieve every general in the army if he refuses to fight when and how I tell him, promote privates, and lead them into battle myself!"

I maintained silence. Tenedos forced calm.

"Very well, Damastes. Who takes over the dragoons? I would have given them to Linerges, but I have a sufficiently difficult task already chosen for him. If he survives the day, he'll get his general's sash."

I had my answer ready. "Petre, sir."

"I should have known. He'll have no trouble going from cavalry to mounted infantry? Very well then. I assume you have a replacement to command your pet Lancers?"

"I do, sir. His name's Bikaner."

Tenedos frowned, then remembered. "Yes. The sergeant who was with us in Kait. Good. It does the army good to see a common soldier brought to high rank. Consider it done. Call the others back, if you would." I started to obey. "No," Tenedos said. "Wait a moment. Two things I'd planned to tell you, and both are for your ears only.

"First, I've sent inquiring spells out, and discovered the name of Chardin Sher's master magician. He's a fellow named Mikael Yanthlus, whose name translates as Mikael of the Spirits. He was once a Maisirian, interestingly enough. I recollect the other mercenary, Wollo I think it was, who was in Achim Fergana's employ. Odd. One day we might find it worthwhile to look into Maisir's affairs, to see why their natives seem bent on traveling abroad and stirring up trouble. But I veer.

"So, now I know this worthy one's name, I have a bit of power over him. That is one thing. The second is that there shall be a battle spell cast, a large one, before we fight, which I must not describe to anyone. But don't be surprised when it begins, although I don't think, if our strategy works, you or your horsemen will be within hearing or sight of it. But if it succeeds, it shall make things most interesting for the Kallians.

"Now, if you'll tell Captain Othman to send for Domina

Petre and tell him he's now a general, and then summon the others back, we can continue."

There were no other objections to Seer-General Tenedos's battle plan, which wasn't surprising. Relieving an officer is generally the end of his career. In fact, most of the officers seemed impressed by Tenedos's firmness. Men are no different from horses in some regards, and can sense an unsteady hand on the reins.

The attack was set for five days hence. I wondered why Tenedos hadn't ordered the usual immediate attack, but assumed his spell would take some time to prepare, or else the stars or moon wouldn't be right until then.

Not that our army sat idle. Yonge's division of skirmishers was sent into the front lines, with orders to prepare for a series of probing actions. He would be reinforced with Linerges's regiment, which had been rebuilt with replacements to about three-quarters of its strength. Four other regiments were placed under Linerges's command as well, and these would form a new division if the battle was successful.

Finally, three regiments of heavy cavalry were detached from my command to be directly under Tenedos's orders. I wasn't upset—it would have been difficult for them to keep up with the rest of my men when the attack began. Besides, all three of them were very staid, very traditional units, unlike the Twentieth Heavy Cavalry of the frontier, more resembling the ceremonial Second Heavy Cavalry that had been wiped out during the riots. I'd frequently had to reprimand their dominas for dragging their feet and being unwilling to accept the new standards. In fact, I rather hoped all three officers, and a good number of their staff, might suffer nicely incapacitating wounds, so I could rebuild the regiments as I wished. Four days later, I was to be ashamed of that wish.

Three days before the attack, all mounted troops except the heavy cavalry and one regiment to secure each flank were pulled back behind the lines. It was hoped that Chardin Sher's sorcerers and spies would see this, and figure we were once more being held in reserve until the front was broken.

Two days before the planned assault, the men of the dragoons were assembled before Tenedos's sorcerers. Curious, I rode over to watch what was going on.

All officers, all warrants, and every fifth man were lined up, and one by one brought before two wizards. One magician held a Kallian sword in one hand, a shield in the other. He touched the soldier on the head with the flat of the blade, on the heart with the shield. The second stood in a triangle formed by tall braziers that sent red smoke curling into the sky, red being Chardin Sher's chosen color. That mage chanted:

"This is your compass
This is your lodestone.
You will be drawn
You will be led.
Follow this sign
You will know the path.
Your feet will feel
Your sword will lead.
You will obey
You cannot turn."

When they were finished, a wizard explained what the spell gave them. If they became lost in the forest, all they had to do was think of Kallians, and they would be drawn in the right direction.

"And when you come on them," the wizard shouted, "you won't need my magic to tell you what to do, will you, lads?"

The men roared, a hungry roar like a lion about to be unloosed. I noted the wizard's name—Gojjam—as being a worthy leader, since I doubt Tenedos had told his magicians to be rabble-rousers as well.

The day before the battle the fighting began, and Tenedos cast a weather spell. The skies closed, and hail whipped down, becoming rain, then snow, then hail once more.

Yonge's skirmishers went forward in various-sized units, and launched probing attacks on the Kallian lines. Of course the Kallians counterattacked, and drove the skirmishers back. Each time, a few men died. An hour later, they'd hit again, in another sector, and again the Kallians would be forced to drive them back. Once an entire Kallian regiment came from the forest edge into the open, and before it could retreat was hit by a combined attack from a column of heavy cavalry and a company of Linerges's infantry. They were pushed back, and, after a pause, another raid was mounted by Yonge's men.

I thought I understood Tenedos's tactics—to drive the Kallians to distraction with these small, stinging attacks, so they'd be paying little attention to other areas of the front—but I was wrong. That was the least part of what Tenedos was doing, although it would be years before I divined the real purpose.

Late that afternoon, my cavalry and Petre's dragoons moved out, some miles west of the Kallian position. We rode to the edge of the woods, dismounted, and, each man leading his horse or mule, began thrashing our way through the forest.

It was terrible going, branches whipping across our faces, across the animals' faces, men stumbling and going down in unseen cracks in the forest floor, horses shrilling and mules braying in anger and confusion, their owners clamping a hand over their muzzles, hoping the clamor of the distant skirmishing would mask our noise. Lance Karjan, just to my rear, proved surprisingly vocal as we pushed on, muttering a steady stream of obscenities, some of which I'd never heard.

It was dark in those trees, dank and freezing. But there was more than the cold to fear—it was as if this forest had never been traversed by man, and was the abode of old gods, gods who were nameless, who paid no fealty to Jacini, but to eldritch deities, demons perhaps, and we all felt chill menace about us.

There were almost 10,000 cavalrymen moving through this forest, with 5,000 dragoons to our rear. We moved in ten columns, each column sure his shit-brained leaders had picked the absolute roughest route.

Eventually the twilight darkened, and the day ended. We

fed our horses from the feedbags tied to our saddles. In these long columns there weren't any officers, any warrant; no one could traverse the line to see how his men were doing. I was just a horseman, no longer a general.

There was only one blessing: One of Tenedos's wizards had developed a spell to keep liquids hot, and so each man had a clay container filled with soup to warm him. That is, if he hadn't smashed it against a tree, as I had mine. Karjan offered me some of his, but I refused, and crouched against a tree, wrapped in my soaked blanket, and gnawed at some dried beef, allowing myself a bit of self-pity in the darkness, worrying about Marán, worrying about myself, worrying about the morrow and how I would do, if we ever broke out of this demon-haunted jungle. It was too cold and wet to sleep, and fairly soon it began raining once more.

But self-pity is a shallow vessel, at least for me, and I found myself grinning at my own misery. We were well and truly lost in this forest that went on forever, and we'd never be seen, but be doomed to wander until time ran out and the Wheel stopped, and Irisu wondered where several thousand of his subjects had gotten off to and looked for us.

Sometime in the night, it froze, and I guess I slept, because I opened my eyes to grayness and long knives of ice hanging from the tree branches around me.

Lucan was looking at me, wondering why I'd chosen to put him through this torture. I fed him once more, and gave him a treat of some brandy-soaked sugar I had in a twist of oiled paper, and we were ready to move on. Now the cavalry marched without the dragoons. They turned to the east, toward the Kallian forces, and, using the spell given them, started for the enemy flanks.

About an hour later, the bedlam of destruction smashed into my ears from the east, and I knew the main battle had begun.

An hour after that, the forest ended, and we were in open brushland once more. A few miles away, the plateau ended, and roads led down toward the Kallian capital. We formed our battle line and sat our horses, waiting.

Yonge's skirmishers had harried the Kallian lines all night, never giving them any rest. Now all would depend on whether the dragoons had been able to reach their position in time.

At first light, a regiment of infantry and another of heavy cavalry had made a frontal assault on the lines. It was suicidal, and the two units were decimated. As the Kallians moved out of their positions, to mop up, the dragoons attacked through the forest from the western flank, smashing out of nowhere.

Mikael Yanthlus and Chardin Sher's other sorcerers had sensed nothing, and so the astonished Kallians were sent reeling, rolling up their own lines as our Numantians drove against them. They tried to hold, but it was no use, and they fell back through the forest. But it wasn't the orderly withdrawal as planned, but a staggering retreat.

The dragoons returned for their horses, then followed the Kallians, so there was a bit more than a half-mile gap between the two armies. This was exactly what Tenedos wanted, he told me later, for he wasn't sure how discriminatory his grand spell would be.

I still shudder to think what it would have been like to be a Kallian, shaken by the dragoon assault from nowhere, trying to save himself, trying not to give in to his fear, when the forest itself attacked him.

Branches reached down, striking like clubs or whips, smashing men to the ground. Roots rose from the soil and tripped men, and then curled around them, strangling them, crushing their bones.

Some Kallians went mad—and perhaps they were the lucky ones—seeing their native earth rise against them. Trees tumbled, with never a warning crack, and fell on command groups. Brush pulled at men, holding them back, keeping them from fleeing, keeping them immobile, as their eyes shot up, hearing the snap of a widowmaker and seeing it tumble down.

Crows rose screaming as their familiar perches shook, and the creatures of the forest darted out of their winter burrows in panic as the forest moved about them, far more than the worst disturbance a storm could bring.

This was the first of the two Great Spells Tenedos launched in the Kallian War. It was impossible. No one could cast it, had ever heard of it being cast before, I learned. But it had been created, created by one man. Men whispered he'd sold himself to demons, but then shook their heads. No. Even that price wouldn't give that much power. No one knew how he could do it, but he had, and so the fear and respect his name carried grew.

I knew not of what was going on, but I did feel a queasiness, a disturbance, but laid it to fatigue or perhaps a chill I'd gotten in the forest. My attention was locked on the snow-touched treeline, and then men came out of the woods, shouting, thousands of them, only a few in any sort of formation. They kept turning to look back into the forest, expecting demons to pursue them, but instead, from their right flank, came the blast of bugles, and 10,000 cavalry men charged.

I've said the Kallians were brave men, and so they were. Commanders bellowed orders, and some men and units had the guts to form squares to repel our charge. We ignored them and smashed into the mass of the Kallian Army.

Our charge lost momentum, and now we were a sword-swinging body of horsemen, trying to beat our way through the rabble. A man lunged with a pike, and I brushed it aside with the flat of my blade and sliced his arm away. Another man aimed his bow, but Karjan was behind him, and he, too, went down. Then something came at me, and I ducked aside, barely recognizing it as a regimental standard on a spear. Lucan reared in fear, sending me falling back across his haunches to the ground.

I managed to tuck and fell across a body, rolling to my feet, sword still in hand. Three Kallians shouted glee, seeing a dismounted officer, and pushed toward me. I moved to the side, so they were in each others' way, parried the first man's thrust, cut his face open, and he lurched back, and I lunged under his arm, spitting the second. The third had his blade back for a slash, but I kicked him in the stomach, then drove my knee into his face as he bent double.

Karjan was beside me, hewing down at the Kallians, his

horse as battle mad as he, lashing out with its hooves. I pulled myself up behind him, and we shoved our way out of the throng, seeing a welcome phalanx of Numantian horsemen ride toward us. Then I was safe, and we were on clear ground, and I shouted to turn, and attack once more.

The dragoons came out of the forest and attacked as we came back on the Kallians from the rear, between them and the safety of their capital. They hit the few resolute units on the field, standing off from their squares and using archers to break them and send their soldiers fleeing like the others, and the killing went on.

Then there was nothing but white flags and shouts for mercy, quarter, surrender,

Less than 25,000 Kallian escaped from the field that day. But among them were Chardin Sher and his master wizard, so the war was not over.

But we'd met the enemy on the field of their own choosing, fought them with our new tactics, and defeated them handily. We'd taken heavy casualties, but only among the heavy cavalry, Linerges's infantry, and the skirmishers. The blood-price was acceptable.

Now the way was open to Polycittara.

We reformed on the far side of that dread forest and made ready to fight on.

The next morning, a letter finally reached me:

> *My dearest husband*
> *I cannot say how ashamed I am of myself for not writing you. I cannot offer any excuses, except that the death of our child struck harder than I thought, and it was as if I was dead myself, wandering about feeling like my heart had become stone, unable to talk, let alone write.*
> *I am weeping now, hoping you might forgive me, for I had no right to feel such selfishness while you, the one who means more to me than life itself, are just as alone, and in desperate danger.*

*I will always be indebted to our dearest friend Amiel,
who dragged me out of my morass of despair, and told me
what a fool I was being. She has given me the greatest
comfort since our son died, and I hope you will love her
as I do for it.*

*Now I realize, we must move on. We have a life
together, and there are other days, and other times. I still
want a child, want several children, but now I want you,
just you. I want to feel your cock hard inside me, feel you
scatter your seed in me. I want the taste of you, warm and
salty in my mouth.*

*Please try to understand me, Damastes, as I am trying
to understand myself. I know I'm very young, and very
foolish, but I am still learning how to love. Please still
love me. I am yours for always, as you know.*

Marán

I'd no more than sealed my response to this, feeling the
leaden weight I'd carried for too long fall away, and hoping the
war was almost over, when my tent flap was torn open and
Yonge stumbled in.

"Drink with me, Numantian," he ordered, and plunked a
nearly empty bottle of brandy down on my table.

I uncorked the bottle, and touched it to my lips, seeing that,
as drunk as he was, he'd barely notice what I did. I was right.
He grabbed the bottle, drained it, and pulled another from a
pocket inside his cloak.

"So, what do you think of our famous victory?" he slurred,
his voice hard, angry.

"I'm sorry to hear of your losses," I said.

"Sorry? Yes, Numantian, I guess you are."

"Yonge," I said, "why are you angry with me? I had nothing to do with what happened."

Yonge glowered at me, then slowly nodded.

"No," he agreed. "No, you didn't. Guess I'm angry at
everybody, and nobody. Nobody but one.

"You know how many men got killed, whittled away, a

man here, a man there, a squad here, a company there? Damn near half my skirmishers.

"They aren't like other soldiers, you know. Takes time to train a man to *not* want to go blazing out with a sword, but take the measure as he's taught, and tell it to others, and let them fight.

"Prob'ly takes longer than to build a cavalryman."

He drank.

"Wonder why that bastard did it to me."

"Tenedos?"

"He's the only bastard I can think of. Told me what to do, and I did it. Did it without arguin', knowing what'd happen.

"Damn the bastard."

"What would you have done?" I said, trying to be diplomatic. Yonge, in a mood like this, was looking for a fight, and I knew the Men of the Hills seldom used fists to settle their differences. Even drunk, I had no confidence I could defeat his knife. "He said he was using you as a feint, to cover the dragoons."

"You believe that?"

"I do."

Yonge stared at me very hard.

"You remember, a long time ago, I said I wanted to study honor from you?"

"I do. But I think you're now a better one for me to study," I said.

"Shit on that. I still think you tell the truth. You don't think there was any better way to start the battle? You don't think my men were thrown away?"

"Why would Tenedos want that?" I said. "He knows how valuable the skirmishers are. Hells, man, he created the force."

"He did," Yonge grudged. "I don't know why we was sacrificed. But I feel we were."

"Why?"

"I don't know." Yonge heaved a deep sigh. "Hells. Maybe I'm just drunk, and mournin'. Maybe that's all." He lifted the bottle, and, to my amazement, finished it.

"Guess I'm not thinkin' straight," he said, and stood. "Sorry to bother you. You're a man of honor, like I said. An' I trust you."

His eyes slid closed, and he toppled. I caught him before he hit the ground, and eased him down. I called for Karjan, and we made a rough bed for the general with my cloak and a pillow. He muttered something about honor and blood, then began snoring. I little wanted to be inside his head in the morrow.

I tried to go to sleep, but the absurd thought stayed with me: Why *had* Tenedos chosen such a sacrificial way to begin the engagement? It was another answer I wouldn't have for years.

Now Tenedos's magic held Chardin Sher firm in its vision, and because of that many lives were saved, both Kallian and Numantian. If he had not been able to track him through sorcery, we might have decided Chardin Sher would retreat to the capital, gone after him, and mired ourselves in street butchery. Probably the Kallian assumed we would do just that, and give him some time to regroup, for he fled past Polycittara, and took refuge beyond.

The Numantian Army ignored the bait of Polycittara and marched after him. Two weeks after Dabormida we came on his final refuge.

It was a huge brown stone fortress, walls many yards thick, that occupied the entire top of a solitary peak that commanded the center of a fertile valley. It was the ultimate refuge, and I think all of us thought the same thing:

We would all die here, under these grim battlements, before we would destroy Chardin Sher.

TWENTY-EIGHT

THE DEMON
FROM BELOW

The nameless fortress had an evil reputation. It had been built centuries before by a meditative order, its battlements intended to give shelter to the priests and simples of the surrounding country men when raiders threatened. But as the centuries passed the order became fascinated with the dark arts, and it was said they were more feared than any brigands. All manner of evil was attributed to these priests, including human sacrifice to demons.

One storm-tossed night, the story went, nearby peasants heard screams from the fortress, screams far louder than any human throat should be able to produce. A few of the bravest chanced peering into the night, and saw all of the citadel's lights flash bright and then go out as if they were a single candle snuffed by a giant hand.

The next day, no one came out of the citadel, and that night it remained dark. So it went for a week until one courageous young man chanced climbing the ramps to the entrance, and found its iron gates blasted open, as if a giant hand had ripped them away.

He entered, and found no sign of any of the priests. Nor was there any indication of what had happened, neither bloodstain nor corpse to be found.

The stronghold sat vacant for almost a century, then an out-law baron took and held it, and once more the valley paid a bit-ter price for "protection." Three generations of this family held the fortress, each lord more baneful than the last.

Finally, Chardin Sher's father mounted an expedition against the current baron and, by deceit, gained entrance. The baron was taken, tried for his crimes, and quartered below the citadel. His women and children were reduced to commoners and sold as slaves. Perhaps the fortress should have been left empty, or even razed to the bare rocks. But it was not. Chardin Sher's father and then his son made it their last refuge, adding to its defenses.

Now it was surrounded by the Numantian Army. There were three choices: to reduce it by sorcery; to attempt to storm it; or starve out Chardin Sher, his magicians, and his retainers.

Tenedos tried magic first, and his assembled magi used the natural force of the season to send storm after storm against the towers. The magicians within, led by Mikael Yanthlus, not only used defensive spells to lessen the effect, but sent their own conjurations against the soldiers below.

The normal spells of apprehension, fear, and such were accompanied with incantations intended to bring sicknesses and plagues on us, fortunately countered by Tenedos's magi-cians before more than a handful of victims were stricken.

The storm spells were cast again and again, and then it seemed they took on a life of their own. It was awesome to watch the dark bulk of the citadel against the night as winds screamed against it and lightning slashed from the skies, thun-der rocking the valley.

It was awesome—and harder on us in some ways than on those inside, for at least they had shelter. We had nothing but canvas, and the winds laughed at our tents and ripped them to shreds. The fields were sodden muck, and the farmers fled the wrath of the Numantians.

One night was marked by bolt after bolt, and it seemed cer-tain the fortress would be, must be, broken and shattered to the smallest stone as it stood against the night, its bulk sheathed with white light. But when the dawn mist blew away it still stood, seemingly untouched. Then someone noticed a narrow crack down one side. We tried to feel hopeful, but if that was the best Tenedos's wizardry could produce it would be a very long siege.

Two days later, Tenedos summoned me. He was not living under canvas, but had taken over a guildhall in the nearest town. I found him there, and was about to jest about how comfortable our leaders chose to live, but clamped my mouth shut, seeing how drawn and gray his features were. He looked far worse than any horseman or private, and I realized this war of spells was as exhausting on him as hand-to-hand fighting would be for me.

I asked his health, and he said he was well, and then inquired as to mine, as to how Marán was doing, was she managing all right, and so forth. He took me into his own chamber, and told me to sit down while he made tea.

He brewed a fragrant, warm concoction, and let it steep. I drew in the smell, and felt the long chill in my bones from living rough for so long dissipate a little. He poured me a cup, and offered a tin of sweets that must have just been sent him by Rasenna.

I took one, just as a small alarm bell tinkled in my mind. I attempted to turn it into a joke, saying that, no doubt, with all this buildup I was about to be asked to do something completely insane, such as storm the fortress single-handed.

"Just so, Damastes," Tenedos said, and there was not an ounce of humor on his face or in his voice.

"Sir?"

"May I sit down?" This was unusual, my commander hardly needing my permission for anything. I nodded. He poured himself some of the tea, then let it sit and grow cold, ignored, while he considered his words.

"Damastes, we must destroy Chardin Sher. There can be no truce, no surrender except unconditional, or he'll try to usurp our rulers again."

"Of course."

"I do not know if the army can stand up to a long siege, quite frankly. We have no training, nor, with our new policies, the supply train that would allow us to keep Chardin Sher's fortress invested. Nor do we have the engines for such a battle, and it would be several months to build or have them built and transported to the faraway area.

"I know it is my army, and they obey me absolutely, but I fear if we just sit here the Rule of Ten will find a backbone somewhere, and begin meddling once more."

"We can hardly take that bastion by storm," I pointed out.

"No," Tenedos agreed. "Nor, although you did not hear it from me, will magic work. I have more power than Mikael Yanthlus, and with my magicians far greater strengths than he and his staff can ever produce. The problem is all he need do is defend, which takes less energy than to attack. The best my mightiest incantations could produce, and this was calling in debts owed creatures of other worlds, was that storm that managed to chip the citadel's paint.

"Pfah! I like this but little."

"So somehow I am going to be the solution to everyone's problems," I said.

"I was serious, Damastes. Let me explain. There is something dark, something evil, about that fortress, as you know if you've heard anything of its history. I don't know what it is exactly, but I have managed to contact this thing, this power, and woo it to do my bidding. You may not ask what its price is, but it is terrible, but not to be paid for some time to come, fortunately.

"But this thing, force, demon, whatever it is, desired something else before it agreed to the bargain.

"If it is to act as I wish against Chardin Sher, I must be willing to prove my sincerity, or maybe commitment is a better word." Tenedos sat silently for a moment, then went on. "A certain service must be performed by someone I love, a service that could mean that person's life, or the force will not grant my wish."

"So I'm to be a hostage?"

"More. You must enter the fortress and, on the floor of its innermost courtyard, draw a symbol and pour a potion out. Then the bargain is sealed."

"I assume I die in the process?"

"Not necessarily," Tenedos said, but he looked very unsure. "If you manage to make entrance, do what you're required, you could well have time enough to escape if you're not discovered."

"And what are the chances of *that*," I said, feeling my guts cold within me. "As a matter of fact, how do I know that this demon or whatever it is will keep its bargain?"

"I'll be truthful. There is a chance of betrayal, but a very slight one. As for you being able to escape, I'll give you all the sorcerous guards I can provide."

"How am I to enter the citadel? Can you change me into a bird? Or, considering the nature of that place, a bat might be more appropriate."

"Of course not." He took me by the arm, and led me to a window and opened its shutter. The winter wind howled around us, but neither of us paid mind, as we stared up at the brooding mass not many miles distant. As Tenedos pointed, I'd already guessed his idea. It was not utterly impossible, just highly so.

Tenedos closed the shutters.

"I shall not press you for an answer, Damastes, my friend, and you now know how highly I prize that title, for you are the only one who is acceptable to my partner-to-be. You don't even have to tell me no. If I don't hear from you within a day or so, well, then, we'll find another way to winkle Chardin Sher out."

I only half-heard him. I opened the shutters, and looked up once more at the fortress. I was reminded what I'd been taught from when I was a child, that a leader's duty is to lead from the front, and then I remembered a proverb I'd heard somewhere, that duty is hard as iron, but death is light as a feather.

Easy words, hard meaning. My mind turned to Marán, and I thought wistfully of her. I desperately wanted to say no to this absurd idea, but could not. Nor could I agree to it. I wondered if our child had been born whole if I'd cling to life so desperately, something a soldier must not do.

I banged the shutters to, and turned to the seer.

"You needn't wait for a reply. I'll go."

A slow smile moved across his face.

"Do you know, Damastes, I never doubted that you would say yes? That's why it took me two full days to find the courage to ask you."

The way in was, of course, up that lightning-cut crack in the walls. Once atop the walls, all that would be necessary was to evade the sentries on the battlements, make my way down the wall, across unknown obstacles, perform Tenedos's task, and then somehow be able to escape with my head more or less attached to where it was most comfortable.

On the way I also planned to end war, disease, and famine with my free hand.

I decided I'd need three other fools to accompany me.

The first was Lance Karjan. I told him what the chances were, and he shrugged. "Sir, how many times since we met have we been dead an' gone already? I'm gettin' used t' the idea by now. 'Sides, if we get away wi' it, which we ain't gonna, it'll be a tale that'll buy me drink for the rest of my life."

"If you're going," I said, "you'll have to go as a lance-major. Bigger death benefits."

Karjan growled, then grinned.

"You'll take any 'vantage, won't you, sir?"

"I will."

He saluted.

One.

I couldn't simply tell my dominas I needed two more men, because I knew I'd be swamped with volunteers. While I considered how to do it, Karjan returned. Behind him was the bulk of Svalbard, that great silent brawler who I now was pleased to see wore the slashes of a lance-major.

"He's goin', too," Karjan told me.

"Lance Karjan told you what I'm going to attempt?"

"He did. Sir."

"You're aware there are *no* chances of surviving?"

"Don't believe that. Sir."

We stared at each other in silence. I was the first to break, knowing how useless it would be to say more.

"Very well. Leave your troop and move up here to my headquarters."

"Thank you. Sir." And the man was gone.

Two.

The third was Domina Bikaner, who insisted he by the gods had the right to go, being who he was and how long we'd soldiered together. I told him absolutely no. The Lancers needed him. He began to argue, and I had to order him to shut up and get out. I was considering who I should ask to finish the suicide team when General Yonge entered my tent without bothering to knock.

"I understand, my friend, that you are planning something completely foolish."

"That's about the best way to put it. How did you hear about it?"

"Never ask that of a man who was his village's best chicken thief before he could walk more than five paces without falling. I want to know why you did not call on me?"

"Because you are a gods-damned general."

Yonge spat on my tent floor, and lifted off his sash. His knife was suddenly in his hand, and the sash was cut in two pieces. He cast it down and ground his heel across it.

"Now I am just Yonge of the Hills."

I swore at him, and he swore back at me. I told him he was being insolent, and he told me I had best watch my tongue, for a Kaiti would not allow anyone, not even a general, to talk like that. Especially if he was Numantian.

"You know I could call for the provosts, or tell Tenedos, and you'd be held in irons until I returned?"

"Do you think I would still be here by the time they

arrived? Listen, you ox of a Cimabuan. I came to study honor, did I not?"

"Honor is not foolishness, dammit!"

"What idiot said that?"

My grin took me by surprise.

"As for that wizard, pah!" Yonge went on. "Do you think I obey him because I'm afraid? I do what I want when I want. For a while it amused me to lead soldiers, to try to teach poor lumbering farm boys how to move as if they were men of the crags. Now it amuses me to do something else.

"Now I plan to climb that fortress to see what is inside. Would you care to accompany me, Cimabuan?"

"How do you know I'm planning to climb it?"

"Because not even you are foolish enough to try tunneling."

Tenedos would be livid, but:

Three.

Two generals and two lance-majors stood in sheeting rain at the foot of the nearly vertical wall of Chardin Sher's last stronghold. Ten feet above us, the crack lightning had smashed into the fortress began.

The storm had raged, on and off, since noon of that day, alternating with periods of calm. It was partially regulated by thirty of Tenedos's magicians, working from a post just behind our front lines. In my pack I carried a small, dark lantern, which I could use to signal the sages. One flash meant lift the storm, two meant bring it down. Three flashes would be sent when—or if—we reached the top of the wall. "I doubt if this will work exactly," Tenedos had said. "But it's worth the effort." Also in the pack were gloves, sock-like covers to muffle my nailed boots if we succeeded in climbing to the ramparts, a flask of tea, three sealed oilskin pouches of spiced chicken, plus some jerked beef and hard candies to suck. The most important item was a quart flask full of the potion that would set off the spell. Beside it was a fat stick of reddish chalk-looking material. I'd spent four hours drawing and redrawing the figure I was to create inside the courtyard, with

Tenedos hovering over me and correcting my mistakes, although both the figure and the symbols that were to accompany it made no sense to me. I asked Tenedos if the rain wouldn't wash the chalk off the stones, and he told me it had a spell cast to prevent that from happening.

I also had a belt pouch with a small hammer and soft iron spikes to hammer into cracks in the wall for climbing aids. Over my shoulder was a fat coil of rope.

I wore dark clothing, fingerless gloves, and a stocking cap. The other three were dressed the same, and had similar gear in their packs.

Each of us carried but three weapons: a dagger and two four-inch pigs of lead. I carried the dagger Yonge had given me for a wedding present, after I'd gotten Tenedos to put a darkening spell on its silver.

We looked up and up, and our way seemed endless. But it was growing no shorter by the looking, and so Svalbard bent, Yonge stepped into his cupped hands, and the big man cast Yonge upward. He caught the edge of the crack, and shinnied up a few feet. Yonge pushed an iron peg in, then dropped a rope for the rest of us to use to start the climb.

Then it began. Yonge in the lead, I behind him, then Karjan and Svalbard, all roped together. We used our hands and the sides of our feet, forced into the crack to move up a step, then another, then another. It was monotonous, wet, and muscle tearing. I thought of signaling for the magicians to try to lighten the storm, but I'd rather be wet than heard.

We went on and on, ever more slowly. Once Yonge slipped, his hands scrabbling on the slippery stone, and his boots crashed down on my shoulders, almost knocking me loose. Then he had a grip, and we were climbing once more.

The way became easier as we went higher, and the crack widened. I'd hoped that we'd be able to move completely inside it, but we weren't lucky, because the wall had been built in layers, and the lightning had only broken the outermost. It was still almost three feet deep, and so we were somewhat sheltered from the weather.

I was reaching for a hold when a bird squawked, and bolted from its nest into my face. I jerked back, and came off, falling the few feet to the end of my rope. Fortunately Yonge had heard the bird's alarm, and had time to brace himself. I swung back and forth like a pendulum, feeling the rope throttle the life from me, then Karjan pulled me in to safety. I took a moment to let my heart reenter my breast, and we climbed on.

I'd hoped the night would be endless, but it wasn't, and we were still climbing when I realized I could see Yonge's boots above me. I cursed, having feared this would happen, and that day would break and we would still be on the wall.

There was nothing to do but move as far inside the crack as we could and wait. I was afraid to keep going, for fear of being heard or, more likely, seen by anyone looking over the parapet.

The magicians saw our plight, and attempted to make it easier by calling up spells and stopping the storm. I clawed out the lantern, blew its wick to life and over and over again, blinked twice . . . twice . . . twice. Better to be wet and miserable than dry and dead. I guess they saw my feeble signal, for the rain started again.

That ended another worry—when it had been clear I saw white dots far across the fields staring up, and knew we'd been seen by our fellow soldiers. I cursed, but there was nothing that could have been done. Warn the soldiers not to look at the wall and assume no Kallian would hear the warning, sorcerously or otherwise? Make the officers order their officers not to look at the fortress? I just hoped not many of the fools would point and draw Mikael Yanthlus's attention.

We drank our tea, chewed our rations, shivered, and stretched our muscles whenever we could. Karjan muttered something about why did following me always mean going straight up. I refrained from reminding him about his volunteering. Yonge grinned and whispered that this crevice was like a vacation home to him; sometime Karjan would have to take leave to Yonge's mountains and see what real climbing was like. That was the best—and only—jest of that rainsoaked day.

Eventually the light died, and we crept out, onto the face of the wall, our bodies creaking at being forced once more into exertion, and climbed on. The crack widened, and we climbed with our backs against one wall and used our feet to "walk" us up on the other. It was excruciatingly painful, tearing at the muscles of my thighs, but I was afraid the crack would open up farther, and then we'd have to use our pegs and ropes.

But it did not. I was moving numbly, one foot, then the other, then push the back up and I banged my head against Yonge's boots. I was about to mutter an oath and wonder why he'd stopped climbing, then I realized:

We'd reached the top of the wall.

I unroped, slipped inside of him, and scrabbled up. I listened, but heard no sound of a sentry. I reached into my pack, took out the dark lantern, and sent three flashes into the night.

I reached up, felt the welcome smoothness of worked stone, and lifted myself out of the crack and through a crenel and was on my hands and knees on a rampart of Chardin Sher's fortress. I looked for sentries, and thought I saw movement, but it was distant on a far wall. Chardin Sher wasn't a fool and leaving his fortress unguarded—there was little point in having the ramparts lined with soldiery, for any attack would be heard long before it reached this point, and with the storm blowing hard all that would be accomplished was to wear out good men. It took some care to spot the few guards since the ramparts were lined with obscene statues of demons, leering defiance at the world beyond.

I hissed, and my three men came up. I guessed the hour close to midnight. There were no maps of the inside of the fortress, and Tenedos had been afraid of alerting Chardin Sher's magicians if he tried to peep inside.

I saw our goal, though, and the path seemed fairly straightforward. Impossible, but straightforward, and I knew there was no impossibility for the four loons who'd managed to reach as far as we had. I whispered a question, and found that all three of my men could swim, so my scheme had possibilities.

The stronghold had been built with a concentric series of walls, so if one line of defense fell, the garrison could fall back to another, and then another.

It looked to me as if we could reach our objective with only one more wall to climb, and so we crept along the top of the rampart to the point I'd indicated. We knotted a rope at three-foot intervals, tied it off to one of the statues, and went down the rope, walking backward, with the rope coming down over one shoulder, then up between our legs and across one thigh.

The small problem we faced at the bottom was that this section of the fortress was the defenders' reservoir. We lowered ourselves into the water, far over our heads, and began swimming. It was harder than I'd imagined to swim with the weight of the pack and our clothes, but at least the other three had the buoyancy of their rope coils. We left mine dangling in the shadows. It would not only provide a fast retreat, but if it was discovered we'd hear the hue and cry and hopefully have time to devise another exit. The pouring rain mottled the water's surface, so we were impossible to see from the walls around us.

The far side of the reservoir was slimy, sloping stone, halfway toward vertical, intended as a runoff so rain could refill the pool. We used our iron pegs, one in each hand, digging them between the stones, and moved steadily upward, four crabs hunting dinner along the shoreline. It should have been fairly easy, but we were tired from the day and two nights on the wall, and our muscles sorely stretched.

But we reached the top, and once more peered through crenellations to look for guards. The storm had lightened, unfortunately, and I could see dimly. This inner keep was better guarded than before, with one sentry on each of the ramparts visible. Very well. I'd hoped to be able to make this sortie without leaving a body to be discovered, but that would be impossible. We flattened close to the rampart, and waited.

The sentry paced toward us, huddled in his cloak, paying little attention to anything except his own misery. Blackness reared out of blackness, and he had not even a moment to cry out as an arm swept around his chest, Svalbard's other great paw cupped his chin, and snapped his head sideways. His neck broke with an audible crack, and Svalbard let the body slip to the rampart, then stared down, his expression calm, as if nothing had happened.

I pulled the sentry's helmet off and gave it to Karjan. Even in this darkness I could see his scowl, but he was the most logical choice. We pulled the body's cloak off, gave it to Karjan, then slid the corpse over the parapet into the reservoir.

Karjan, with the Kallian's spear and cloak, the too-small helmet forced over the top of his head, would pose as the sentry—so no one would see bare walls and give the alarm—as well as being our rear guard.

We pulled the muffling covers over our boots, saw steps not far away, and went down them, zigging back and forth, until we reached ground level.

Our way led through long stone corridors, and I lost direction twice, and had to retrace my steps. I heard voices several times, and we went by doors with light shining under them, but encountered no one. The Kallians were either asleep or achamber in front of a blazing fire at this hour, and I blamed them not, feeling the darkness of the ancient building in my bones.

We went up steps and down a passageway. Ahead was a solid iron door, standing open, that led into the open.

I went through it, and the door slammed behind me with a clash of metal, and a bar dropped into place, sealing Yonge and Svalbard on the other side!

Elias Malebranche came out of the darkness.

"I *felt* you coming, Numantian," he hissed. "I have a touch of the Talent, and my master's sorcerer was kind enough to give me an amulet to help. I'd hoped to encounter you on the battlefield and slay you there, but you have come to me, instead. So we can settle our private business privately."

His hand touched his waist, and the knife came out.

"Third time lucky, Damastes."

I said nothing. Talk in battle is for buffoons and the overconfident. My own dagger was in my hand, and we circled each other. Malebranche was a far better knife-fighter than I, but I hoped his arrogance would help me. Not only had he spoken, but he had not given the alarm. He wanted the glory of killing me and ending our mission all to himself.

Players on a stage portray a knife fight as a series of lunges and thrusts for the vital areas. It's most dramatic, but also completely unrealistic. A real knife fight either ends on the first thrust, when your opponent is surprised and, hopefully, his weapon is still sheathed; or else is an unbelievably gory affair, with the two battlers slashing away, trying to wound or cripple the other before attempting the killer stroke.

Malebranche's knife flickered, and I wasn't able to pull back in time. Pain burned the back of my forearm, but fortunately the Kallian hadn't been able to sever the tendons of my hands, as he'd intended. He came in once more, and I kicked hard, my boot connecting with his lower leg, and he gasped, bent, and I cut him. I'd aimed for his neck but missed as he backrolled away, back to his feet.

"That is the end for you, Damastes. It is a pity you'll not live to witness the coronation of Chardin Sher as king of Numantia. Perhaps I'll take your widow to my bed, as recompense for the time you scarred me. Think of that, Damastes, as you go down into death."

He slid around, toward my weak side. As he did, his guard was open for a moment, and I thrust. But it was a deception, and his free hand snapped out, and sent my dagger spinning away, and his blade darted.

I tried to pull back, but stumbled on the slippery cobbles, and he cut deep into my inner thigh. I almost shouted in pain, but clenched my teeth, went down, rolling, reaching for my knife.

But it lay nearly five feet away from my scrabbling hand, and I heard Malebranche's boots come forward, and the next thing I'd feel would be his knife between my shoulder blades.

I rolled, hand still outstretched, and then, impossibly, my dagger whirled through the air and was in my hand, and I had a flash recollection of the spell Tenedos had put on it after the demon-snake attacked us.

Malebranche was striking at me, but I parried, blade clanging blade, then smashed both feet up and sent him floundering. I had my feet under me, and limped toward him.

He struck, and my blade seemed to hum in my grip, reaching out of its own volition, brushing his thrust aside, gashing open his chest. Now I saw fear on his face, and he moved back, and I closed, moving cautiously. Back and back we went, and a stone wall was not far behind him. He glanced once over his shoulder, knew he was trapped, and broke.

He hurled his blade at me, and it spun in the air, hitting me in the chest with the pommel, hurting, but not harming, and he turned and ran, darting around my guard, heading for another passageway. He'd shout alarm in seconds, and my hand was in my pouch, on one of the lead pigs, and I hurled it with all my strength.

It crashed into the back of his head, and I heard his skull crunch. He crumpled, and lay motionless. I hobbled to him, and kicked him over. His face stared up, horrible fear his last expression. I checked for a pulse, and found none.

The third time had, indeed, been the fortune.

I ran as fast as I was able back to the iron door and lifted the bar. The door came open and Svalbard stumbled into me. I saw no sign of Yonge.

"He went to find another way," the big man whispered. He saw Malebranche's body. "Are there any more?"

I shook my head, just as the hillman ran into sight. He saw the open door and the two of us, and there was no explanation needed at the moment. We ripped strips of cloth from my tunic for crude bandages for my wounded thigh and arm. I felt no pain nor stiffness, my body reveling in the death of my foe and the savage joy of battle. We dragged Malebranche's corpse into the shadows and went through that other corridor and found our goal.

The innermost keep of the castle was built most peculiarly, as a pentagon, and I remembered the tales of the priests and their dark magic and wondered if they'd held their ceremonies here. It was quite empty, which I well understood, feeling the chill and something else around me. I wondered for a moment how Chardin Sher and his men could stand the aura I felt, but put it aside. Perhaps they didn't sense it at all, but I did because I was an enemy of Kallio. But I had no time for speculation.

I took the flask with the potion and the drawing stick from my pack, and hurried to the center of the keep. I took a deep breath, calming myself, then carefully drew the figure as I'd been taught.

I finished within a few moments.

I opened up the flask, and upended it over the center of the symbol I'd made. I gagged; the potion smelled worse than anyone could imagine, the stink of burning corpses, the reek of fresh-spilled blood, the moldy odor of long-forgotten tombs filling my nostrils.

Then the flask was empty.

Tenedos had told me I must flee as quickly as I could once the spell had set. He said he would feel it begin to work, and begin his own casting from outside the walls, but we must be away from the fortress before the incantation took effect, or face the same doom he hoped to bring on Chardin Sher.

We hurried back through the corridors, making more sound than we had before. A door opened, a woman peered out, saw the three of us, and slammed and barred the door as we neared, yet I heard no outcry.

We retraced our steps, and I marveled I was able to remember them so precisely, and found the stairs leading up to the inner wall. Atop it, Karjan, the false sentry, still paced his rounds.

Gladly he doffed his helmet and cloak, cast the spear aside, and we tied a rope to one of the crenels and went down that sloping wall into the reservoir.

The icy water hit and burned at my wound, and I knew I'd have the grace of not feeling pain for only a short time longer.

The rope we'd left hung down into the water, and we pulled our way upward. I was very glad we'd taken the time to knot it at intervals before descending.

We untied it, ran to where the wall cracked, doubled a rope

around one of the crenels, and slid down it to the end, pulled one end of the rope until it fell down to us, then crawled into the crack.

We were about to climb down in a normal manner, but I heard a roar. At first I though the storm was building, but then realized the sound came from everywhere, from *inside* the wall as well as beyond. We had to take a great chance, and hammered three iron nails into the stone, looped a rope around them, and tugged. They held firm, and we used the rope to backwalk down as we had before, although the chance of a peg pulling free and dropping us to our deaths was very great. My leg throbbed agony, but I ignored it.

The nails held, and again and again we did the same, while the clamor grew and grew, and we could feel the wall vibrating. Once a peg pulled free, and Karjan almost fell, but he caught himself and continued down.

I looked down, and saw to my amazement that the ground was no more than thirty feet below us. One more rope-length, and I reached for more nails. The wall around me was shaking harder and harder, and we'd run out of time.

"Jump!" I shouted, and we sprang out into the blackness. We fell and fell, and I braced for the crack of breaking bones when we landed.

But I landed in muck, sliding and tumbling away from the wall, covering myself from head to foot. I found my footing and ran as hard as I could, limping, the other three in front of me. Karjan came back, threw his arm around my shoulders, and we ran on.

I was afraid to stop, afraid to turn and look back. Trees rose in front of us, and I saw our front lines, and a sentry, fear making his voice quaver, challenged us.

Yonge shouted the response, but I don't think it would have mattered, for the man was gaping at the fortress.

Now I allowed myself to stop, my lungs searing, and see what we'd fled from.

The ground was shaking, as if in an earthquake, and the thundering was deafening. I saw flames flickering from the stronghold above us, as if the stone itself was burning, yet was never consumed.

The ground rumbled again, and I lost my footing and fell, and then a bellow reverberated through the night.

A monstrous figure rose through the flames, stretching, growing, and I saw its V-mouth gaping, fangs glistening. I saw arms, four of them, each ending in claws, and I swear I could see, even at this distance, that all of them held men, their screams unhearable against the din.

The demon, the force, bayed triumph at the skies, finally holding complete thrall over its kingdom, and lightning flashed down from the heavens and bathed it.

I heard a whimper, and saw Karjan on his knees, head bowed, praying, and knew there was no shame in it. I also knew the gods could not be listening on this night.

The monster turned, gazing about, its arms thrashing against the stone walls, smashing them and sending them tumbling, and again the demon screamed its joy, and the storm echoed its howls.

The beast grew and grew, and I feared Tenedos had unleashed true chaos, and wondered if this could be a male manifestation of Saionji.

At that moment a bolt of pure energy, a searing blue, as blue as the finest summer day, came down. It was not lightning, but appeared like it.

It struck the monster full on the breast, and it screeched, another bolt came down, the ground shook once more and the demon was gone, and we were staring at nothing but the night, the storm raging against the torn stones where a fortress had once reared proudly, but now there was naught but ruin.

In this manner died Chardin Sher, Mikael Yanthlus, their sorcerers, retainers, and advisers, although no bodies were ever found in the wreckage of the citadel.

The war was over.

TWENTY-NINE

RETURN TO NICIAS

With Chardin Sher's death, the rebellion vanished as if it had never existed. Kallian soldiers deserted their formations, threw away their weapons, and traded their uniforms and any money they had for a scrap of clothing that suggested they'd always been civilians.

Couriers galloped in from the east, carrying the congratulations of the Rule of Ten, and requesting Seer-General Tenedos to return home immediately for his triumph.

He refused, saying the victory belonged to all of us, and we would share in it equally.

We buried our dead, treated our wounded, and made our way back through Kallio.

At each village and town we were met with cheering citizens, as if we'd defeated some foreign army. Somewhat bemused, we marched on, wondering at the fickleness of man.

We diverted toward Polycittara, and its elders, in panic, declared the capital an open city. They offered tribute. The soldiers would get an appropriate medal, officers would get silver, and generals, Tenedos, and the Rule of Ten gold.

Tenedos announced that the Rule of Ten had decided they needed no more gold, and he would not allow any of his men to accept a tin medal from a former enemy. I grinned when I heard this, knowing Tenedos certainly hadn't bothered to consult the Rule of Ten about the matter.

The Polycittarian leaders whimpered, and Tenedos said because of their intransigence the amount of the tribute was doubled, and if any further delay was made he would either double it again or allow the army three days of license in the city.

Within the hour wagonloads of gold, silver, jewels creaked out of the city's gates toward us, and when the soldiery found out it was to go to them, rather than far-distant bureaucrats whose only muscles were in their penhands and asses, they cheered Tenedos as if he'd personally promised each of them a step up on the Wheel in their next lives.

Of course, being soldiers they quickly wanted more, and there were suggestions that we should take the gold and loot the city anyway, but Tenedos forbade it. There were rumblings of discontent, and one half-company deserted, determined to celebrate in their own way.

Tenedos sent the Lancers out after them before they could do any worse than destroy a tavern, burn a hamlet, and ravage two women, and marched them back to the army's camp at lance point.

He called for representatives from each unit to assemble, had hasty gallows built, marched the entire half-company, plus its commanding officer, into the great square formed by the soldiers, and hanged every single one of them. That ended any further thoughts of freelance mayhem.

He summoned the city elders, told them what he'd done, said he could have required greater reparations, but he knew the Kallians would need their gold to rebuild. "Now is the time," he said, "for all of us to remember we are Numantians. Our dispute is over, and we are one nation once more."

We marched on, back the way we came. I felt satisfaction when we crossed the Imru River. We had avenged our defeat and our dead well.

Orders were waiting at Cicognara. Tenedos *must* leave the

army and return to Nicias for his honors, or face the displeasure of his rightful rulers, the Rule of Ten.

Tenedos ignored their order, and sent out commands of his own by heliograph and messenger. All ships worthy of travel on the Latane River where to go immediately to Cicognara. He reiterated what he'd said: All the army would be honored in Nicias, or none.

There was no response whatsoever to his disobedience from the Rule of Ten. They huddled in Nicias, afraid of what might come next.

The ships arrived, wave after wave of them, everything from the speedy *Tauler* and her sisters to cargo lighters and yachts, their arrival marking the coming of spring, the Time of Births.

We streamed aboard ship, and set out. It may sound like we held to the harsh discipline of the war, but this was far from the case. As long as a soldier could stumble to a required formation and be able to stand erect for his duties the exact extent of his sobriety was ignored. At nightfall there was no roll call, nor did provosts comb the transports to make sure there was but one set of legs coming from under a blanket, since many of the ships had arrived with women or boys who were eager, either for free or for silver, to thank the army for holding the nation together. Meals were cooked by quartermasters, but if a man chose to eat elsewhere at the invitation of a grateful civilian, it mattered little.

I was blind to all the revelry. All I wanted was to return home and Marán. At least her letters had resumed their regularity. She wrote at least once, frequently twice a day, and each time mail met us on our journey north I was inundated with scented documents of love.

I shook myself out of my fixation, though, and wondered what would happen when we reached Nicias. What would Tenedos do next?

His first move was ominous—for the Rule of Ten. As our motley fleet left the delta, he sent word to each ship that it was *not* to dock in Nicias, but rather disembark the troops at the tiny fishing village of Urgone, upriver from the capital. We would set up camp there, and not enter Nicias until "the proper time." It was obvious he intended to keep the army together, and hold it as a threat in being against the Rule of Ten.

Soldiers aren't stupid, and by now almost everyone realized something strange was happening, that there was conflict between the Rule of Ten and Tenedos. Some hotheads were heard to remark that if it came to that, since they hadn't been permitted to loot Polycittara, Nicias would be an acceptable stand-in.

We built a fortified camp, and busied ourselves rebuilding the army with new uniforms, weapons, supplies. We received replacements, but Tenedos ordered them into temporary regiments, saying they'd be permitted to join regular formations within a short time, but not at the present time. Tenedos didn't want the fervor of his veterans to be watered down. I sensed he must move quickly, however, because the army was at high pitch.

Nicians streamed out to meet us, but most of them were politely told by the sentries they could not enter the camp at the moment.

There were exceptions.

I rode back to my tent one tired afternoon, and found Lance Karjan waiting. He appeared most smug, and I asked him what made him so self-satisfied. He smiled more broadly, and said nothing whatsoever, but I might wish a bath before joining my officers in the mess. Or, if I chose, I could eat alone. In any event, I was to hand over my sword and belt—generals weren't supposed to look shabby.

I frowned; I was hardly the reclusive sort. I gave him my weapons belt, told him I'd bathe and change into mess gear and be ready to eat within the hour, and entered my tent.

Marán stood quickly from the chair she'd been waiting in. She wore only a thin, white robe with blue flowers on it, and a matching gown, slit to her upper thigh. Its neckline was low, curving just above her nipples. She was barefoot.

I saw, hanging from a peg on the crude framework I used for my wardrobe, her riding costume.

"Welcome home, my husband," she murmured, not looking up at me.

I was frozen. I'd dreamed of this time and now it had arrived.

She lifted her eyes.

"I . . . I am sorry," she said. "For what I did."

Once more that punished animal look was on her face. I found words, and my legs, stepped forward, and took her hands.

"Marán," I said. "You did nothing wrong. Not when I was gone, not now, not ever.

"I love you."

I saw tears well in her eyes.

"Here," she whispered. "Give me your coat."

I unbuttoned it, and let it slide to the ground. She came close, ran her fingers over my bandaged forearm and grimaced. Then she kissed my nipples through my shirt.

"I forgot how sweet you smell when you sweat," she said, and lifted her head to me.

I smelled flowers as we kissed, and blood began to hammer against my temples. I put my arms around her, feeling her warmth through the thin gown. After a time I pulled back slightly.

"Marán, grant me a favor. I don't want you to be thinking I'm some sort of magistrate, judging what you do or don't do. I'm your partner, not your lord. I'm going to do things wrong . . . hells, I know I already have. I'm but human, and expect mercy and forgiveness, so I guess I'd better grant you the same right, hadn't I? Please stop being so hard on yourself."

She stared at me, then buried her head against my shoulder. I felt her tears through my shirt.

"What is the matter?"

"Nothing," she said. "Nothing at all. I just . . . I guess I just never thought I had any right to be happy. I was, for a while. Then our baby died, and I felt like I was being punished."

"For being happy?"

She nodded.

"Did anybody ever tell you you're silly sometimes?"

She nodded once more. "I know I am."

"And did anyone ever tell you aren't supposed to be crying when your husband comes home from the wars?"

"I'm sor—" and I cut off her words with another kiss. I slid my hand down her side, til I reached the slit, moved inside it, and stroked the satin of her buttocks. She didn't move her lips from mine, but her hands crept up and unbuttoned my shirt, and I let her loose long enough to slip out of it. I could feel her nipples firm against my chest.

"I said I wanted something in one of my letters," she said, "and I mean to have it."

She unbuttoned the fastenings of my trousers, and slipped them down over my boots. She gasped, seeing my still-bandaged thigh.

"Oh, my love, they hurt you."

"I'm healing. It hardly bothers me now."

"I shall be your nurse," she said. "And take care of your every need." She knelt, and touched my rising cock with a finger. "I've missed you," she murmured, and took its head in her mouth. She worried me gently with her teeth, then ran her tongue across its very tip.

"Now, Damastes, if you are as needful as I am, let me taste you," and she took me in her mouth, moving her lips down along my cock's shaft, her tongue coiling, caressing, and I had my hands around her head, pulling her hair around me, and gasped as my long-held semen gushed.

She kept moving her head and the joyful agony grew, and then subsided. She rose to her feet, her mouth wet with me, and swallowed.

"That was to make sure we would have our full share of pleasure."

I stood, and embraced her once more. As we kissed, I slid the robe down from her shoulders, then pulled at the knots holding her gown up, and it fell about her waist.

Pregnancy had made her breasts grow, and now they

curved like beautiful persimmons. She curled a leg around me, and rubbed my calf with her heel. My cock stiffened against her stomach, and she caressed my balls gently.

I carried her to my small camp cot and laid her down on it. I stood over her, bestriding the cot. She lay with her head back, then opened her eyes and looked up at me, and smiled, dreamily. She pulled her gown up until it pooled in her lap. She brought one leg up, then the other, and let her thighs fall apart.

"Did you dream about me, my husband?"

"Every night."

"I dreamed about you, and tried to find a bit of pleasure in my own ways. But they were nothing compared to you."

Still smiling, she began stroking her sex, and put one finger, then the other, inside herself, moving them in and out gently.

"I am wet, Damastes," she moaned. "I am ready for you. Come love me, come fuck me now."

I knelt on the coach, and as I touched her wetness with my cock she jerked. I entered her, but only until the head was buried, then moved it slightly in and out.

"All the way, put it in all the way," she said, but I continued the slight motions. "Oh, love, please, please, it's been so long, oh, split me, tear me, oh, fuck me!"

I withdrew slightly and she suddenly hooked her heels under the cot's sideboards, and levered herself up until I was buried in her. She cried out, and I fell across her, pounding as her hips drove against me, her hands pulling at my back, her mouth open, gasping, our wet lips sliding across each other, and we were one again.

"Soldiers of Numantia," Tenedos's amplified voice boomed across the vast formation. "You have served your country, and me, as well.

"I promised you rewards for your sacrifices, and you believed me, and have been most patient. In Polycittara I gave you a taste of what I promised. There shall be more, much more, in the days to come.

"I shall begin with six of my best soldiers.

"All of them are generals, and richly deserve the rank. They are heroes as well.

"This day, I am creating a new rank, the rank of tribune. Here is its symbol of office." He held up an onyx rod, about two feet long, with silver bands around either end.

The six of us standing at attention before Tenedos were amazed. There'd been no clues as to why he called this army-wide formation, nor why he'd called us up from the heads of our own units.

"My tribunes will hold the highest commands, and will be answerable only to me.

"Now I shall name them. You know them by name and reputation, but I shall have a few words to say about each.

"My first tribune shall be Damastes á Cimabue. He was the first to follow me, and has been the bravest of the brave, from Kiat to the final destruction of Chardin Sher, serving in every conceivable way. Tribune á Cimabue, I honor you for your service."

He walked forward, and handed me the first staff. I heard the army roar approval behind me. I was incapable of speech, never having dreamed of such an honor. Tenedos must have known what I was thinking, because he smiled, and said softly, "You see what happens when you listen to a madman in a mountain pass?" I managed to salute, and he stepped back. The others would come to him.

"The second is General Hern, a man who has always led from the front, always obeying my commands, and always providing an example." Hern received his baton as well.

"The third is General Myrus Le Balafre, our best swordsman and a man who leads by example. He needs no medals, for his scarred body shows how he has given his life to Numantia." Le Balafre took his baton, and walked back beside me. I whispered congratulations, and he nodded thanks. "I guess I'll stay around for the peace," he replied. "Life looks like it shall be interesting now."

"The fourth," Tenedos's voice thundered, "is General

Yonge. I wish all who are not native Numantians to note this honor, and recognize that there shall be no prejudice for or against people from one state or another, nor against those who choose to enter my service from other nations." I was waiting for Yonge to shout something outrageous, but the occasion seemed to have overwhelmed him. Knuckling tears from the corner of his eyes, he took the baton and stumbled back to our small formation, forgetting to salute the seer-general.

"The fifth is General Cyrillos Linerges, who returned to the army in its hour of need, and has risen through the ranks rapidly as he proved again and again his leadership and bravery." Linerges, an arm still bandaged from the battle with the Kallian Army, beamed.

"My final appointment is to General Petre, a man who fights as hard with his brain as his sword. He should be a study for you young officers that time spent studying the art of war instead of gaming or wenches can be profitable. General Petre has done as much to form this army as anyone, and this is his reward." Petre, humorless as ever, marched to Tenedos, took the baton, saluted snappily, and about-faced. He saw me looking at him, and a smile crossed his face for just an instant. Then his expression became as wooden as usual and he returned to ranks.

"Six men," Tenedos said. "They are but the beginning, and an example. I know there are men out there listening who shall one day carry this black rod, and further honor themselves, their family, their state, and all Numantia."

"That," Tenedos said, "was the first arrow of my campaign."

"So the Rule of Ten knows nothing about your creating this new rank?"

"They do now."

"What do you suppose they shall do?"

"I'm not sure. That's why I asked you to join me with the special detail I asked for."

That "special detail," nearly 200 men, rode behind us as we clattered into the outskirts of Nicias. They were all volunteers, then hand-combed for toughness of mind and body. There were almost as many officers as enlisted men. Among them were Tribune Yonge, Domina Bikaner, and hard fighters like Regimental Guide Evatt, Sergeants Karjan, Svalbard, and Curti, and others I knew not but whose dedication had been attested to by their officers.

They carried not only their swords, but daggers and, hidden under their dress uniforms, truncheons.

Tenedos had personally given them their orders before we rode out of camp, and told them they could be called in various-sized groups, and then named men to each group.

We were heading for the Palace of the Rule of Ten.

"I am delighted," Speaker Barthou said, "to honor you, Seer-General Tenedos, for having served us so well."

"I served not only you, sir, but our homeland of Numantia." Tenedos stood in the center of the great audience chamber. I stood just behind and to one side, as he'd ordered.

"We have arranged a great triumph for the army," Barthou went on, "then feasts, ceremonies, celebrations, all that Nicias can do to show its gratitude." There were cheers, and for the first time Barthou appeared to notice that the balconies were full of soldiers in uniform. He looked worried.

"We thank you," Tenedos said. "But in fact there is more Nicias can do, and must if proper honor is to be shown. Brave service is best rewarded with real gifts."

"What do you mean?" Barthou looked upset; this was clearly not going as planned.

"First, gold. Pensions for the men who must be invalided out of service. Compensation for men who were crippled, losing an arm, an eye, or whatever. More, sir. Numantia is a vast country, and there is much land unworked. I would suggest that the Rule of Ten grant small holdings to those veterans who leave the service."

"That's unheard of!" Barthou blurted. I looked at Scopas, Tenedos's sometimes ally, and he, too, looked surprised, then a calculating expression crossed his face.

Boos and shouts came from the gallery. The Rule of Ten's guards looked more nervous than their masters. Tenedos turned, and stared up at the soldiers, and there was an instant silence.

Before Barthou could continue, Scopas rose.

"Excuse me, Speaker. But, as you say, the noble seer-general has presented some unusual ideas. I think we should withdraw and consider them."

Someone shouted from the balcony, "How long, y' bassids? Y' gonna forget about us like allus?"

Scopas looked up and addressed the anonymous jeerer.

"We shall be out for less than an hour, sir. You have my promise."

Barthou was about to protest, but I saw Scopas move his head slightly.

"Very well. Within the hour."

The Rule of Ten filed out.

"Before we continue," Barthou said, "I have some announcements to make." The man looked gray, ashen, as if his life had been threatened.

"First, let us congratulate the men Seer-General Teredos proclaimed tribunes. We find this a worthy idea, and are sorry we did not devise it ourselves."

The Rule of Ten turned their attention to me. I kept my face blank, but I thought, So, you are trying to woo me, and the other five as well. What will you offer?

"We wish to offer our own rewards as well," Barthou went on. "I note that Gen—Tribune á Cimabue, Count Agramónte, is with us. Tribune, it honors us greatly to name you life-baron. We invite you to choose the remainder of your title at your leisure.

"We also wish to give all tribunes an annual salary of fifty thousand gold coins and will provide estates as well, these estates to be maintained by the government.

"Baron and Tribune á Cimabue, Count Agramónte, since you were the first to be named to the rank, we grant you the Water Palace, to be used as you see fit during your lifetime.

"Other tribunes will be given similar gifts.

"Now, Seer-General—"

"Before you give me anything," Tenedos interrupted, "what of the land grants I spoke of?"

"They shall be made, sir," Scopas said. "We shall set up a commission to begin giving these grants out within a year."

Tenedos stared at him.

"A year, eh? That should be discussed. But go on."

I heard a rumble from the troops in the balconies.

Scopas indicated to Barthou he had the floor again.

"Seer-General Tenedos," Barthou said, "you are created a hereditary baron, and one hundred thousand gold coins per year and an estate for your reward now, with other honors to follow."

Barthou paused, expecting, no doubt, Tenedos to babble thanks. But the seer said, coldly, "That is not nearly adequate."

"What?"

"I think we should withdraw to your chambers once more and discuss this matter," the sorcerer said.

"There's no need to do that," Barthou protested.

"This situation is entirely out of hand," his newly appointed lapdog, Timgad, blurted.

"No," Tenedos corrected. "The matter is well under control, in spite of what you gentlemen think. Now, shall we retire for a few moments?"

There was hasty agreement. The Rule of Ten rose, and started for the exit. Tenedos turned to me and signaled.

"Tribune?"

I spun. "Ten men!" I shouted, and there was a clatter as soldiers ran down the stairs from the gallery. Among them were Svalbard and Karjan.

"What is *this*?" Timgad protested.

"You shall find out shortly." Timgad was apoplectic, and Scopas took his arm and dragged him out.

"How could you bring armed soldiers into our most private chambers?" Barthou hissed.

"I invited them because I don't trust you," Tenedos said calmly. "However, I mean them only as personal protection, not as a threat."

I nearly smiled, knowing the ten hard men against the wall behind me hardly presented a pacifistic image.

"So what is it you desire?" Scopas said. "This matter, as Timgad said, *is* getting out of hand."

"Many things. We shall start with what's been said already. The matter of land for my soldiers shall be handled immediately, not within a year or so. Second, those whom you name barons, like Tribune á Cimabue, shall be given hereditary ranks, instead of the shameful life-peerages."

"How dare you dictate to us?" Barthou shrilled.

"I dare, because of those men who stand behind me. I dare, because I am a true Numantian. I dare . . . because I dare."

"Go on," Scopas said grimly.

"You are given forty-eight hours from this moment. At the end of that time, you are to announce that the Rule of Ten is withdrawing from actively governing to an advisory position, and that you have finally found the emperor you were ordered to name, and supposedly have been seeking all these decades."

"And what if we don't?"

Tenedos stared at Barthou until he looked away.

"A year ago, the army was in the streets of Nicias, doing your bidding, bringing peace," he said. "If you do not obey my orders, it shall rule Nicias with the sword once more.

"And you shall bitterly rue the consequences.

"You cannot change what will happen. I shall be emperor, with or without your bumbling approval. The time has come for changes, and I have been chosen by Saionji to make them.

"Think well, think wisely," Tenedos said grimly. "For the blood shall be on your hands."

Without farewell, without salute, he stalked out, paying no heed to the gabble and shouts from behind.

THIRTY

THE CROWN

I stood beside the altar, the high priest at my side. He held a heavy box in his arms, a box made of solid gold and crusted with gems.

The huge temple was full. Every nobleman and -woman who could reach Nicias packed its main floor and balconies.

The center aisle was lined with soldiers. All of them were tribunes or generals.

Trumpets blared, the great doors opened, and Tenedos entered as the audience stood. Instead of seer's robes, he wore the simple uniform of an army officer, but without badges of rank or decorations.

Music from an unseen orchestra swelled, and Tenedos paced slowly toward the altar. As he passed each officer, the man knelt in obeisance, and the men and women behind them bowed humbly.

He reached the foot of the altar and stopped.

"Are you the man named Laish Tenedos?" the priest asked.

"I am he."

"You are chosen by the Rule of Ten, in the names of Umar, of Irisu, of . . . of Saionji," the priest stumbled over the last-minute addition to the ritual, and I heard gasps from the audience, "of Panoan, and all the rest of those mighty beings who created and watch over Numantia, to lead us.

"Laish Tenedos, I require you to promise that you shall

govern wisely and well, frequently consulting the gods to ensure you rule in wisdom, mercy, and justice, never treating your subjects with cruelty or disdain, never leading them into war without justification."

"I so vow."

"Then I proclaim you emperor of Numantia."

He opened the box and took out the single gold circlet.

"Tribune Damastes á Cimabue, Baron Damastes of Ghazi, Count Agramónte, you have been chosen the most worthy to crown the emperor. Take this diadem from my hands, and place it on your ruler's brow."

I lifted the circlet. As I did, I saw Marán in the audience, her face a beacon of love and hope.

I placed the circlet on Tenedos's brow, then knelt, bowing my head.

And that was how the Seer King came to the throne.

On that day we stood on the summit of the highest mountain. All the world's glory spread below us.

It was the beginning of the end.

ABOUT THE AUTHOR

CHRIS BUNCH is the co-author (with Allan Cole) of the Sten series and the bestselling Anteros trilogy. As a solo writer, he is the author of the Shadow Warrior science fiction series from Del Rey. Both Ranger and airborne-qualified, he was part of the first troop correspondent for *Stars and Stripes*. He edited outlaw motorcycle magazines and, as a freelancer, wrote for everything from the underground press to *Look* magazine, *Rolling Stone*, and prime-time television. He is now a full-time novelist living in Washington State.

1003-c

• A MAN BETRAYED

At Castle Harvell, demented Prince Kylock commits murder to seize the reins of power. Harvell's two young refugees are torn apart by the storms of war: headstrong young Melliandra is captured by brutal slavers and Jack, whose wild power works miracles, falls prey to a smuggler's lying charms.

"A highly successful, popular fantasy epic."

—*Dragon* magazine

(0-446-60351-1) $5.99 USA, $6.99 CAN.

• MASTER AND FOOL

In the fortress of Bren, mad King Kylock and the wizard Baralis spread their sadistic terror across the shattered kingdoms. Meanwhile, the fallen knight Tawl and Jack, the baker's boy, meet in a quest to save widowed Melliandra and her unborn child. Soon sons will turn on fathers and dread secrets will be revealed, as Jack and Kylock clash in a magical apocalypse.

"Jones stamps it all with a distinctive touch."

—*Locus*

(0-446-60414-3) $5.99 USA, $6.99 CAN.